BURN

Linda Howard is the award-winning author of many *New York Times* bestsellers. She lives in Alabama with her husband and golden retriever.

Also by Linda Howard

Dying to Please
Cry No More
Kiss Me While I Sleep
To Die For
Killing Time
Cover of Night
Drop Dead Gorgeous
Up Close and Dangerous
Death Angel

BURN

LINDA HOWARD

piatkus

PIATKUS

First published in the US in 2009 by Ballantine Books, an imprint of
The Random House Publishing Group, a division of Random House, Inc.,
New York
First published in Great Britain in 2009 by Piatkus

A CIP catalogue record for this book
is available from the British Library

ISBN 978-0-7499-0921-5 (HB edition)
ISBN 978-0-7499-0923-9 (TPB edition)

Typeset in Caslon 540 by Phoenix Photosetting, Chatham, Kent
Printed and bound in Great Britain by MPG Books, Bodmin, Cornwall

Papers used by Piatkus are natural, renewable and recyclable
products sourced from well-managed forests and certified
in accordance with the rules of the Forest Stewardship Council.

Mixed Sources
Product group from well-managed
forests and other controlled sources
www.fsc.org Cert no. SGS-COC-004081
© 1996 Forest Stewardship Council
FSC

Piatkus
An imprint of
Little, Brown Book Group
100 Victoria Embankment
London EC4Y 0DY

An Hachette UK Company
www.hachette.co.uk

www.piatkus.co.uk

To the lovely people who work at the Christmas Place in Pigeon Forge, Tennessee, which is one of the magic places in the world. Thank you all for the use of your first names for some of the characters in this book.

And to our beloved girls, our golden retrievers, Honey and Sugar, who are now romping together in Heaven. It has to be true that all dogs go to Heaven, because where else would such pure love go?

BURN

Prologue

Present Day, onboard the *Silver Mist*

This was the vacation from hell.

Jenner Redwine sat frozen on the barstool, trying to re-member what Bridget had told her and reconcile it with the nightmare that was actually happening. She'd been told that a man and a woman would argue at some point during the evening. The woman, Tiffany, would leave, and the man, Cael, would then approach Jenner. She'd been instructed to appear interested, and accommodating. She was to do exactly what he said, otherwise they would kill Syd, the only real friend she had in this world.

The scene wasn't unfolding as she'd been expecting. Tiffany wasn't leaving the bar. She was screaming and stomping and throwing a drunken temper tantrum, though of course she wasn't really drunk. She was accusing Cael of sleeping with Jenner even though this was the first night on the ship and no one had slept with anyone yet—probably—because of the early hour. Cael had approached Jenner *before* the argument started, though of course she hadn't yet

1

realized who he was. He'd stood next to her at the crowded bar to order drinks, and he hadn't said anything suggestive. No, nothing about this night was playing out the way Bridget had briefed her, other than that a very public argument was taking place.

Cael would finesse the details, Bridget had said. He certainly had. Jenner had no idea what would happen next, which was probably a good thing. She wasn't an actress, couldn't play along like a practiced con who rolled with the punches. They obviously could.

The man who had jostled Cael earlier had joined in the argument, as loud and drunken as Tiffany, telling her she didn't know what she was talking about and she was drunk and should go to her cabin and sleep it off. He was determined to take the blame for starting the unpleasantness, which was nice of him even if he was drunk. Or maybe he was one of *them*, Jenner thought, because she didn't know him and, really, he could be anyone.

The only people she couldn't be suspicious of, she realized, were the people she already knew. She might not know who she couldn't trust, but she definitely knew who she *could*, for all the good it would do her. Whatever was going on, she was in on it, sink or swim, because of Syd. Her friend was being threatened, and Jenner wanted to be pissed. If she could get pissed, then she wouldn't be so afraid.

She wanted to be able to do something to get these people out of her life—and Syd's. Instead she was terrified that no matter what she did, things wouldn't work out well for either of them. Being so afraid of what might come next, and not *knowing* what would happen next, made her feel helpless, and that wasn't a trait she admired in anyone, least of all herself.

Maybe it was time she took control of some of the details, the way she had by going out on the balcony when Faith had been standing guard. She slipped off the stool and tried to edge her way around Cael, as if she were trying to escape the scene, but Tiffany saw her and shrieked, "Don't try to run off like you're Little Miss Innocent! I saw you flirting—"

"I don't know you," said Jenner, interrupting her even as Cael turned and subtly shifted his position to block her avenue of escape. "And I don't know him, so leave me out of your nasty little tantrum." She caught the eye of someone she knew from Palm Beach, Leanne Ivey, and gave a helpless, I-don't-know-what's-going-on shrug. Leanne gave her a sympathetic look in return.

Faith suddenly detached herself from the crowd and approached Tiffany, putting her arm around the black-haired woman's shoulders and softly saying something to her. Tiffany responded by bursting into tears, and Faith gently led her away, putting an end to the dramatics. Almost simultaneously, Faith's husband, Ryan, limped up to Cael. "That was nice of you to give her your stateroom," he said in a perfectly pitched tone that was just loud enough for those around them to hear.

Cael shrugged. "I could hardly toss her out, could I?" He was still keeping Jenner blocked from leaving, and now he and Ryan had her sandwiched between them. She was trapped, as surely as if they'd each grabbed her by an arm and held on tight. Not that it mattered. She had nowhere to go, though surely her expression plainly said she wanted to get away.

The *Silver Mist* was a big ship, filled with people . . . surrounded by water. Even if these people weren't threatening her friend, where would she go if she managed to escape? Cael would find her, no matter where she tried to hide. Much as she hated to play along, she didn't want to find out what he might do if he didn't get his way.

"There was a mix-up on our suite," continued Ryan, "and we have a two-bedroom instead of one. You're welcome to take the other room, if you like."

"Much obliged. But first I'll check to see if another stateroom is available. Have you heard if the cruise is sold out?"

Jenner wanted to scream. The two men sounded so normal, as if this were a perfectly natural conversation. She knew it was anything but, though no one else would realize what was going on. She supposed that was the plan, but this chatting was like sandpaper on her nerves.

Ryan lifted one shoulder. "I haven't heard. But if there isn't, you can definitely stay with us. I've already cleared it with Faith, so don't think she'll mind." He looked at Jenner then, giving her a friendly, almost gentle smile. "What a way to start the cruise, huh?"

"With a bang," she agreed, once more trying to slide sideways around them. She could barely take in a breath with the two men towering over her, closing her in. They stole her air, and she needed to breathe. She felt as if she were being crushed, though neither of them was actually touching her. And then . . .

Ryan reached out and took hold of her elbow, a gentlemanly gesture that nevertheless anchored her in place. "Have you two actually met, or were you just caught in the explosion?"

"No, we haven't met," Cael said, even though Ryan had asked the question of her.

"That makes the whole scene even more ridiculous, doesn't it?" Ryan said with a rueful laugh, man to man. "Jenner Redwine, this is Cael Traylor."

"Pleased to meet you," said Cael, extending his hand, and Jenner had no choice but to extend her own. His hard warm fingers enfolded hers, and she felt calluses on his palm. She looked up and met cold blue eyes that were watching every move she made, reading every flicker of expression that crossed her face.

They had set up a situation that showed both Cael and herself in a more positive light, she realized, than if he'd dumped Tiffany and immediately made a move on her. Bridget must have passed along the comment that Jenner had made, that hooking up with sleazoids was out of character for her. They didn't want anyone suspicious of their sudden "romance." By making Tiffany look obnoxious and drunk, they had tilted public sympathy toward the new couple. And now here they were, being properly introduced by a man who was, to all appearances, perfectly harmless and acceptable.

Slick, she thought warily. These people were slick. It wouldn't pay to underestimate any of them, not that she could do anything except play along with whatever scenario they set up. That didn't mean she'd roll over and play dead; that wasn't in character for her, either.

Her chance would come when Syd was safe. She had to believe that Syd would be released unharmed, and she had to believe that somehow she would be able to make these people pay for what they were doing to her, and to her friend. To dwell on any other possible outcome would have the power to incapacitate her—and she couldn't let that happen. Until her chance arrived, she had no choice but to do whatever this Cael told her to do.

It was the thought of survival—and payback—that kept her from screaming as she stood and made small talk with Ryan and Cael, keeping it casual and inconsequential for the people who were still avidly listening. Cael thanked Ryan again for the offer to use their extra bedroom, then he turned and retrieved Jenner's drink from the bar, as well as the Ghostwater he'd ordered.

He looked at the Ghostwater, grimaced, then set it aside. "That was for Tiffany," he said to Jenner. "She'd had one already, and insisted on having another. That's how I knew they hit hard and fast."

She nodded, but didn't reply. Let him work a little harder at this instant romance.

He looked around the crowded bar. For the most part, everyone had returned to their own conversations. The music had started up again. He nodded to a couple of people—acquaintances or more of his own group?—then said, "Let's get out of this crowd and walk. I could use some exercise."

"You two go on," said Ryan, not giving Jenner a chance to accept or decline. "I'll see how Faith is doing getting Tiffany settled."

In short order Jenner found herself strolling beside Cael on the sports deck, because the Lido deck was too crowded with both chairs and people. Even though they were just one deck above the Lido, the noise level was considerably diminished, and they had very little company. They didn't talk; she stared straight ahead as she marched along, at least until he caught her arm and pulled her to a slower pace. "You look like you're trying to run away from me."

"Imagine that," she said sarcastically. She hated that he had such a smooth, deep voice, that he was tall and good-looking and well-dressed. She'd been expecting a common thug, someone she could dislike on sight. After all, he was a kidnapper, a low-life scum. A kidnapper was far worse than a mooch, no matter how good-looking he might be. Her heart was thumping hard and fast, from fear, from dread, from the effort she was making to appear, at least from a distance, that she was in the beginning stages of a shipboard romance.

"Think of your friend," he replied without inflection, but lowering his voice even more. Sound carried on the wind, and up here the breeze caused by the ship's movement was even more brisk, lifting her hair away from her face. She shivered, rubbing her hands over her bare arms.

"I am thinking of her. That's the only reason I haven't pushed you overboard."

"Then you'd better think harder, because you're doing a piss-poor job of selling the idea that we've got a thing going."

"Who am I selling it to? There's no one up here," she retorted, and that was mostly true. There were a few couples strolling around, like them, and a lone man who had come up for a cigarette and was standing well away from everyone else. She wasn't as good an actress as they'd like her to be, and no amount of threat could change that. She definitely wasn't like them, able to pretend to be someone she was not on command.

"I decide when you need to sell it, not you. And I'm telling you to sell, now." Effortlessly he swung her around to face him, so close that once again his body heat wrapped around her. The ship was well lit, but the black night that enclosed them threw harsh shadows across his face, making his bone structure look harder and more severe. He looked down at her for a long moment, then moved his hands to her waist and pulled her full against him. "You're not taking your friend's health as seriously as you should."

"I've done everything you've told me to do!" She'd hated it, but she'd played along. What choice did she have? Panic laced her tone, because did that mean they'd already hurt Syd?

"Kiss me like you mean it," he ordered, and bent his head to hers.

She didn't. She couldn't. Even though his mouth was warm and his lips firm, his taste pleasantly clean, she couldn't make herself forget who and what he was or that Syd's life was at stake. She stood stiffly, holding her breath, her arms at her sides as he kissed her. If he had an ounce of compassion he'd realize that she was terrified and he'd back off, but she suspected that was an ounce more than Cael possessed.

"Sell it," he growled against her mouth, and deepened the kiss, slanting his mouth over hers, using his tongue to explore deeper. Jenner shuddered under the rebellion that shook her but she thought of Syd and obediently lifted her arms to twine them around his neck.

Still, she tried to hold her body away from his, tried not to let her breasts or hips touch him. She didn't want to touch him any more than she had to. From a distance she should look willing enough to anyone watching, and that should satisfy him. He overcame her stiffness by pulling her solidly against him, fitting their bodies together like lovers and holding her there. She felt the hardness of his muscled shoulders under the silk of his shirt, felt the thick ridge of his penis begin to get even thicker, firmer.

Oh, God. Blind panic swept over her. He had an erection. He wasn't like other men, she couldn't trust that he'd rein in any unwelcome sexual interest, that he'd take her "no" seriously. She tried to back away just enough to ease the pressure of his body against hers, but he held her so tight it was impossible. She was completely at his mercy, assuming he had any . . . and how could she assume anything except the worst about him, considering? What did he intend to do to her? She was afraid she knew, and there was nothing she could do to stop him.

Was the same thing happening to Syd? She had been so focused on not getting Syd killed, and now she had to accept that other things could happen, that neither of them would get out of this unscathed. Her earlier thoughts of payback seemed trivial now. She wanted to survive; she didn't want to be hurt. She wanted the same for Syd. There were no more thoughts of what would come after, just the terror that came with moment-to-moment survival.

"Don't," she whimpered, unable to stop the plea. She hated herself for begging, when what she wanted to do was spit in his face, hated herself for letting him see how frightened she was.

"Then act as if you mean it," he said for the second time, kissing her again.

Enraged, helpless, she did.

Part One

DUMB LUCK

Chapter One

Seven years earlier . . .

Jenner Redwine's cell phone rang as she was trudging across the parking lot to her car. That would be Dylan, she thought with a flash of annoyance as she fished the phone from the bottom of her denim purse; she'd had the phone for just five weeks, and already he'd developed a pattern. She bet she knew what he wanted, too. She thumbed the Talk button, said "Hello," and waited to see if she'd won the bet with herself.

"Hey, babe," he said, as he always did.

"Hey." If he'd had an ounce of sensitivity he'd have noticed the distinct lack of welcome in her voice, but "sensitivity" and "Dylan" were direct opposites.

"You off work yet?"

As if he hadn't been watching the clock, she thought, but didn't say it. "Yeah."

"How about stopping at the Seven-Eleven and picking up a six-pack, okay? I'll pay you for it."

He hadn't yet, she thought grumpily, and she was getting

tired of it. His dead-end job paid more than hers, but he was mooching his beer off her. *Last time,* Jenner promised herself as she said "Okay," and hung up. If he didn't pay her this time, this was her last beer run.

She had just clocked out at the end of second shift at Harvest Meat Packing Company, she was exhausted, and the bottoms of her feet throbbed from standing on the concrete floor for the past eight hours. Dylan's job at a machine shop was first shift, which meant he'd been off work for roughly those same eight hours, but he hadn't bothered to get his own beer. Instead he'd been watching her television and eating her food.

Having a steady guy had seemed like a good deal at first, but Jenner didn't suffer any fool gladly, even when the fool was herself. Unless Dylan pulled off a miraculous recovery, she'd shortly be placing him in the "mistake" column. She'd give him this one last chance—not because she thought he'd come through, but because somehow she needed this one additional bit of evidence to push her past the point of no return. Hanging on to people when she should let go was a character flaw, but she knew herself well enough to accept that she *had* to give him this one last chance, or uncertainty would eat her alive.

Reaching her battered blue Dodge, she unlocked it and pulled hard on the door handle—the driver's door tended to stick. After initially resisting her effort, the door suddenly gave way with a creak of rusty hinges, and Jenner staggered back. Controlling her irritation, she got in, slammed the door, and stuck the key in the ignition. The engine fired right up. The Blue Goose didn't look like much, but it was reliable, and that was all she asked. At least she had *something* she could depend on, even if it was just a beat up, rusty car.

The 7-Eleven nearest her duplex was a few blocks out of

her way, but certainly close enough that Dylan could have gone there with very little effort. The shop was brightly lit, and the parking lot packed despite the late hour. Jenner wedged the Dodge into a space that was as tight as too-small panty hose, but what the heck; what did another ding matter in a car that was practically one big ding?

She shoved her shoulder against the door and, sure enough, it swung open with too much force and banged the car beside her. Wincing, she contorted herself so she could slide through the small opening, and rubbed her finger over the ding in the other car in an effort to smooth it out—not that the owner was likely to notice one more, considering this car was almost as bad as the Goose.

The combined smells of exhaust, gasoline, and hot asphalt hit her in the face. Typical summer smell, and all in all she kind of liked the smell of gasoline. Kerosene, too. Weird, but not something she wasted time worrying about.

The bottoms of her sneakers stuck to the softened tar of the parking lot as she trudged across it. The air-conditioned coolness of the convenience store washed around her as soon as she made it through the door. She wanted to stand for a moment, just absorbing the cold air. The heat wave that was cooking the Chicago area seemed to suck every bit of endurance out of her. Damn, she was tired. She wanted to be at home where she could kick the shoes off her aching feet, peel out of her sweaty jeans and shirt, and flop across the bed so the breeze from the ceiling fan could blow across her mostly naked body. Instead, she was buying Dylan's beer. So who was the loser? Dylan, or herself?

She glanced at the curiously long line at the counter, and had an *aha!* moment as suddenly it clicked: lottery. She had to be tired, not to have realized immediately what was going on. A huge jackpot had been building, and the drawing was

tomorrow night. That was why the parking lot was full and
there was such a long line at the counter. Every now and
then she played the numbers, and a couple of times she'd
won a few bucks, but for the most part she didn't bother.
Tonight, though . . . hell, why not? Let Dylan wait for his
beer.

She grabbed a six-pack, then joined the queue, which
wound between two aisles to the back of the store, then
snaked halfway up another aisle. She passed the time by
examining prices, looking at candy, and trying to decide
which numbers to pick. She was sandwiched between two
guys, both of whom smelled like stale beer and equally stale
sweat, and who both kept making occasional comments to
her, which she mostly ignored. Did she have some invisible
sign on her head that said, "All losers apply here"?

Then again, maybe they just wanted her beer. On a hot
summer night, beer had to rate pretty high—maybe even
higher than a tired Clairol blonde in an ugly blue shirt with
the words "Harvest Meat Packing" embroidered on the
pocket. Though when she was on the job she had to wear
coveralls and a plastic head-cover, the packing company
required that their employees wear the company shirts to
and from home, figuring they'd get free advertising. The
employees even had to buy the damn shirts—but at least, if
she quit, she got to keep the shirts . . . until she threw them
away the first chance she had.

On the other hand, these two bozos maybe looked at the
shirt and thought, "Hey, she has a job! And beer!" She hated
to think this shirt could be a come-on.

Eventually, the slow shuffle of the line brought her to the
counter. She plunked down her money and bought three
tickets, mainly because three was supposed to be a lucky
number. She chose three sets of numbers at random,

thinking of birthdays, telephone numbers, addresses, and anything else that occurred to her. Then, dropping the tickets into her bag, she trudged back out to her car. The vehicle that had been parked beside her was gone, and a pickup truck had taken its place. The truck was parked so close there was no way she could get the driver's side door open. Muttering a curse under her breath, she unlocked the passenger door and managed to wiggle in, then she had to climb over the console. At least she was skinny and limber, otherwise she'd never have managed.

Her cell phone rang as she was wedging herself under the steering wheel. She jumped, banged her head, and cursed again. This time it wasn't under her breath. Digging out the phone, she punched the button and snapped, *"What?"*

"What's taking you so long?" Dylan demanded.

"Buying the damn beer, that's what's taking so long. There was a line."

"Well, hurry it up, will ya?"

"On my way." If her tone was grim, he completely missed that little detail, but then, Dylan seemed to miss a lot of signals.

Each half of the duplex where she lived had its own tiny drive, a luxury she appreciated as she didn't have to park on the street. At least, normally she didn't. Tonight, Dylan's Mustang was in her drive, so she had to hunt for a space. By the time she found one, trudged back to her place—where every light was on—she was all but breathing fire.

Sure enough, when she went in, the first thing she saw was Dylan sprawled on her couch, his work boots propped on her coffee table, a wrestling show blaring on her television. "Hey, babe," said Dylan with a smile as he got up, half his attention remaining on the television. He took the six-pack from her hand and fished one out of the carton. "Shit, it isn't cold."

She watched as he picked up the opener he'd already fetched from the kitchen—so he wouldn't have to go to the trouble of waiting for his brew—popped the top off the bottle, and lifted the beer to his mouth. He dropped the top onto the coffee table, and settled himself back on the couch.

"How about putting the others in the fridge on your way to change clothes," he suggested. She always changed clothes as soon as she got home because she couldn't stand wearing the ugly polyester shirt one second longer than necessary.

"Sure thing," she said, picking up the carton. She told him how much the beer was.

He gaped at her. "Huh?"

"The beer." She kept her voice very even. "You said you'd pay me for it."

"Oh, yeah. I didn't bring any money with me. I'll pay you tomorrow."

Ding. She heard the little bell that said he'd passed the point of no return. She waited for a sense of being set free, but instead all she felt was tired. "Don't bother," she said. "Just get out, and don't come back."

"Huh?" he said again. Evidently he was having problems with his hearing, along with his problems thinking. Dylan was good-looking—*very* good-looking—but not nearly good-looking enough to make up for all his shortcomings. Okay, so she'd wasted almost four months of her life on him; she'd know better next time. The first sign of mooching, and the guy was out.

"Get out. We're done. You've mooched off me for the last time." She opened the door and stood there, waiting for him to leave.

He heaved himself to his feet, arranging his face in the charming smile that had blinded her at first. "Babe, you're just tired—"

"Damn straight. Tired of you. Come on." She made shooing motions. "Out."

"Jen, come on—"

"No. That was it. You had no intention of paying for the beer, and I have no intention of giving you another chance."

"If it meant that much to you, all you had to do was say so. You don't have to go off the deep end," he charged, the charming smile vanishing and a scowl taking its place.

"Yes, I do. I like the deep end. The water's nice and cold there. *Out.*"

"We can work—"

"No, we can't, Dylan. This was your last chance." She glared at him. "You either walk out this door, or I'm calling the cops."

"All right, all right." He stepped onto the miniscule porch, then turned to face her. "I was getting tired of you, anyway. Bitch."

She closed the door in his face, then jumped as he slammed his fist into the wood. That was evidently his parting gesture, because about ten seconds later she heard his car start, and she watched through a tiny opening in the curtains as he backed out of the driveway and left.

All right. Finally. She was boyfriendless, and it felt good. Better than good. The sense of relief and freedom finally showed up and she took a deep breath, feeling as if a ton had been lifted from her shoulders. She should have stood up for herself sooner, saved herself some grief. Another lesson learned.

First things first. She walked back down to where she'd parked the Goose, and pulled it into her driveway where it belonged. Then, as soon as she was safely inside her place and the doors were locked, the curtains snugly pulled, she called her best friend, Michelle, as she went back to the bedroom and began stripping out of her clothes. Breaking up with a boyfriend was definitely something a best friend should hear immediately.

"Dylan's history," she said as soon as Michelle answered. "I just gave him the boot."

"What happened?" Michelle sounded shocked. "Was he cheating on you?"

"Not that I know of, but that doesn't mean he wasn't. I got tired of him mooching."

"Damn. He's so good-looking, too." The shock faded into regret, and a sigh came down the phone line.

Jenner sat down on the bed to peel off her sweaty jeans, holding the phone cradled between her head and shoulders. "Yeah, but stupid. Let's not leave out stupid."

Michelle was quiet for a moment—barely—then her voice picked up enthusiasm. "So! The night's young, and you're free. Want to go out?"

That was why she'd called Michelle, Jenner thought. Michelle was always up for a party, and she needed to get out of the Dylan rut she'd let herself sink into. She forgot about her aching feet. She was twenty-three, she had just dumped a loser, and she'd get over being tired. She wanted to celebrate. "Sure. Give me time to shower. I'll meet you at the Bird," she said, naming their pre-Dylan favorite bar.

"Woo hoo!" Michelle shouted. "Bird, watch out! We're back!"

She and Michelle made a pretty hot team, if she did say so herself. Michelle was barely over five feet tall, with a mass of curly black hair, big brown eyes, and curves in all the right places. Jenner herself was of medium height and on the skinny side, but when she took time with her hair and makeup and put on something short and tight, she held her own. An hour later, they hit the door at Bird's, whooping with delight and singing "Hit the Road, Jack," inviting all the women present to sing along in the chorus. Jenner changed "Jack" to "Dylan," which didn't work quite as well, but who cared? She was having fun, and there was no shortage of guys wanting to dance with her.

She ended up stumbling home at dawn, thankful for the first time that she worked second shift and could get in some sleep. She hadn't drunk that much, just a couple of beers over the past five hours, but fatigue had sucker-punched her. Maybe twenty-three wasn't as young as she'd thought it was, because while she'd bounced back for a while, the bounce hadn't been all that high and now she could barely put one foot in front of the other.

She did remember to set the alarm clock, fell facedown across her bed, and didn't move until the alarm went off eight hours later. She lay in bed blinking at the ceiling and trying to remember what day it was. Finally everything clicked—oh, yeah, it was Friday—and the first thought that followed was that Dylan was gone, gone, gone. The second thought was that she had to go to work. She jumped up and hit the shower, humming a happy little song in honor of her freedom, and with remarkable good humor put on a clean ugly blue shirt. Not even the shirt could depress her today.

Why hadn't she realized before how *over* she and Dylan were? Why had she let him keep hanging around? Sure, it hadn't actually been that long, but she'd let the situation go on a good four or five weeks longer than she should have, kind of hoping it would improve when she knew damn good and well it wouldn't. It never did. She had to learn to see around that big blind spot she had. Well, not quite a blind spot. She'd known Dylan wasn't what she'd wanted him to be, just like her dad wasn't the dad she wanted. She'd given up on good old dad a long time ago, but at first, for a couple of weeks, Dylan had shown real promise. Then reality had set in, and it hadn't been pretty.

She got through her shift at work, and faced the weekend off with the same sense of lightheartedness. She could do what she wanted, when she wanted. And what she wanted was to go out again with Michelle, so they made another night of it and closed down Bird's again.

It wasn't until dinner break at work on Monday that she heard about the lottery. She was in the dingy break room with her coworkers, unenthusiastically chewing on a ham sandwich and chasing it with a Pepsi, listening to them talk about how there'd been a jackpot winner this time, but no one had come forward with the winning ticket. "It was sold over at that convenience store on Twenty-seventh," said Margo Russell. "What if the ticket was lost? I'd shoot myself if I lost a ticket worth three hundred million!"

"Two hundred and ninety-five million," someone corrected.

"Close enough. What's five million, one way or another?" Margo joked.

Jenner almost choked. She sat frozen, unable to swallow the bite of sandwich in her mouth. Her throat felt paralyzed, along with the rest of her. The convenience store on Twenty-seventh Street? That was the store where she bought the beer.

The thought, the possibility, could barely form itself. Could *she* have . . . ? Sheer terror, the sense of standing on the edge of a cliff and teetering back and forth, made sweat form along her hairline.

Then common sense asserted itself, and the world around her swam back into normal focus. She chewed and swallowed. Nah, things like that didn't happen to people like her. She doubted she'd won even five bucks. There had been a lot of people in there buying lottery tickets. The odds against her winning had to be at least a thousand to one, maybe two or three thousand to one. She hadn't paid any attention to the drawing on Friday night, hadn't checked the newspapers, hadn't watched any news, because she'd been too busy having fun with Michelle. The lottery tickets were still right where she'd dropped them, in the bottom of her denim bag.

Several issues of that day's newspapers were scattered around the break room. She picked one up and began flipping through it, looking for the lottery numbers. Finally she found the notice and tore it out. A glance at the clock on the wall told her she had five minutes before they had to be back to work.

Her heart was pounding as she hurried to her locker and with shaking hands spun the dial on the padlock. Don't get excited, she scolded herself. Getting her hopes up just meant a bigger letdown. The odds were heavily against her. This was just to make sure, so she wouldn't spend the rest of her shift wondering about it—kind of like making sure Dylan was a loser and a jerk so she wouldn't spend the rest of her life wondering if she'd made a mistake in dumping him. After she'd checked the tickets and satisfied herself that she hadn't won, she'd joke about it with Margo and the others, just like she'd joked about Dylan with Michelle.

Grabbing her bag, she dumped it upside down in the locker, completely emptying it. Two lottery tickets fell free, and she grabbed them. Where was the third one? What if she couldn't find the third one? What if she never found it and no one claimed the jackpot? She would go the rest of her life knowing she'd probably missed the chance to have two hundred and ninety-five million dollars.

Calm down. You didn't win. She never expected to win

23

when she bought a ticket, she just bought them because the possibility gave her a little buzz, a little moment of "what if."

She took a deep breath and scrabbled through the pile of stuff, heaving a big sigh of relief when the missing ticket was finally in her hand. She compared the numbers to the numbers on the scrap she'd torn from the newspaper, and almost laughed when reality smacked her in the face. None of the numbers matched. So much for her panic over not immediately seeing the ticket.

She looked at the next ticket, and looked again. 7, 11, 23, 47 . . . Her vision wavered; she couldn't see the remaining numbers. She heard herself gasping for breath. Her knees went weak, and she leaned against the open locker. The lottery ticket dropped from her suddenly nerveless fingers, and absolute panic washed over her even though the ticket had gone no farther than the floor. Sinking to her knees, she grabbed up the ticket and once again began comparing the numbers, laboriously concentrating on each one: 7, 11, 23, 47, 53, 67.

She checked the scrap of newspaper again, then again, looking back and forth between it and the ticket. The numbers didn't change.

"Holy shit," she whispered. "Holy shit."

Carefully she slipped the ticket and the scrap of newspaper into her front jeans pocket, climbed to her feet, closed her locker, and clicked the padlock, then numbly went back to work putting on the ugly coveralls, the white cap that covered her hair. What if she was wrong? What if this was some joke? She'd look like a fool if she told anyone.

She'd check it out tomorrow. Maybe she'd turn on the news in the morning and find the jackpot had been claimed, and when she looked at the ticket again she'd see that she'd read one of the numbers wrong.

"Are you okay?" Margo asked as Jenner slipped into place. "You look kinda green."

"I just got too hot." The instinct to keep everything quiet was too strong for her to ignore, even with a good-hearted soul like Margo.

"Yeah, this heat is miserable. You need to drink more water."

Somehow she made it through the rest of her shift, somehow she managed to drive home, though she gripped the steering wheel of the Blue Goose so tightly her hands ached. She was breathing too fast, gulping in air, and her lips were numb, her head swimming. She blew out a big sigh of relief when she finally steered the Goose into her driveway, cut the headlights, killed the engine. Just as if her heart wasn't galloping a hundred miles an hour, she got out and carefully locked the Goose's doors, went up the steps to her creaky little porch, unlocked her own door, and stepped inside the safety of home. It wasn't until then, after relocking the door behind her and she was safe, that she pulled the ticket and the piece of newsprint from her front jeans pocket, laid them side by side on the coffee table, and forced herself to look at the numbers again.

7, 11, 23, 47, 53, 67.

They were the same on both pieces of paper.

She checked them one more time, then did it again. She got a pencil, wrote down the numbers on the ticket, then checked that against the piece of newspaper. Nothing changed. Her heart began to race again.

"Holy shit." She swallowed hard. "I've won the lottery."

Chapter Two

Sleeping was impossible. The clock ticked into the small hours while Jenner paced back and forth, stopping occasionally to look at those numbers: 7, 11, 23, 47, 53, 67. They didn't change, either on the ticket or the scrap of newspaper, no matter how many times she checked them. Maybe the newspaper had made a typo in one of the numbers; maybe there'd be a correction in the next edition. And maybe she was crazy, for almost wishing the numbers were wrong, but . . . holy hell, two hundred and ninety-five million dollars!

What was she supposed to do with that kind of money? Five thousand, yeah. She could handle five thousand. She knew exactly what she'd do with it: pay off the Goose, buy some new clothes, maybe go to Disney World or something like that. She'd always wanted to go to Disney World, no matter how hokey that sounded. Five thousand bucks would be easy.

Even twenty thousand, she'd have no problem with. Fifty thousand . . . she'd buy a new car, sure, maybe find a small house that was fixable, but run-down enough that she could afford the payments, and use the rest of the money as a down payment. She was okay with renting—she didn't have to do any repairs, though getting the landlord to do anything was a pain in the ass—but owning her own place would be kind of nice, too.

Beyond fifty thousand, though, was scary territory. She didn't know anything about investments or crap like that, and while she didn't have any experience with extra money, *real* extra money instead of just a twenty here and there, she was pretty sure she wasn't supposed to stick it in a bank and just let it sit. She was supposed to *do* things with the money, move it around according to the mysterious ways of the market, put it to work.

She didn't know how to do any of that. She knew what stocks were, sort of, but had no real idea what a bond was or what it did. Scam artists would be waiting in line to take advantage of her—good old Jerry, her dad, would be first in line—and she was lost as to how she could protect herself.

After yet another look at the ticket, nausea overwhelmed her and she ran to the bathroom, hanging over the cracked old toilet for a long time even though nothing except hot water came from her mouth. Finally she took some deep breaths, and bent over the sink to splash cold water on her face. Then she braced her hands on the cool porcelain and stared at herself in the mirror, knowing that the reflection she saw was a lie. According to the mirror, nothing had changed, yet she knew that *everything* had changed, that the life with which she was comfortable no longer existed.

She looked around the bathroom, at the dingy tile on the floor, the cheap fiberglass shower, the flyspecked mirror, and she almost collapsed under the overwhelming sense that what she saw wasn't real. All of this stuff suited her fine. This was where she belonged. She was comfortable here, in a run-down, aging duplex in a going-downhill neighborhood. In another ten years this area would be a slum, and she'd have moved on to some place that was pretty much on the same level this one was now, and she'd have been okay with that. This was her life. She scraped by, she managed to pay her bills, and she and Michelle had the occasional blast at Bird's. She knew where she fit in this world.

But this was no longer her world, and the sickening realization was enough to make her bend over the toilet once more, her stomach heaving. The only way she could keep things the same was to never claim the winnings, and, yeah, like *that* was going to happen. She wasn't stupid. Nervous and nauseated, maybe, but not stupid.

She would be saying good-bye to almost everything from this life. She thought of all her friends, both casual and close, and of them all she thought only Michelle would stick. She and Michelle had been friends practically from the day they'd met, back in high school. She'd spent as much time at Michelle's house, probably more, than she'd spent at her own home—wherever that had happened to be, with Jerry dragging her from place to place and always leaving behind a couple of months of unpaid rent. The way he figured it, he paid rent for only two or three months out of the year, and the rest of the time he got to live in a place for free because it usually took the landlord a couple of months to kick them out. In Jerry's world, only fools paid rent every month.

Jerry was going to be a problem. It wasn't a question of *if* he'd cause trouble, but *how much.*

Jenner had no illusions about her dad. She hadn't seen him in months, didn't even know if he was still in the Chicago area, but as sure as the sun rose in the east he'd turn up as soon as he heard about the lottery, and do whatever he could to get his hands on as much of the money as possible.

Therefore, she had to take steps to protect the money before she claimed it.

She'd read about people setting up plans and stuff that sheltered the money, sometimes waiting weeks before going public that they'd won. That's what she would do. She'd keep working at Harvest until she actually got the money, but as soon as possible—today—she'd find someone whose job it was to know what to do with this kind of cash.

By three a.m., she was exhausted, both physically and mentally. She stripped down and climbed into bed, then set her alarm for eight just in case she was able to doze off. She had too much to do to risk oversleeping. Around dawn, she fell into a fitful sleep, waking often to check the clock, and finally getting up before the alarm went off. After taking a shower, she nuked a cup of instant coffee and sipped it while she blow-dried her hair and put on makeup.

At eight thirty, she was watching the clock as she flipped through the phone book's advertising pages. There was nothing under "money handlers," which was frustrating, because how the hell else would it be listed? Maybe there was something under "banks." What she learned was that there were a lot of banks in the Chicago area, and most of them advertised themselves as "full service" banks. What was that? Maybe they pumped gas for your car and checked the oil. Banks cashed checks, right? What else was there? Unfortunately, the ads didn't say what those services were, so she was still in the dark.

She slammed the phone book shut and angrily paced the kitchen. She hated feeling ignorant, hated that she couldn't look up what she wanted in the yellow pages, because she didn't know how things were listed. But she'd never had a bank account, mostly because she never had much money and a bank account seemed stupid. She paid her bills either in cash, or by money order. That wasn't the wrong way to do things, was it? Lots of people handled their bills that way— most of the people she knew, in fact.

Already she was running into that wall she'd sensed—the wall between the life she knew and the life all that money would automatically bring with it. Other people had managed, and she would, too. She could figure things out.

Opening the phone book again, she looked up one of those full-service banks, checked that the clock had ticked past nine, and dialed the number. When a woman answered in a modulated, professionally friendly tone, Jenner said, "I saw your ad in the phone book. Exactly what does 'full service' mean?"

"It means we offer financial planning and investment services, as well as financing for home, autos, boats, unsecured personal loans, and a variety of checking and savings plans that can be tailored to your needs," the woman said promptly.

"Thank you." Jenner disconnected, having found out what she needed to know. *Financial planning.* She should have thought of that. She heard the term on television all the time. The financial markets were always doing something, going up, going down, spinning in circles and evidently doing everything except kissing its own ass.

Lesson number one: What she thought of as "money," people with a lot of money thought of as "finance."

Going back to the advertising pages, she looked up "Financial Planners." There were a number of listings, including some she'd seen in commercials. There was also several subcategories, for mutual funds, stocks and bonds, investment and brokerage firms.

She read the listings under "Financial Planning Consultants" three times, then chose Payne Echols

Financial Services. Their ad was more than a simple listing, but less than a full page, which she figured made them established but not the biggest firm in town. The big boys might secretly make fun of her, or, worse, take advantage of her. A midsize firm would be more likely to count its blessings, and treat her better.

Choosing a firm was just one decision, but that one small step made her feel better. She was in control of this. She didn't have to do anything she didn't want to do. If she didn't like the people at Payne Echols, she'd choose another investment firm.

She blew out a small breath and dialed the number. On the second ring, another of those professionally modulated voices said, "Payne Echols Financial Services. How may I direct your call?"

"I don't know. I want to make an appointment with someone, as soon as possible."

The woman paused briefly. "May I ask what sort of services you require? Then I'll know which of our financial planners have the proper expertise."

"Ah . . ." Jenner thought quickly, wary of blurting out the truth. "I've received an inheritance, about fifty thousand, and I want to invest it." She plucked the number out of midair, but it seemed like a good number, big enough to need advice but not big enough to attract attention.

"Hold, please," the woman said, returning to her smooth tone. "I'll connect you."

"Wait! Who are you connecting me to?"

"Ms. Smith's assistant. She'll book your appointment."

There was a half-second of dead air, then some generic tinny music began assaulting her eardrums. What were they trying to do, bore her into hanging up? Why didn't companies play lively music, something interesting?

She waited a few minutes, trying her best to ignore the awful music. How long did it take to switch a call? She tapped one toe, growing vaguely annoyed. Just as she was beginning to think about hanging up, there was a faint click and another smooth female voice said, "Ms. Smith's office, how may I help you?"

She was getting tired of all these impersonal, perfect voices. Would these people be fired if they ever revealed anything as mundane as interest? "My name is Jenner Redwine. I'd like to make an appointment with Ms. Smith."

"Certainly, Ms. Redwine. When would you like to come in?"

"As soon as possible. Now."

"Now? Well . . . Ms. Smith does have an opening in forty-five minutes. Would it be possible for you to be here by then?"

"I'll be there."

Jenner hung up, then securely tucked the lottery ticket and scrap of newspaper in her wallet, dropped the wallet back in her denim purse, then went outside and unlocked the Goose. The driver's door stuck, as usual, and she swore under her breath. Forty-five minutes wasn't very long, in Chicago traffic, and she didn't have time to wrestle with the door. Gripping the handle, she gave it one more tug and the door flew open, almost knocking her butt on the ground.

"The first thing I do," she muttered, "is get a new car." It didn't have to be a fancy car, just something *new*, without a single ding, and with nonsticking doors. And after that . . . she didn't know. She couldn't think much about "after that." One step at a time, and the first step was getting the money organized and settled.

As she drove she thought about calling Michelle, telling her what was going on. She even fished her cell phone out of her bag, thumbed in the first couple of numbers, before she hit the End button and dropped the phone back into the bag. Michelle would think she was just joking around, but . . . what if she didn't? That wariness surfaced again. Jenner wanted everything settled and protected before the news got out.

The Payne Echols offices were downtown, where parking was at a premium, but when she drove past she noticed the firm had a private parking deck attached, and watched over by a guard to keep the general public out. She pulled up to the orange barricade arm and rolled down the window. The guard looked at the Goose and she could almost see the doubt running through his brain. "I have an appointment with Ms. Smith."

"Your name?"

"Jenner Redwine."

He punched a few keys on a small computer, evidently confirmed that her name came up on the approved list, and raised the barricade. Jenner drove though, parked in the first empty slot she came to, and hurried to the entrance.

As soon as she opened the door, a sense of uneasiness rippled down her spine. The Payne Echols offices were cool, austere, and so quiet she could hear herself breathing. The main colors were gray and brown, as if the decorator had been deathly afraid of color. The abstract paintings on the walls each had a touch of blue, but even that was subdued. There were a lot of very impressive plants, so perfect they couldn't be real, but when she poked her finger into a planter she found dirt. Hurriedly she stuck her hand behind her back and tried to dust the dirt from her finger as she crossed to a desk half-hidden behind more plants.

Behind the desk was a slim, business-suited brunette, who lifted her head at Jenner's approach and said, "May I help you?" Her tone was perfectly neutral, just like her surroundings, but once again Jenner had a sense of being sized up and dismissed.

Keeping her own voice as blank and calm as the receptionist's, she said, "Jenner Redwine. I have an appointment with Ms. Smith."

"Please have a seat. I'll notify Ms. Smith's assistant."

Jenner perched on the edge of an uncomfortable gray sofa. Straight ahead of her was one of the abstract paintings, which looked to her as if a blind monkey had painted it. How hard could it be? All that was needed was a couple of paintbrushes, a canvas, and whatever colors happened to be lying around. Haphazardly apply the colors, and presto, one big ugly painting.

Some men in suits walked past, and she could spot a few people in the offices that were within her limited field of vision. They were all busy, focused, on the phone or poring over papers, or tapping on a computer keyboard. She didn't see any women.

Evidently Ms. Smith wasn't in any hurry to greet her new client. Uneasily Jenner wondered just how trustworthy financial planners were. She'd have to trust her instinct when it came to deciding whether or not to use Ms. Smith, because no one she knew had enough money to know squat about investments and taxes and stuff like that. She had only the yellow pages and her common sense to guide her.

Finally a stick-thin woman appeared from a carpeted hallway and approached. "Jenner Redwine?"

"Yes." Jenner quickly stood, gripping her bag.

"I'm sorry to keep you waiting. I'm Ms. Smith's assistant. If you'll come this way . . . ?" She indicated the hallway, and led Jenner at a brisk pace down the long expanse.

They walked past large, slickly decorated offices, visible

through open doors. Other doors were closed, so Jenner had to use her imagination about their appearance and inhabitants. As they went down the hallway, the offices became smaller in size, the furniture plainer. She began to think she should have picked a number larger than fifty grand for her white lie, because evidently Ms. Smith wasn't very high in the Payne Echols pecking order.

The assistant stopped in front of a door, tapped lightly, then turned the knob. "Ms. Redwine to see you," she said, stepping back so Jenner could enter the small office, then closing the door and presumably returning to her even smaller cubbyhole.

A somewhat stocky woman with too-short hair stood up behind a slightly battered desk and with a tight smile extended her hand to Jenner. "I'm Al Smith."

"Al?" Jenner repeated. Maybe she'd heard wrong.

The tight smile widened the barest bit. "It's short for Alanna. No one calls me that." From the complete lack of humor in the comment, Jenner suspected no one dared. Al Smith continued, "I understand you have a small inheritance you're interested in investing."

Small? No one Jenner knew would call fifty grand "small," but in a place like this, even to the inhabitants of the less-than-lavish offices, it was probably chump change. Again she perched on the edge of her seat, and studied Al Smith across the expanse of desk.

Ms. Smith couldn't be called a pretty woman. Not only was her dark hair too short, she didn't wear much makeup— if any—and the gray suit she was wearing made her look boxy. If her lack of wrinkles was anything to go by, she was probably not much older than Jenner, but the image she projected added ten years to her age. Her eyes were disconcertingly pale, her gaze direct, and she didn't look as if she laughed very often.

Jenner didn't trust easily. Just because this woman worked for a top-notch financial planning firm, didn't mean she was reliable and honest. She did like the no-bullshit attitude, though.

"Can I ask you a question?" she finally said.

Ms. Smith looked faintly interested. "Of course, but I might not answer it."

"Fair enough. How long have you worked here?"

"A little more than two years." She didn't seem surprised by the question. "It's obvious I'm low man on the totem pole here. That doesn't mean I'm not good at my job. I'll work my way up."

"How old are you?"

Ms. Smith gave a bark of laughter. "That's more personal than I expected, but I don't mind telling you. I'm twenty-seven. Yes, I'm young. I understand your concern. But I'm here to help, and I won't always be in one of the back offices."

The straightforward ambition appealed to Jenner more than any generic, diplomatic reassurance would have. She glanced around the small office, thinking that Al Smith might be leaving it sooner than she'd expected. Her gaze fell on the shelf behind the desk. There were a couple of plants, smaller and less perfect than those in the lobby, and some simply framed snapshots of Ms. Smith and another woman smiling into the camera, their arms looped around each other's shoulders. The pose struck Jenner as somewhat romantic, and she stared at the photos a moment too long.

Ms. Smith glanced over her shoulder at the photos, and her mouth tightened. "Yes, Ms. Redwine, I'm a lesbian—but don't worry; you aren't my type. Skinny little blondes don't appeal to me."

Judging from the photographs, Jenner would say Ms.

Smith preferred tall, curvy redheads. To each his—or her—own.

Jenner smiled, relaxing. She liked this plainspoken, up-front woman. "I don't have an inheritance," she admitted, digging into her bag and pulling out her wallet. Opening it, she pulled out the newspaper clipping and laid it on the desk in front of Ms. Smith. Next she took out the lottery ticket and placed it beside the piece of newsprint.

Ms. Smith gave her a curious look, then picked up a pair of glasses and slid them in place. She looked down at the two pieces of paper, and Jenner watched her expression change as she realized what she was seeing. "Holy sh— Excuse me. Is this what I think it is?"

"Yes."

Al Smith abruptly sat back. With one finger she adjusted her glasses, as if to make certain she was seeing properly. She looked back and forth from the newsprint to the lottery ticket, comparing each number much as Jenner had done. Finally she lifted her head, and looked her new client in the eye. For the first time there was a twinkle there as she said, "I think skinny blondes just became my type."

Jenner was surprised into a snort of laughter. "Sorry. My type comes with a penis. Besides, your redhead could probably beat me up."

"She could," Al admitted. She and Jenner grinned at each other, two tough-minded young women who recognized similar qualities in each other. They were both used to working hard for what they had. Al no doubt made way more money than Jenner did, but she was still fighting and clawing her way up the career ladder.

Jenner didn't know anything about investments, but she understood people, and how the pecking order worked. That lottery ticket represented a huge stepping-stone to Al, just as it did to her. By bringing in this size of an account, Al would leapfrog over everyone else on her level, and would quickly move into one of those larger offices. With her added influence, she would gain other accounts, and the effect would snowball. If she was half as good as Jenner thought she might be, Al Smith could one day have her own investment firm, or at least be a senior partner at Payne Echols.

Al sobered, surveying Jenner over the top of her glasses. "Most lottery winners are broke within five years, no matter how much they win."

A chill rippled over Jenner's skin. She couldn't imagine how she could possibly lose that much money, but the possibility made her feel a little sick to her stomach. "That's why I'm here. I don't want to be broke in five years."

"Then you'll have to be very careful. The only way to completely protect the money is to set it up in an irrevocable trust that will pay you X amount every year—or every month, however you wanted to set it up—but you'd lose control of the principal, and you don't strike me as the type of person who would like that."

Everything in Jenner rebelled at the idea of letting someone else have control of her money, even though the act would be voluntary. *Irrevocable*. She didn't like the sound of that.

"That's what I thought," Al said drily, reading Jenner's expression. "So . . . whether or not you're insanely rich in five years, or broke and working a dead-end job, is entirely up to you. If you can't turn down the moochers, you'll go through this pretty fast. I'd strongly recommend either an irrevocable trust or getting the winnings in a yearly payout rather than lump sum. Lump sum is the smartest choice, *if* you can leave it alone."

"I can leave it alone," Jenner replied, thinking of Jerry. "I want it protected, invested, where no one can get to it without my in-person say-so. My dad—" She stopped, her expression wry. "He's the main one I'll have to watch out for. Let's just say he doesn't believe in working for what he has."

"All families have one like that," Al observed. "Okay, let's start working out a plan. Lump sum, you'll probably get about"—her fingers danced over a calculator—"a hundred and fifty million dollars."

"What?" Jenner sat up straight. "What happened to the other hundred and forty-five million?"

"Taxes. The government gets what it wants before you get anything."

"But that's almost half!" She was outraged. Yeah, a hundred and fifty million was still an incredibly hefty amount of money, but . . . but—she wanted the rest of it, too. She'd won it, fair and square. Yeah, she'd known, vaguely, that she'd have to pay taxes, but she hadn't realized the hit would be that big.

"Sure is. If you add up all the taxes—income, social security, sales taxes, the taxes on gasoline and the phone bill and everything else, it isn't unusual for people to end up paying over sixty percent to the government, but a lot of it is hidden. If the average guy realized how much Washington is sucking out of his pocket, there'd be riots in the streets."

"I'll carry the pitchfork," Jenner muttered.

"I bet you would. Still, we can put a hundred and fifty million to serious work." She put some more numbers into the calculator. "A return rate of four percent would give you an annual discretionary income of around six million, without ever touching the principal. And four percent is a low estimate. You should make more."

Okay. Wow. Six million a year, without drawing down the

principal at all. She didn't need six million, she could live on a lot less, so that much could stay in her investments, working and earning. The more she had, the more interest it earned, and her worth kept growing. She felt as if a door had just opened, and she could see what was inside the room. She *got* it.

All she had to do was be smart, and not blow it.

Al launched into a mini-lecture about the variety of investments available—stocks and dividends, Treasury bills, and high-level debt. Jenner didn't pretend to understand it all, but she absorbed what she could and asked a hundred questions. She set her own requirements: no one would be moving her money around without her permission. She didn't want to find that Al or anyone else at Payne Echols had decided to invest her money in a risky stock or whatever, and she'd lost everything. She wanted to be the final word on every decision. She also didn't want anything at her house that would leave her open to theft. She wouldn't put anything past Jerry. He'd do whatever he could to get his hands on the money. People like him were a big part of the reason most lottery winners were broke within five years.

Al set to work formulating a plan. A small part of the money—a hundred thousand—would be put in a bank for Jenner's immediate use. Most of it would be in a savings account that she could easily access, moving money to checking as she needed it. She would also need a safe-deposit box where she could keep all her papers, and no one else could get to them unless she personally granted that person access. Al would work up an investment plan, and when Jenner claimed her winnings she could have the money transferred directly into those accounts.

Jenner breathed a sigh of relief. She wouldn't claim the money until everything was in place, but Al said she'd put everything else on the back burner and get all the paperwork prepared. In another week, at the latest, she'd be ready.

Once the plans were hammered out and she was back in the Goose, Jenner blew out a huge breath. She'd walked out of Payne Echols somehow . . . changed. She was part of the financial world now, and it felt strange, but exciting. Her heart was beating faster, and she felt like laughing and dancing. She wanted to celebrate. She was a multimillionaire! Well, almost. Soon. A week at the most.

She glanced at her watch. Michelle would be at lunch. Grabbing her cell phone, she paused for a split second as she considered how expensive cell minutes were—maybe she should wait until she was home, and use the regular phone—then reality smacked her in the face again and she laughed. Her cell phone bill didn't matter anymore. She dialed Michelle's number.

Michelle answered with a crisp, "What's wrong?" because Jenner almost never called during the day.

There was no easy lead-up, no way other than to blurt out the truth. "I won the lottery."

"Yeah, right. Seriously, what's up? Is Dylan pestering you? Has the Goose died?"

"No, the Goose is fine. I won the lottery," Jenner said again. "The big one. Two hundred and ninety-five million, though I've just met with a financial consultant and she says after taxes I'll end up with a lump sum of about one-fifty. Million."

A long moment of silence stretched out. Finally Michelle said, in a small, faint voice, "You're serious."

"As a heart attack."

The next sound was a piercing scream. Jenner laughed, then screamed along with Michelle. She sat in the Goose, cell phone to her ear, and laughed until tears ran down her cheeks. Her life had changed and she knew it, but at least Michelle was there for her.

"If you're pulling my leg, I'll kill you," Michelle finally choked out.

"I know. It's hard to believe. I just checked my ticket last night, and I've been scrambling since then to get things set up. You're the first person I've told—well, except for the financial person. *Don't* tell anyone else yet."

"My lips are zipped. Oh my God. I can't believe it. You're rich!"

"Almost. Soon. Maybe next week."

"That's close enough!" Michelle whooped again. "Girlfriend, we are going to celebrate big time at the Bird tonight, and drinks are on you!"

Chapter Three

Habit was a weird thing. Either that, or she still couldn't quite believe what was happening to her. Whatever the reason, Jenner went in to work her regular shift at Harvest that night; celebrating with Michelle would have to wait until afterward. She didn't make the phone call to begin the process of claiming her winnings, either, even though Al was hard at work getting things ready. She felt almost as if she were prodding a sleeping tiger, and once that tiger woke up, everything would be out of her control and in the tiger's.

She wasn't ready to tell the world yet. She wasn't ready to abandon all the normal aspects of her life. So she put on the ugly polyester shirt once again, went into work, and donned the coveralls and hair covering. She joked with Margo, she ate her usual sandwich, she did her job—and all the while she had the weird sense of being in two worlds at the same time, as well as feeling sharp, unexpected pangs of grief. She might never see these people again, and though she wasn't close friends with any of them, they were still a huge part of her everyday life. As soon as she went public, she probably wouldn't be able to do ordinary things, at least for a while.

And really, would she want to work in a meat-packing plant once she had all that money? No, she wouldn't, not for a single minute. But for now, this moment, she didn't have the money and ordinary things felt special, as if she should savor them and commit them to memory.

After work, though, she changed clothes and she and Michelle hit Bird's, where she bought their drinks, they danced almost nonstop, and they laughed at everything and nothing. Happiness fizzed like ginger ale in her veins. She was young, and she was *rich*! How could life get any better? So what if she was spending most of her cash, and payday was still three days away? She had gas in the Goose, food in the house, and celebrating with Michelle was more important than worrying about money. In a few days, she'd never have to worry about money again.

Morning brought reality with it. Once again, there were calls she had to make and things she had to do.

Jenner took a deep breath and dialed a very important number. When the call was answered, she had to take a second deep breath. "I have the winning ticket," she said baldly. "What do I need to do?"

"Are you the sole ticket holder?" The man who had answered sounded almost disinterested. Maybe they got a lot of calls from people claiming to be the winner. Probably she was something like the fiftieth person to call. Grimly she imagined all those other people trying to claim her winnings. She could just see them sitting at home working on manufacturing a fake lottery ticket, trying to get it just right, hoping they could get the money and disappear before the real winner came forward.

"Yeah. Yes."

"You'll need to bring in the winning ticket, of course, as well as a photo form of identification, and proof of your social security number—if not your actual card, then a pay stub, or something like that, that shows your number."

Jenner tried to think where her social security card might be, but she came up blank. She couldn't remember the last time she'd seen it. Maybe she could find one of her pay stubs, though. What on earth had she done with the last one? She began to panic. If she couldn't find a pay stub, what would she do?

Wait until she got another paycheck, that's what. The commonsense reply loosened the sudden tightness in her chest, let her breathe again. "Okay, what else?"

"That's it. Ticket, identification, social security verification. When will you be coming in?"

"I don't know." That depended on how long it took her to find a pay stub—*if* she could find one. "Tomorrow morning, probably. Definitely by Friday afternoon. Do I need to make an appointment?"

He gave a little laugh. "No, that isn't necessary. Our office hours are from eight thirty to four thirty." He gave her the address, which was on the seventh floor of a building downtown, close to city hall. She'd never been to city hall, but she bet parking was a bitch. She'd be better off taking the bus, instead of driving.

After thanking the man and hanging up, she began tearing through her closet and old purses, looking for her social security card. She'd always been careless with it, because, hell, she had the number memorized, and it wasn't as if she had anything anyone would want. Well, now she *did* have something millions of people would want, and she steadily swore under her breath at her own stupidity as she looked in every pocket of every old wallet she could find. She would never, ever again be so careless. If she ever found that damn card, it was going in the safe-deposit box, which she didn't have yet, with the rest of the important stuff she didn't have yet, but soon would.

Finally she gave up. The card was probably long gone, incinerated in some trash dump somewhere. She'd had it when she got her driver's license, obviously, but renewing the license didn't require one, so she hadn't kept track of it—and she'd moved at least three times since getting her license.

That left a pay stub for proof. She didn't keep her pay stubs, either. She usually either dropped them in her bag when she got her checks cashed, or put them in the Goose's glove compartment. She didn't let the Goose get filled with clutter, because the poor thing looked bad enough as it was, but she couldn't remember when she'd last gathered up all the pieces of paper that seemed to accumulate.

She hurried outside, unlocked the passenger door, and leaned in to open the compartment. Napkins from fast-food places practically exploded outward, along with ketchup squirt-packs, little salt and pepper packets, drinking straws, melted peppermints, gum—and two crumpled pay stubs. Jenner grabbed them, closing her eyes as she held them to her chest and sent a silent thank-you upward in case God was listening or something.

She took all of the debris and the pay stubs inside, where she carefully stored one of the stubs in her purse with the ticket. Then she took a pair of scissors and carefully cut the remaining pay stub into tiny bits, which she flushed down the toilet. From now on, she had to be careful with every bit of paperwork.

She checked the time: almost noon. She didn't have enough time now to get downtown and back before going to work, and something in her still wouldn't let her blow off her job. *Maybe next week*, she thought. Duh! She'd better find out how long it would take to actually get the money, because she had to live until then.

She grabbed the phone and hit Redial. When the same guy answered, she asked, "I called a little while ago. After I bring in the winning ticket, how long does it take to actually get the money?"

"Four to eight weeks," he replied.

"Holy sh—! You're kidding." She was flabbergasted. Damn good thing she hadn't quit work yesterday!

"No, processing the claims are time-consuming, but we take pains that no mistakes are made."

"Thanks," she said, hanging up. She wanted to kick something. Eight weeks! She couldn't even wait eight weeks to claim it, because the processing wouldn't start until she did so. The sooner she got to the office, the better—and then she'd *still* have to work at that damn meat-packing plant for maybe two more months.

There was only one person she could call to vent, so she dialed Michelle's number.

"Two months!" she said, incensed, when Michelle answered. "It'll take them almost two months to get the money to me!"

"You're shittin' me."

"I wish."

"How hard can it be? All they have to do is cut a check!"

"Tell me about it. So, no more celebrating for a while," Jenner said glumly. "I blew most of my cash last night, and I have two more months of rent to worry about. Damn it."

"Damn it," Michelle echoed. "Crap. I was looking forward to doing some serious shopping, maybe putting in some vacation time somewhere cool, but if it takes two months to get the money then summer will be over."

"I know." Jenner sighed. The heat was killing her, and

getting away sounded great, but it wasn't going to happen. "I guess that plan will change to going somewhere warm this winter. I'm going downtown tomorrow morning to start the ball rolling. The longer I put that off, the longer it'll take to actually get the money."

"I'd love to go with you, just to watch," Michelle said wistfully. "But I can't take off work, so you remember every detail, okay? I want to hear everything."

"Promise."

The next morning she took extra pains with her hair and makeup. Her roots were showing some, but not too bad, so she made a zigzag part on top to hide the darker color. She put on the clothes she wore to funerals—a white, short-sleeve, button-up blouse paired with a dark blue pencil skirt and white strappy sandals—because the weather was just too hot to put on panty hose and high heels. Besides, she had a run in the only pair of panty hose she owned, and thanks to the celebration with Michelle she didn't have any extra cash to buy another pair. She had enough cash for the bus, and that was about all, until she got her next paycheck.

Strange how, in the space of a phone conversation, she could go from quitting work in two days to pinching pennies by not buying a new pair of panty hose.

She used the bus ride to compose herself, and get her thoughts ordered. Another talk with Al had cleared up a few more points. Al said if Jenner wanted, she could set up a blind trust, to keep Jenner's identity secret, but was there really any point? When Jenner Redwine, who didn't even have a bank account, suddenly quit work, bought a new car, and moved to a better place, everyone she knew was bound to figure something was up. Besides, Michelle couldn't keep a secret forever. Jenner loved her, but Michelle tended to talk first and think later. Setting up a blind trust would also mean hiring a lawyer, which would be more delays, besides what the lawyer would charge. She just wanted to get everything started.

She got off at the nearest bus stop, found the correct building, and took the elevator up to the seventh floor. When she opened the door, everyone in the room turned to look at her. Her heartbeat hitched. Did anyone in the room breathe as she approached the long, tall counter? She didn't think so.

Three other people—maybe they'd won some of the smaller payouts—were seated in the small waiting area. One was reading a magazine, but the other two watched her. What were they waiting for? God, was she supposed to sign in and wait her turn? This was nerve-racking enough, without having to wait.

An older woman pasted on a good imitation of a sincere smile when Jenner reached the counter. Swallowing hard, Jenner reached into her bag and took out the winning ticket, as well as her pay stub and driver's license, and placed them all on the counter.

"I won," she half-whispered, trying to keep everyone else in the room from hearing.

The woman picked up the items, looked at the ticket, and a wide grin split her face. "Yes, you certainly did." She nodded to the people in the waiting area behind Jenner, and they all got up from their chairs. Jenner turned, and a flash went off in her face, momentarily blinding her. The woman and two men fired questions at her, talking on top of each other; she couldn't pick out a single question that made sense, everything was jumbled so. She backed up and found herself pinned against the counter, unable to go either left or right.

One of them stepped on her left foot, and abruptly she'd had enough. "Hey!" she said loudly, almost shouting. "Back it up, okay? One of you almost took my toe off." The three reporters momentarily paused, and Jenner took advantage of the brief silence to announce, "My name is Jenner Redwine."

Chapter Four

YOU CAN'T UNRING A BELL.

Jenner stared down at the legal-size sheets of paper in her hand, trying to make sense of what she was reading. She'd just gotten out of the Goose, in the employee parking lot at Harvest Meat Packing, when a nondescript man had approached.

"Jenner Redwine?"

You'd think she'd have learned by now, because the past two weeks, since she'd gone public with the winning ticket, had been filled with people who wanted her to invest in a surefire business proposition, or give to charity, or give to them, or any number of variations on the theme of Give Me the Money. She should have run as fast as she could. Instead, startled, she'd turned and said, "Yeah?"

The man extended a thick envelope to her, and automatically she took it. "You've been served," he said, then the asshole winked at her before turning and hurrying away.

Served?

"I don't have a red cent yet!" she yelled furiously at his back.

"Not my problem," he called as he jumped in a white Nissan and drove away.

Jenner tore open the envelope and unfolded the stapled-together sheets of legal-size paper, quickly scanning them. Sheer rage engulfed her, making her literally see red. In that moment, if she'd been able to get her hands on Dylan, she'd have strangled him.

"Trouble?" A coworker sneered at her as he passed. "Who knew being rich would be such a bitch?" He laughed at his own joke as he entered the plant, and everyone in the vicinity laughed, too.

If she'd only known, if she'd had any idea, she'd have set up a blind trust and never gone public. She wouldn't even have told Michelle, not until she actually had the money. Not that Michelle hadn't been great, but these past two weeks had been hell—and now this. Now Dylan was suing her for half the winnings, claiming . . . whatever it was he was claiming, that they'd lived together and shared expenses and went in on the winning ticket together, along with a bunch of other bullshit.

Hounded to death was a reasonable description of what Jenner's life had been like for the past two weeks. Practically from the minute her name had been released as the jackpot winner, her phone had rung. And rung. And rung. All hours of the day and night, the phone rang, until she had finally unplugged it, more or less permanently. Charities, long-lost relatives—usually so long-lost she hadn't even known she had them—people offering her the opportunity of a lifetime to get in on the ground floor of a great business opportunity, friends who wondered if she could help them out of tight spots . . . the list was endless. At first she had patiently explained to each and every one that she hadn't received a single dime yet and possibly wouldn't for months, but she'd soon learned that reality hadn't made a dent in their persistence. Most people simply didn't believe her.

She fished out her cell phone and called Al, who had become her voice of sanity, her anchor. "I'm being sued for half," she said baldly when Al answered. "An ex-boyfriend— who I broke up with before the drawing, and I can prove it, because I called a friend and we went out to celebrate."

"Did you live together?" Al asked briskly.

"No. Never. He wore out his welcome pretty fast."

"I know you don't want to do it, but you have to hire a lawyer. The suit has to be answered and dealt with, or he wins by default." Al had been recommending an estate lawyer and Jenner had been resisting, not wanting to take on that expense when getting the money would take so long, but Jenner recognized necessity when she was staring at it.

"All right, one lawyer coming up. Can Dylan win anyway?"

"I doubt it. A lawyer can tell you more about that than I can. He probably just wants you to pay him to go away, because lawyer fees can add up fast. When your lawyer contacts his lawyer, don't be surprised if he makes an offer to settle out of court for, oh, fifty thousand or so."

"I'm not giving him one red cent, no matter how much a lawyer costs," Jenner said between gritted teeth. She glanced at her watch, then at the employees' door. She was going to be late clocking in if she didn't get a move on. "I gotta go, I'm going to be late."

"I keep telling you: quit."

"I have to have something to live on until the money comes through."

"So borrow fifteen, twenty thousand from the bank. They'll gladly give it to you just on your signature alone, no collateral required. Take a vacation, get out of here until everything settles down."

Al had been recommending that from the time Jenner's name went public, but Jenner was still too close to getting by from paycheck to paycheck to be so cavalier about going into debt for that much money. Twenty thousand was a lot of money to her, one fifth of the amount she'd settled on for discretionary cash. To her, that would be money wasted, blown on basically nothing, and she just couldn't make herself do it. Not yet, anyway. Things were getting so uncomfortable at work, she wasn't ruling anything out.

"I'll think about it." That was the first time she'd given in, even a little, on her stance that she had to work. "I don't know how much longer I can take this." She felt guilty for admitting even that much of weakness, as if she had already moved to Wussville. She ended the call and trudged toward the plant entrance.

But it wasn't just all the people asking for money, or even Dylan. It was everything. It was the way her coworkers had celebrated with her, at first—before the snide comments started. They resented her for still being there. What was she doing working when she didn't need the money? She was taking a job from someone who really *needed* a job—meaning a relative, a friend, whoever they knew who was unemployed. Her explanation about how long it took to get the money was no more than wasted breath, because to them she had options, so therefore she had no excuse. And maybe she didn't. Maybe she'd just do as Al suggested, borrow some money, and get away, which would give her the added bonus of being somewhere Jerry couldn't find her, at least for a little while.

Her dad had shown up almost immediately, as she'd

known he would. It had started with a phone call, the morning after her name was in the newspapers. "Hey, baby girl!" he'd boomed, all jovial and loving, as if it hadn't been months—almost a year—since she'd heard from him and had no idea where he was. "Way to go! We gotta go out and celebrate!"

"Where are you?" Jenner asked, not responding to the "celebrate" idea. Too many people wanted to "celebrate" with her, which of course meant she'd pick up the tab. After the first couple of "invitations," that had gotten old fast. Michelle was one thing, because Michelle had picked up the tab for Jenner during bad times, but anyone else? Uh-uh.

"Huh? Oh, nowhere important," Jerry said blithely. "I can be there in a few hours."

"Don't bother. I have to work. And it could be two months before I get any of the money."

"Two months!" The blitheness changed to shock. "What's taking so long?"

Good old Jerry, she thought. At least he didn't pretend he wanted to see her because she was his daughter and he loved her, or any other sentimental sludge. "The claim has to be processed," she said, giving her stock answer.

"Yeah, not to mention the state gets to keep the interest that two hundred and ninety-five million dollars earns while the 'processing' goes on," he groused.

"That, too." By her admittedly rough estimate, in two months the state would earn about a million dollars in interest—and there was nothing she could do about it, so it seemed pointless to waste time fretting that the money could have been in her account and earning her that kind of interest.

"Well, never mind. We can still celebrate."

"Only if you're buying. I'm broke." That should put an end to any celebrating he wanted to do, she thought. In Jerry's world, other people paid for stuff while he went along for the ride.

"Well, you said you had to work, so if you gotta, you gotta. I'll catch you some time tomorrow, okay?"

He had, and every day since then, too. If he wasn't on her front porch in the morning, wanting to have coffee with her—though of course he didn't want to have the instant she had on hand—he was on the phone, showering her with fatherly attention that was all the more disconcerting because he'd never shown any before. She didn't know how to get rid of him, because he ignored the hints that she didn't intend to become Handout Central for him—if you could call blatantly *telling* him so a "hint." The thing with Jerry was that he was so focused on what he wanted that everything else sort of bounced off him.

She didn't know how to make him go away. She even had to admit to a tiny part of her that still hoped, somehow, this time Jerry would just be happy for her and wouldn't try to relieve her of as much of the money as possible. Faith and hope were two different things: She had no faith at all in him, but she still hoped the leopard would change its larcenous spots.

Regardless of that, she took precautions. She didn't leave her bag where he could get into it. If she had to go to the bathroom while he was in her house, she took the bag with her. Everything related to the lottery, and the financial arrangements she'd made so far and the others she was making, was locked away in a safe-deposit box that she'd spent a hefty chunk of her paycheck to rent. The key was on the ring with her car keys, and they were in her pocket unless she was in bed; then she slipped them inside her pillowcase—just a normal precaution for a daughter to take, to prevent her father from boosting the Goose.

As she entered the plant, a supervisor approached. "Jenner, I need to have a talk with you before you clock in."

"I'll be late," she protested, glancing at the clock.

"Never mind that. Let's go in the office."

A cold, sick feeling coalesced in her stomach as she followed the supervisor, Don Gorski, into his small, shabby office, constructed of white-washed concrete blocks, with an unpainted concrete floor, and occupied by a beat-up metal desk, some metal filing cabinets, and two chairs.

He dropped heavily into the chair behind the beat-up desk, but didn't ask her to be seated. Instead he rubbed his jaw, looking everywhere but at her, and heaved a sigh almost as heavy as his ass was.

"You're a good worker," he finally said, "but you've been causing a lot of disruption around here in the past couple of weeks. People—"

"I'm not causing the disruption," Jenner said, heat edging into her voice. "I'm doing my job the way I always do."

"Then let me put it another way: You're the *cause* of the disruption. Reporters calling, showing up at the gate, people complaining. I don't know why you're still here. You don't need the job, and there are plenty of people who do. So why don't you do everyone a favor and quit?"

The unfairness of it made her want to beat her head against the wall. Instead she straightened her shoulders and set her jaw. "Because I need to eat and pay my rent and utility bills, just like everyone else," she replied, her tone just short of a snarl. "Believe me, as soon as I get some money to live on, I'm outta here. Until then, what am I supposed to do? Live on the street?"

He sighed again. "Look, I'm just doing my job, too. The guys up front want you to go."

Frustrated, infuriated, she threw her hands up. "Fine. Then fire me, so I can collect unemployment until the money comes through."

"They don't want—"

"I don't care what 'they' want. I care about being able to live." She leaned forward and planted her hands on the desk, anger evident in every line of her body. "I've paid unemployment taxes since I was sixteen, and never collected a dime. If you want me gone—without a lawsuit being filed, and believe me when I say that very shortly I'll be able to afford a lawyer good enough to keep this company tied up in court for years, and will cost way more than a few weeks of unemployment benefits—then that's the deal. Fire me, okay the unemployment, and I'm out of here. Mess with me in any way, and the legal fees will bankrupt this company. Are we clear on this? Take the deal to the guys up front, and get back to me."

She stalked out of the office, changed into the ugly coveralls and hair cap, and clocked in. She was late for the shift, but so what? She didn't give a damn. In fact, with fury still running through her veins, she felt pretty good. Okay, so she didn't have any money yet, but what she did have were options, and she'd just exercised one.

None of the people around her spoke or made contact, not even Margo. Jenner ignored them as studiously as they ignored her. Several of them had gone to management to complain about her, she figured, exaggerating how much of a distraction her presence had been, blowing up the case for asking her to leave. Maybe she should have brought boxes of doughnuts every day, treated everyone, but, damn it, she didn't have the money! What was so hard about that to understand?

pillowcase—just a normal precaution for a daughter to take, to prevent her father from boosting the Goose.

As she entered the plant, a supervisor approached. "Jenner, I need to have a talk with you before you clock in."

"I'll be late," she protested, glancing at the clock.

"Never mind that. Let's go in the office."

A cold, sick feeling coalesced in her stomach as she followed the supervisor, Don Gorski, into his small, shabby office, constructed of white-washed concrete blocks, with an unpainted concrete floor, and occupied by a beat-up metal desk, some metal filing cabinets, and two chairs.

He dropped heavily into the chair behind the beat-up desk, but didn't ask her to be seated. Instead he rubbed his jaw, looking everywhere but at her, and heaved a sigh almost as heavy as his ass was.

"You're a good worker," he finally said, "but you've been causing a lot of disruption around here in the past couple of weeks. People—"

"I'm not causing the disruption," Jenner said, heat edging into her voice. "I'm doing my job the way I always do."

"Then let me put it another way: You're the *cause* of the disruption. Reporters calling, showing up at the gate, people complaining. I don't know why you're still here. You don't need the job, and there are plenty of people who do. So why don't you do everyone a favor and quit?"

The unfairness of it made her want to beat her head against the wall. Instead she straightened her shoulders and set her jaw. "Because I need to eat and pay my rent and utility bills, just like everyone else," she replied, her tone just short of a snarl. "Believe me, as soon as I get some money to live on, I'm outta here. Until then, what am I supposed to do? Live on the street?"

He sighed again. "Look, I'm just doing my job, too. The guys up front want you to go."

Frustrated, infuriated, she threw her hands up. "Fine. Then fire me, so I can collect unemployment until the money comes through."

"They don't want—"

"I don't care what 'they' want. I care about being able to live." She leaned forward and planted her hands on the desk, anger evident in every line of her body. "I've paid unemployment taxes since I was sixteen, and never collected a dime. If you want me gone—without a lawsuit being filed, and believe me when I say that very shortly I'll be able to afford a lawyer good enough to keep this company tied up in court for years, and will cost way more than a few weeks of unemployment benefits—then that's the deal. Fire me, okay the unemployment, and I'm out of here. Mess with me in any way, and the legal fees will bankrupt this company. Are we clear on this? Take the deal to the guys up front, and get back to me."

She stalked out of the office, changed into the ugly coveralls and hair cap, and clocked in. She was late for the shift, but so what? She didn't give a damn. In fact, with fury still running through her veins, she felt pretty good. Okay, so she didn't have any money yet, but what she did have were options, and she'd just exercised one.

None of the people around her spoke or made contact, not even Margo. Jenner ignored them as studiously as they ignored her. Several of them had gone to management to complain about her, she figured, exaggerating how much of a distraction her presence had been, blowing up the case for asking her to leave. Maybe she should have brought boxes of doughnuts every day, treated everyone, but, damn it, she didn't have the money! What was so hard about that to understand?

Because that wasn't how they wanted things to be, she realized. In their fantasy of making it big—maybe by winning the lottery—a win brought instant wealth, an end to all problems and money worries. They'd have been happier if she'd bought a new car, regaled them with tales of big new condos and houses she was thinking of buying, letting them live vicariously through her. Instead she had remained the same: broke. She'd let them down, discredited their fantasies, and now they didn't want her around.

Within an hour, though, Don Gorski approached her. "I have papers for you to sign," he said, and she followed him, not to his office, but to a larger office up front, one occupied by two men she'd seen around but whose names she didn't know.

"We agree to your offer," one of the men said, putting his finger on a single sheet of paper and pushing it across the desk toward her.

Jenner picked up the sheet and carefully read every word. In exchange for her promise not to file any lawsuits against Harvest Meat Packing or them personally, her unemployment compensation would be approved. There was a place for her signature.

"Two things," she said. "Actually, three. There's only one copy, which I assume you'll want to keep. I'll need a copy, too. Also, there's no date specified for where you'd approve the unemployment, so you could hold out a few weeks, figuring I'd get the lottery money before the claim went through, and then it would be denied. The third thing is, there's no place for your signatures. I'm not going to be the only one signing this."

Al had drummed it into her head that she didn't sign anything without reading it, and especially not unless she understood every word. She'd told Jenner some things to look out for, but Jenner's own street smarts, plus a lifetime of dealing with Jerry, who took advantage of every loophole he could find or invent, made it tough to put anything over on her. She'd picked up some of Al's jargon, too, so she could speak these guys' language. She saw in their eyes that she'd sprung all their little traps.

She handed the paper back to the man who'd pushed it toward her. "I'll have those changes made," he said without a hint of argument, and stepped out of the office.

They stood in silence, waiting for his return. Almost fifteen minutes lapsed. When he did come back, there were two sheets of paper in his hand. Jenner took them, carefully read them and saw that places for their signatures had been added—in fact, one signature, that of the the owner and president of Harvest Meat Packing, was already present—and that her unemployment claim was to be approved effective that very day. She took that to mean they wanted her to clock out and leave. Fine.

Silently she scrawled her name on both sheets, watched as they signed in the appointed places, then she took one of the sheets and carefully folded it.

Gorski escorted her back to her locker, where she stripped out of the coveralls and plastic cap, handed them to him, gathered her stuff—there wasn't much—and walked out the door for the last time.

The sun was still shining. She checked her watch; less than an hour had passed since she'd clocked in. Even though she'd left her window rolled down a little, when she opened the Goose's door, heat rolled out and punched her in the face, so she stood there a minute and fished out her cell phone while she waited. First she called Al. "I've been fired. Looks like I'll be borrowing some money after all. I've never done this before, so tell me how I go about it."

After Al finished explaining the process and what she should do, Jenner climbed into the Goose and cranked it. As she rumbled out of the parking lot, she called Michelle.

"Hey, want to go on vacation?"

Chapter Five

She was late. She was supposed to meet Michelle at seven and it was already eight thirty. Still, though walking the distance to Bird's would make her even later, Jenner parked her new car a block away from the bar—she didn't want any dings marring it. So what if it wasn't a luxury car? It was a Camry—loaded, but still a Camry—because she couldn't get her mind around paying two years' worth of her former salary for a car. She'd had the Camry only a couple of weeks, and she was proud of it. She still inhaled deeply every time she got in it, drinking in the delicious new-car smell.

She was tired. She sat in the quiet car for a few minutes, her eyes closed. If she hadn't promised Michelle she'd meet her tonight, she'd have gone home, which was still the duplex because finding a new place to live was taking much longer than picking out a new car, and crashed. Who knew that managing a shitload of money would turn out to be damn near a full-time job?

Al was great—and was in the process of moving into a better office already—but Jenner insisted on being involved, which meant she spent a lot of time at Payne Echols. She wanted to understand what was going on, why Al was doing what she was doing, and what all the headache-inducing terms meant. She trusted Al, but Al might not always be around, and Jenner didn't want to be forced to rely on someone else. Her instinct was to get educated, and get control. For too much of the time since she'd picked that winning ticket, she hadn't had any control over events. Now she did, and the relief was almost staggering.

The money was hers, now. She'd gone through an excruciating ceremony where cameras flashed in her eyes while she smiled until her facial muscles screamed, and her hand cramped from holding one end of a huge cardboard check—which the lottery people had been careful to tell her wasn't real and couldn't be cashed, as if she were the village idiot and couldn't have figured that out on her own—but at last it had been over and the paperwork finished, and she'd begun stepping back into anonymity . . . she hoped. The media had gone away, of course. Now, if she could just get settled in a new place and get on with life, she'd be a lot happier.

Parts of it had been fun. She and Michelle had gone on a great shopping binge, and she'd not only replaced her own wardrobe, but Michelle's, too. Purses, shoes, good jewelry, silk blouses, sharp and sexy dresses . . . it had been great. But one of the most disconcerting things she'd learned was that, after a few days, she got bored with shopping. She would never in a million years have thought that would have happened, but there it was. Being able to spend money was great. After the initial glee and spree, though, she hadn't seen anything else she'd wanted, and boredom had set in. That still felt like some kind of betrayal by the universe.

Her life had definitely changed. Most of her old friends had fallen by the wayside already, while she'd become very friendly with her lawyer, William Lourdes. He was a shark, but he was *her* shark. He'd smiled when he'd read the suit Dylan had filed against her. In short order, after Lourdes had filed a countersuit, with prejudice, against Dylan that would have taken everything he owned, Dylan had dropped his suit and dropped out of her orbit. Bill, as Lourdes insisted she call him, had then set about setting up her estate to protect it from all the human vultures who would try to get a piece of it should something happen to her.

Sitting there in the dark car, Jenner felt a tiny smile move her lips at the very idea that she, Jenner Redwine, had an *estate*. Wow.

She also had both a savings account and a checking account at a bank—a bank where the tellers and managers called her by name, and where she was always treated with both kindness and courtesy. A mere two months ago, having even a small checking account hadn't been on her radar. Now she seemed to spend a lot of time at the bank, moving things in and out of her safe-deposit box, because she couldn't leave any type of paperwork at the house, not with Jerry still hanging around.

He hadn't given up, but then she hadn't really thought he would. She'd bought him some clothes, even given him a hundred here and there, but without any real hope that he'd leave. She knew her dad. He would play it straight for a while, try to ease her suspicions, then he'd come up with a good reason why he needed a new car, or try to talk her into buying him a condo, or something like that. A few hundred dollars wouldn't even make a dent in Jerry's ambition.

Finally she gathered her energy and climbed out of the Camry. She didn't have to shove her shoulder against the door to force it open, the way she had with the Goose. She hadn't firebombed the Goose, though she'd thought about it.

The poor thing looked like crap, but the motor was dependable, so she'd donated it to a charity. There'd been a time when she'd needed that ugly car; someone else needed it now. Thank God that someone wasn't her.

Her energy level picked up as she slung her new, expensive purse over her shoulder and walked toward Bird's. An evening of laughing and dancing was just what she needed; she'd feel better after a beer. Michelle would already be a drink or two into the evening, and a dance or two—or three—ahead of Jenner, but that was okay, because Jenner didn't think she'd be able to keep up with her tonight.

The bar was packed and incredibly noisy—it was a Friday night, after all—so she had to look around the milling bodies for a while before she spotted Michelle, sitting at a table with three other regulars. From the number of glasses and bottles on the table, Michelle and the others had more than a two-drink jump on the evening.

Jenner was almost at the table before Michelle spotted her. "Woohoo!" she yelled. "Love the hair!"

Jenner resisted the urge to touch her hair, which was now black, with spiky little strands on top. She had gotten it done just that morning. The new style was elegant and sexy and edgy, but most of all, it made her look so different that few people recognized her. After the last couple of months, she figured that was a good thing.

She pulled up a chair and sat, looking around for a waitress. "I'm wearing the shoes," Michelle announced, turning so she could lift her foot high enough for Jenner to see. The shoes had been outrageously expensive, over five hundred bucks, but seeing the undiluted delight on Michelle's face as she'd tried them on had made Jenner think they were well worth it. But then Michelle had been oddly terrified to wear them, afraid they'd get scuffed or she'd break a heel, or something. She had often tried them on at home, then put them safely away. This was the shoes' first outing, and Jenner clapped her hands.

"About time," she said.

"Are they hot, or what?" Michelle asked, turning her foot this way and that as she admired the rhinestones on the delicate straps. She lifted her foot even higher, so the two men and woman who also sat at the table could see. Across from the table, a man whistled as Michelle's lifted foot maybe gave him more to admire than just a shoe. She laughed, stuck her tongue out at him, but put her foot back on the floor.

"Next time," she said to the other three, "I'm going to get the matching purse. It was *amazing*. The leather felt like butter, it was so soft."

Before Jenner could say anything, the cocktail waitress arrived with a loaded tray. As she began passing out the new round, she glanced at Jenner. "What'll you have?"

"A beer," Jenner said. As tired as she was, she was wary of drinking very much; she'd limit herself to the one beer and go home in an hour or so.

"Your tab's up to ninety-four fifty," the waitress said to Michelle, her tone saying that she wanted to see some cash or a credit card before anything else was ordered.

"Put it on her tab," Michelle said carelessly, picking up her colorful drink and tipping the glass in Jenner's direction. "She'll take care of it. That's what she's food gor. I mean, *good for.*" She laughed at her silly mistake, waving her hand so that the contents slopped over the edge of the glass; she stopped to swipe her finger over the rim before sticking it in her mouth. "Oops," she said.

Oops? Was Michelle talking about the spilled drink, or what she'd just said?

Jenner blinked, sitting back in her chair. She almost didn't believe what she'd heard—almost, but not quite. Maybe a tiny part of her had been waiting for it, but then again, maybe not, because this *hurt*. Michelle, too?

She probably should have seen it coming. Not that she minded always picking up the check now, it was just that she was always *expected* to do it even when, as now, she hadn't even had a drink yet. And the other three people . . . she knew them only because she'd often seen them here, but very casually; she didn't even know their last names. Why should she buy their drinks, too?

The prospect of fun had faded like a cheap T-shirt, fast and ugly.

"Actually, cancel that beer," she said to the waitress. "I can't stay." She readjusted the shoulder strap of her purse as she stood. "I just wanted to stop by and let you know, since you were expecting me," she said to Michelle. "I knew it'd be so loud in here you'd never hear your cell phone ring."

Michelle stared at her, the smile sliding from her face. "What the hell?"

"I'm tired," Jenner said.

"Yeah, because shopping and counting money all day is so exhausting." Michelle laughed at her little joke, and so did the others at the table.

Jenner didn't laugh. "I gotta go," she said, turning on her heel and trying to escape before she said something she wouldn't be able to take back. She and Michelle had been friends a long time, but she could sense that relationship was suddenly teetering on the point of no return, and she didn't want it to tip over. Michelle was half-drunk—maybe three-quarters—and tomorrow she would apologize and they'd go on as before. Jenner hoped that was what would happen, anyway.

67

She made it to the door and stepped out, into relative coolness and quiet, before Michelle caught her and grabbed her shoulder. "You can't go," Michelle said, no longer laughing, and not sounding quite as tipsy. "I didn't bring any cash with me. You have to pay for our drinks."

Reluctantly Jenner turned and looked Michelle in the eye. Michelle tossed her dark curls, her expression defiant. Behind them, bar patrons were drinking, talking, laughing, dancing. A few squeezed out past them, and some people squeezed in to take their places. Finally Jenner said, "You just expected that I'd be here and that I'd pay for everything."

Michelle's expression changed to incredulity. "Well, yeah," she said, as if that was the most obvious thing in the world.

Fatigue slammed down on Jenner's shoulders. Was what Michelle expected really any different from her dad, and Dylan, and the endless parade of charities and cons that had stopped calling her only because she'd disconnected her landline? At least Michelle had been there for her in the past, which the others hadn't been. That counted for something. She opened her purse, intending to give Michelle enough cash to pay for her evening. Maybe tomorrow they could get things straightened out. Maybe when Michelle hadn't been drinking she wouldn't be in such a bitchy mood.

"You know," Michelle said, her full mouth twisting in a little sneer, "you've changed since you won that damn money. You used to be fun. You used to think about something besides money, money, money. Now you're just—"

"Your personal ATM machine?" Jenner shot back, her tone scorching as she pulled a stack of bills from her wallet. She had changed? Sure she had. Everyone around her had changed, so was she supposed to remain the same, untouched by what was truly a gigantic shifting of her world? She had to deal with them, so damn straight it had changed her.

Michelle's expression hardened, and her eyes narrowed. "I don't like you very much, anymore. The people who used to be your friends aren't good enough for you now, just because you can buy things."

"You liked me and my money fine when I was spending it on your shoes and jewelry, and your new couch," Jenner pointed out. "You liked me when I bought every single meal we ate out, when we went on vacation together, and when I paid for every round we drank in this place." She took Michelle's hand and slapped the bills into it. "Well, here it is, all I have on me. Have fun."

Michelle's fingers clenched around the money, but the sneer didn't leave her face. "Bitch," she said.

The word stunned Jenner. Even though she'd stood up for herself, she had still been expecting that, tomorrow, she and Michelle would make up. Now, staring at the venom in Michelle's face, hearing it in her tone, something in her realized there was no apology coming tomorrow.

"Good-bye," she managed to say, a choking sadness keeping her tone oddly gentle, then she turned and headed down the sidewalk. She heard the door bang as Michelle went back inside. The immediacy of the sound told her Michelle hadn't paused, hadn't even looked back.

That was that, then. Hurt congealed in her chest, making it difficult to breathe. Michelle had been there for years, always ready to laugh and party. They'd consoled each other through breakups with boyfriends, head colds, and past-due bills. They had lived in the same world, but now they didn't.

She unlocked the Camry with the remote and slid into the

driver's seat. Her hands trembled as she tried to fit the key into the ignition. She was so tired she wanted only to go home, but she'd just given Michelle every cent she had and she needed to get some cash. She didn't like not having any cash on her. In the past she'd been broke plenty of times, and she didn't like it. She'd very quickly grown accustomed to never being without some money.

There was an ATM in Bird's—very handy for the bar patrons—but she didn't want to go back in there. Sadly she realized she'd probably been to Bird's for the last time, another touchstone in her life that was sliding away into the past. Mentally she searched the area. There was another ATM just a few blocks away, but she didn't like the neighborhood. Instead, because it felt safer, she drove to the nearest branch of her bank—she didn't like paying user fees, either, so she preferred using the bank's—and pulled up to the ATM.

A cool breeze whipped around her as she got out of the car and approached the machine. She'd withdraw a couple of hundred to replace what she'd given Michelle, and that would be more than enough to tide her over the weekend. She tapped in her account number, and PIN.

INSUFFICIENT FUNDS.

She stared at the little screen, blinking at the words as she tried to make sense of them. She knew, roughly, how much she had in her account, but she hadn't balanced it in over a week. Still, there should be around twenty-five thousand, give or take a few hundred.

She was tired, though, and upset; she'd probably punched in the wrong number. She tried again, and this time she was very careful, making certain every number was correct.

The same message flashed on the screen: INSUFFICIENT FUNDS.

At this hour, the bank was dark and there was no one to help her. She thought a moment, then entered a different request, this time to see her account balance. Probably this machine was malfunctioning, and was giving the same message to everyone who tried to get money from it. For that matter, maybe the machine was empty, and it was telling her *it* had insufficient funds. The idea was almost funny, and she smiled a little, but then the smile froze on her lips.

Three dollars and twenty-two cents?

She stared at the impossible number. She *knew* she had more than that, thousands more than that. What had happened?

Automatically she got back in the car and started it, put it in gear. All the way home she turned the situation over in her mind, feeling sick as she worked through details.

Someone—and she had only two someones whom she suspected—had gotten his hands on her checkbook and written himself a check for twenty-five odd thousand. Dylan, or Jerry? It had to be one of them. They knew where she lived, and they were both determined to get something from her. They both wanted their cut of her good fortune, their fair share for—what? Breathing?

She'd tagged Dylan for a moocher, but she wasn't sure he'd steal. Even if he did, he wouldn't be bold enough to take it all. He'd steal a few checks, write one here and there for a couple hundred dollars, hoping she wouldn't notice, and if she did then he'd hope she'd cut him some slack instead of going to the cops. That was Dylan.

But her dad . . . Jerry Redwine would take all he could get and then he'd run.

She felt that inner door slam that signaled yet another end. She wouldn't hear from him again. He wouldn't call. There would be no more awkward lunches, no more offers to get in on the ground floor of some great opportunity he'd dreamed up. Her latest refusal had evidently convinced him she couldn't be fleeced, so instead he'd stolen from her. He was gone for good this time, because he'd known there was no getting past this.

The certainty that he was the culprit ate through her like acid. How had he done it? He couldn't have gotten her ATM code—and besides, ATMs would dispense only a limited amount of cash from an account—but somehow he must have gotten his hands on her checkbook.

She'd been so careful whenever he was in the house, always taking her purse with her if she went into another room, or locking it in the trunk of the car if she'd known ahead of time that he was coming over. But what if she hadn't known he was there? What if he'd lurked outside, waited until she was in the shower or even in bed asleep, then quietly slipped the lock and let himself in? She could easily see him doing that. In hindsight she realized she should have installed an alarm, but she hadn't wanted to spend any money on a place where she wasn't going to be living much longer, and she'd let it slide. She was still in the habit of avoiding relatively small expenses, because they were outside her experience, and now it had cost her big time.

When she got home she took out her checkbook and carefully went through it, looking at the numbers to make sure none were missing. The books each had twenty-five checks in them, and she kept only one book at a time; the others were in the safe deposit box. She knew what checks she'd written, because she kept a careful record. The blank check on top was the next one in sequence. They were all there . . . except for the very last one in the book.

She looked up the last time she'd balanced the account,

and carefully began subtracting the amount of each check she'd written. The total was more than she'd thought. She'd had a balance of twenty-seven thousand, four hundred three dollars and twenty-two cents. Jerry had even taken the four hundred. Heck, he'd evidently even done the math himself, to see how much he could write the check to himself for. If he hadn't, if he'd left her a few hundred, it might have taken her days longer to realize what he'd done.

And this was it. He'd finally done it, finally gone past her limit. This was turning out to be a hell of a day. First Michelle, and now Jerry, though actually Jerry had made his move first, even though she'd just found out about it. She hadn't seen him since Wednesday. Two days, then. He'd have left immediately, because he wouldn't be certain she wouldn't turn him over to the cops for forgery.

She wouldn't. Let him have the money. Let this mark the complete end. She'd been waiting for this moment from the second she realized she'd won the lottery, wondering how much it would cost her, and now she knew: twenty-seven thousand, four hundred dollars.

She sat in the silent duplex, feeling exhausted and empty, and suddenly she had a moment of clarity. She'd known all along that winning the lottery would change her life, known that some of the changes would be jarring, but she hadn't expected how complete the change would be.

Part Two

BAD LUCK

Chapter Six

Seven years later

"We have a situation developing," the familiar voice said on Cael Traylor's secure, encrypted cell phone.

Cael could put both a name and a face to the voice, because he'd made a point of being able to do so. Finding out what he wanted to know had required a cross-country drive, but driving had kept him off the radar, which he wouldn't have been if he'd flown. Any time his name showed up on a passenger list, certain elements of the U.S. government learned of it. Not Homeland Security, not the State Department, but certain people who handled black ops, such as the man who was currently talking to him on his phone.

"Details," he said briefly, turning off the television and wheeling away from his computer so he could concentrate. He didn't take notes; a paper trail could come back to bite him on the ass. He did take precautions to make certain he was never hung out to dry, but notes weren't part of his routine.

"We've picked up some transmissions from the North Koreans that make us suspect they've established a source for some technology we'd rather they not have."

Cael didn't ask what that technology was—not yet, anyway. At this point he didn't need to know. If at some point he decided he *did* need to know, then he wouldn't proceed without that information. "Who's the source?"

"Frank Larkin."

Cael's interest level shot up several degrees. Larkin was a multimillionaire who was one of the behind-the-scene powers in Washington, D.C., with a lot of friends and contacts in high places. He had jumped on the green bandwagon with so-called environmentally friendly businesses and products that were questionable at best, and were probably outright cons. Cael didn't get emotionally involved in causes, but in his opinion it took a particularly sleazy type of bastard to take advantage of people who were trying to do something good.

"He pulls a lot of juice" was all he said, his tone neutral. Because of Larkin's connections, anything they got on him would have to be ironclad—and even then there was no guarantee that anything would ever be done. On the other hand, in a lot of these cases no formal charges were ever brought. The "problem" was taken care of, and would look like a heart attack or a stroke, at least on paper, while the bullet hole in the back of the head would somehow escape the medical examiner's notice.

Cael had done his share of wet work, but that was for another country, in another decade. His true specialty was surveillance, so what he was being called on to do was get the goods on Larkin, not take him out.

"Specifics," he said.

"Larkin is one of a consortium that's expanding into

luxury ship cruises. The first ship, the *Silver Mist,* is scheduled to go into service very shortly. Before that, however, her maiden voyage will be a special two-week charity cruise to Hawaii. The passengers will all be the super-elite, all the proceeds from the cruise will be donated to charity, and there's a huge public relations push going on. Larkin will be the host of the cruise. We think he'll be meeting with the North Koreans while he's in Hawaii, but the place and time won't be set until shortly beforehand. We need to know when and where."

Cael mulled that information over. The computer age had changed espionage; actual prototypes or products didn't have to be stolen. Instead, the specs could be transmitted in the blink of an eye, and the receiving country or agency could proceed from there. The North Koreans were famously paranoid; a face-to-face meet, especially on foreign soil, posed far more risk to them than a simple file transmission.

"Something's off," he said. "Why would the Koreans agree to that? Why the need for a face-to-face meet?"

"We don't know. There may be something else going on that we haven't unraveled yet. What we *do* know is enough."

Cael gave a mental shrug. In the end, it didn't matter why the Koreans would agree to such a risky move, just that they had. "When's the cruise?"

"Two weeks."

Not much time then. "Can you get me and my people booked? We'll need the suite next to Larkin's."

"How many rooms do you need?"

"Two," he replied. He and Tiffany would take one room, Ryan and Faith the other. In fact, the best arrangement would be Ryan and Faith in the suite adjoining Larkin's. This cruise was just the type of thing they would do, so their presence wouldn't be in any way remarkable. "And I'll need two people embedded in the ship's crew."

"Names."

He provided them, his thoughts already moving ahead. He would also need someone on the security staff, and putting one of his people there at this late date was probably impossible. Therefore, he needed to buy someone who was already on staff. He relayed that requirement, too.

"I'll have everything set up. Get your people ready."

They both hung up. Cael left his chair to get more coffee. He'd been awake and at the computer for more than an hour, but it was barely five o'clock in the morning, California time, too early to call any of his people and put them on alert. Instead, he took his cup out onto the porch and sat in one of the comfortable rocking chairs, stretching his long legs out to prop them on top of the porch railing. Dawn hadn't yet rolled across the mountains to the east of him, but the birds and insects were producing an anticipatory symphony. He listened to them, enjoying the songs and solitude, the soft feel of the early-morning air on his bare chest.

His house was the only one in sight, and he liked it that way. The house itself was two-story, made of timber and rock so that it blended into its surroundings, not so big as to attract notice but large enough that he could be comfortable. The security array was more extensive than normal, but not immediately apparent. He'd installed at least half the precautions himself, so no company would have a set of schematics that could be used to breach his defenses. Maybe he had a touch of paranoia himself, but the way he looked at it, he'd rather spend some extra money than be caught with his pants down. He was in a dangerous business—not as dangerous now as what he'd done before, but in his type of work you didn't win many friends.

Trust was the keystone in his relationships, both professional and personal. Professionally, he didn't trust the people he worked for, but he did the people he worked with. He had a good group assembled. They didn't work together exclusively, but more and more the others were turning down jobs that hadn't come through him.

He hadn't set out to be the head of anything. For that matter, he hadn't set out to work in the world of black ops. A combination of birth, circumstance, and natural talent had gradually led him to where he was now, and he had to admit the job was a good fit.

He'd been born in Israel to American parents. His mother was a nonpracticing Jew; his father a laid-back Mississippi Delta boy who didn't give a hoot one way or the other. The fact that his mother didn't practice the religion she'd been born into was a sore spot with Cael. "If you aren't willing to follow the customs that pertain to you," he'd once groused to her, "why the hell couldn't you have left my foreskin out of it?"

"Stop complaining," she'd retorted. "You didn't need it."

"But I might have *wanted* it, and now I'll never know, will I?"

Just as a matter of principle, he didn't like the fact that one of his body parts had been removed without his permission.

He'd lived in Israel until he was ten, and had grown up speaking three languages: Hebrew, English, and Southern. Later on he'd added Spanish and German, with a smattering of Japanese that he was gradually expanding. Moving to the United States had been a big culture shock to him, but one he liked. He may have spent his first ten years in Israel, but he'd always been aware that he was an American. This was where he belonged.

Even so, he retained a deep fondness for Israel, and

because he'd been born there he had dual citizenship. When he was eighteen he'd decided he wanted adventure, and he'd served a stint in the Israeli army, where he'd exhibited certain talents that brought him to the attention of Mossad. He'd done some jobs for them, before maturity and a desire to live brought him back to America, where he'd belatedly gotten a college degree in business administration.

There was no getting away from fate, he mused. His degree had come in handy, with the string of car washes, Laundromats, and other cash-rich businesses he owned. He'd built a fortune for himself—smallish, but still a fortune. The truth, however, was that those cash-rich businesses provided a convenient way for him to launder the money he earned from his real livelihood, which was mostly finding out things that other people wanted to keep hidden. The people who paid him didn't exactly provide 1099s at the end of the year, and he had to have some way to account for his money to the IRS. He did have some of it salted away in Switzerland, but the whole point of money, to him, was to put it to work. To do that, he had to have it in the United States. Thus the low-rent businesses, which had turned out to be a gold mine. No matter what, people washed their cars and clothes.

While he'd nursed his coffee, dawn had gradually arrived. He could see the mountains now, the deep green forest around him, see the birds that sang. His stomach reminded him that he'd been up for hours, and it was time for breakfast. After breakfast, he'd start calling his people, and get a plan put in place.

Crystal chandeliers glittered overhead; in fact the entire ballroom seemed to glitter, from the chandeliers to the crystal glasses on the tables, to the jewelry decorating hair and ears, throats and hands, to the sequins and crystals on gowns and shoes and evening bags. Everything glittered.

Jenner stifled a sigh. She was so damn tired of glitter, so bored with these endless charity functions even when they were for a good cause. Why couldn't she just write a check and be done with it?

Even if she'd enjoyed the social aspect of these things, wine tasting, followed by an expensive dinner, which was then followed by an auction for overvalued objects she didn't want or need wasn't Jenner's idea of fun, and yet here she was. Again.

It was Sydney's fault, of course. Sydney Hazlett was Jenner's only real friend among the south Florida elite, and Syd often begged Jenner to attend these things to give her support and backup; in an odd reversal of circumstance, nature—whatever—the young woman who had been born to a life of luxury, coddled and catered to all her life, suffered from an almost paralyzing lack of confidence, while Jenner, who had come from nothing, could stare down anyone and shrug off any slight, which meant the one doing the slighting was, at best, unimportant to her.

That was how Jenner had survived these seven years after leaving Chicago. She had to admit that, by and large, people here had been polite, even gracious, but they hadn't welcomed her into their inner circles. She had many acquaintances, but only one friend, and that was Syd.

According to Syd, her attendance was mandatory, which meant Jenner's was, too. So as much as she wished she could just write a check to the children's hospital and call it done, she had to endure these tedious events—and she'd still end up writing a check.

She didn't even like wine, which she supposed was an

indication of her very red blood and her low-brow, blue-collar upbringing. Give her a beer and she was much happier. She barely managed to keep from shuddering at each sip, and thank *God* she could spit the nasty stuff out. At least with dinner she'd be able to get her favorite drink, a teeter-totter, which was a delicious blend of half champagne and half sparkling green apple juice. She couldn't stand champagne on its own, but mixed with apple juice it was great. All the servers and bartenders at these events knew what she drank, without having to ask.

Where *was* Syd, anyway? They'd be sitting down to dinner any minute, and after being coerced into attending this thing, she'd like to have someone she could talk to. Jenner was feeling decidedly grumpy that she'd endured this to give Syd company, and her friend wasn't even here. She should have expected it; Syd was often late—partly, Jenner suspected, because she dreaded these functions even more than Jenner did, but her tardiness was usually about fifteen to thirty minutes. This time, she'd missed the entire wine-tasting, which had lasted for over an hour.

Jenner was thinking about slipping outside and calling her when Syd said behind her, "You're blond again. I love the shade."

Jenner turned, smiling wryly. "You're late. If I'd known you were going to miss the entire wine-tasting, I wouldn't have shown up, either."

"I just couldn't—" Syd looked down at herself with a sigh. She looked fine to Jenner. Her gown was classic in line and construction, the cream color looked great with Syd's honey-blond hair and golden skin, and Syd herself was very pretty, with her natural sweetness evident in her expression. But Syd was hypercritical of herself, always fearing she didn't measure up to her father's exacting tastes, afraid people were making fun of her, second-guessing her clothing decisions, which of course meant she never wore the first thing she tried on—at least not without trying on several other outfits before, in despair, she went with her original choice.

On Syd's behalf, Jenner would have hated Mr. Hazlett, except he so obviously adored Syd and tried in a number of ways to prop up her fragile self-esteem, and was hugely relieved and grateful to Jenner for being Syd's friend. J. Michael Hazlett did indeed have impeccable taste; he was handsome, urbane, and completely comfortable in his skin, as well as being a formidable businessman. But he never said anything the least critical to Syd, and would have fought tigers to protect her. It was hard to hate someone who not only wasn't a villain, but who actually, in his own endearing, slightly clumsy masculine way, tried to show his daughter how special and lovable she was. She and Mr. Hazlett had become coconspirators, always trying to make certain one of them was available to lend Syd support if she needed it.

Just like now.

"You look great, as always," she said to Syd. "But leaving me to handle a wine-tasting on my own just isn't right."

"I'd rather talk about your hair than my tardiness," Syd replied, smiling. "I still say blond is the most flattering for you, it makes you look so alive and bright. Though the auburn was striking," she added hastily. "And the black was very elegant. What *is* your natural color, anyway?"

"Dishwater blond," Jenner retorted. Though she hadn't seen it in years, she recalled the exact, unexciting shade. A psychiatrist could probably have a field day on why she changed hair color so often, but it was her hair, and if she wanted to change it she could, so who cared what an analyst might think? She'd loved having black hair, loved the edgy, kick-butt feeling it gave her. The red hair had been surprisingly sexy, and she'd liked that, too. When she got bored with this pale blond, she'd probably go back to the red for a while.

There was a signal for everyone to take their seats at the elegantly decorated banquet tables, each seating eight. By Jenner's count, there were fifty tables, which meant four hundred people were in attendance. An orchestra, seated in the balcony, began softly playing, providing a pleasing background without being so loud they intruded on the conversation below.

As Jenner took her seat, holding the slim skirt of her long black gown so she wouldn't catch her heel in it and pitch face-forward into the table, she remembered her first charity dinner, almost seven years ago. She'd done her best to mingle beforehand, to introduce herself to people, but she'd felt enormously out of place and uncomfortable. No one had spat on her, but neither had she been made to feel welcome.

At dinner, she'd found herself sitting at a table with seven strangers and a daunting array of silverware and glasses, which had all but paralyzed her with uncertainty. She'd thought, "Holy shit, five forks!" What was she supposed to do with five forks? Use a fresh one for each bite? Defend herself from the others at the table?

Then the pretty young woman across the table had caught her eye, given her a friendly, conspiratorial smile, and very discreetly lifted the fork on the outside of the setting. There hadn't been anything derisive in her attitude, just an honest offer of aid, which Jenner had gratefully accepted. She'd gotten through the dinner, realized that the order of utensil use was very simple, and in the course of that dinner also realized that the young woman across the table was genuinely sweet and friendly. Afterward, they had gravitated toward each other so they could really talk, and by the end of the event each had found a friend.

Strange how much she'd changed since then, Jenner thought, and yet one thing hadn't changed: She still didn't truly fit in here. She'd left Chicago behind, and in truth no longer felt like the girl she'd once been, the one who had been so bitterly hurt by family and friends alike, but her sense of not belonging was as strong as ever. Here she was, thirty years old. She'd lived in Palm Beach for six years. In those six years, she'd attended a hundred or more of these charity events, gone to cocktail parties, pool parties, whatever—and to the others of this social set she was, and would always be, the working-class meat packer who'd gotten lucky and won the lottery. She would never be one of them, no matter how casually friendly they were to her. If not for Syd she probably would've moved on, looked for somewhere else to live, but instead she'd made a home here.

She'd filled those seven years by staying busy. Al had warned her, years ago, that most people who win the lottery end up broke within five years. Jenner had been determined not to be one of those people. With Al to help with the investments, a good accountant, a couple of attorneys—and, oddly enough, a head for handling investments herself—Jenner was richer than she'd been the day she claimed her winnings . . . over twice as rich. Even with the recent stock market tumble she was financially sound, thanks to her diverse portfolio. The market might be drastically down, but her own losses were less than twenty percent. These days she even managed a portion of her investments herself, through an online account—though Al, who was now a senior partner at Payne Echols, took care of the rest.

Managing that much money took a lot of time, much more than she'd imagined way back when she'd first picked Payne

Echols out of the yellow pages. Add in the charities she supported, the ever-changing list of classes she took—in art, in gourmet cooking (French *and* Italian), in cake decorating, judo, skeet shooting, ballroom dancing, pottery, computers, snorkeling, even parasailing—and her days were full enough. Occasionally aimless, but full.

She'd tried gardening and knitting as well, but she hadn't enjoyed either of those. Though Jenner often felt as if she still didn't know who she was or what she wanted to do, she definitely knew that she was *not* Suzy Homemaker. She was good in the kitchen, but she'd rather be surfing the Web. And except for the occasional lunch she'd prepared for Syd, who was she going to cook for? If she was the only one there, she'd rather pick up something from the deli down the street and save herself the trouble.

She had a luxury condo with all the security bells and whistles, and someone to clean it. She had great clothes. She had a great car, a beautiful little BMW convertible. She dated occasionally, but not very often. If a man wasn't in her financial league, then how could she ever truly know whether he liked her for herself or if he was just interested in her money? Her experiences with Michelle, Dylan, and her dad had definitely left emotional scars.

She knew she was unduly critical of the people she socialized with, knew that most of her uncertainty stemmed from herself, but protecting herself by holding most people at a distance was a damn sight easier than dealing with the hurt and repairing the damage if her suspicions were proved correct.

They were actually pretty nice people, she thought, looking around the table. They gave millions and millions to worthwhile charities every year, and it wasn't because of tax deductions, either. Jenner had made the horrifying—to her—discovery that, at her financial level, almost nothing was deductible. She didn't even get a personal deduction. So these people gave because they wanted to do good, to make a difference, and not because it in any way benefited them financially. That they combined social events with their giving wasn't a horrible thing to do. Why not get together with friends before writing those huge checks?

She liked most of them, but she wasn't close to any of them, except for Syd. Syd also suffered from Jenner's dilemma when it came to men; she, too, wondered if someone wanted to go out with her because of her father's money rather than being interested in her. And regardless of how sweet Syd was, how genuinely friendly and nice, how could Jenner say she was wrong in feeling the way she did when Jenner suffered from the same doubt?

After dinner, the auction part of the evening began. She and Syd went into the adjoining room and walked among the tables where the donated items were on display. Nothing there called to her, though she supposed she'd do her part and bid on at least a couple, whether she wanted them or not. There were small white envelopes and thick, rich paper for the attendees to use to place their silent bids. After a quick perusal of the items, Sydney bid on a facial and massage at her favorite spa—for much more than she would have paid by simply booking the services—and Jenner bid on a pair of unexciting pearl earrings. If she got them, she would donate them to a center for abused women. She passed a lot of stuff on to the center. Sometimes, even a piece of jewelry could do a lot for the self-esteem of a woman who had been beaten down to the ground.

After the auction was over—neither of them won, but they both wrote checks anyway—there was dancing, which was as far removed from the dancing Jenner had learned at Bird's as caviar was from tuna. As they watched the elegant couples sway and twirl, Syd asked, "Are you excited about the cruise?"

Jenner racked her brain, but drew a blank. "What cruise?"

"What cruise?" Syd echoed, staring at Jenner was if she were insane. "The charity cruise. Didn't you read about it in yesterday's paper? You *are* going, aren't you?" She looked suddenly anxious. "Dad has to be in Europe for some meetings at the same time, or he'd go, so I have to go in his place."

Okay, Jenner could already see where this was heading. Everyone who was anyone would be expected to go on this cruise, as the charity circuit took to the high seas. And if Syd went, then she'd want Jenner to go along for company and support. And, what the hell, she'd probably go. She hadn't been on a cruise before, but she liked the water, liked her snorkeling and parasailing lessons, so why not?

"I didn't read the paper yesterday," she said—a lie, because she'd read the stuff that interested her. "Fill me in."

"It's the maiden voyage of the *Silver* . . . Something. Or maybe it's a Crystal Something. I don't remember." Syd waved away the ship's name, because it truly didn't matter. "It's the most luxurious boutique ship in the world, and before it goes into service its maiden voyage is being used to raise money for charity. All the proceeds from *everything* will be donated, from the passenger fees to the casino take. There'll be an art auction, a masquerade ball, a fashion show where you can actually buy the garments and they'll be tailored to fit you . . . oh, all sorts of stuff. Doesn't it sound like fun?"

"At least it sounds interesting," Jenner allowed. "When is it, and *where* is it?"

"Um . . . I'll have to get back to you on the 'when,' but the 'where' is a two-week cruise in the Pacific."

"Hawaii? Tahiti? Japan?"

"Uh—farther south than Japan. Does anyone cruise to Japan? Anyway. Hawaii or Tahiti. One or the other. Or both. I don't know. They're both pretty, so who cares?"

Jenner had to laugh at Syd's reasoning, because she was absolutely right. They could be cruising up and down Lake Erie, and they'd still go, because it was for a good cause and that was what they did.

"Okay, I'm in. Tell me more."

Syd's expressive face filled with relief. "Thank goodness," she breathed. "I was afraid I'd have to go by myself. Dad booked one of the penthouse suites, so from what I understand we'll each have a private bedroom. This ship is supposed to be gorgeous; every stateroom is at least a mini-suite, with a balcony, but there are way more true suites than there are on any other ship in the world—for right now, at least."

"Which line owns the ship?"

"I don't think there's a line. I think it's a consortium of people, because one of the co-owners, Frank Larkin, is hosting the voyage. Dad knows him."

That wasn't surprising; J. Michael Hazlett knew everyone.

Still, two weeks of isolation, of peace and quiet, sounded very nice. She would sleep, see new places—something she'd discovered she loved to do—and eat great food. On the flip side, there would be many nights like this one, nights where she rubbed shoulders with the rich and powerful who would make up the very exclusive passenger list. And after all, she was now one of those rich and powerful.

Two weeks . . . Maybe she didn't want that much peace and quiet. She felt suddenly uneasy. "I don't know about being out of touch that long," she said.

"Silly. There are phones in all the rooms, and Internet

access. Most ships just have an Internet cafe, but this ship has full wireless service."

So long as she could get to a computer, she could keep on top of things, so Jenner relaxed. She was a little paranoid about staying informed, maybe because she hadn't actually *earned* her money and she was always, in the back of her mind, afraid it would slip away as easily as it had come. She didn't have survivor guilt, she had dumb-luck guilt.

"Maybe we'll meet a couple of someone specials while we're at sea," Syd said, smiling wryly.

"Yeah," Jenner said, "like the ship won't be filled with people we already know, and this set is lousy with young, handsome, straight, available men who don't care one way or another that between us we could fund our own small country."

Sydney covered her mouth and coughed to hide a laugh. "You're so jaded."

"And so right."

Syd's smile faded, became a little sad around the edges. "Maybe it's just us. No one else seems to worry about being married for their money, they just go ahead and live their lives."

"And get divorced," Jenner pointed out, then wished she hadn't, because Sydney's mother and father had gone through an extremely bitter, acrimonious divorce when Syd was twelve, a terribly vulnerable age, and that had surely played a part in making her so unsure of her own worth as opposed to her material worth.

It hadn't helped that, after less than a year, her mother had relinquished custody of Syd to her father and moved to Europe with her new husband. Syd's whole life had been full of emotional upheaval, including a broken engagement.

By contrast, Jenner considered herself heart-whole. She'd

had crushes, sure, and a couple of times when she was younger thought she was in love, but that was it. Since she'd won the lottery, she'd been way too wary to let anyone get close to her, and perhaps that was more a reflection on her than it was on the men who might have shown an interest in her if she'd been more approachable. Perhaps *she* was the one who couldn't forget she'd been a meat packer, maybe *she* was the one who thought no one would want her for herself.

The stray thoughts made her impatient with herself. It wasn't that she'd entirely given up on men, or that she believed every man on the planet was either greedy or snobbish. But how did a woman in her position go about finding the men who were neither, and how could she tell? She hadn't figured that out, yet.

A week later, their arrangements were made. The cruise ship *Silver Mist* was sailing from San Diego, and the publicity surrounding a ship full of millionaires, billionaires, and assorted glitterati was at fever pitch—at least in their circle. Jenner imagined the average Joe couldn't care less about a bunch of rich people taking a cruise and the ship's owners donating all the proceeds to charity. Unless it directly impacted them . . . well, big hairy deal.

Realizing that didn't stop her from looking forward to it. This was her first cruise, and she was vaguely excited.

Sydney was truly excited about the cruise, though she suffered her normal anxieties about the social events onboard. But she had a friend from college who lived in the San Diego area, and she decided to fly out ahead of time for a visit beforehand.

"You should go with me," she cajoled Jenner. "You'd really like Caro, and she'd love to have you. If you're uncomfortable staying at her house, though, you could always get a suite at the Del Coronado. It's a great old hotel, and the Navy SEALs train on the beach right in front of the guest rooms. If you just happen to run into one, you wouldn't have to tell him right away about the small country thing."

"Now, there's a match made in heaven," Jenner retorted. "He could overtake the small country, and I could buy it. We'd have all bases covered."

Navy SEALs notwithstanding, she resisted Syd's arguments. For one thing, Caro hadn't invited her, even though she was fairly certain Syd had already broached the subject with her friend before asking Jenner. She could imagine Caro's agreement with the plan had been fairly tepid, hence she'd left the actual invitation to Syd.

But she and Al had a face-to-face meeting scheduled, which they didn't often have an opportunity for these days. She and Al had become good friends, and she wanted to catch up on how things were going in Al's life. All things considered, she'd rather visit with Al than suffer through a slightly awkward vacation with Syd's college friend.

It wasn't lost on her that her two best friends were single women named Al and Syd. How weird was that?

"Thanks, but I need to make this meeting with Al. Her flight back to Chicago is Monday afternoon, so I'll have that evening to finish packing, then I'll take an early flight out and, with the time change, arrive in San Diego in plenty of time to meet you at the port. You enjoy your visit with Caro, I'll do the same with Al, and then you and I will spend two nice, lazy weeks cruising around the Pacific."

"I can't wait to see the ship," Syd said, hugging her knees. They were on the balcony of Jenner's condo, watching the sky change as the sun set behind them. "All of the suites are decorated differently, and the one Dad reserved is gorgeous, all white and silver with touches of blue. It looked really serene and calming, at least in the pictures on the Internet.

Not that I imagine we'll be spending a lot of time in the suite, other than sleeping there."

"Then who cares how it looks?" Jenner asked what she considered a very practical question.

"I don't want to sleep in an ugly room," Syd said indignantly. "Anyway, there's something planned for every night, and plenty to do during the day."

"You've been on a cruise before, right?"

"Of course. It's a lot of fun. All sorts of classes, which you'll like, plus things like spas, movies, dance contests, and unending food. We'll need a different gown for every night."

"Packing will be a bitch," Jenner said, thinking with horror of how many suitcases would be required. Not only would she evidently need fourteen evening gowns, but the shoes, the evening bags, and the jewelry that went with them. "Gaaa."

"Who cares? It's all for a good cause. Bring that gorgeous strapless black gown you bought last month, just in case you meet that handsome, straight, nonjudgmental available billionaire we're always looking for."

"The SEAL sounded more likely."

"But you have to be prepared, just in case. You never know what'll happen."

Chapter Seven

Frank Larkin read over the passenger list, noting the names he knew and their stateroom assignments, particularly those that adjoined the owner's suite. The *Silver Mist* was due to sail in two days, and every detail had to be perfect. The assignment of the suites adjoining his owner's suite bothered him. On one side was a couple he didn't know, either personally or by name, and suspicion sharpened his gaze as he stared at the names, Ryan and Faith Naterra. Had they requested the suite next to his for any specific reason? Or had they simply requested one of the top suites—almost everyone had—and they'd simply been lucky enough to be among the first to sign up?

Frank didn't believe in luck. He also didn't believe in assuming there was no ulterior motive in asking for those suites. Rather, there was definitely an ulterior motive; everyone breathing had an ulterior motive. That ulterior motive might not involve him personally, but the possibility was always there.

Either way, he didn't know Ryan and Faith Naterra, and that made him suspicious.

His head ached. It always did, a dull, ever-present reminder that there was, after all, something he couldn't overcome. Briefly he massaged his temples; he knew that wouldn't ease the pain, but the action was so instinctive he couldn't stop himself. He had become so accustomed to the pain that most of the time, until recently, he'd seldom noticed it was there. Lately, though, he seemed to feel a small point of heat inside his head that was like a worm gnawing through his brain.

Was that the cancer? Could he actually feel the tumor growing? His doctor said no, but how could the bastard know? Had *he* ever had brain cancer? Had *he* ever had to live—yeah, fucking bad pun—with the knowledge that his brain was being eaten by disease and there was nothing he or anyone else could do to stop it?

The doctor had tried to explain that his brain wasn't being "eaten," that the disease was adding cells that didn't have the normal brain function, blah blah blah, and what the fuck difference did it make? It was killing him anyway. And he could still feel that kernel of heat. He could take the pain; it was relentless, but not excruciating. What he couldn't take was the enraging loss of control, the helplessness. Well, fuck that. He wasn't going to die curled in a ball, whimpering with pain and pissing himself because he couldn't control his bladder any longer. He would go out his way, and by God, no one would ever forget Frank Larkin.

But now wasn't the time, not quite. Before that time came, he had a lot of things to arrange.

"Find out about this Ryan and Faith Naterra," he said to Dean Mills, his head of security. "I've never heard of them, and I don't like it."

Dean was a stocky man in his early forties with close-cropped white-blond hair and sharp blue eyes. The stockiness disguised a powerful musculature that most people underestimated, but what Larkin prized him for had nothing to do with physical strength and everything to do with an extremely useful blend of intelligence and lack of ethics. Dean was ruthless in getting the job done, whatever the job happened to be. He looked briefly at the information the Naterras had provided when they booked the cruise, said "Will do," and went off to dig up every scrap of information about them he could find.

Larkin went back to the passenger list. Most of the names were familiar to him, even if he didn't know the people personally. Those who could afford this cruise belonged to a small, relatively close-knit group of the super-rich who had money to burn on something like this charity cruise, so being acquainted with most of them wasn't difficult, if you moved in the same circles. Larkin didn't, but he moved in a circle of movers and shakers that overlapped with them on social occasions.

He'd made a damn good living off these people, so it made good business sense to be familiar with as many of them as possible. Right now, he was raking in more money than he could count on his "green initiative" companies and programs. The rich idiots felt guilty about having so much money and were eager to do something to save the planet. Fine with him. He was more than happy to take their money and plant a stupid tree somewhere, just like a bunch of other hucksters who couldn't believe their good fortune. Most of the so-called green industries were nothing more than cons—the only green concerned was the folding kind—but if it made people feel better then he saw no reason why he shouldn't profit from it.

Still, the easy profits fed into his already intense contempt for the gullibility of the very people who bought his "products" and gave to his trumped-up causes. By and large, Americans were idiots, falling all over themselves in their asinine desire to "save the world," or whatever quixotic notion was in favor at any given moment. Some people admired their idealism, but they were idiots, too. The smart people saw how to make money off them, and seized the moment.

He'd made his share of money, manipulating government policy to set up conditions under which he could better run his cons, so that now he had more money than he could ever possibly use. Yet what good did it do him. No amount of money could provide him a cure, or even a reasonable treatment to give him more than another month or so—and he would still be deathly sick during that time anyway, which made the whole effort a waste of time.

Dean knocked briefly before reentering the spacious office, making Larkin aware that his thoughts had been drifting, wasting time that had become so precious, he almost refused to sleep until he was so exhausted he couldn't put it off any longer.

"Nothing suspicious," Dean reported. "They live in San Francisco, they've been married almost six years, no kids. He inherited money from his stepmother, who was one of the Waltons; she had no kids of her own, and she married Naterra's father when the boy was just three, so he was practically hers. He's dabbled in a few things, including Microsoft."

Nothing there that was suspicious. Larkin read over the printout Dean gave him, and even he couldn't find a single detail that gave him pause.

But would there be? Wasn't that the point of someone being in deep cover? He thought of the meeting that was set up in Hawaii, thought of how many governments were after the North Koreans, and said, "Change the staterooms. Shuffle everyone around."

"People chose—"

"I don't give a shit what they 'chose.' It's my fucking ship, and I want people moved around. I don't want anyone next to me who asked to be there, understood? If anyone complains, tell them there was a regrettable computer error and it's too late to make changes." As no one would board for another forty-eight hours, that was complete bullshit, but they wouldn't find out about it until they were actually on board, so the excuse would hold. And if it didn't . . . he didn't care. If dying had any benefit at all, it was that it was very freeing. He'd seldom followed any rule it didn't suit him to follow, but now he had absolute freedom, because nothing had any meaning.

He glanced back at the passenger list. While most of the passengers assigned to his deck were married couples— young and old, but mostly older because they tended to have the most money—there was one "couple" different from the rest: Sydney Hazlett and Jenner Redwine. Sydney was the daughter of J. Michael Hazlett, who had originally booked the cruise but then had to cancel for business reasons, and sent his daughter to represent the family instead. Redwine was some blue-collar dolly who'd won the lottery and hung around the fringes of Palm Beach society, trying to fit in. But she and Sydney were best friends, and they were a known quantity. There wouldn't be even a hint of a threat from those two.

"Put Hazlett and Redwine in the Queen Anne Suite," he ordered. "And . . . Albert and Ginger Winningham in the Neptune." Most ships had numbered suites, not the *Silver Mist*. The suites in the lower decks were numbered, but on his deck each suite had some pretentious name to make them seem more important. Those particular suites were the ones on each side of his.

Albert Winningham was eighty-four and hard of hearing. His wife, Ginger, was arthritic and wore glasses as thick as the bottom of a Coke bottle. If Larkin had been in the mood to be amused by anything, he'd have laughed. He'd be perfectly safe, wedged between two airheads and Mr. and Mrs. Deaf and Blind.

Dean made a note of the arrangements. He would make certain the changes were made. "Anything else, sir?"

"Has the ship been swept for bugs?"

"Twice."

Something in Dean's carefully blank expression alerted Larkin that he must have asked that question before. He rubbed his forehead. "We can't be too careful," he muttered. "Are you certain the entire crew has been vetted?"

"All five hundred and twenty have had a thorough background check, and been interviewed twice, by either Tucker, Johnson, or me."

It was unfortunate that such a large crew was necessary, but the service on a luxury boutique ship had to be impeccable to help justify the exorbitant cost, and that meant crew had to be available to handle any possible detail. But as extensive as a background check could be, could anyone really trust what was found online? It seemed to Larkin that no check was ever thorough enough. He knew, because he had manipulated his share of them.

Dean was satisfied with the crew that was in place, so Larkin supposed that would have to do. If anything went wrong . . . well, Dean was expendable. Everyone was.

"We have a problem," Tiffany said flatly. "Sanchez checked

the passenger list this morning. The suites have been switched around. Ryan and Faith aren't next to Larkin."

Cael sat up in bed, cell phone to his ear. "The paranoid son of a bitch," he muttered as he turned on the lamp, a mellow pool of light spreading across the floor. "Who has the two suites now?"

"An older couple, Albert and Ginger Winningham, have been put in the Neptune. That was the suite Ryan and Faith had, and the positioning was perfect. The suite on the other side, the Queen Anne, now has Sydney Hazlett and Jenner Redwine in it. The arrangement of rooms makes that suite more problematic, but do-able."

Cael went across the room to his computer and woke it from sleep mode, then pulled up the suite diagrams in question. All he had was the Platinum suite, which was the owner's suite, where Larkin would be, and the Neptune suite. The sitting room of the Neptune exactly corresponded to that of the Platinum.

"I don't have the Queen Anne," he said. "Can you shoot that to me?"

"Hold on."

He heard the tapping of keys, then a melodic tone on his computer signaled a message had just downloaded. He clicked on it, then opened the PDF that showed the floor plan of the suite in question.

"I see what you mean." The common wall between the two suites had the bedrooms situated on it. That was no problem from the Queen Anne side; if they had to use that suite, the room they'd be in didn't matter, but the fiber-optic surveillance they had to install was more likely to feed them useful information if it went into the Platinum's living room, rather than the bedroom. Still, as Tiffany had said, it was do-able. More difficult, but do-able. He'd need access to

Larkin's suite, though, instead of just threading the wires through tiny holes between the two suites. The job had just become exponentially more dangerous.

His mind raced. Larkin was notoriously suspicious of everyone and everything, but lately he seemed to be taking his paranoia to new extremes. So, even though Cael hadn't seen this coming, he wasn't really surprised. He just wished he'd thought of the possibility beforehand so they'd have a fallback plan. He hated having to improvise, because that upped the odds that something would go wrong.

"The passengers in the suites can't be moved again," he said, thinking aloud. "Larkin put them there for a reason, and if we have Sanchez switch them around Larkin will know something's up." A plan was forming, one that involved one of his group switching out with one of the people in either the Neptune suite or the Queen Anne.

"The old couple's very well known. Anything involving them will attract a lot of attention, plus I gather they aren't in the best of health." Tiffany might not know exactly what he was thinking, but she was sharp enough to know it would involve the passengers currently assigned to one of those two suites.

"What about the other two guys?" Two gays, obviously, which meant Tiffany wouldn't be of much use. He himself was paired with Tiffany—professionally, not personally—so perhaps he could move Matt into the primary position on this job. Cael was a little uneasy with that. Matt was damn good at what he did, but his acting skills didn't extend to portraying a convincing gay. Besides, Matt had already been hired on with the crew, so moving him to the passenger list would send up all sorts of red flags. No, he'd have to do this himself.

"Wrong-o," Tiffany said, having already pulled up their info on her computer. "They're both women. Sydney—spelled with a 'y' instead of an 'i,' is an heiress. Jenner Redwine won the MegaMillions lottery several years back. They're best friends, but not lesbian. At least, if they *are* lesbian, they're so deep in the closet they could pass as garment bags."

"Are they, or not?" A tinge of impatience laced his deep tone. Although he appreciated the garment bag analogy, he didn't have time for humor.

"Going strictly by instinct . . . no. They're straight. And they're stand-ins for Sydney's father, who had to cancel. My reading is that Sydney was asked to take her father's place, and she asked a friend to go along for company. Hmmm. The suite that was originally booked was a two-bedroom, but the Queen Anne is just one bedroom."

"That could be a problem for them."

"No, it's okay. The king beds can be separated into twins. Besides," she retorted, "women don't have the same hang-ups about sharing a room that men do. With members of the same sex, that is."

He ignored the jab. Tiffany was always trying to ruffle his feathers—that was her nature. His attention to and concentration on the job was legendary, so of course she had to try to jolt him out of his mental tracks.

The sudden kink in their plans had kicked his mind into high gear. "Find out everything you can about Hazlett and Redwine. I want their travel plans, I want to know how they think, what kind of people they are."

"I'm on it."

"Ryan and Faith go to backup," he said. "We can't move them around again—that'll alert Larkin. You and I become primary."

"All right!" She sounded disgustingly cheerful. There was nothing Tiffany liked more than being in the front lines.

After hanging up, Cael did some research on his own. They had very little time to get a plan in place, so he had to lay as much groundwork right now as he could, which involved waking up some people who'd be unhappy about the hour. Tough shit. He was awake, doing his job, so they could wake up, too. He didn't have time to be considerate.

On this special charity cruise of the *Silver Mist*, before the luxury ship went into commission, he had chosen Ryan and Faith as primaries because they genuinely moved in some fairly rarified financial circles. It just so happened they both had a taste for adventure, and good skills. If Larkin hadn't shuffled the passenger list around, they would have been good to go.

Cael studied the faces he'd pulled up on the computer screen. Tiffany would do deep discovery on the two women, but he could get a feel for what kind of people they were. Hazlett was the prettier of the two, with dark blond hair and classically even features, but there was something soft in her expression. Redwine, on the other hand, was more cute than pretty, and the candid photos of her showed some attitude. The pictures he pulled up also showed that she changed her hair color about as often as she did her shoes. That could mean she had a streak of adventure in her, which meant she could be a liability. On the other hand, did Hazlett have the backbone to do what would have to be done?

It was a judgment call. Hazlett would be more pliable, more easily influenced, but her nerves might not stand up to the job. Redwine's nerves would stand up fine, but she'd dig in her heels and cause problems the whole time.

He stared longer at Redwine's photo. Tiffany might dig up something that changed his mind, but he didn't think so.

The job was what was important, and carrying off the ruse would take guts, which he didn't think Hazlett possessed. So . . . Jenner Redwine it was. If she gave him any trouble, well, he'd just have to handle it—and her.

"Hello, sweetheart," he said softly. "We're about to become lovers."

Chapter Eight

The morning the ship was supposed to depart on the two-week cruise, Sydney got up very early—she hated rushing around. She invariably did something stupid when she was rushed, like the time she'd put on one each of two different pairs of shoes, or when she'd once forgotten to put on any jewelry at all for a formal dinner. She tried to be composed and together, but it rarely worked. This time, she didn't want to be in such a rush that she forgot to bring all her luggage, or left her passport behind. On that thought, she double-checked to make sure it was in her bag.

This past week had been fun, drowsing by the pool, shopping, talking into the wee hours. Sydney had really enjoyed spending time with Caro. There were very few people with whom she could truly relax, and Caro was one of them. Her personality was laid-back, nonjudgmental, and she saw everything through a filter of good humor. It didn't escape Sydney how completely different her two best friends were, though she loved both of them.

Well, not *completely* different. Jenner *did* have a sense of humor, though it tended toward the wickedly ironic. On the other hand, there was nothing about Jenner that was laid-back; even when she was relaxing, she seemed to hum with energy. She was more wary than outgoing, somewhat prickly, and as fierce in her likes as she was her dislikes.

Maybe it was Syd's own unrelenting sense of inadequacy that had made her notice Jenner when they'd been seated at the same table at a charity dinner. To the casual observer, Jenner would have looked composed, contained, everything about her discreet and understated, from her gown to her makeup to her jewelry. Syd, on the other hand, was so hypersensitive to others' expressions, looking for any hint of derision or disapproval, that she saw the tiny flare of uncertainty in Jenner's eyes as she gave the silverware a brief, panicked glance. Immediately Syd knew that Jenner was out of her depth, that this was the first formal dinner she'd ever attended, and that she had no idea how to handle the admittedly excessive array of forks and spoons.

Normally, making the first move, whether it was initiating conversation or anything else, was agonizing for Syd and she had to psych herself up beforehand; that night, however, what she'd done had been so simple, and as easy as breathing, that she hadn't had to think about it at all. She'd caught Jenner's eye, subtly lifted the correct fork, and made a lifetime friend.

She'd been so afraid at first that her father wouldn't like Jenner. He was no one's fool, and after her disastrous engagement had ended he'd become ferocious in making sure no one else took advantage of her. Jenner's background wasn't exactly shining; winning the lottery wasn't regarded with the same amount of respect as was working twenty hours a day and making astute decisions that affected thousands of people, hopefully for the best. There was no skill or talent involved in winning the lottery; it was just a matter of luck. And she was newly arrived in south Florida, so no one knew anything about her other than the most superficial information; what concerned Syd's father most was whether or not Jenner would be a loyal friend, or if she was merely using Syd as a means of working her way into society.

To her surprise, the two of them had hit it off. Jenner didn't give a flip about society, she was who she was, and that included being Syd's friend—period. There was no rhyme or reason when it came to hitting it off with a person, she supposed. It just happened, sometimes, and she was so glad one of those times had been with Jenner.

Normally, the thought of two solid weeks filled with one formal event after the other would have almost paralyzed Syd with dread, but somehow being on a ship made things different. The whole atmosphere was just easier. Being on a ship meant being in a completely different world, where the outside couldn't intrude. There weren't any phone calls to field, and people were more preoccupied with relaxing and having fun than they were with how they or anyone else looked. She enjoyed cruises in general, and this one not only promised to be fun, but it would raise money for several very good causes. She only hoped Jenner had fun, too; Jenn was such a control freak—at least when it came to staying on top of business, because she wasn't that way with anything else—that getting away from it all would either be a great relief, or frustrating for her, and Syd had no way of knowing which way she would fall until they were actually at sea.

But even if Jenn did freak out at first, maybe then she'd relax and they could have fun. The world would be fine without her for fourteen days. There was no one else in the world Syd enjoyed spending so much time with; Jenner's take on the world was so pithy that it was hilarious. Then, too, Jenner had some of the qualities Syd admired but didn't possess: strength, self-confidence, the balls to look life in the eye and dare it to blink first.

Syd heaved a little sigh. She herself didn't have any balls—at all, not even peanut-size ones. Maybe one day.

The limo arrived at Caro's right on time to pick her up. While the driver, whose brushed gold name tag said he was "Adam," loaded her vast amount of luggage into the trunk, Sydney gave Caro a long, heartfelt hug, they made many promises that they'd get together again and wouldn't wait so long next time, then Syd bounced down the steps to the limo. She cast a quick, anxious look at the driver. She *did* have an enormous amount of luggage, and she wanted to apologize, to explain that she'd packed to be away from home for two weeks and there were all these social events on board the ship and— She bit back both the apology and the explanation. First, to his credit, Adam wasn't scowling or looking impatient or anything. Second, he was a tall, good-looking, well-built man, and that type always made her excruciatingly aware of her own shortcomings, one of which was the urge to apologize for everything.

She settled into the seat and placed her bag next to her, thinking that when she signed the credit card receipt for the limo she'd add to the tip that had already been figured into the cost. Anyone who handled that amount of luggage without complaint deserved an extra tip.

As the limo pulled away from the curb Sydney stared out the window at the sun-drenched hills, and the blue of the Pacific off to her right. It was another beautiful day; every day she'd been here had been perfect. The prospect of another fourteen days of beautiful weather loomed in front of her, making her smile.

She checked her watch, a diamond-studded Cartier her

father had given her on her eighteenth birthday. She was going to be one of the first passengers on the ship, but if Jenner's plane was on time and her limo made good time through the traffic, it was possible she'd arrive at about the same time. Syd was relieved that she wasn't going to be late this time. She knew she had a terrible habit of not being on time, and she really tried not to be late, but like almost everything else, time seemed to be beyond her control. She never *intended* to be late, just the opposite, but . . . She'd try to do better, especially while they were on the cruise.

She didn't pay much attention to the landscape as Adam drove at a leisurely pace through the upscale neighborhood that surrounded the gated community where Caro lived. It wasn't as if she knew her way around San Diego anyway, so the landmarks meant nothing to her. Instead, she let her mind wander as she thought about the days ahead, the sunbathing on their private balcony, the wonderful food she really shouldn't eat but would enjoy immensely because everyone knew cruise calories didn't count. Maybe she'd even drink a little too much now and then, and dance with a handsome Latin ballroom instructor. Uh-huh. Sure. She wasn't known for her ability to cut loose. So she *wouldn't* drink too much—she never had—and as she already knew how to ballroom dance, she probably wouldn't dance with an instructor, either. But she and Jenner would relax, enjoy themselves, maybe flirt a little even if it was only with someone who was safely in his seventies, and have a real vacation.

With a slight jerk, the limo halted at a stop sign, and the door locks clicked. Confused, Sydney glanced at the driver, because all his other stops had been smooth as silk, and why were the door locks just now engaging? Usually they automatically clicked down as soon as the car was put in gear.

The passenger door across from her opened and a dark-haired women slid into the seat, then closed the door with a firm bang. Sydney gaped at her, too startled to do more than make a few incoherent noises. The car started forward again, and once more the door locks clicked. Confused, she realized the first click had been when they *unlocked*, which meant he'd put the gear in Park.

"Adam—" she began, alarm pushing aside her startled confusion as the car picked up speed. She scooted to the edge of the seat, gripping the door handle as she reached forward to tap on the partition separating them. Surely he realized they'd picked up an unwanted passenger. He should be pulling to the curb, turning around and telling the woman—

"Just sit still, Ms. Hazlett," the woman said in a calm tone. She took her hand out of the pocket of her tracksuit to reveal an ugly black gun. "If you do exactly as we tell you, you won't be hurt."

We.

The driver was in on it. He'd deliberately stopped so the locks would disengage and the woman could get in. Everything had been prearranged; he'd known she would be there.

For a long, dizzying moment, Sydney held her breath. She clutched her purse because it was literally all she had to hold on to. Kidnapping was always a possibility when someone had money, and her father had a lot of money, but security in their circles was mostly limited to *home* security. She knew a few people who employed personal security guards, but very few, because for the most part people just lived their lives as normally as possible. So far as she knew, her father had never had a kidnapping threat. And yet, here she was in a locked car with two strangers, one of whom was holding a gun on her.

Don't panic. Don't panic. She told herself that over and over. If she panicked, she would lose control and start crying and screaming, and somehow it seemed important not to do that. All she could think was how upset her father would be if she were killed, so she shouldn't do anything that would force these people to shoot her.

Everything would work out. They would ask for a ransom, her father would pay it, and they would let her go. This would all be over in no time.

She'd seen their faces. Wasn't that a bad sign? Hadn't she read somewhere that kidnappers who intended to let their victims go after they got the money always concealed their faces, so they couldn't be identified? If a kidnapper made no attempt to conceal his—or her—identity, they usually didn't intend to let the victim live.

"People are expecting me," she blurted desperately. "I'm supposed to go on a cruise. I was on my way there—" But they knew that, didn't they? After all, "Adam" was her driver. He'd been supposed to take her to the dock. She lurched into a different tack. "I have money. Cash—"

"We won't want your money," the woman said. She was tall, with short dark hair and the sort of leggy elegance of a model, though she wasn't particularly pretty. Her tone wasn't harsh or vicious, which Sydney would have expected given the gun in her hand.

"But . . . I . . ." Sydney's voice trailed off, because her mind went blank. If they didn't want her money, what *did* they want?

"Stay calm," the woman said. "Do exactly as we tell you, and when this is all over you and your friend will be allowed to walk away, completely unharmed. But if you pull any John Wayne shit, your friend will pay the price for it. Understood?"

Sydney's thoughts splintered again. They'd grabbed *Caro*? If they don't want money, then why? And even more ridiculously—John Wayne? *Her?*

"We already have Ms. Redwine," the woman continued. "In a little while, we'll set up a call for you to talk to her. That way you each will know the other is okay—for now."

Not Caro. *Jenner.*

A bubble of hysterical laughter rose in her throat, threatening to choke her. Oh, God, Jenner was the one they should be having the John Wayne talk with, not her.

"Calm down," the woman said sharply, seeing how rapidly Sydney's control was fraying.

Sydney gripped her bag so tightly her knuckles turned white, her chest heaving with the force and speed of her breathing. Her lips felt numb. "What do you want?" she whispered, and tears stung her eyes. Quickly she wiped them away, not wanting to appear any weaker than she was, even though she knew the woman had already seen them and knew very well what they meant. They *wanted* her to be afraid. They wanted her to be so terrified that she'd do whatever they said, when they said it. Well, congratulations—she was there already.

"Just do as you're told" was the only answer she got. "If you cooperate, you'll be treated well. This experience doesn't have to be unpleasant."

The limo made a smooth turn. Ahead, several hotels loomed on either side of the street, some taller than others, some sterile and generic, others more welcoming. Sydney stared blindly at them. There were always a lot of people around hotels; maybe she could attract someone's attention, though the windows of the limo were tinted so dark she didn't see how. And what if she did? What would happen then? Would this woman shoot her?

"We're going to walk into the hotel," the woman said in a low, even tone, "without incident, without any sign that we aren't the best of friends. I repeat: Do as you're told, and you and Ms. Redwine won't be hurt. We're going to check in, and you're going to hand over your credit card and sign the registration paperwork the way we've both done hundreds of times before, then we'll all go up in the elevator. I'll be watching. I'll know if you do anything different, if you try to scribble a message or roll your eyes at the clerk . . . *anything*. If you do anything out of the ordinary, Ms. Redwine will pay the price."

That threat froze whatever idea Sydney might have had for trying to run, make a quick escape. Jenner's life depended on her, on what she did or didn't do. Oh, God, she'd never been able to act worth a damn. What if she couldn't even manage to check into a hotel without looking as if the bitch next to her was holding a damn gun on her? She wasn't an actress, she wasn't brave, and she didn't have an intrepid bone in her body. What if she screwed this up?

She couldn't. She couldn't let Jenner down. She had to get this right.

The limo turned, and came to a stop under a large, curved portico where hotel guests arrived and left by taxi, or left their own vehicles for the valet service. A burly hotel doorman in a burgundy uniform stepped forward and opened the passenger door. The woman slid out, and stood waiting, so close to the car that the doorman couldn't close the door, while Adam got out and silently opened Sydney's door. She swung her legs out and stood, carefully not looking at him. If the woman was armed, it stood to reason that he was, too, otherwise the woman wouldn't have gotten out of the car and left Sydney inside.

Adam stood just a shade too close to her, not so close that

he would attract attention, but close enough that she had no hope of darting around him and making a break for it. If it hadn't been for Jenner, she might have tried something desperate like that, but they had her as effectively hogtied with their threats as if they had actually used rope to secure her.

The woman came around the car, smiling, and looped her arm through Sydney's. "Take care of the tip, Adam, please," she said pleasantly, then marched Sydney inside the hotel.

With no other choice, Sydney sucked in a deep breath, steadied her weak knees, and did exactly what the woman had told her to do. Her heart was pounding so hard and fast she thought she might faint, and her voice sounded high and squeaky to her own ears, but she handed over her platinum American Express card, she signed her name, collected the key cards—three of them—at the woman's whispered direction, and turned all three of them over to her. When the hotel clerk asked if she had luggage, the woman smiled and said, "Our driver is bringing up our bags," and that was that.

They went to the bank of elevators, the woman punched the "up" button, and casually glanced around, studying everyone and everything around them. The elevator arrived with a pleasant little tone, the doors smoothly opened, and they stepped inside, along with several other people. The woman punched the button for the top floor—the twenty-fifth—and they shot up. An older woman got off on fourteen. A young man exited on seventeen. When he was gone and the doors had closed behind him, Sydney blurted, "How do I know Jenner is all right?"

The woman squeezed Sydney's arm and glanced up at the camera in the corner of the elevator car. Frustrated, Syd turned so that only the back of her head faced the camera. "On TV, there's no sound on elevator surveillance tapes."

The woman smiled, a completely humorless stretching of her lips, and whispered, "This isn't TV."

On the twenty-third floor, another woman joined them.

They reached the twenty-fifth floor, exited the elevator, and the second woman fell into step with them. Sydney darted a frightened glance at her and was met with a cool look that sent chills down her spine. She was with them, then—whoever "they" were.

Silently she followed the first woman, with the second one pulling guard duty. They took a right, then walked all the way down a long hall to the double door at the end. A suite, then.

The woman took one of the key cards, swiped it, and opened the door. A firm hand on Sydney's back ushered her into the foyer, then turned her to the left, toward the parlor. Immediately the first woman went over to the window and closed the curtains, while the other one, behind Sydney, turned on the lights. She also turned the air-conditioning to a cooler temperature. Sydney stood beside the round dining table and watched them, feeling more impotent than she ever had in her entire life. What was going on?

The second woman had long brown hair pulled up into a ponytail. She was prettier than the first woman, but her body was just as taut and muscled. She pulled off her jacket, and Sydney saw a knife in a sheath at the small of her back. A knife! What was this, Charlie's Angels gone bad?

But somehow the knife was more frightening than the gun. Guns made noise—well, unless they were silenced, and the gun she'd seen hadn't been—and brought people running. A knife was silent; her body might not be found for days.

She plucked up her courage. "*Now* will someone tell me what's going on?" She tried very hard not to let her fear show, but she heard her voice waver in the middle of the sentence.

The first woman said, "You don't need to know. You just need to do what you're told. My name is Dori, and this is Kim. Please sit down while we wait for Adam."

Sydney sat. She tried to calm herself, but it wasn't easy. Would they have told her their names if they intended for her to survive? She could describe them, she knew their names. Of course, the names could be fake, but the fact that they'd made no effort to disguise their faces still wasn't good.

The enormity of it all suddenly hit her like a slap in the face. She gulped and tried to control the violent shaking that seized her, tried to stop the tears that suddenly welled in her eyes and dripped down her face, but all of her willpower was useless against her sudden despair and she covered her face with her hands, sobbing. She didn't cry just for herself. She cried for her dad, who would be in so much pain and blame himself, if this kidnapping proceeded as she suspected it would and she ended up dead—or worse, she simply disappeared and he never knew what happened to her. And Jenner . . . was she being held this way? Had she been met at the airport by more of these people, was she also taken to a hotel somewhere for God knows what purpose?

Dori and Kim left her alone for a couple of minutes, then a soft but strong hand gripped Syd's arms and pulled her up, to an unsteady standing position. Those hands remained in place, literally supporting her.

"First things first," Dori said, gently taking the bag Sydney had continued to clutch. She opened the bag and searched through the contents, removing both Syd's iPod and her cell phone, a nail file, two pens, a safety pin, and anything else that was remotely useful. In a moment of bad timing, the cell phone began to ring. Sydney jerked, startled by the tone, and automatically reached for it.

Dori silently took the phone and slipped it in her pocket.

Kim took Syd's arm and led her back through the foyer, past the double doors, toward the bedroom. "In a little while, we're going to call Ms. Redwine. Use the time to pull yourself together. You're going to give Ms. Redwine instructions, and if she does as she's told and you do as you're told, everyone will be all right. I give you my word."

She sounded sincere. It was all Syd could do not to laugh in her face. Was she supposed to *trust* these people? She'd do what they said, because she had no choice, but their "word" didn't mean a thing. What kind of fool would take comfort in the word of a criminal?

They stepped into a spacious corner bedroom. Light poured into the room, which was decorated in blue and beige—mostly beige. There was a king-size bed, a comfortable-looking chair by the window, and a private bath.

"In a day or two we'll let you call your father, since it's possible he'll hear that you aren't on board the ship."

Yes, Syd could imagine that happening. An e-mail or a phone call from someone aboard the *Silver Mist* could cause all sorts of complications.

"You'll tell him you were too ill to make the trip, you must have caught a virus, but you're feeling better and you'll spend some more time in San Diego, with Caro, until Ms. Redwine returns from the cruise."

"If I'm better, then why don't I just fly to Hawaii and join the cruise there?" Sydney blurted.

Kim stared at her, then gave a shrug. "You're feeling better, but the virus is still holding on."

"You're not going to . . . ask him for money?" Why else would they be holding her?

"No," Kim said briefly, and her expression hardened. "Here's the situation, Ms. Hazlett. You'll notice this bedroom has no walls common to another room. There are

119

two outside walls, and the emergency stairwell runs beside the third wall. We're on the top floor, so, barring an emergency, of course, traffic in the stairwell will be limited."

That was true. Some people took the stairs as a matter of course, for the exercise, but from the twenty-fifth floor?

"If you scream for help or bang on the walls," Kim continued, "no one will hear you but us. However, we're hoping you'll continue to cooperate. You won't be completely confined; maids will come in and you'll need to be in the parlor with us while they're here. We'll also be ordering room service, and you'll take your meals with us."

Room service that would be charged to her American Express, Sydney thought bitterly. That really pissed her off, that she was being made to finance her own kidnapping.

"If we see even a hint that you're not cooperating fully, if you do something silly such as try to signal one of the maids, our people who're holding Ms. Redwine will be informed." Her eyes turned cold. "You really don't want to do that."

While Sydney stood there, maddeningly impotent, Kim went around the room and collected the pens and notepads that the hotel provided. She disconnected the phone, leaving the phone itself sitting there so the maids wouldn't notice it was missing, but taking the cord with her. She went into the bathroom and checked there. While she was out of sight Sydney stood there, looking longingly at the door, but chained by her fear for Jenner.

Kim came out of the bathroom and nodded approvingly when she saw Sydney still standing in the same place. "Good choice," she said, knowing of course that running had been considered. "Especially since Dori is standing in the foyer and you wouldn't have made it outside."

Just then there was a sound in the foyer as someone knocked briskly at the double doors. Sydney's heart leapt, but then she heard the sound of the door opening and Dori said, "Good Lord! There's enough luggage there for three people!"

Sydney's face burned.

"Do the math," Adam said, amusement in his deep tones. "This was a two-week trip. Most women need more than two tracksuits and three changes of underwear for that length of time."

"I wash out my underwear every night," Dori said, her tone as annoyed as Adam's was amused.

"Just saying. You aren't exactly in a position to judge whether this is a lot of luggage or not."

Their banter spoke of a long relationship but not, to Sydney's ear, of anything romantic. Then Adam came into the bedroom, easily carrying two of her heaviest bags. "We'll need to go through everything, make certain she doesn't have anything in here that could cause us any trouble." He hoisted the bags onto the bed. "You take these two," he said to Kim. "Dori and I will handle the others." He flicked a quick, impersonal look at Sydney. "How's she holding up?"

"*She's* holding up just fine," Sydney snapped, infuriated that he talked over her as if she weren't there. She was lying, of course, because she wasn't holding up fine, but at least she wasn't a limp puddle on the floor.

"Good deal," he said, smiling at her.

She met the smile with a stony gaze. How dare the bastard smile at her?

His expression remained pleasant, because of course he didn't care if she was upset or not, didn't care what she liked or didn't like.

Turning, he started into the foyer to help Kim with searching the rest of Sydney's bags, but he stopped in the bedroom doorway and pulled a small gadget out of his pocket. Flipping out a screwdriver head, he whistled softly as he dismantled the lock on the bedroom door.

Even though logically she knew the flimsy lock wouldn't have kept them out, she had been looking forward to at least the illusion of privacy. Now that was gone, as casually and easily as getting a drink of water.

Her knees wobbled again, so she sat down in the chair and dully watched as all her belongings were sorted through. Kim wasn't careless with the fragile fabrics; she took each garment out separately, and neatly laid it aside, but she was extremely thorough in her search, even checking the lining of the suitcases. Good God, what did they think she was, a spy?

At last the chore was finished. Pausing at the door, Kim said, "We'll bring your cell phone to you in a little while, so you can call Ms. Jenner. Until then, make yourself comfortable."

Comfortable? *Comfortable?*

Sydney supposed that was possible, at least physically. The bedroom was nice enough. This wasn't a luxury hotel, catering more to the business crowd, but it was decent. But how could she be comfortable when she was a prisoner, when Jenner was, too, somewhere—and they were both likely to die before this was over?

And she still didn't know what the hell these people wanted.

Chapter Nine

Jenner checked her watch as the plane landed in San Diego. The flight was almost two hours late, and even though she wasn't worried about missing the ship—it didn't sail until four p.m.—the weather delay in Dallas had been both annoying and tiring. Despite her changed financial circumstances, she wasn't exactly a seasoned traveler. She had never been to Europe, for instance. A lot of the Palm Beach crowd would fly to Switzerland every winter for the skiing, but she wasn't interested in learning how to slide down a mountainside on two skinny planks, so she had no reason to go. One day she wanted to go to Australia, maybe, and there were a couple of other countries she'd like to see, but so far she simply hadn't traveled all that much.

When she did fly it was first class, but she didn't belong to any of the airlines' clubs and didn't really see a lot of difference between sitting in one place or sitting in another. Sitting wasn't what she wanted to do; she was too restless, too antsy after the long flight. So she'd walked the Dallas–Fort Worth airport for two hours, trying to get in some exercise, but constantly dodging around more slowly moving people or, worse, getting trapped behind them was about as relaxing as driving in rush-hour traffic. Still, at least she'd been moving.

She had tried to call Syd from Dallas, to let her know about the storm delay, but the calls went straight to voice mail. Syd was scrupulous about turning her phone off when she was in a restaurant or any other social situation, because she was so hypersensitive about disturbing or annoying others, but she often forgot to turn the phone back on right away. Jenner wasn't as polite; she would set her phone to vibrate instead of ring, but she never turned it off. What had once been a luxury was now an absolute necessity, like air, water, and Stuart Weitzman shoes.

By now, though, when Jenner hadn't shown up on time, Syd would have remembered to turn on the phone and tried to contact her. As the plane taxied toward the terminal, Jenner thumbed the power button on her phone and waited for the system to connect. All over the first-class cabin, she could hear the various tones that signaled almost every other passenger was doing the same thing.

There was no message. Maybe downloading messages from her carrier took a few minutes, though the guy beside her was intently listening to his messages. Just before the plane reached the Jetway, she checked again. Still no message.

Surely Syd should have called by now. Maybe her message had been dropped. Jenner thumbed in Syd's cell number as the tone sounded that released passengers from their seats and everyone stepped into the aisle, gathering their carry-on bags. Jenner followed suit, slinging her bag over her shoulder and nodding a thank-you to the man who stepped back to allow her to join the queue that jostled and snaked its way forward. She still held the phone to her ear as she stepped off the plane, listening as the ringing stopped and the call went to voice mail. She left another message, then clicked off and slipped the phone back into her bag.

Even if Syd were late, too, which wouldn't have surprised Jenner, she would have called. Jenner began to feel a little worried.

Still, things could have happened. Syd's cell phone could have a dead battery, or have completely stopped working, and she hadn't discovered either of those possibilities until she was already on the ship. Her purse could have been stolen. Or she was on the ship, had been leaning on the rail of their balcony, and had dropped the phone overboard. Any number of things could have happened, which were all not only more likely but were also all better than the real worry she had, that Syd had been in an accident and couldn't call.

Jenner had notified the limo company that her flight would be late, but its actual arrival time had pretty much been anyone's guess, so she hoped no wires had gotten crossed there. The first thing she saw when she reached the baggage claim area, though, was a uniformed Hispanic man holding a sign that said "REDWINE." She signaled him and he hustled over to collect her luggage, which took its own sweet time arriving. The carousel didn't start turning for a good fifteen minutes, and while one of her bags appeared almost immediately, the other didn't show up until most of the other bags were gone.

Every additional delay ate at her nerves. She hated being late, even by as much as one minute. The discipline of getting to work on time, clocking in, getting docked money if she was late, and the possibility of getting fired if she was late more than a few times a year, had drilled punctuality into her brain and habits. The fact that none of these delays were her fault, or under her control, almost made it worse because that meant she was helpless. She had to go with the flow, and the flow today was sluggish.

"Is this all your luggage?" the driver asked, pulling out the telescoping handles of each suitcase and gripping each one.

"Yes, that's all." Syd had taken a mountain of luggage, but Jenner had repacked several times so she could fit everything into just two bags. They were big bags, though, and so heavy she couldn't lift them. She just hoped she hadn't forgotten anything vital, because it wasn't as if she could run out and pick up whatever it was, though she imagined any decent cruise ship would be well stocked with whatever necessities might be forgotten by careless passengers. This particular cruise didn't include as many port calls as most cruises did, due to their destination and the nature of the cruise, so surely the shops onboard would carry a larger variety of items.

"How long will it take to get to the cruise ship terminal?" she asked the driver, once more checking her watch. Time was slipping away from her. "I don't want the ship to sail without me."

He grinned, a flash of white teeth in his dark face. "I'll get you there in plenty of time, I promise."

Thank goodness, traffic cooperated by being delay-free, helped by the fact that lunch hour had already come and gone and the evening rush hour hadn't begun yet. Sooner than she'd expected, the limo was pulling into the impressive loading area. The *Silver Mist* loomed over the terminal, which was itself easily three or four stories high. Jenner caught her breath at her first sight of the ship. While she knew it wasn't a huge ship, going more for luxury than quantity, the size of the thing still took her by surprise. She saw ships all the time, living where she did, but she'd never been this close to one before.

And the *Silver Mist* was beautiful. All of the cruise ships she'd seen were gleaming white, with different trim and sterns, but this one wasn't exactly white. It wasn't exactly gray, either, but somewhere in between. The paint gleamed and shimmered, almost like . . . a silver mist. Duh.

An enormous parking lot was across the street, but she imagined very few, if any, of the passengers on this cruise had driven themselves to the terminal. The only vehicles she saw were limos. Her driver pulled up to the luggage area where a swarm of men were unloading, tagging, and reloading a mountain of luggage. She had printed her luggage tags from the Internet site, and the tags listed the suite number, which was how the bags were delivered to the correct staterooms.

As soon as the porter saw her luggage tag and looked at her paperwork, he said, "There was a mix-up on the suite assignments on this deck. When you get aboard, there'll be someone in a red jacket waiting in the elevator vestibule to tell you which stateroom is yours. Your luggage will be set aside until we get the correct number."

Her anxiety level ratcheted upward even more. She was tired, she was worried about Syd, and she didn't want to deal with mix-ups. She didn't want her luggage to be "set aside," because what if the ship sailed without it? But this was one more thing she couldn't control, so she mentally threw up her hands and gave up. "What am I supposed to do now?" she asked the porter. "I've never been on a cruise before."

He smiled. "Then you're in for an experience. You'll love it." He pointed toward the entrance to the terminal. "Go in there, and take the escalator up. The concierge will take care of you, get you checked in, and show you aboard the ship."

Syd had told her that the passengers who booked the suites were checked in separately, and before the others, but on this particular cruise everyone was a VIP, so she had no idea how the order of check-in would be handled. On the other hand, most people were staying in the smaller mini-suites, so the ones who had booked the most expensive suites would still get the star treatment. Maybe.

She followed the porter's directions, got private, individual service checking in, and was escorted to security, where her photo was taken and scanned into a facial recognition software program. She was given her key card and her ship's card, which she'd need for identification, drinks, and anything else she bought while onboard, then she crossed from the terminal to the ship via a covered walkway. A red-jacketed attendant was there, checking room assignments and sending people in the right directions. When he saw Jenner's card, he called up and alerted someone to Jenner's presence, then directed her to the correct elevator with the assurance that someone would meet her when she got off the elevator at the penthouse deck.

The hallways, corridors—whatever they were called on a ship—were full of activity as people strolled around, crew members delivered luggage, and acquaintances stopped to talk and thus blocked the rather narrow passageway. Jenner saw a couple of people she recognized, but waved instead of stopping to chat. She wanted to get to the suite and find Syd. She reached the elevators and punched the "up" button for both of them, then got in the one that arrived first.

Another red jacket was waiting for her when the doors slid open. "Ms. Redwine?" the woman asked, smiling. "Please come with me, I'll escort you to your suite. I'm so sorry for the confusion. The suite you had booked was lovely, but I think you'll be very happy with the one you've been assigned. It's next to the owner's suite. Your steward, Bridget, is waiting for you."

The attendant started briskly down the corridor and Jenner followed; she wanted to ask if Syd had arrived, but at the pace the woman was walking figured she'd find out herself in about five seconds anyway. They passed an impressive set of double doors that had to be to the owner's suite, then stopped at the next door down as a compact but sturdily built young woman with coppery red hair and calm blue eyes approached. "This is Bridget," the attendant said. "Bridget, this is Ms. Redwine. I'll leave you to your duties." Then she hurried back the way she'd come, talking into her radio phone as she raced to meet more arriving passengers and conduct them to their newly assigned quarters.

"I'll be taking care of you and your quarters," Bridget said, swiping her own key card and unlocking the door. She held it open for Jenner to enter. "If there's anything you need, please don't hesitate to call me."

Jenner stepped into the living room part of the suite. In the past seven years she'd become accustomed to luxurious homes, but this room, in gold and white, screamed of elegance and old-world charm. The walls were decorated with oil paintings, not reproductions, and the frames were ornate. Beyond the wall-to-wall draperies was a sun-drenched balcony that called to her, even though they weren't at sea yet.

"Sydney?" she called. "Syd?" When there was no answer, she turned to Bridget. "My friend, Sydney Hazlett, hasn't arrived yet?"

"One moment," said Bridget, taking out her radio phone and punching in a number. Her smile remained calm and unflustered. Probably late-arriving passengers were part of the job description. A moment later she disconnected the call without saying a word to anyone.

Puzzled, Jenner said, "Is she here?" The words were

scarcely out of her mouth when her own cell phone rang. Retrieving it from her bag, she glanced at the caller ID and breathed a sigh of relief. Syd—finally! "Never mind, this is her," she said to Bridget, turning away as she answered the phone. "Syd, I just got here. Where are you? I've left two messages."

There was a moment of silence, then Syd said in a tight voice, "Jenn. Do what they say."

Jenner halted. "What?" She had one of those moments of blank confusion, because while the words made sense, the context didn't.

"I'm okay, they haven't hurt me, but you have to do what they say or . . . or they will."

"*What?*" Jenner asked more forcefully, actually taking the phone from her ear to stare at it for a second before putting it in place again. "What are you talking about? Do what *who* says? Is this a joke?"

A man's voice, deep and unexpected, interrupted. "This isn't a joke, Ms. Redwine. Do what you're told, and at the end of the cruise both you and Ms. Hazlett will be released unharmed. Cause any trouble, and you won't see your friend again."

Her entire body seemed to lose all its heat. Shocked, abruptly terrified, Jenner began to shiver. "Who is this? Put Syd back on the phone *right now.*"

Instead, the silence of dead air was all she heard. She looked at the phone again and saw that the call had been ended.

Gently, Bridget reached out and took the phone from Jenner's nerveless fingers, slipping it inside her own jacket. "There's no need to panic," she said. "We don't want to harm either of you, but we'll do whatever's necessary. As the man said, do what you're told, and you'll be all right."

Chapter Ten

If there was one thing Jenner disliked, it was someone telling her to do what she was told. Anger began to boil in her veins. She'd been away from the tough streets of Chicago for a long time, but the old instincts remained. Her eyes narrowed and her chin lowered even as she took a step back to better assess her enemy.

"Don't try it," Bridget gently advised. "I can take you without breaking a sweat."

Now that she had a good look at her, Jenner had to admit that was probably true. She herself was in good shape, but Bridget's solid muscles showed under her trim uniform. Jenner had often wished for bigger boobs, but right now she didn't give a damn about boobs, she wanted big muscles to go with those judo classes she'd taken.

The bad thing was, Bridget probably had more training than some classes that taught basic self-defense. And even more than muscles, she had something else: Sydney. Just the thought of her friend being held by people, whoever they were, was enough to squelch Jenner's almost overwhelming urge to fight fast, fight dirty, and scream her head off at the same time.

Nevertheless, she was compelled to say, "If Syd is hurt in any way, I'll hunt you to the ends of the earth." Maybe that wasn't the smartest thing to say to someone who held all the cards, but she meant it, and the absolute truth of that glittered in her eyes—for all the good it did.

"Whether or not she's hurt is completely up to you, and how good an actress you are," Bridget returned, unperturbed.

Actress? They thought she was an actress? What was going on? She'd fallen down the rabbit hole, Jenner thought, looking around the room for clarification, because, once again, what she'd heard didn't make sense. "I'm not an actress," she said, bewildered. "Do you have me mixed up with someone else?" That was far-fetched, but actresses did tend to be blond and skinny, and she *was* both permanently skinny and temporarily blond, so at least the possibility existed. "I'm Jenner Redwine. I've never acted in anything in my life!"

"Then you'll need to learn fast," said Bridget. "And there's no mix-up. I wish we didn't have to do this, but circumstances changed"—she shrugged, as if to say *what can you do?*—"and here we are. So have a seat, Ms. Redwine, and I'll tell you what we want from you."

Jenner didn't see that she had a choice, but it still galled her to have to do as directed, which was proof that she never had been and never would be any kind of actress, good or bad. She sat down on the curved gold damask sofa, her expression mutinous and her eyes still flashing a promise of retribution.

Bridget sighed. "Better Cael than me," she murmured, half under her breath.

"What? Who?" Jenner demanded, having caught only half of that.

Bridget sat, also, which Jenner thought was probably against all sorts of steward rules, but hell, she obviously wasn't a real steward, she was involved in a kidnapping, so why would she care about a little rule like not sitting down in one of the staterooms? "First," she began, "there are several of us onboard, and, no, I'm not going to tell you who everyone is. You'll meet a few of us, but there are more. You'll be watched at all times."

Clever, Jenner thought. She had no way of knowing if that were true or not, if she was being watched by unknown people, or if Bridget was saying that just to keep her in line. Either way, she'd have to assume the statement was true, because Syd's life hung in the balance.

Her doubt and frustration must have shown on her face, because Bridget sighed again. "Don't overthink it, just go with what I tell you."

"Yeah," Jenner said with heavy irony. "Because you're so trustworthy."

Bridget's lips tightened a little, but her tone remained calm. "Whether or not I'm trustworthy has nothing to do with the situation."

That was interesting, Jenner thought. A kidnapper who cared what the victim thought about her? She mentally filed that little tidbit away. Right now, Bridget and whoever was helping her had the upper hand, but every bit of information Jenner could glean might eventually come in handy. She might be able to play one of them against the other. But so what if she did? How would that change Sydney's situation, except for the worse? It wouldn't. She had to remember that, not let her anger and natural resistance lead her to do something rash. She had to remember Sydney.

"The phone in here has been disabled," said Bridget, indicating the phone on the wall. "Likewise the phone in

133

the bedroom. Feel free to check them if you don't believe me."

Believe her? Hah! Thinking how stupid she'd feel if she didn't check the phones and later found out Bridget had lied, Jenner promptly got to her feet and checked them both. They were corded phones, or they were supposed to have been, but both cords were gone, so, yes, the phones had definitely been disabled.

Bridget had silently followed her into the bedroom, watching her. "You're right," Jenner agreed, stating the obvious. "No phones." They were going to a lot of trouble to make certain she didn't contact anyone, despite holding Syd's safety over her head. Either they thought she might be stupid enough to do something that would endanger Syd, or they took no chances, period.

Bridget inclined her head in acknowledgment, then said, "Here's what's going to happen. The first night at sea, there's no formal dinner because everyone is too busy getting settled, but the casual restaurants and bars are open. You'll go out to eat alone. If anyone asks, Ms. Hazlett had to cancel at the last minute because of a stomach virus. In a day or so, she'll be allowed to call her father and tell him the same thing, in case someone here onboard sends an e-mail or text message to her father, asking if she's okay."

That meant they planned on Syd still being alive a couple of days from now, Jenner thought, and went cold at the realization that the exact opposite could so easily have been true.

"After you eat, go out to the Fog Bank, which is the aft bar on the Lido deck—"

"Where's aft?"

Bridget paused, as if she wasn't certain whether or not Jenner was pulling her leg.

"Look," Jenner said testily, "I've never been on a ship before. I intended to rely on Syd to lead me around until I got things figured out, but you screwed that up, so if you want me in a particular place at a particular time, it's up to you to get me there."

"Aft is the rear of the ship," replied Bridget with grim patience. "This suite is on the left side, the port side, of the ship. When you leave the room, turn right, and you'll be heading aft."

"Okay. Aft bar, Lido deck. Where's the Lido deck?"

"The elevator buttons are named instead of numbered, as I'm sure you noticed when you took the elevator up to this deck. The Lido deck is the fun deck. The top deck is usually the sports deck, and the second deck is the Lido. The Lido is where games are played—"

"How appropriate," Jenner murmured.

Bridget's jaw clenched ever so slightly. Her calm was beginning to show a few cracks. Still, she ignored Jenner's interruption and continued, "A couple will get into an argument. Their names are Cael and Tiffany. They're sharing a stateroom, but they'll break up, very publicly. Then he'll approach you, and it'll be love at first sight."

"Unlikely. I'm not the impulsive type. And I'm not known for picking up sleazoids."

"Pretend," Bridget said briefly, through clenched teeth.

"That I've suddenly lost all my common sense and taste? Ooookay."

"Oh, jeez," Bridget said under her breath. Then, more loudly, "Cael's a good-looking guy, so your taste won't come into question. He'll hit on you, and all you have to do is act smitten. He'll finesse the details, come back here with you, and from then on you're his headache, I hope."

"So he'll be my guard?" she asked warily. Being at a man's

135

mercy made her uneasy, as it would any woman with an ounce of common sense.

Finally she'd asked a question that seemed to please Bridget, if her wide, bright, shark smile was any indication. "He's more than that. He's the boss. How healthy your friend stays depends entirely on how happy you make Cael."

The big ship eased away from the dock, but Jenner missed the excitement of departure on her very first cruise because she was literally being held hostage in her own suite. Bridget had other duties to fulfill, but another woman had taken her place. This one called herself Faith. Whether or not that was her real name was anyone's guess. She was tall and slim, as classically lovely as Syd, and had the same sort of style—the one that screamed Old Money. Her thick brown hair fell in a perfectly cut swath down her back, and her discreet makeup emphasized her high cheekbones and large hazel eyes.

Over the years Jenner had learned how to recognize designer clothing, so she knew Faith was wearing Roberto Cavalli sandals that cost upward of eight hundred dollars. The diamonds in her bracelet, and the big solitaire nestled against her wedding ring, were genuine. Had she stolen them, or was she rich? And if she was rich, why was she involved with kidnappers?

Regardless of Faith's beauty, and her good taste in clothes and jewelry, she, too, had that very fit, toned look that said she worked out regularly. And even if she wasn't Bridget's equal in the ass-kicking department, so what? Jenner was still over a barrel, because of Syd.

Syd must be terrified. Where were they holding her? Had they hurt her, maybe slapped her around, to make her do what they wanted? The image of someone hitting sweet, vulnerable Sydney made Jenner tremble with rage. Syd had never harmed anyone. She had no idea how to fight, and emotionally she was defenseless against any type of violence.

Jenner wrenched her thoughts away from Syd, because otherwise she'd become so angry she couldn't think straight, not that she could anyway. Her thoughts seemed to spin in circles, as she asked herself the same questions over and over despite the complete lack of answers. Who were these people? What did they want? Evidently not money, because they weren't holding Syd for ransom. Instead, they were holding her as a means of forcing Jenner to do . . . what? Act as if she'd fallen in instant lust with this guy Cael? To what end?

Did they have some kind of long con going on? From bitter experience with her dad, she knew cons, knew how they worked. If this was a con, it wasn't like any she'd ever heard of before. Cons manipulated people into behaving in stupid ways, they didn't involve elaborate kidnapping schemes—that took the con into the realm of a federal offense.

So, no con was involved. To go to this much trouble and expense, and to have as many people involved in the game as they did, they were serious. She knew of at least four people on this ship—Bridget, Faith, and the unknown Cael and Tiffany—and she'd talked to one other man, the one who had Sydney. That was five people, at a minimum. Probably more than one person was with Syd. And if she believed Bridget, there were other people on the ship who wouldn't be identified to her, so she wouldn't know if she was being watched or not.

What terrified her was that they were letting her see their faces, giving her their names. The names could be fake, but their faces weren't. Did that mean they weren't worried about anything she might later tell the authorities? Maybe they didn't intend for her to return alive from this cruise. After she'd done what they wanted, all it would take was a simple tip over the balcony rail, and she'd be gone.

But what about everyone else aboard the ship? There were people here who knew her, knew Syd. If she was supposed to be carrying on a torrid shipboard romance with a man she'd just met, others would notice. She'd have to introduce him to people they encountered, so even more people would be able to describe him. Not only that, he'd gotten aboard by going through the same security procedures as everyone else. His photograph was in the facial recognition program. There was no way he could hope to get away, unless he destroyed the entire ship and everyone on it.

Recognizing how far she'd strayed from the shoreline of logic, Jenner mentally paddled back into shallow water. These people weren't on a suicide mission. They had a definite purpose, and they needed her to carry it out.

So . . . that meant she had an edge with them. They needed her. They'd gone to the extreme of kidnapping Syd to use as leverage against her, to make certain she did as they wanted. This probably meant they wouldn't hurt her, but Syd didn't have that protection.

She tried to think of some way, any way, that she could thwart them, but finally she had to admit that she was infuriatingly helpless. Jenner hated being helpless. She hated feeling vulnerable, not knowing what to do or where to turn. She hated this strange woman sitting in her suite and calmly reading the book she'd brought, paying no more attention to her than if she were a fly—less, even, because she'd at least have swatted at a fly.

Deciding she'd rather be swatted at than dismissed, Jenner got up and went to the balcony door.

"Please sit down," Faith said, her tone as courteous as if she were offering coffee or tea.

"I will," Jenner returned, "out on the balcony." Her heart thumped hard from the fear that they might take this out on Syd—could they have a severed pinkie finger, or ear, or any other body part, delivered to her at sea?—but this was nothing other than a small push to discover her boundaries. They had to realize that, if they actually did hurt Syd, they ran the risk of pushing Jenner so far she balked. This was a balancing act they were all engaging in, with neither side wanting to push the other into anything rash. She banked on that as she stepped out onto the balcony.

Warm, moist air wrapped around her. The movement of the ship created a breeze that kept the temperature pleasant. Going to the rail, she gripped it and leaned over just a little, looking to her left to see the sunlit coast of California and Mexico falling behind as the *Silver Mist* steadily moved southwest—more west than south—toward Hawaii. Even leaning out that little bit was enough to make her head swim, so she retreated to the deck chairs and sat down in the one farthest from the door, stretching out her legs and relaxing against the high chair back.

Faith followed her onto the balcony, bringing her book with her, and took the chair that was closest to the door, so Jenner would have to get past her if she tried to bolt. That had occurred to Jenner beforehand, so she'd deliberately chosen the one she had just to reassure her guard that she wasn't going to try anything stupid.

Being outside was calming, with nothing but the sea and sky surrounding them. She slipped off her shoes, feeling a little of the tension drain from her bones. The deck flooring was teak, with small cracks between the individual planks to allow the water to drain away. Other than the top railing, the balcony was enclosed only by panels of clear Plexiglas that didn't obstruct the view. White gulls wheeled and soared, shrieking as the silver giant plowed through the foam-topped waves that swirled with all shades of blues and greens. Under different circumstances, this would have been wonderful.

As far as she could tell, there was no one on the balconies on either side of them, though she supposed it was always possible someone could be quietly reading as Faith was doing, or even napping. This early into the cruise, though, most people were likely exploring the gorgeous new ship or meeting up with friends, or both.

"Tell me about him," she prompted, meaning this guy she was supposed to hook up with.

Faith looked up from her book, frowning a little as she glanced in both directions before shaking her head in refusal. Even though she had to have made the same assessment that Jenner had made about the possibility they could be overheard, she wasn't willing to take the chance.

Raising her voice, Jenner shouted, "Hello, neighbor! Anyone there?"

Faith sat upright, looking alarmed, as if she was thinking about clapping a hand over Jenner's mouth and dragging her inside. But no one answered, not from either side, or even above or below, though Jenner didn't think sound carried well from those directions. From what she'd noticed so far, the ship was far quieter than she'd ever imagined it would be. Other than the sound of the ocean rushing by, she could hear only the deep, distant rumble of the powerful engines.

She lifted one shoulder in a careless shrug. "See? No one's there. You can talk."

"No," said Faith. "I can't. You'll find out soon enough." Nothing Jenner said budged the woman, though she gave it the old college try until Faith completely lost patience and ushered her back inside.

"Soon enough," as it turned out, was a little after nine that night. At seven, Faith had walked with her to the outdoor cafe on the Lido deck, where she smilingly introduced a tall, dark-haired man, who carried a cane and walked with a slight limp, as her husband, Ryan. Ryan had shaken Jenner's hand without even a hint that he was anything other than delighted to meet her, though of course he had to be one of Them. Okay, that made five people that she knew of.

Then Ryan and Faith had left her to eat alone. She went through the buffet line and had a plate filled with food she randomly indicated, without paying attention to what she was getting, then she sat at a small table close to the rail. She was acutely aware that she was being watched, by at least those two. Others would be watching her, Bridget had said, and she wouldn't know who they were.

The tension made it almost impossible for her to choke down any food, but she kept at it long after she'd lost any vestige of appetite. The longer she could put off going to the bar, the better. Despite what she'd asked Faith, she had no desire to meet this Cael person, didn't want to know anything about him. So she lingered over her dinner, then got dessert, a lemon mousse that was so light she didn't feel as if she were choking when she swallowed it. Under different circumstances she would have enjoyed it, but now it was just another delaying tactic.

When she couldn't put it off any longer, she asked one of the attendants to point her toward the aft bar, the Fog Bank, which turned out to be through a set of swinging doors directly behind her. She went through the doors and found much the same setup as the cafe: The bar itself was under a roof, but most of the tables were in the open air. A band was playing dance music, but not so loud that people had to shout to carry on a conversation, which was a nice change from the usual. The dance floor was crowded with both singly gyrating bodies and couples who were actually dancing together.

From the literature she'd read about the ship she knew there were several bars, but this one was humming with activity. Perhaps people were excited by the first night at sea, and no one wanted to be inside, which made the Lido deck the place to be. Stars were shining overhead, the ink-black ocean waves were gleaming with silver caps, and a brisk breeze tugged at hair and clothing. Even as tense as she was, Jenner felt something magical at being on the glowing ship surrounded by the vast, empty ocean. There were no other lights in sight in any direction, emphasizing how alone they were.

A single stool at the bar came empty, and Jenner squeezed onto it. There were so many people around she wondered how she was supposed to spot one particular couple, especially since she didn't know what they looked like. Well, that was their problem; they knew who she was, so it was up to them to get close enough to attract her attention. And maybe she'd make it even more difficult by keeping her back turned to the crowd.

The bartender smiled at her. "What can I get you?"

"A teeter-totter," she replied.

"Have you tried a Ghostwater yet? It's the ship's signature drink." He indicated the drink another of the trio of bartenders was handing across to a passenger; the liquid was a pale gray concoction, and wisps of what looked like fog rose from the tall, skinny glass.

142

"I'd pass on the Ghostwater, if I were you," a man advised from her left as he angled one broad shoulder in to the bar. "They pack a big punch. But I'll have one."

Jenner automatically looked up, because the man was seriously encroaching on her personal space, and found herself just a few inches from a pair of very blue, very intent eyes. For a split second time froze, her heartbeat thumped hard against her rib cage, and the bottom dropped out of her stomach. Hastily she looked down, breaking eye contact. He was so close she could feel his body heat, so close his hard chest was actually touching her shoulder; a belated alarm skittered along her nerve endings. She didn't like strangers touching her, didn't like the way she was being crowded, especially by a man as tall and powerfully built as this one. She tried to shift away, but the crowd around the bar was so dense she couldn't move without putting some muscle into shoving people.

"One teeter-totter and one Ghostwater, coming up," said the bartender, turning away to mix the drinks.

She stared straight ahead, unwilling to make eye contact again. Was he hitting on her, or was he just trying to get a drink at a crowded bar? Either way, she couldn't afford the distraction. Her field of vision was blocked on both sides now, so she couldn't see what was going on around her, and so many people were talking she wasn't certain she'd be able to tell if anyone was arguing. As soon as she got her drink she needed to move, find a more isolated corner.

"Are you here by yourself?" the man asked, and because they were so squashed together his voice was practically in her ear, his warm, pleasant breath brushing her cheek.

"No," she said, because she wasn't. At least four people were here with her, watching her, even though she was sitting alone. She still didn't look up at him again.

"Pity," he said. "Neither am I."

His voice had taken on a deep, warmly intimate undertone that, against her will, brought her gaze back up to his. The bottom dropped out of her stomach again. She had seen men who were better-looking, but damn if she'd ever seen one who oozed more masculinity than him. What was bewildering was that there was no one facet of his appearance that set him apart. He was tall, but not unusually so; muscled, but not muscle-bound; short dark hair, blue eyes, a hint of five o'clock shadow on a strong jaw. He was simply dressed, in black slacks and a white silk shirt with the sleeves rolled up on his forearms, and yet he seemed more elegant than any of the other men, who were no slouches in the dress department themselves. Taken as a whole, he was quite a package, and that had more to do with the aura that surrounded him than it did with any individual feature.

The bartender set their drinks in front of them. Relieved by the interruption, Jenner reached for her ship's card but the man beat her to it, handing over his card to the bartender and saying, "Both drinks."

"Sure thing."

Now she had to look up at him again, though she really, really didn't want to. She aimed her gaze at his nose, because those blue eyes were too unsettling. "Thank you." She kept her tone as neutral as possible.

"You're welcome," he said, reaching past her to accept his card back from the bartender. Just then the ship rolled slightly to the left, the first real movement she'd felt, but even as slight as it was that was still too much for a few people who had already had too much to drink. There was a commotion to the right, a yelp, then the man beside her was suddenly moving, both arms coming around her to brace against the bar as he shielded her with his body. He made a soft "oof" as someone landed against him, and for a moment he was crushed against her, his chest to her back, her head against his shoulder.

"Sorry," someone said, just as the man also said "Sorry," and straightened away from her.

"Damn you." It was a woman's voice, dripping with inebriated scorn and fury. "I saw that! You can't even get a drink without putting your hands on another woman."

Uncomfortably Jenner looked around. A curvy brunette with exotic sloe eyes was standing just behind them. She was overdressed in a skintight red cocktail dress that ended just a few inches below her ass, and she teetered precariously on five-inch heels, though whether that was because of the ship's movement or the amount of alcohol in her blood was anyone's guess. She was glaring at them, her chandelier earrings glittering as she tossed her head.

Jenner felt him sigh, felt the rise and fall of his chest. "You're drunk and you're making a scene," he said quietly. "Let's go back to the table."

The man who had initially stumbled looked around, blinking as he tried to make sense of the situation. He was sober enough to say, "No, that was my fault—"

"I know what I saw!" she said shrilly, dismissing him as she advanced closer to the man who had just saved Jenner from being knocked off her stool. "I don't know why you asked me along—"

"Neither do I." His tone was hard and grim. "But I regret it more every minute."

"That's easy to fix! Get your clothes and get out, you bastard." Her voice rose to a shriek of outrage, and tears began to melt her mascara into black rivulets running down her cheeks. More and more people were falling silent, turning to watch the scene, and Jenner began to feel as if she

145

were caught in the middle of a train wreck with no way of escaping. She looked desperately around, hoping she could slip away.

He tilted his head, his expression turning hard. "I don't believe you can kick me out of my own stateroom, Tiffany, but I'll tell you what: I'll let you have the room, because I'd rather sleep in the laundry than spend another minute with you."

Tiffany!

Oh my God. Horrified awareness swept over Jenner like ice water. This was Cael.

Chapter Eleven

The scene got uglier and uglier. Tiffany's face turned an unbecoming red as she began shrieking and sputtering incoherent insults. Cael didn't respond. He didn't have to. He let his expression say it all for him; he might as well have been looking at an insect. Beside him, Jenner Redwine was frozen on the barstool, her expression both stunned and horrified.

Before he'd called Tiffany by name, she'd been merely uncomfortable, and a little embarrassed at inadvertently being sucked into a scene. He'd been paying close attention to her, though, and he knew the exact instant she'd made the connection and realized who he was. She really hadn't suspected. He'd made the call not to coach her on the changes they'd made to the scenario, because he'd thought her reaction would be more believable if she was caught by surprise. He'd been right.

Redwine hadn't been the only one caught by surprise, though.

Funny how seeing her in person could give him a completely different reaction from what he'd expected looking at her photograph. Seeing her picture, he'd thought she might be trouble, but then he'd dismissed her. Seeing her in person, he *knew* she was trouble, but there was no dismissing her.

She wasn't a tall person, a little under average height, and she was thin, but on her it looked normal and not like she had starved herself. For one thing, even though she had small breasts, she had a nice, round ass. It wasn't big, just . . . round. He liked round. In this case, he liked it too much.

She hadn't dressed up. Faith had reported that she hadn't changed clothes at all. But even in simple oatmeal-colored pants and a sleeveless emerald-green blouse, she stood out from the crowd around her. Yeah, that could be because he'd been watching for her, but even looked at objectively she was different: the erect way she carried herself, the reserve, the way she had of looking at people that made them start surreptitiously checking to see if they'd spilled something on themselves. There was a subtle, underlying aggression in everything she did, in her very posture, that said Jenner Redwine would fight for what she wanted and God help anyone who got in her way.

He'd have to watch her every minute, because she wouldn't be intimidated into quietly going along with what she was told to do. No sooner had that realization flashed through his brain than she was slipping off the stool and edging away, looking for all the world as if she was just trying to escape an unpleasant scene.

Tiffany, bless her, also saw what was happening and shrieked, "Don't try to run off like you're Little Miss Innocent! I saw you flirting—"

"I don't know you," Jenner interrupted. Cael took the opportunity to shift his position, subtly blocking her avenue of escape. She shot him a bladed look from narrowed green eyes. She looked as if she would gladly have brained both of them. "And I don't know him, so leave me out of your nasty little scene." Then she evidently caught the eye of someone she knew because she gave a sort of what-can-you-do shrug. Good girl; that looked completely genuine. Maybe she was a better actress than she'd let on to Bridget.

On cue, Faith approached Tiffany, putting her arm around Tiff's shoulders and softly talking to her. Tiffany started crying, real tears dripping down her cheeks—how in hell did she do that?—and Faith finally led her out of the bar. Silence spread around them. Then Ryan limped up to Cael, concern in his eyes. Ryan was a hell of an actor, too. He did have a limp, but a very slight one. When he was in public, though, he always exaggerated it because that was part of his persona, and Cael had never, not once, seen him forget. "That was nice of you to give her your stateroom," Ryan said, just loud enough that everyone around them could hear what he was saying.

Cael shrugged. "I could hardly toss her out, could I?" He and Ryan automatically positioned themselves so Jenner was blocked, with no way to slide past them. She looked so frustrated he had to fight to control a grin.

"There was a mix-up on our suite," continued Ryan, "and we have a two-bedroom instead of one. You're welcome to take the other room, if you like."

"Much obliged. But first I'll check to see if another stateroom is available. Have you heard if the cruise is sold out?"

Ryan shrugged. "I haven't heard. But if there isn't, you can definitely stay with us. I've already cleared it with Faith, so don't think she wouldn't like it." He switched his gaze to Jenner, smiling. "What a way to start the cruise, huh?"

"With a bang," she said a bit sharply, once more trying to slide sideways around them.

Ryan reached out and took hold of her elbow, holding her in place. "Have you two actually met, or were you just caught in the explosion?"

"No, we haven't met," Cael said before Jenner could respond. The less she had to improvise, the better.

"That makes the whole scene even more ridiculous, doesn't it?" Ryan said with a rueful laugh, man to man. "Jenner Redwine, this is Cael Traylor."

"Pleased to meet you," said Cael, extending his hand. The brief flash in her eyes said she'd rather touch a cobra, but she held out her hand and he took it, keeping his touch gentle but holding on longer than he should have. Her fingers were slim and cool, her skin soft, and despite everything she firmly gripped his hand in return. She looked up at him, and for a brief moment their gazes locked. He kept his expression blank, but that one glance was enough to see the rebellion brewing in her. He needed to get her out of here, and fast.

He and Ryan talked awhile longer, making things look normal for the people who were still standing with their heads half-cocked to hear what was being said. He thanked Ryan again for the offer of their extra bedroom. Finally he turned and retrieved Jenner's drink from the bar, as well as the Ghostwater he'd ordered. It was a potent combination of Grey Goose vodka, absinthe—the real stuff—and a couple of other things. He wouldn't have touched one on a bet, but hundreds of people were sipping the foggy drink as if it were water.

He looked at the Ghostwater, grimaced, and set it aside. "That was for Tiffany," he said to Jenner. "She'd had one already, and insisted on having another. That's how I knew they hit hard and fast."

She nodded, but didn't reply. That was good. The less she

150

talked right now, the better. All he needed was for her to follow his lead.

He glanced around the bar. The music was playing again, and most people had returned to their own conversations. He nodded to a couple of people he recognized, then said, "Let's get out of this crowd and walk. I could use some exercise."

"You two go on," said Ryan. "I'll see how Faith is doing getting Tiffany settled."

The Lido deck was too crowded for any kind of real walking, plus he wanted to get Jenner mostly alone, so they took the stairs. In short order Jenner found herself strolling beside Cael on the sports deck, which was mostly empty. They didn't talk; she stared straight ahead as she marched along, as if she were in the military and had to walk a fifteen-minute mile. He caught her arm and pulled her to a slower pace. "You look like you're trying to run away from me."

"Imagine that," she said sarcastically. Oh, yeah, she had a mouth on her. The bad thing was, every time he looked at her he liked that mouth more and more.

"Think of your friend," he replied without inflection, but lowering his voice even more. Sound carried on the wind, and up here the breeze caused by the ship's movement was brisk. It blew her hair back and plastered her clothes against her body. *Good wind*, he thought, admiring the shape of her small breasts. She shivered, rubbing her hands over her bare arms and coincidentally shielding those breasts from his view.

"I am thinking of her," she snapped. "That's the only reason I haven't pushed you overboard."

"Then you'd better think harder, because you're doing a piss-poor job of selling the idea that we've got a thing going."

"Who am I selling it to? There's no one up here," she

retorted. That was mostly true. There were a few people walking around, couples, and one man standing by himself and breathing through a cigarette. Cael recognized him as Dean Mills, the head of Larkin's personal security detail. Had he just come up here for a smoke, or had Larkin sent him? Regardless, this had to look real.

"I decide when you need to sell it, not you. And I'm telling you to sell, now." He swung her around to face him, not quite touching, but close. Startled, she looked up at him, and something in him seized, frozen, as for a split second he imagined her looking up at him just this way when he pulled her beneath him. Ruthlessly he shoved the idea away. There was no place for shit like that in this job. Nevertheless, they had to make this appear real. He looked down at her for a long moment, then moved his hands to her waist and pulled her full against him. "Kiss me like you mean it," he ordered, and bent his head to hers.

She didn't. She stood as stiff as a mannequin, her arms at her sides, her lips stubbornly closed.

"Sell it," he growled against her mouth, and deepened the kiss, slanting his mouth over hers, pushing his tongue inside to taste her. She shuddered, then slid her arms up and wrapped them around his neck.

Still, she tried to hold her body away from his, and that wouldn't do, not with Larkin's man watching. Cael tightened his grip, pulling her tightly against him, breasts and hips and thighs. The contact hit him low in the gut, and he felt an erection begin to stir. He held her there, knowing she felt it, using his automatic reaction as a weapon to bring her into line. She didn't know whether he had any intention of hurting either her or Sydney Hazlett in any way, and by God he meant to keep it that way, because that fear was his only means of keeping her in line.

"Don't," she whimpered, and the fact that she begged told him how frightened she was. He could feel her heart, hammering away in her chest, and he pushed away the instinct to comfort her.

"Then act as if you mean it," he said again, and kissed her a second time.

She hesitated for a split second, then did as he ordered. Maybe fear wasn't a natural reaction for her, because now all he felt was anger, humming through her like an electric current. She plastered that skinny body against him and kissed him as if she were trying to set him on fire with her mouth. His erection shot to full attention, and he backed her against the rail, holding her there with all his weight as he met her ferocity with his own.

Shit. This was more real than he'd bargained for.

Like everyone else at the Fog Bank, Frank Larkin watched the nasty little squabble taking place at the bar. He recognized Jenner Redwine, because he'd studied her photograph when he had her and the Hazlett woman reassigned to the suite beside his, but he didn't know the squabbling couple.

"Who is that?" he asked Keith Gazlay, an industrialist from Seattle. Gazlay was a sharp-eyed man who was there with his third trophy wife; they kept getting younger, and this latest one was younger than his children—at least the three by his first wife. He'd had a second family, a girl and a boy, with his second wife—the first trophy wife—who had been a mere fifteen years younger than him. Number one had taken him to the cleaners, and their relationship was bitter; after that, he'd been smart enough to get prenuptial agreements.

"I don't know," replied Gazlay, eyeing the screaming

woman's breasts, which were about to pop out of her tight red dress. "But I'd like to."

Evidently marriage number four was already in trouble. Frank hid his contempt for Gazlay and turned to signal Dean Mills. He had a brief word with his chief of security, then turned back to watch the rest of the show while Dean followed his instructions.

The black-haired woman was drunk and unreasonable, not listening to anything anyone said. The man she was screaming at was watching her with a distant, dismissive look on his face that said he was finished, regardless of any apologies she might offer the next day. Another man was trying to explain that the whole incident was his fault, while Jenner Redwine looked acutely uncomfortable and kept trying to edge away, only to be prevented by the crowd, which had thickened around the scene.

Dean Mills returned, his voice low as he imparted the information Frank had requested. The man was Cael Traylor, from northern California; he owned a series of restaurants, car washes, and Laundromats. The woman was Tiffany Marsters, who evidently did nothing except fuck for her bread and board.

Dean didn't elaborate on his recital; he didn't have to. They both knew that businesses such as Traylor's were an excellent cover for money-laundering, so he was probably dirty. Frank found that reassuring. A man who had something to hide wasn't likely to go poking his nose into anyone else's secrets.

Frank's head was aching, the pain more intense than usual. The music was making the throbbing worse, and even his vision seemed to be throbbing. He'd had to put in an appearance tonight, the first night, so he pushed the pain away. No one could know there was anything wrong with him, or the vultures would be picking his bones before he was dead. All of them were vultures, rich vultures who thought their money made them better than everyone else. He'd show them. Once and for all, he'd show the world how stupid they all were, how he'd always been smarter and laughed at them as he took their money.

Someone else whose face he recognized moved into the scene by the bar: Faith Naterra. She and her husband, Ryan, had originally been booked into one of the suites adjoining Frank's. He watched as she approached the Marsters woman, putting an arm around her shoulders and leading her away.

This was better than a soap opera, and just as idiotic. Now Ryan Naterra had gone up to Traylor and was talking to him, evidently introducing him to Jenner Redwine because the two shook hands. He turned back to Dean. "See what's going on," he murmured, and Dean melted into the crowd. Shortly afterward, Traylor and the Redwine woman left the bar, with Dean discreetly following.

Frank suspected he'd just seen Traylor seize the opportunity to dump a woman who was more trouble than she was worth, and latch on to one who was worth a few hundred million. That was fine with him; it wasn't as if either of them was going to live much longer, anyway.

Chapter Twelve

Jenner was almost hyperventilating with terror by the time they reached her suite. The more frightened she was, the angrier she became. No matter how often or how deeply she had to kiss him in public, she'd be damned if that meant she'd let him do whatever he wanted in private. Her willingness to touch him, and be touched by him, stopped at the door.

He was a damn good actor, and that scared her even more, because it put her at an even greater disadvantage. How would she know what to believe, and what not to believe? He was so convincing in his role that, if she hadn't known better, her heart would be pounding at being the focus of so much male intensity. He wasn't playful, he wasn't giving her time to get to know him better; every move he'd made, every look he'd given her, had been those of a man who had his sights on a woman he wanted.

In real life, Jenner would have been running for the hills if any man had tried to be so dominant with her. She didn't like bossy men and didn't tolerate them. Cael was more than just bossy; he was downright ruthless, and the knowledge had her so scared her teeth were almost chattering.

He took her tiny red leather shoulder bag from her and opened it, taking out the key card for the door. She stood mutely, gritting her teeth to keep from grabbing the bag back. No one who knew her would ever believe for one minute that she'd let a man get away with such high-handed behavior, but who, besides Syd, really knew her? She and Syd were such close friends precisely because neither of them fit in with the rest of the crowd.

Someone was coming down the passageway toward them. Jenner carefully didn't look to see who it was, instead keeping her head down and her gaze focused on his hands as he inserted the card in the lock and the little light flashed green. They were big hands, but well-shaped and hard, with a look and feel to them that she recognized. He worked out, long and often, and he had quite a bit of training in the martial arts. Her little bit of judo would be useless against him.

Removing the card, he opened the door and ushered her inside, his callused palm warm on the small of her back.

As soon as they were inside and the door was closed behind them, though, Jenner whirled away. Her cheeks red with temper, she spat, "I will *not* let you rape me, is that understood?"

"Keep your voice down." Clamping one hand on her arm just above her elbow, he forced her farther into the room, away from the door. He paused then, his cool gaze raking her, her red bag still in his hand. "Correct me if I'm wrong, but I think the definition of rape means there isn't any 'letting' involved. You can rest easy, though; I'm not interested."

"Yes, I felt how uninterested you are," she snapped, then wished she hadn't, because she really didn't want to be discussing the state of his penis. His reassurance had failed in its purpose because she didn't feel reassured at all. She was still practically jumping out of her skin from nervousness, and her instinctive reaction was to fight.

He looked amused. "You don't know much about men, do you?"

"More than enough, thank you! *Hey!*" The last word was yelped as he dragged her through the bedroom door to the left. The bottom dropped out of her stomach and, just like that, panic washed over her in a tidal wave, obliterating thought. She exploded into a flurry of movement, fighting him for all she was worth. She punched him with her free hand, pulling back as hard as she could in an effort to break his grip on her arm, twisting, trying to stomp his feet, elbow him in the gut, head butt him—anything and everything she could do, without any strategy in mind except the blind need to *fight*. He grunted when her first blow hit his jaw, then he thwarted most of her efforts by simply turning his body so she was left with no target except his shoulder and back. His hard grip never once loosened. Infuriated, terrified, she used the only weapon she had left and bit him, sinking her teeth into the back of his upper arm.

"*Shit!*" he said between clenched teeth, and with a twist of his body she went airborne, sailing across to land with a teeth-rattling bounce on the bed. Desperately she twisted, trying to regain her balance and roll off the bed on the other side but he pounced with the quickness of a snake striking, snagging her wrist and dragging her bodily off the bed to sling her into the bedside chair.

The violent speed of the move left her sprawled in the chair, disoriented and stunned, unable to make her body move for several valuable seconds. He pulled a plastic restraint from his pocket and slipped it over her hand, then with two hard jerks secured her to the chair. Straightening, he glared down at her, his blue eyes cold and glittering.

"Bridget said you were a pain in the ass," he growled, "but she forgot to mention you're also rabid."

Breathing hard, trying to make her head stop spinning so she could make sense of the situation, Jenner mutely stared up at him. What was—? He wasn't—?

"I thought you were—" she began, then stumbled to a halt.

"Don't think," he advised in a tone that was close to a snarl. "You aren't good at it." He took out a cell phone and thumbed in a two-digit number. "Bring a bucket of ice," he said, still in a clipped tone that said his temper hadn't faded. "The little bitch bit me." Even from where she was sitting, Jenner could hear the laughter from whoever was on the other end of the call.

Oddly, being laughed at didn't seem to bother him. His mouth quirked in a half smile as he listened. "You were right about that," he said, and flipped the phone shut to end the call.

"I'm not a bitch," she said, feeling compelled to defend herself. Her voice was embarrassingly shaky. "I was scared."

He ignored her. Moving to the bed, he opened her bag and upended it, dumping out the contents. There wasn't much; the bag was too small. A lipstick, her ship card, breath mints, driver's license and passport, a credit card, and some loose cash, all scattered across the bedspread. No cell phone, because Bridget had taken it.

He examined the bag's small zipper compartment, but it was empty. She didn't have so much as a nail file or fingernail clippers; Faith had gone through the tote bag she'd carried onboard and removed everything that could remotely be considered a weapon or a tool. Jenner longed for those fingernail clippers now, because they'd snip right through the plastic restraint that bound her to the chair. She couldn't go anywhere or do anything about the situation, because of Syd, but she'd love to show him what she thought of his dinky little plastic ties.

She would also love to stab him with a nail file, but even if she had the file in her hand it wouldn't do any good, because of the airline restrictions that prohibited metal files. Hers was the kind made of soft foam stuff, meaning it was absolutely useless for anything except smoothing a rough spot on a fingernail. She wondered if she could sue Homeland Security for depriving her of a weapon, even so much as a metal fingernail file, when she needed one.

He moved on to the closet, which was located on the other side of the bedroom, on the passageway wall. Through the open door she could see that her luggage had been unpacked, which meant Bridget had been back in the suite. Cael examined every garment, looked in every pocket, every shoe, every handbag, even though Bridget would have done the same thing while she was unpacking. The fact that he was searching everything again could mean either that he didn't trust Bridget, or that double-checking the details was a matter of course for them. She hoped it was the former, but suspected the latter. So far, these people were frighteningly efficient.

Bridget knocked on the door, delivering the bucket of ice. Cael left Jenner restrained in the chair and went to let Bridget in. She heard Bridget say, "I have the ice you requested, sir."

"Thank you. Put it on the table, please."

"Yes, sir."

Their formality was obviously in case anyone in the passageway overheard them. The door closed, then Bridget appeared in the bedroom door, grinning like a jackass when she saw Jenner cuffed to the chair. Cael moved past her and retrieved a hand towel from the bathroom, then returned to the parlor. Bridget withdrew without saying anything, though her eyes were bright with enjoyment. Which she enjoyed the most, Jenner biting Cael or Cael tying Jenner to the chair, was up in the air.

"Ouch," Bridget said a moment later. "That left a bruise. Here, lean forward."

From where the chair was positioned in the bedroom, Jenner couldn't see even a sliver of the living area, but she could hear them very easily and knew they would be just as attuned to any noise she made. She stared at the plastic cuff holding her to the chair. She could probably work it free, given that only one hand was restrained, but what would she gain other than the satisfaction of having thwarted him? She couldn't go anywhere, she couldn't call for help. She couldn't do anything that would endanger Syd. She might as well sit right where she was.

At least she could use the time to recover both mentally and physically from her fright. She felt as if she'd been through a super-stringent workout, then been forced to run five miles. Her breathing was still too fast, her heart still beating too hard. The adrenaline burn had left her feeling weak and woozy, but her mental wheels were beginning to turn again.

First and foremost, she had to accept that, for good or ill, she was in this with them. They had Syd. She, therefore, had to do whatever she could to make sure they succeeded at whatever plan they had, because that was the only way she could do Syd any good. Doing what they wanted in public didn't mean she wouldn't raise hell by whatever means she could when they were in private, but if they wanted her to act as if she was madly in love with the bastard, then she'd give them an Oscar-worthy performance.

An ache in her arm finally got her attention and she looked down, to find the outline of his fingers plain in her flesh where he'd gripped her while she was trying to fight. He wasn't the only one who sported a bruise, she thought, then realized something else.

"Hey," she called. "I need some ice, too."

"Tough," Cael replied, evidently not inclined to share his ice with her.

"A shirt will cover your bruise," she snapped. "I don't have anything long-sleeved to cover my arm, and not one person on this ship who knows me would think I'd put up with abuse for one minute. So you'd better bring me some ice, to help these bruises go away."

Both Cael and Bridget reappeared. He was shirtless, holding the makeshift ice pack in his hand. She didn't want to see all those muscles, so Jenner quickly looked away from the hair-dusted expanse of his chest, shifting her gaze to Bridget as she lifted her arm to show the reddened stripes.

"I'll get the ice," Bridget said, turning back into the living area and returning in a few seconds with the ice bucket. She carried it with her into the bathroom, where she raised her voice a little to ask, "What did you two do, have a bare-knuckle street fight as soon as you were through the door?"

"*She* had one," Cael muttered. "All I did was toss her ass in the chair and tie her there."

That was literally true, Jenner realized. He hadn't retaliated, hadn't struck her, and had in fact tied her to the chair only after she bit him. But if he thought he got brownie points for that, he was sorely mistaken. "I don't owe you an apology," she said fiercely. "Kidnappers don't get apologized to, because they deserve what they get." Still, he hadn't really hurt her. Scared her out of ten years of her life, yeah, but in retrospect she had to admit that had probably been inadvertent.

Something was going on here, something beyond the obvious. But what?

Bridget came out of the bathroom with ice wrapped in another towel, which she folded around Jenner's arm. The cold immediately began to ease the stinging ache.

"Do you have everything you need?" she asked Cael. "I have to get back, in case anyone else wants something."

"If everything on my list is here, I'm good to go," he replied.

"It's here. I checked it all twice."

"I'll get started. Call me if he heads back to the suite."

Bridget nodded and let herself out.

Who was "he"? Jenner wondered. Because she wasn't likely to find out anything unless she asked, she said, "Who are you talking about? Who's 'he'?"

"None of your business," he replied, removing a duffle bag from the closet. She'd never seen the duffle bag before, so Bridget had to have placed it there.

"Excuse me, but all indications are it's very much my business who he is," she said, indicating the plastic tie with a wave of her hand. She wished he would put on a shirt, because she was getting tired of having to avoid looking directly at him.

"Shut up or I'll gag you."

He just might do it, too, she thought, forgetting that she didn't want to look at him and glare, which was wasted because he wasn't looking at her. He was removing the contents of the duffle bag and laying everything out on the bed. There was an array of electronic equipment, the use of which she couldn't begin to guess at, wires and gadgets and tools that looked like—

"Is that a drill? Why do you need a drill? What are you drilling?"

163

"Holes to screw your coffin shut," he growled. "Shut up."

Oh, the satisfaction of getting under his skin. Served him right. She waited a minute, waited until he looked as if he was getting deep into concentration, then said sulkily, "I need to pee."

His head fell forward and he closed his eyes.

"I can't help it. Everyone needs to pee. Even Darth Vader needed to pee, though I don't know how he managed it without taking off his life-suit. If you hadn't made me drink that teeter-totter I wouldn't need to pee now, so it's your fault." If she could have thought of anything else outrageous to say she'd have said it, because she wanted—needed—to see what he would do when pushed, how far he'd go.

Grimly, not saying anything, he picked up a pair of wire cutters from the tools on the bed and snipped open the plastic that bound her to the chair. Only then did she realize that he could have pulled the cuffs much tighter than he had, because he'd easily been able to slip the wire cutters between her skin and the plastic.

With her newly freed hand she held the towel of ice to her arm as he escorted her to the bathroom. She didn't know why he thought she needed an escort, because there was no way out of the bathroom other than back through the bedroom. From a previous visit, when Faith had been guarding her, she also knew there was nothing in the bathroom that could be used as a weapon, unless she could convince him to step on a bar of soap, slip, and bash his head when he fell.

"Don't lock the door," he ordered.

Jenner considered how far she wanted to push him, and decided she'd gone far enough for right now. Baby steps. After all, she had no real idea how he'd react if she really tested his patience. She didn't know him, didn't know what he was capable of. She didn't want to inadvertently push the wrong button and get Syd harmed, just because she was laying groundwork and exploring her limits. So she didn't lock the door, and she did pee, just in case he was listening.

As she was washing her hands she looked at herself in the mirror. A pale, exhausted face stared back at her. God, what time was it? Glancing at her wristwatch, she realized there was a very good reason why she looked exhausted. She'd been up since before dawn, Eastern time, and it was now two a.m. Eastern, eleven p.m. Pacific—almost twenty-four hours.

He opened the door. "That's long enough. Come on out."

She finished drying her hands, examined the reddened skin on her arm where she'd been holding the ice, and decided she didn't need any further application. She unfolded the hand towel and shook the ice into the basin, then neatly hung the towel over the rack to dry. As she left the bathroom he turned to precede her, keeping himself between her and the door, and she saw the swelling, purplish spot where she'd bitten him on the triceps. He needed the ice far more than she did. Unless he went swimming, though, he wouldn't be taking off his shirt.

She stared at his back, at the deep furrow of his spine bisecting all those muscles, and wished to hell he'd put a shirt on *now*.

"I'm exhausted," she said, to take her mind off the manscape in front of her. The only time she'd ever let good looks get in the way of her common sense had been with Dylan, all those years ago, when she was just twenty-three, and even then the insanity hadn't lasted long. She was made of tougher stuff now. "Whatever you're doing, it can wait until tomorrow. Lock me in here, sleep sitting up against the door, I don't care. Just let me get some sleep."

"What I'm doing can't wait until tomorrow," he replied

shortly. "And the more you interrupt me, the longer it'll take. So sit down and shut up. Got it?"

She got it. If she hadn't, the fact that he pushed her down into the same chair and slapped a real pair of handcuffs on her, fastening her to the chair, would have gotten her attention.

She stared down at the metal shackling her wrist. Somehow this seemed far more alarming than the plastic cuffs. These were real handcuffs, and whatever these people were doing, they were serious as a heart attack about it.

Chapter Thirteen

Cael lay on his stomach on the bedroom floor, drilling a small hole in the base of the wall that separated this suite from Larkin's suite. Larkin could return to his suite at any time, though his duties as host of the cruise might keep him occupied for an hour or so longer, depending on who wanted to talk to him. If Cael didn't get this done before Larkin returned, they'd be both blind and deaf this first night at sea. He didn't like that option, so he ignored everything else and concentrated on what he was doing. He wanted ears in that suite, if nothing else.

Normally, concentrating wasn't a problem. Normally, however, he didn't have a woman with attitude yammering at him nonstop.

He'd been right about her having the guts to carry off the act he needed. He'd also been right about her causing trouble. Just for once, he wished he'd been wrong. This would have been so much easier if she'd been more like Sydney Hazlett, who was frightened and had cried some but hadn't shown any sign of fighting back. She'd been told the same thing that Redwine had been told, that her friend's

167

safety depended on what she did, that each was hostage for the other. The difference was that, according to his people holding Hazlett, she was quiet. Redwine was anything but quiet.

He silently cursed Larkin for being a paranoid son of a bitch and switching the suite assignments around at the last minute. Until then, the plan had been simple enough. From the suite Ryan and Faith had originally had, on the other side of Larkin, they could have set up all the surveillance necessary to gather information: his phone calls, his onboard meetings, his visitors. If Ryan and Faith had been in place, none of this elaborate charade would be necessary, the kidnapping wouldn't have been necessary. The surveillance equipment would already have been installed and tested, and they wouldn't be forced to settle, for now, on eyes and ears in the bedroom instead of the living area—and *he* wouldn't be forced to listen to the nonstop commentary on what he was doing.

"What are you, a thief? What are you doing? Is that a camera?" He could hear her shifting around in the chair, probably trying to get a better look at the equipment neatly arranged on the floor beside him, as well as what he was doing. "You're going to an awful lot of trouble for a run-of-the-mill perv."

Cael stopped drilling and checked his progress. Drilling through a wall on a ship wasn't exactly like drilling through a wall in a house. The requirements for stability and noise reduction were different, the wiring was different, the codes were different.

Larkin's suite was a big one, about thirteen hundred square feet, with the living room on the other side, adjacent to the suite Ryan and Faith had booked. In the middle was the dining room, and on this side was the bedroom. The equipment he was using was sensitive enough to pick up everything said in the bedroom, and part of what was said in the dining room. No way would it pick up the living room sounds. They'd have to get a bug on his phone, and if Larkin had a computer with him they'd also have to get access to it. They'd have had to do that in any case, but the layout of the rooms would have eliminated most of his problems—and the biggest problem that would have been eliminated was sitting handcuffed to the chair behind him.

If they got through this without her blowing the whole scheme wide open with her mouth, it would be nothing short of a miracle. He would have to ride herd on her every minute of the day to keep her under control; he wasn't sure any of his other people could do it.

She'd already gotten under Bridget's skin, and rattled Faith. Tiffany . . . nothing rattled Tiffany, but with the scene they'd set up, absolutely no one would believe that Tiffany and Redwine could become buddies, so Tiffany spending any amount of time with her was impossible. Matt couldn't do it, because his cover as a ship employee wouldn't let him be in her suite, either. That left Ryan, and as good as he was, he was also a married man and he and Faith were known to be very happy, so what excuse could he have for being in Redwine's suite? Moreover, Larkin was so paranoid that if either Faith or Ryan, the original occupants of the suite adjoining his, suddenly began spending a lot of time in the suite on the other side of him, he would go nuts.

That left Cael. *God help me*, he thought wryly.

"Whatever your plan is, it isn't going to work. No one is going to believe that you and I are together. I know some of the passengers on this cruise, and you're so not my type, plus they won't believe I'd ever bring you back to my suite for the night right after you just broke up with your girlfriend."

169

If she kept kissing him the way she'd kissed him up on the sports deck, they would. He stifled that particular memory before it could fully form, because the last thing he wanted right now was to get turned on. He focused on his work, threading two very thin cables, one with a tiny microphone on the end, the other with an equally miniscule camera, through the hole he'd drilled and into Larkin's bedroom. According to the layout of the suite Bridget had given him, and the exact measurement he'd used to place the hole, the camera and mic were just beside the large plant that filled the empty space in that corner of the bedroom.

He could have used a single cable that incorporated both audio and video, but in his opinion they weren't as sensitive as the ones with dedicated functions. If he'd been threading the cables through a solid core, the task wouldn't be half as delicate, but instead he was moving them through empty space. The camera was already operational, inserted just an inch or so, and he used the video from it to guide the audio cable toward the small hole on the opposite side of the wall. Once the audio was in place, he taped the cable so it wouldn't move, then began working the video cable toward the same hole. The biggest problem was that, at the slightest touch, the audio might fall out of place.

That was exactly what happened. As soon as the video cable touched the audio, the audio cable fell sideways. Silently cursing, he began all over again. He was sweating by the time he got both cables securely in place, but just barely through the hole so they weren't noticeable. He checked the read-out on the monitor, held his breath as he made minute adjustments to the camera until he was satisfied with the angle, then heaved an inward sigh of relief when both cables remained in place. Carefully he duct-taped both to the floor and wall.

"What kind of name is Cael? You were named after a vegetable?"

Now that he was finished, he gave her a cool look. "It's spelled C-A-E-L, and yes, it's pronounced just like kale. You don't have any room to talk. What kind of name is Jenner?"

She shrugged. "According to my dad, my mother had a huge crush on Bruce Jenner. She couldn't name me Bruce, so she named me Jenner. Of course, that's according to dad, so take the story with a grain of salt."

How could she keep that mouth going? She was exhausted; her face didn't have any color except for the dark circles under her eyes. He suspected she still had some fight left in her, though, just as he also suspected he was about to catch the full brunt of that fight when she realized how they were going to spend the night.

First things first, though. Taking out his cell phone, he called Bridget. "Everything's up and running. Get some rest."

"Glad to," she replied. "How's the prisoner?"

"Mouthy."

She laughed. "Yeah, intimidated she isn't. Call if you need help."

Cheerful thought. He didn't want to battle with Redwine, he just wanted to catch some sleep himself. He rotated his shoulders, working out the kinks and feeling the soreness in his triceps where she'd bitten him. She'd really clamped down, too, like a skinny, blond pit bull. She was lucky he hadn't strangled her, because the urge had definitely been there.

He went into the bathroom and relieved himself, then splashed cold water on his face. He'd looked at the shower, wishing he could risk it, but he didn't dare turn his back on Redwine that long. Even though she was safely shackled to the chair and couldn't free herself from it, she might be stronger than she looked and be able to pick up the chair and carry it. He didn't think so, because ship furniture was heavier than regular furniture and she was skinny, but he wouldn't bet the bank on it.

She must have been too tired to even try it, because when he stepped out of the bathroom she was sitting exactly as she had been. If she hadn't been such a pain in the ass, he might have felt some sympathy for her.

Instead, he grimly braced himself for the next battle.

"All right, Mike Tyson, let's go to bed."

Jenner was so exhausted that for a minute the words didn't register. *Mike Tyson?* Then she realized he was referring to her biting him, which gave her an insane desire to laugh, but hard on the heels of that came comprehension of the rest of his sentence and all desire to laugh completely vanished.

She sprang to her feet, at least as much as she could while handcuffed to the chair. "What do you mean, *let's go to bed?* I'm not sleeping with you! You can sleep on the damn couch out there. There's no separate door out of the bedroom, so there's no reason to—"

"Your only options are whether you put on the pajamas I saw in the closet or sleep naked," he cut in.

Sleeping naked was so far out of the question that it really wasn't a choice of options at all. He knew it, too, because he smirked as he came over and released her from the handcuffs. The clamp of metal was instantly replaced by the clamp of his hand as he urged her toward the closet. "Go ahead and change."

She stumbled to the closet and selected a pair of pajamas at random, then went into the bathroom while he stood guard outside. His high-handedness made her so angry she could barely think. There was absolutely no reason for this, other than showing her who was boss, as if she didn't already know.

Quickly she stripped down and washed off her makeup as fast as possible, because she wouldn't put it past him to jerk the door open at any time. After she put on the pajamas, though, she took the time to brush her teeth just as she always did. She should have brushed faster, because he opened the door without warning and caught her with a foamy mouth.

She almost choked on the toothpaste, because the open door revealed more of him than she'd ever wanted to see. He'd used the time to remove his shoes and pants, and was wearing only a pair of black boxer briefs that revealed just how hard and muscled he was, and a lot more besides. After her first startled look she turned away and spat the toothpaste into the basin. "Where was I going to go?" she snapped. "Down a drain pipe?"

"You're skinny enough," he returned.

She ignored the impulse to deny that, and instead said irritably, "Call Bridget to bring your pajamas."

He looked amused. "I don't own any."

"Then put your damn clothes back on!" It was bad enough he'd been without his shirt for hours. Now he was practically naked, and the inherent threat made her skin crawl as if she were covered with ants.

"I'm not sleeping in my clothes. If you have any virtue, it's safe with me, so stop acting like a Victorian virgin."

"I'd say I have more virtue than you, considering who's the kidnapper here," she fired back.

"Yeah, yeah. Come on, Cujo, stop delaying and wipe the slobber from your mouth. I'm bushed."

Jenner glanced in the mirror and saw the toothpaste still foamed on her lips. Unaccountably embarrassed, she quickly rinsed and spat, then wiped her mouth before charging back into the fray. "At least put your pants back on. That way I won't have to bleach my eyeballs if your little ding-dong accidentally falls out."

"You and your eyeballs will live, no matter what my ding-dong does." His tone was flat and unyielding; his eyes glittered briefly, but she couldn't tell if he wanted to laugh or smack her down.

He caught her arm and hauled her out of the bathroom. While she'd been in there changing clothes, he had not only removed his pants, he'd turned out all the lights in the suite except for the bedside lamps, and he'd also turned down the bed. Her entire body ached at the sight of those smooth white sheets. If only he weren't here, she'd have whimpered with joy at the thought of actually lying down.

"Get in," he directed, steering her toward the far side of the bed, away from the door leading into the living room. She was too tired to argue anymore. Her spirit was willing, but her body said if she didn't get some sleep soon she'd fall down. Silently she crawled between the sheets and pulled the blanket up over her. He turned out the lamp beside her, then went around to the other side of the bed and got in beside her.

Her eyes were already closing, despite her best effort to glare at him. They popped open when his hand closed over hers. Cold metal snapped in place around her right wrist, then he calmly fastened the other handcuff around his left wrist and stretched out his right arm to turn out his lamp.

Darkness engulfed them, and Jenner stared upward in shock. Damn him, he'd handcuffed her to him! Now what?

174

Chapter Fourteen

She was too tired *NOT* to sleep, but she didn't sleep well. Being handcuffed to someone wasn't comfortable, especially when that someone outweighed her by about a hundred pounds, and every time he moved he pulled her with him. The same wasn't true when she moved, though, mainly because of that hundred pounds. She couldn't budge him.

In the restless doze that was the best she could manage, she drifted in and out of awareness. Sometimes she half-dreamed she was in the bar again, in those moments before she realized who he was, feeling the heat of his body when he leaned in so close to her, feeling tension coil and knot deep in her belly at her first startled look into those blue, blue eyes. She hadn't let a man get to her in a long time, but there'd been something in his deep, smooth voice and the look in those eyes that had tempted her.

Acknowledging that she'd been tempted pissed her off enough to wake her up. She lay there for a few minutes, blinking at the ceiling. He was lying only inches away and she could feel his body heat; she hated to admit it, but that heat felt good. Somehow the blanket and coverlet had gotten kicked away. *Somehow?* Like there was more than one candidate for kicking blankets off the bed? In her world, blankets were for wrapping up in, not kicking away. Even though she was wearing pajamas and was still covered by the sheet, she was cold. For one thing, the tank style of the top left her arms completely bare—and those bare arms were also completely uncovered.

Grumpily, barely awake, she tried to tug the sheet higher around her neck, but the fabric was securely tucked under his heavy arm and wasn't going anywhere. Annoyance brought her the rest of the way awake, and she turned her head to glare at him, for all the good that did, given how dark the room was.

She was lying on her back, her right arm raised up and back, with her hand tucked almost under his chin, because that was where his left hand was. And where his left hand went, her right hand also went, whether she wanted it to or not. Even more annoying, she could feel the warm puffs of his breath on her hand.

She took another moment to orient herself. The heavy curtains blocked out most of the ambient light, so the bedroom was very dark. Only the slight lessening of darkness ahead and to the right indicated where the open door to the living room was. His breathing was slow and deep; he was asleep, damn him. After everything he'd put her through, it wasn't right that he should be able to sleep while she couldn't, especially when it was his fault that she couldn't sleep. Though, come to think of it, she'd rather he be asleep than awake.

But—damn it, her shoulder hurt with her arm twisted up and back in that position. She shifted a little onto her right side, trying to ease the strain but at the same time not get any closer to him, but that pulled the sheet even farther down and she couldn't use her right hand to pull it up again. Awkwardly she fumbled with her left hand, but the angle was wrong and she needed an extra joint in her arm to get the sheet where she wanted it.

Dilemma: She could either freeze, or she could wake him up.

It was his fault she was freezing. It was his fault her shoulder was hurting. But if he was asleep, then she didn't have to be scared of him and fighting for all she was worth to keep him from realizing that.

She hated being frightened, but she was. She was terrified for both Sydney and herself, because she didn't know what was going to happen and maybe she'd be even more terrified if she did. Just because she did everything they wanted her to do—whatever that was—didn't mean that at the end of this she and Syd would walk away unharmed. Letting either of them go would be sheer stupidity, and so far none of these people struck her as being stupid.

If she knew what was going on, what they wanted, maybe she could reason with them. They weren't after money— both she and Sydney were rich—and if money were the object then they didn't need her, they could simply have grabbed Syd and demanded a ransom. True, with her added in that would have doubled the money, but she didn't have any family they could bargain with for the ransom. She didn't know where Jerry was, hadn't heard from him at all in the seven years since he'd stolen twenty-five thousand from her, and even if he had been in a position to pay a ransom for her . . . good luck with that was all she could say. She doubted her father would have paid even a hundred bucks to keep her alive.

So . . . money didn't come into the equation, especially when she factored in what she'd seen tonight, after Cael had brought her back to the suite. He'd drilled a hole in the wall, threaded some wires through the hole, checked a monitor and some sort of recording device. And he'd ignored her the entire time he was working, no matter what she said. His concentration on the task at hand had been impressive, because she'd worked hard at getting his goat.

Were they spies? Whether a real *spy* spy or industrial–type spy, Cael was definitely doing some spying.

She felt her scalp prickle with alarm. The whole thing seemed too James Bondish, but they had to be. Nothing else made sense. There were too many of them, and they had too many apparent resources. The pertinent questions were: Who did they work for, on whom were they spying, what did they want, and, the most pertinent question of all, were they supposed to kill anyone who got in their way or threatened the success of their operation?

If she knew who was staying in the suite next door, at least one of those questions would be answered, but probably knowing who had hired these guys would tell her a lot about how far they would go. So far, everyone she'd met was either American or had received enough extensive training to pass for one. If they were government spies, that meant they weren't likely to kill either her or Syd . . . she hoped. A lot of different factors came into play with industrial spies, though, such as how much money was on the table, because she doubted they'd get paid if they didn't deliver the goods. Put enough money in front of some people, and what moral boundaries they had seemed to melt away. Probably no one got into the business of being an industrial spy if his moral boundaries were very sturdy, anyway.

The situation began to solidify for her. Okay, they were spies. They were after something—probably information, considering how much trouble they'd gone to to get a wire into the next suite—and they needed her to . . . provide cover. That was *it*! She was nothing but cover for them! They had probably had this suite booked, but when the assignment snafu occurred and the suites were switched around, they needed a reason to be in this suite without raising suspicion! But how could they have known far enough ahead of time to get this whole charade orchestrated?

That was easy to figure out because, obviously, they had people working as crew members, in various capacities. Bridget was one. Jenner had no idea how far ahead of time a steward found out who was in which suite, or when a steward was even allowed onboard; she could have found out, or it could have been someone else. Maybe one of the ship's officers was working with them. Throw enough money at a problem, and anything was possible.

In the long run, other than confirming that they had people watching her whom she hadn't met, how they'd discovered the suites had been reassigned didn't matter. She and Syd had been the unlucky ones to get this suite, and Cael had cooked up the scheme to grab Syd and hold her hostage as a means of forcing Jenner to act as if they were lovers, so he could have access.

She could be completely off base with all this supposition, but she didn't think so. Everything fit. They *needed* her, and now that her nerves had settled down some and she could think, she realized that she had a modicum of power. Not much; she couldn't make them let Syd go free, and as long as they held Syd she couldn't notify ship security or even kick Cael's ass out of her stateroom, but there was one very important thing she *could* do. She'd have to be careful, because until she had evidence to the contrary she had to assume that these were the bad guys, but the fact that Cael hadn't strangled her earlier gave her a tad more confidence than before.

Because she might lose that confidence if she waited, and because she hated feeling powerless and afraid, she shoved at his shoulder. "Hey!" she said, not quite shouting but definitely raising her voice.

He didn't bolt upright, which would have been very satisfying, but she succeeded in finding out that he woke up instantly alert because without hesitation or confusion he growled, "This had better be good."

"From my point of view, none of this is good," she shot back. "I'm cold, you've kicked the blanket off, you have the sheet locked down like a prison, you have my arm twisted so my shoulder is about to be dislocated, and you're *breathing* on me!"

"God forbid I should *breathe*," he muttered.

"Isn't that amazing? God and I agree." She yanked her right arm. "Handcuff me to the bed, or something. This is ridiculous."

"Take a look at the bed. There's nothing to handcuff you to, no posts, no handy little iron rings. This is as good as it gets. The only other option is if I toss you overboard."

Jenner plowed on, ignoring what he said because she wanted to finish before she lost her nerve. "And what's more, I talk to Syd every day or I don't cooperate with you at all. Got that?"

Silence. He hoisted himself to a sitting position and switched on the lamp. She blinked and instinctively shielded her face with her left hand until she became more accustomed to the light, which seemed unreasonably bright for such a small lamp. Then, because she didn't like it that he was sitting up and she wasn't, she struggled to an upright position herself. Too late, she remembered that she wasn't wearing a bra; when she'd changed into her pajamas she'd been too tired to think of keeping her bra on underneath the tank top. The ribbed knit was thin; she was so cold her nipples had to be almost poking through the material. *Well, tough.* She'd be damned if she'd squeal and jerk the covers up like some scared little girl.

He scrubbed his hand over his face, his beard scraping against his palm with a sandpaper sound. He looked tired, his eyes a little puffy from sleep, his dark hair mussed, but his voice was cold and flat. "You aren't in a position to give any ultimatums."

"I haven't been able to sleep, so I've been thinking instead," she replied just as flatly. "I've decided I'm in exactly that position. You need me to give you cover for being here, in this suite. I don't know why, I don't need to know why, I just know that you do. Fine. My cooperation depends on whether or not I talk to Syd every day, and what she tells me. If she's okay, I'll play along to the best of my ability. If she's hurt in any way, the deal's off. That's nonnegotiable."

"As long as I hold her, you'll play along, regardless."

"You know what? That threat will work only as long as I trust you not to hurt her, and I have to tell you, there's no trust on the table. The only way I'll know for sure she's still alive and unhurt is if I talk to her myself—*every day.*" The risk she was taking was so huge she felt nauseated, but at the same time she knew she couldn't back down. This was the only way she could keep Sydney safe, the only weapon she had, so she'd be stupid not to use it.

He watched her, his eyes hooded. She held her breath. At least he was thinking about it, considering all the angles. He had nothing to lose—unless Syd was already dead. Oh, God, if he refused, what would that mean? That they'd killed Syd immediately after the initial phone call?

The thought was like a knife in her chest. What would she

do without Syd? There wasn't a sweeter, nicer person in the world; she didn't deserve any of this happening to her, but to think that she might have been murdered—*no!* Jenner surged to her knees, her lips trembling and tears stinging her eyes. "You bastard," she said raggedly, barely able to breathe. "If you've hurt her—"

With a lightning quick move he caught her left arm before she could even think of swinging it. "Settle down," he said sharply, and to make sure she did, he exerted enough twisting pressure on her arm that she cried out and clumsily half-fell, half-sat on the mattress. The pressure immediately eased, but he retained his grip. "Do *not*, by God, bite me again, because you won't get away with it a second time. She's fine."

"Then let me talk to her," Jenner insisted, those damn tears overflowing her eyes and dripping down her cheeks. "Now. Let me talk to her now. *Please.*" She didn't care that she was begging. She wouldn't beg for herself, but she'd beg for Syd. Because he was still holding her left arm she lifted her right hand to swipe at the tears, only his hand came with it, and swatted her on the forehead. "Ow!" Startled, she jerked back and glared at him through her tears.

Slowly, not taking his eyes off her, he shook his head in disbelief. "If I were Catholic, I'd be calling in an exorcist," he muttered. "We're *handcuffed together*! What the hell did you think would happen?"

"Unlike you, I don't have a lot of experience with handcuffs!" She sniffed and lifted her hand again to wipe her eyes, but much more slowly this time.

He exhaled an exasperated breath, tilting his head back to stare at the ceiling. "Do you have any idea what time it is?"

She'd removed her wristwatch before she washed her face, so it was still lying beside the bathroom sink. Leaning to the

side, she tried to see the digital clock on the table beside him. "Three twenty-six. Why?"

"Because it's that time in California, too."

"So? Do you think I care if your goons don't get their beauty sleep?"

"You should," he replied grimly, "since they're the ones taking care of your friend. You don't want them grumpy."

"You're their boss. Tell them to play nice."

Briefly he closed his eyes. He said, "Fuck," then opened his eyes again. "If I place the call," he said wearily, "will you lie down and shut up? I don't care if you sleep or not, just *shut up*."

"I'll lie down," she promised. "Whether or not I shut up depends on whether or not you let me have some cover, and whether or not you stop breathing on me. I feel like I'm in some horror movie."

He released her arm and, muttering words under his breath that sounded like "possessed" and "carnivorous" and a couple of other things she couldn't catch, he grabbed his cell phone off the bedside table and speed-dialed a number. The connection took longer than normal; they'd already been at sea for almost twelve hours so they were hundreds of miles from the coast. The call was probably bouncing off a satellite or two. Finally he said, "Wake up Ms. Hazlett. Redwine wants to talk to her. Yeah, I know what time it is. I'd like to get some sleep, too, but that won't happen until she talks to Ms. Hazlett. Just put her on, and save the bitching, unless you want to swap places with me." He paused, listening. "Didn't think so. I figured Bridget had already been in touch." Another pause. He pinched between his eyes. "Yes, she bites. Damn it, put Hazlett on the phone!"

Grimly he put the cell on speaker and handed it to Jenner. She grabbed it and eagerly said, "Syd?"

A male voice, the same male voice she'd talked to earlier, said, "Hold on a minute." She heard muffled sounds, something that sounded like a knock, then a mumble of frightened, confused words that were definitely in Sydney's voice. Syd didn't wake as easily as Cael had; Jenner hated hearing the fright, but the sleepy confusion was so like Syd that she had to smile.

"Jenn," Sydney said, sounding panicked. "Are you okay? Has something gone wrong? Have they hurt you?"

"No, I'm fine," Jenner said, and began to cry. She tried not to let the tears sound in her voice, because that would scare Syd even more and she didn't want to do that. "I was just so worried about you I had to make sure you're okay."

"I'm okay and you're okay. Okay." Syd suddenly gave a watery chuckle, as if she, too, were fighting back tears. "That sounded like some dorky self-affirmation course. But this is a good idea. We'll talk every day, *won't we?*"

"Yes, we will." She gave Cael a meaningful glare, and figured that somewhere in California, Syd was doing exactly the same thing to her captor.

"All right, that's enough," Cael said, taking the phone from her. "Let's all try to get some sleep now." He closed the phone and replaced it on the bedside table. Reaching down with one brawny arm, he grabbed the blanket and coverlet from the floor and flipped them up on the bed. "There," he growled. Growling seemed to be a habit with him. Maybe he'd been a bear in some former life.

Silently Jenner reached with her left arm, gathering the covers and trying to bunch them all on her side of the bed, then she stretched out and gathered them over her.

Sighing, Cael turned out the lamp and lay down beside her. He pulled the blanket more securely around her, tucking it in. "There. Are you satisfied?"

"My feet are still cold, but I feel better." She added reluctantly, "Thank you for letting me talk to Syd." She definitely felt better. Knowing that Syd was still alive, that her sudden panic had been unfounded, was such a relief that she felt almost limp. Snuggled under the silky sheets and nice warm blanket, she decided not to say anything if he breathed on her again.

She was so tired. Her reaction to the warmth, the relief, hit her like a tidal wave. She actually felt herself being sucked under, into sleep.

Just before she reached oblivion, she felt a pair of large, warm feet being tucked under her cold ones.

Chapter Fifteen

Normally Jenner jumped out of bed wide awake, which was probably more from early conditioning than from nature. Until seven years ago, she'd never had the luxury of sleeping as late as she wanted, of lazing around in bed even after waking. Even when she'd been a little kid, getting up and going to school had been her responsibility, because Jerry had seldom been awake that early, and sometimes not even at home. Getting up and hitting her stride had immediately become so deeply ingrained in her that she did it even when there was no longer any need. Her mornings now usually involved nothing more pressing than sitting on the balcony reading the morning paper while leisurely drinking coffee, but, by damn, she had a right to it.

This morning, however, even after she woke she couldn't make herself get up right away. Instead she kept dozing, lulled by the darkness and the subtle rocking of the ship. Gradually she realized that the darkness wasn't due to the hour, but that she'd pulled the covers over her head. She was toasty warm from head to toe, she was comfortable, and she was . . . not handcuffed.

Galvanized, she bolted upright out of the nest of covers.

Her first wild hope was that she was alone in the suite, that either she'd just had a wild, *Dallas*-type dream or that a single night of surveillance had given them the information they wanted and they'd all disappeared in a submarine or something. That hope was immediately dashed to bits, because Cael was sitting in the chair beside the bed where he'd handcuffed her the night before.

He had an earbud in place, but when she jumped to her feet in the middle of the bed he glanced up and said drily, "It erupts."

Deflated, she sat down with more force than grace. "How did you uncuff me without waking me?"

"You were sleeping like Dracula at high noon. I thought about pouring cold water on you, but I appreciated the peace and quiet too much."

He'd shaved, she realized; the shadow was gone from his jaw. That meant he'd showered, leaving her alone in the bedroom. To test her cooperation, maybe? Would it have been the kind of test where Bridget waited right outside the door to see if she tried anything? Or had he not played any games and had Bridget here in the suite, watching her? Probably the latter, because she couldn't see him taking any chances, if what they were doing was important enough to rate all this trouble. She knew she wouldn't, if she were in his position.

He was also wearing different clothes, khaki pants and a royal blue silk shirt that darkened the blue of his eyes to something approaching breathtaking. Bridget must have brought his clothes from the stateroom he'd been sharing with Tiffany. Jenner couldn't believe how soundly she'd slept, with all that activity going on.

Then she realized something else, something that stole

the breath from her lungs: He was watching the movement of her breasts under the flimsy tank top.

She wasn't easily embarrassed, but heat flooded her face. Last night she hadn't given a damn whether or not she was wearing a bra, but she'd slept since then, finally, and moreover she'd slept with him. Even though she'd been cocooned in the covers, he'd been mostly naked, and a muscled body like that wasn't one she could easily forget, though she intended to do her level best to ignore it.

Or maybe not. She found herself jamming her finger at him. "Don't even *think* I'll go all Stockholm syndrome. You got that?"

"God save me," he returned. "But if you don't want a man to look, then don't bounce up and down in front of him. Not that yours are big enough to do much bouncing, but they do wobble a little."

"What they do is none of your business. Just keep your eyes north." There didn't seem to be any way she could drive that point any further, so she went on to a different subject. "I'm going to take a shower and wash my hair, so I'll be awhile."

"Don't take too long," he advised, glancing at his watch. "You have forty minutes."

That ticked her off, because she hadn't put a limit on his bathroom time. Her shoulders stiff, she marched to the closet and got out the clothes she was wearing that day. She couldn't find her toiletries, though, and began going through all the built-in drawers in frustration.

"What are you doing?"

"Looking for my shampoo and stuff."

"Everything's already in the bathroom. Didn't you notice last night when you washed your face?"

Last night she'd been practically comatose, so, no, she

hadn't noticed anything. She'd even brushed her teeth without wondering how her toothbrush and toothpaste got in the bathroom. Wheeling, she took her things into the bathroom and jerked the door shut. Everything was there, from perfumed lotion to hair spray. Her shampoo was sitting on one of the shelves under the sink.

Forty minutes, huh? She thought about locking the door, but didn't want to provoke him—he might retaliate by making her leave the door open at all times, and she didn't want that. When she was in the bathroom was probably the only time she'd be alone. The time limit meant she couldn't have a long soak in the whirlpool tub, not that she was the soaking type anyway. Her normal routine was to jump in the shower and jump out again as quickly as possible, so that was what she did. She'd been issued a challenge, and she met it head-on.

The bathroom came furnished with a hairdryer, a good one. Her hair was fairly short, so drying it didn't take long, and her current style was more windblown than sleek. Her makeup during the day was no big deal, just eye shadow, mascara, and lip gloss, so that didn't take a lot of time. She was out of the bathroom well within his time limit.

He raised one eyebrow, which was damn annoying because she couldn't control her own eyebrows that way, and took a leisurely sip of coffee.

Coffee. Her attention zeroed in on it like a bear on honey. She had the beginnings of a headache that said she'd better get some caffeine soon, in any form. "Is there any more coffee?"

Coffee might mean food, too. She hadn't eaten much the night before, and they were several time zones past her normal breakfast hour. A glance at the clock told her they'd even gone past her normal lunchtime.

"You might have time for a cup," he said, getting up. He glanced at the surveillance equipment, evidently assuring himself it was still working, then escorted her into the living room. The small dining alcove was to the right, tucked in a nook close to the door. A tray bearing a coffee carafe, another cup, and a variety of sweeteners and creamers was in the middle of the round table. "Sit," he said, and when she did he deftly handcuffed her to the table leg.

Mentally she rolled her eyes, but the coffee carafe had the lion's share of her attention. There wasn't any food in sight, but right now coffee was her number one priority. At least this time he'd handcuffed her left hand, instead of her right. Setting the clean cup upright, she poured the coffee and gratefully took her first sip.

She'd had exactly four sips when there was a knock on the door, and a half-second later Bridget unlocked it and stepped into the suite, crisply announcing herself as she shut the door. "Lifeboat drill, five minutes," she added.

So that was why he'd given her the time limit, though he could have explained. Jenner glared at him as he removed the handcuff key from his pocket and freed her from the restraints. "Less than half a cup of coffee. Was that worth the trouble of the cuffs?" she snapped.

"Keeping you under control is worth any amount of trouble. Now behave," he ordered, giving her a look that said he meant business.

"Bite me," she returned as she got to her feet.

Bridget coughed, but the sound was suspiciously like a laugh.

His eyes narrowed. "If I were you, I wouldn't mention the word 'bite,' " he advised as he took her arm.

Bridget went into the bedroom, and returned with a pair of orange life jackets that had been stored in the closet. She said, "When the alarm sounds, take the PFDs and report to Muster Station Three. Directions are on the back of the door."

Jenner hadn't had enough coffee, and she was starving. She would much rather call room service and get some food, instead of reporting to any Muster Station. "We can't play hooky?"

"No," Bridget replied. "Lifeboat drills at sea are a serious matter. They have to take place within twenty-four hours of sailing. Roll will be called, and anyone missing will be tracked down and instructed to report to the appropriate Muster Station."

"And we aren't going to do anything to draw attention to this suite, are we?" Cael asked in the insufferable tone of an adult dictating to a wayward child.

"What if someone comes in to clean the suite and finds all your toys?" she taunted.

"They won't," said Bridget. "This suite is my responsibility. Pay attention to what you're doing, and leave my job to me." Cael caught her eye, she nodded briefly, and left.

"What was that about?" Jenner asked.

"Nothing you need to know."

"Do I need to know what a PFD is? It sounds sexually transmitted."

"Personal Flotation Device." He nodded toward the orange life vests. "When the drill starts, don't get any ideas . . . about anything. All rules still apply, and they will until we get back to San Diego. You do exactly as I say, when I say it."

"Yeah, yeah," she said.

The alarm brought an end to that particular exchange, and was followed by a calm voice over the shipwide intercom. Cael picked up the life jackets—PFDs—that Bridget had

191

placed over a chair, and tossed one to Jenner. He paused to take a quick look at the map on the back of the door, where there were simple directions to Muster Station Three.

"Smile, sweetheart," he said as he took Jenner's arm and ushered her into the passageway, where they immediately ran into two older ladies who were grinning as they exited the stateroom across from them. Evidently a lifeboat drill was a lot of fun to some people, Jenner thought. Personally, she'd rather be cozied up to breakfast—or lunch. She was so hungry she didn't care which.

The ladies were dressed in casual cruise wear, including straw hats, walking shorts, deck shoes, and their bright orange PFDs. One was tall and slim to the point of being bony; the other was short and stocky. Together, they were wearing enough diamonds to open their own jewelry store.

"We're going to Muster Station Three," the tall one said. "I assume you two are headed in the same direction?"

"We are," said Cael, smiling at them. Jenner wanted to kick him, because that smile was warm and genuine and made him look entirely too human.

"I'm Linda Vale," said the tall lady.

"Nyna Phillips," the other lady added, her smile a little shy. She had a really sweet face.

"I'm Cael Traylor, and this is my friend, Jenner Redwine."

"Pleased to meet you," said Linda Vale. "We were in the Fog Bank bar last night. That must have been very distressing for you. I'm glad things worked out."

Nyna winked at Jenner. "If I were twenty years younger, I'd have been bumping you out of the way."

"Bump away," said Jenner cheerfully.

The two ladies laughed, thinking she was joking. Cael squeezed her arm, giving her the silent message to behave, or else.

She gave him a smile as dazzling as she could make it. "Just kidding. He's a gem, a man among men, a real prize. He stepped into my trap, and he's mine now. There's no escape."

All three women laughed. Cael slanted a look down at her that promised retribution.

"We should have dinner together one night," suggested Linda.

"I'd love to," Jenner said, too enthusiastically. Cael gave her arm another squeeze, one she interpreted to mean that she wasn't here to make new friends or do a lot of socializing. As far as he was concerned, she was here for one thing and one thing only, and that was to provide cover for him. If he thought he could keep her locked in the suite for the entire time, then he was in for a rude awakening.

"Ladies, we should be moving," Cael prompted, because neither Jenner nor the two older women seemed inclined to do anything other than stand there and talk.

"Do we take a left?" Linda asked, her expression confused as she looked first one way and then the other down the passageway.

"Yes, ma'am, you do," he said, holding out his hand to indicate they precede him.

"I'll take your word for it," she said as they began walking down the passageway. "I usually have a good sense of direction, but so far this ship has me completely confounded. If we really needed to get on a lifeboat, then I'd better have an angel on my shoulder whispering in my ear and telling me how to get there, or I'll never make it."

Behind them another door opened. Cael glanced briefly over his shoulder at the sound, and Jenner did likewise, driven by nothing more than simple curiosity. Two men exited the suite with the double doors, PFDs in hand, and followed them down the hallway. It only made sense that they would all be at the same Muster Station.

One of the men behind them had the look of a sentient tank. He was just medium height, but so powerfully built he looked almost as wide as he was tall. His hair was so blond it was almost cotton white, and cropped very close to his head. He had restless eyes that continuously swept forward and back, noting anything and everything around him. *Hired muscle*, Jenner thought, but *smart* hired muscle.

So the target of Cael's surveillance must be the other man. He looked fiftyish, with graying hair, but toned and fit, with a tan of the particular hue that said it was the best tan money could buy. She didn't have time to see more than that, because Cael hustled her forward with more speed than grace.

"Hurry," he said. "We shouldn't be late." Linda Vale and Nyna Phillips obediently picked up their paces, too, though Jenner was pretty sure he hadn't been talking to the older ladies.

He didn't want her anywhere near the man, Jenner realized. She still didn't know who he was, but at least she knew what he looked like.

"So," she whispered conversationally, "that's him?"

"Not your concern."

"You made it my concern, numb-nuts."

He slanted a glittering blue glance down at her. "It'll be a miracle if we make it to Hawaii without you getting tossed overboard."

The lifeboat drill was unexciting. All Jenner learned about escaping from a sinking ship was how to put on her PFD, and where to go in case of an emergency, though she supposed that was basically all she needed to know. She'd have liked to see a lifeboat actually launched, but when she thought about it realized the difficulty involved in getting the lifeboat back in place, considering they were secured to the ship at least two stories up from the water line, maybe even more, and the ship was cutting through the ocean at a pretty fast clip. Being inside one of those suckers when it was launched was probably a trip, too, one she hoped she never took.

The man who had come out of the double-door suite was sitting two tables over from them at the Muster Station, which was actually one of the indoor cafes. Cael tried to position his chair so he was blocking her view, but he was thwarted by Nyna Phillips, who pointed toward the man and said, "That's one of the co-owners of the ship. He's hosting the Cruise for Charity, so we'll probably see more of him than we will of the captain."

"Really?" asked Jenner, delighted by this opening. "I had no idea that's who he is. What's his name?"

Nyna thought for a moment. "I'm sure I heard, but I can't recall. Memory's the second thing to go, you know."

"What's the first?" Linda Vale asked, leaning forward with a grin that said she expected something salacious.

"I don't remember," said Nyna, completely deadpan, and they both burst into laughter.

As soon as the drill was concluded, the gray-haired man and his bodyguard disappeared. Jenner forestalled being hustled back to the suite and handcuffed to a table or chair by exclaiming how hungry she was, and inviting both Linda and Nyna to eat lunch with them on the Lido deck, in one of the outdoor cafes. The two women accepted with pleasure, and Cael had no choice but to go along, though the look he gave Jenner when the other two weren't looking said he wasn't taking this lightly. He fished his cell phone out of his pocket, called someone, and spoke very briefly before closing the phone.

The outdoor cafes were buffet-style so lunch was very casual. Jenner sucked down some more coffee, ate enough to make up for not having had breakfast, and in general did everything she could to postpone going back to the suite. Linda and Nyna, however, soon excused themselves because of some classes they'd signed up for. Jenner watched them walk away, giving a little sigh of regret. She wished they could have stayed longer. Not only did they seem genuinely good-hearted, now she was once again alone with Cael.

Despite his reluctance to have lunch, now that it was over he didn't seem to be in any great hurry to return to the suite. He lounged in his chair, somehow managing to look elegant, indolent, and dangerous all at the same time. For all his surface sophistication, there was something predatory about him that lingered just below that layer of gloss. He was the type of man women noticed, she thought again, but not just women. She caught several men, perhaps more aware than others, giving him slightly wary, sidelong glances as if they wanted to make certain they knew exactly where he was.

Suddenly she got it. He *wanted* to be seen. Specifically, he wanted to be seen with her. He was cementing the idea of them as a couple, and she had promised to cooperate fully.

"Let's go for a walk," she said, standing and holding out her hand to him. "I could use the exercise after being so tied up this morning."

That blue gaze lashed her as he took her hand and stood, then slid his other hand around her waist and turned her toward the railing. "You're living dangerously, Redwine," he murmured, just loud enough for her to hear.

She smiled, turning her face up to him as if he was flirting with her. "Relax, big boy." She kept her voice as low as his. "You still hold all the cards, except for one. We'll go for a simple walk, and you can use the opportunity to show everyone how nuts we are for each other."

His arm remained around her waist as they strolled along the railing. Jenner lifted her face to the sun, trying to will herself to turn her mind off and relax for a moment. This is the first full day of a two-week cruise; she would be with Cael, under his control, for another thirteen days, and if she didn't find some way of dealing with the stress she'd crack under the strain. She would talk to Syd every day, and that way they would both be reassured that the other was still alive, but she also needed some respite from constantly worrying at the situation like a dog going at a bone.

She forced herself to look around at the ship. From the moment she'd first set foot onboard yesterday afternoon, she'd been too preoccupied to pay much attention to her surroundings. The *Silver Mist* was supposed to be something special, as far as ships go, and she wanted to take a look at her.

As Bridget had said, the Lido deck was the fun deck. People clustered around and in the pools, and teak deck chairs seemed to cover every square inch. Some sort of game was going on by one of the pools, and the sound system boosted the emcee's voice to an almost painful volume. Cael winced and turned Jenner in the opposite direction, and for once she was glad to follow his unspoken instructions.

If it hadn't been for Cael's presence, she thought, Syd would have been right: She'd have enjoyed the cruise. She did love the ocean. She'd become accustomed to its presence over the past seven years, but the gray-green Atlantic was nothing like the vibrant colors of the Pacific.

The deep water was a gorgeous navy blue, but every so often the light would change and she'd catch a glimpse of aqua and turquoise. With no land in sight, the sensation was of being alone in the world—if being with about a thousand other people could be called "alone"—on a bright and pristine floating city.

She could smell the newness of the ship, she realized. It was everything: the paint, the carpet, the upholstery, even the wood of the deck. Everything was new and fresh, and under different circumstances she'd have loved it.

Cael's arm remained around her waist, the heavy weight a constant reminder to behave. To anyone watching, of course, they would look like new lovers, enthralled with exploring this strange and exciting connection they'd found. Only Jenner knew that his grip was a bit too tight, and she blew out a small sigh of frustration. Where the hell did he think she was going to go if she ran? They were on a *ship*, for God's sake. It wasn't as if she could jack a car and escape. Besides, as he so often reminded her, there was Syd.

He probably heard the sigh, because he snuggled her closer and bent his head to kiss her temple, then settled his mouth close to her ear. "Make it look good."

She turned her head, dipped her chin. "I'm too scared," she said, putting a little whine in her voice and managing not to snort. She *had* been terrified . . . but she wasn't now. Odd. Maybe the body and mind could handle terror for only so long, then some sort of coping mechanism kicked in and held the terror at a distance.

He did snort. "Bullshit. You don't scare worth a damn. So act as if you love me, honey, because otherwise there's no point in having you out here and I'll drag you back to the suite. Do you want to spend the rest of the cruise handcuffed to a chair?"

She definitely didn't, so she angled her shoulder toward him and smiled up at him. Only he could see, so she fluttered her eyelashes at him like some nitwit overwhelmed by his testosterone. He needed her out here, she thought. Maybe he could explain away her absence from the many shipboard activities that most of the passengers were already taking advantage of, and maybe no one would think anything of it if she didn't attend any of the formal dinners or auctions, the events that were the whole purpose of this Cruise for Charity. Maybe he could make these people believe that she'd throw all sense to the wind to take up with him, even though she wasn't known for mindless, reckless affairs.

Most of the people onboard ship didn't know her, but enough of them did that he couldn't make her all but disappear for two weeks without questions being raised. He had to let her out of the stateroom, he had to allow people to see her, talk to her. She had to attend the scheduled events.

Too bad she couldn't think of a way to use the exposure to her advantage. She was surrounded by people, but if she screamed for help . . . then what? She'd look as if she'd gone insane, because Cael hadn't done anything in front of anyone that would make anyone look at him with doubt. He'd been charming to Linda and Nyna, attentive to her, and from the way he was looking down at her the casual observer would think he was downright besotted.

And if she screamed for help, what would happen to Syd?

Because she couldn't see any way out of the situation, she turned her thoughts instead to *why*. He'd gone to a lot of trouble for a peek and a listen into someone's stateroom. She didn't know the name of the man in the next suite, but if he was a co-owner of the ship then he was very wealthy, because ships like this had to cost billions and billions of dollars to build and outfit. So, in the real world, wealth equaled influence. Who was he? What were they trying to find out about him? Maybe he had a kinky lifestyle and they were trying to get pictures for some sort of blackmail scheme. That scenario kind of worked for her, except for the way they were going about it. Having an entire team of people aboard a cruise ship like this had to have cost a small fortune, then add in the expenses of the team that had snatched Syd.

That led her back to spies. Industrial espionage. But that usually involved theft of data, or even the actual hard product, so what were they doing here spending so much time watching a man on a cruise?

No matter which angle she considered, this still didn't make sense to her. Whatever Cael and his people were planning, there had to be better ways to get it done, though from what she'd seen they were so well-organized that if there was a better way she imagined they would've found it. So, what the hell was going on?

The threat to Syd had her effectively bound, restricting what she could and couldn't do. Not that Cael was going to leave her unsupervised or unbound, but he *could*, and she wouldn't do a damn thing to take advantage of being free, because of Syd. One phone call from Cael or any of his people, and Syd could be in serious trouble. No matter what, Jenner thought, because of Syd she had to play along.

She took Cael by surprise, turning out of his grip, leaning back against the deck rail and facing him with her feet firmly planted, her gaze narrow and intent. "Tell me what you're up to."

"No." His response was immediate and flat, no room for negotiation, no thinking about it.

"I can't figure it out—"

"You aren't supposed to figure anything out, you're supposed to do as you're told and keep your mouth shut."

He slid his hand over her arm, a movement that looked like a caress, except for the way his fingers clamped around her elbow. "That's enough face time. Let's go."

"I'm not ready to go." She wanted to stand there and argue with him, maybe dig a detail or two out of that stone wall.

He leaned in, too close, too warm, too big. His mouth moved against her cheek. "I swear to God, I'll throw you over my shoulder and carry you back to the room, and just think what a show that'll be for the other guests. Then I'll cuff you hand and foot to the chair, and you won't get out of the room again until the cruise is over. I can do this without you, Redwine."

Her heart thumped, she couldn't take a deep breath, and still, she saw the truth, knew it deep in her bones. "No, you can't. If you could, you never would have involved me at all."

"Watch me." He wrapped an arm around her waist again, pulled her away from the rail, began to lift her.

"Wait!" Putting on an act was one thing, but making a spectacle was another. And he'd do it; he'd really throw her over his shoulder and carry her off, and most people would grin, thinking they knew exactly what would happen when he got her to a private place.

He stopped. Her body rested against his, but wasn't being crushed. Anyone watching would think it an embrace between lovers, rather than a threat, but she could see into those cool blue eyes and knew he wasn't bluffing.

Her heartbeat got even faster, harder. Something about his eyes pulled her in, sucked her into heightened awareness of him on a physical level. She fought to keep her expression blank, to not let him know he was getting to her. Damn it, she shouldn't be affected by his touch, by being pressed against that tall, muscled body, but she was. He should be physically repulsive to her, and the fact that the opposite was true told her she'd have to resist just that much more, build her wall even higher.

He was waiting for her to say something, and she wrenched her thoughts back in order. What was . . . ? Oh, yeah. She'd told him to wait.

She took a deep breath. "You don't have to carry me," she said. "I'll go peaceably, Marshal."

One corner of his mouth twitched. "Good." He eased her down and slightly back, but he didn't release her.

The wind blew her hair across her eyes and she pushed it back as she looked up at him. "But maybe you could do me a favor and let up a bit. In case you haven't noticed, we're on a ship, in the middle of the Pacific. I have nowhere to go, except overboard, and I'm not crazy. I don't want to do anything that will cause Syd to get hurt. As long as you have her, I'm going to play along. Maybe it makes you feel more in control to keep a steel grip on my arm, but it isn't necessary. If I have to be a part of this, then it'll play better if I don't look like a prisoner."

He took a moment to consider, then said, "That sounds reasonable." Just as Jenner began to relax, he added, "But this is *you* we're talking about, so 'reasonable' makes me suspicious."

Frustrated, she went on tiptoe and put her lips to his ear. He immediately tensed and gripped her waist with both hands, as if he were ready to chuck her overboard if she bit him again. He just might do it, too. She caught his earlobe with her teeth and very gently tugged, then released. "You're such an asshole," she whispered as lovingly as possible. "Somehow, some day, I'm going to make you pay for this."

He slid one hand downward and patted her ass. "I don't doubt it for a minute."

Chapter Sixteen

Cael considered himself a calm sort of guy, someone who always kept his cool, who stayed on top of a situation. That said, Jenner Redwine would be lucky if he didn't strangle her in her sleep before this cruise was over. He should put in for combat pay; after all, he had the wound to prove he'd been in a battle.

She was the most annoying, prickly, difficult . . . funny . . . woman he'd ever met. He didn't want to think she was funny, though half the stuff she said had him biting the inside of his cheek to keep from laughing. He wanted to toss her overboard and be done with it. She was so skinny, she wouldn't even make much of a splash. He took a minute to enjoy the vision he had of the little *plop!* she'd make when she hit the water, though she'd probably spoil the moment by giving him the finger as she went under. Women like her should have "Troublemaker" branded on their foreheads, so people would be warned ahead of time. If he'd known before what he knew now, he'd be dealing with Sydney Hazlett, tears and all, and counting his blessings while Redwine would be in California driving other people crazy.

But he hadn't known, and now he was stuck with her. He had the upper hand and he intended to keep it, but she fought for every ounce of power she could possibly get even though the cards were stacked against her. He had the advantage of knowing what was going on, knowing that with the people and power he had behind him he couldn't lose, no matter what happened.

Even if worst came to worst, she couldn't cause legal trouble for him. She and Sydney Hazlett would both be released unharmed, no ransom had been requested, and even though legally he and his crew could be nailed for unlawful detainment, she was too smart to file charges. She herself would have gone to a lot of trouble to convince everyone around them that they were lovers, so any complaint she had afterward would look as if she was merely pissed off because they'd broken up. She couldn't win, but she didn't know the rules of the game and so she kept playing as hard as she could. He would have felt sorry for her . . . if it were possible to feel sorry for a cross between a badger and a pit bull.

After escorting her back to the suite, he left her under Bridget's watchful gaze while he went down to the stateroom he'd been supposed to share with Tiffany, before this whole thing unraveled around them.

Any room Tiffany occupied for longer than an hour always looked as if a bomb had gone off in it, and the stateroom was no exception. The massive amount of jewelry and insanely high-heeled shoes she'd insisted were needed for the job were scattered everywhere; clothes had been dropped on the floor; luggage was opened, drawers were pulled out and half-filled. She was sharp and sexy and lethal as hell, and she was also a world-class slob.

She sat on the bed, long legs crossed and a high-heeled

sandal dangling from her toe, her full attention on her task as she disassembled a chunky, noisy bracelet and removed a tiny but suspicious-looking—to any security guard worth his salt—device. She glanced up at him, a preoccupied expression in her sloe eyes. "How's Redwine holding up?"

"Fine," he replied, not about to tell her, or any of them, all of the ways Redwine had found to be a royal pain in the ass. They were getting way too much enjoyment out of the situation as it was. Besides, in all honesty, he couldn't blame Redwine for doing all she could to bust his chops. He sure as hell wouldn't be taking this shit lying down, if he was in her position.

Tiffany didn't have his patience, which wasn't saying much. He wasn't patient at all, but he had iron control, which was something else entirely. Tiffany said, "If she starts to break, we can drug her and keep her that way for the rest of the trip. Might be easier on you."

Easier on him, definitely, but Redwine was right; her complete disappearance from the social events of the cruise would raise questions he didn't need raised. "So far it hasn't come to that, but I'll keep it in mind."

Tiffany handed him the button camera. In a different place, on a different job, she'd have been assembling firearms. However, getting weapons, even Glocks, aboard a cruise ship was such a bitch he'd made the decision not to even try. It wasn't as if they actually needed weapons on this job, because it was surveillance only. Still, he felt half-naked without the familiar weight of his 9mm Sig Sauer resting against his right kidney.

As Tiffany put the jewelry back together, sans button camera, she looked up at Cael. "Anything on Larkin yet?"

"No." So far, the man was as innocent as he'd been in the last three weeks, while the other team had been on him.

Keeping such a close eye on Larkin while he was at sea was probably unnecessary, but then again, what better place to put together a deal with the North Koreans than in the middle of the Pacific Ocean? "We're hoping to get Matt or Bridget into Larkin's stateroom today, tomorrow at the latest, to get the parlor eyes planted." It would've been so much easier if Larkin had accepted Bridget as his steward, but he'd brought his own along. Paranoid bastard.

Cael didn't have all the details, but Larkin was suspected of being the middle man between a traitorous defense contractor employee and the North Koreans. They didn't know what sort of information was being sold, but the government evidently thought it was important enough to go to a lot of trouble to shut down the deal. They didn't want just Larkin, they wanted his contacts on both ends of the deal, as well as details on whatever information had already been passed on. That meant they would be taking photos of everyone Larkin spoke to, which was why he had so many people onboard: having the same people hovering around all the time would make anyone suspicious, much less Larkin. They had to swap out times and positions, and they had to use in-place surveillance on his suite. He had to be followed, even aboard the ship. So far he was making things easier than they'd expected, by spending a lot of his time in the suite.

There was a soft knock and Tiffany got to her feet, instantly alert. Going to the door, she looked through the peephole, then pulled the door open.

Faith stepped into the room, with Ryan close behind. Neither of them said anything until Tiffany had closed the door. The room was secure—all of their rooms, including Redwine's suite, had been swept for bugs—but they couldn't be sure about the passageway.

Ryan could have delivered the button camera to Cael with

a handshake, but Cael liked to pull his people together for a face-to-face every so often. They could communicate by their secure cell phones, though using that method with Bridget and Matt was problematic because of their jobs, but everyone meeting in person triggered an extra sharpness that wasn't there in phone calls. Maybe it was being able to read each other's expressions, maybe it was simple group chemistry, that being together heightened the sense of being a team, but he'd often seen problems solved within minutes of simply getting together as a group, after they'd been working for days on something by e-mail or cell phone.

They had a pretty good setup for spending time together, except for Bridget and Matt. With their jobs they could have any number of reasons for talking with any passenger, but it wasn't like they could all get together for tea. On the other hand, either of them had perfect excuses for coming to Redwine's suite at any time, Bridget because she was the steward, while Matt could be delivering room service, plus they could speak to him on deck as he was rearranging deck chairs or whatever.

They couldn't afford to have everyone gathering in Redwine's suite, where Larkin or his security detail could possibly see them coming or going and, depending on who had witnessed the scene with Tiffany the night before, wonder why in hell she was so friendly with them. Plus Ryan and Faith had originally been booked into the suite on the other side of Larkin, so Cael didn't want them anywhere near it. Tiffany's stateroom, on the other hand, was on a lower deck, and they could come and go without anyone being the wiser. Except for the public areas, ships were more private than most people realized. Part of it was the way they were designed, with different sections of staterooms served by different elevators, so there wasn't a great deal of cross traffic. He had passed exactly one person in this section on his way to Tiffany's room, and that was soon after getting off the elevator. Basically, no one paid any attention to anyone else.

The suite Ryan and Faith had been reassigned was on the opposite side of the ship from Larkin's suite, but still on the same deck, so while they could probably get together there without any problem, Tiffany's stateroom was much safer.

"Is the key-logger program set?" Cael asked Faith, who was their computer expert. Expert, hell, she was a hacker, and she was scary good.

"It's done," Faith said crisply. "Anything Larkin types on his laptop, we'll collect. I have the computer set to transmit the data whenever he logs onto the Internet, and in fifteen-minute intervals thereafter."

"You know," Cael mused, "I used to enjoy using a computer, before I found out what hackers like you can do from the comfort of their own living rooms." He was just glad Faith was on his team, instead of working against him.

A lot of passengers brought their laptops with them, so there was nothing at all suspicious about Faith having hers— a ridiculously pink Dell, to which she'd stuck a few whimsical, sequined appliqués. The *Silver Mist* came equipped with a cell tower, so wireless Internet was available shipwide, and no one had to be out of touch if they didn't want to be. Except for the sequins, Faith's computer looked deceptively ordinary. It was not, and neither was she.

They made quick plans for the evening, making sure that wherever Larkin was, when not in his suite, one or more of them would be nearby. Each member of the team was equipped with miniature cameras to document who Larkin met with, in case one or more of his contacts was aboard the ship. Odds were that any business done would take place in

Larkin's suite, but they had to be prepared for anything. Bridget or Matt would gain access to the suite's parlor as soon as possible, and then they'd be set.

Tiffany made a sour face. "Tonight I'll get gussied up and try to work my womanly charms on Larkin. God, I hope he doesn't bite." She used the term to mean she hoped he didn't take the bait, but Cael could see the slight movement of her lips as she fought to contain a smile. Faith looked up at the ceiling, pretending she hadn't heard anything. Ryan grinned outright.

"Ha, ha," said Cael. He'd never live it down, that Redwine had managed to sink her teeth into him. If he hadn't been trying so hard not to hurt her he could have put her down and out in one second flat; this grief was what he got for being a gentleman.

"He's creepy," Tiffany continued. She wasn't crazy about the idea of spending any time with Larkin, but it was another possible avenue of gathering information. Was he a talker? Did he try to impress women by telling them how important he was, and let tidbits slip? Not likely, but not impossible, either. Cael wouldn't ask anyone on his team to have sex with anyone they didn't want to have sex with, but if she could get into Larkin's suite and plant some backup surveillance, all the better.

"After watching that fit you threw last night, he'll probably run far and fast if you come on to him," Ryan said soothingly, then ruined the effect by grinning again. "I know I would."

She merely gave him a "you wanna bet?" smirk. A lot of men would be willing to put up with more than that to spend time with a woman like Tiffany.

"Bluetooth sniffer?" he prompted, to get the discussion back on track.

"Working," replied Faith. "We have him covered as much

as possible, short of one of us actually being in the suite with him."

They went over the various aspects of their surveillance methods. If Larkin got suspicious and wanted his suite swept for bugs, Cael could use a remote to disconnect the batteries. If the bug wasn't working, a sweep wouldn't pick it up. For the hardwired bugs he'd threaded into Larkin's bedroom, he could simply pull them out. The hardwired stuff was more reliable and harder to detect, but sometimes they had no choice but to go wireless. Most jobs, like this one, he went with a combination of the two.

He checked his watch; Bridget had been on guard duty for an hour, which was a long time for her not to be taking care of her duties as steward. "I have to relieve Bridget," he said, wondering what mischief Redwine had gotten up to in that hour. Anything was possible. He might get there to find Bridget had both cuffed and gagged her, something he'd considered doing himself. He wasn't worried that Redwine had escaped, because Bridget could take her with one hand tied behind her back, but that didn't mean she hadn't gotten up to some mischief-making. She was way, way too curious about what they were doing and what was going on, which was understandable, but the less she knew the better, because she couldn't let slip what she didn't know.

When he keyed the door and opened it, he held his breath until he saw Bridget calmly sitting on the couch, laptop on the coffee table in front of her, earbud in place, making use of the time by going through as much of their recorded audio/video as possible, to save him the trouble.

Redwine was nowhere in sight. Cael felt his testicles draw up, as if she might attack him from behind at any second. "Where is she?" he asked, dread in his tone.

Bridget looked up. "She's taking a nap," she said, as if that were the most normal thing in the world.

Unbelievable. Cael rolled his eyes upward, ruefully shaking his head. "Why can't she ever do that when I'm here?" he asked, of no one in particular.

Right on cue, she appeared in the bedroom doorway, her eyes sleepy-looking and her hair tousled. Her gaze focused on him like a laser. "Oh, it's *you*," she said in tones of loathing, before giving him a huge, completely fake smile that looked more like a tiger snarling. "Welcome back, lover."

Chapter Seventeen

Larkin had to go to the casino soon for the first of the cruise's organized charity events. All proceeds from the casino—from the entire cruise, actually—were being donated to charity, but there were too many passengers for all of them to fit inside the casino at once, so the organizers had divided them into groups, based on their deck name and room number, and a hundred at a time were allowed in the casino for one hour. The person who won the most money in that length of time got a prize; Frank didn't know what the prize was, and didn't care. It would be something pricey, of course—this crowd would expect nothing less.

It occurred to him that this ship, this cruise, would become the stuff of legends, just like the *Titanic*. Everything the passengers did, the music they listened to, the fashions they wore, would be studied and analyzed as if all of it were important, when in fact none of it was.

He didn't have much of an appetite, but when he did eat he preferred to eat alone. On occasion he couldn't manage to keep down what little he ate, so privacy was important. Dining with the other passengers was out of the question; he didn't want anyone noticing that he didn't eat much and that he sometimes gagged on his food. No one knew he was sick, other than his doctor, and he wanted to keep it that way. He'd ordered a sandwich—tuna salad on a croissant, because God forbid anything as simple as regular bread should be served on this ship—some fruit, and a bottle of water, and he'd do what he could to choke down some of it before he was forced to make an appearance in the casino.

The tumor in his brain had taken away so many of the joys of life. The constant headache made him jumpy, and some days the pain was worse than others. He didn't dare take more than over-the-counter painkillers, because anything more would cloud his mind. He'd all but lost interest in food, though he knew he needed to eat, and he missed the enjoyment of a good meal. Sex was another appetite he'd lost. His body was rebelling against him, taking away all of life's pleasures, and it infuriated him. Wasn't it bad enough that he was going to fucking die? Did the damn cancer have to rob him of *every* possible bit of enjoyment and satisfaction? He was damned if he'd let it.

His personal steward, Isaac, took care of most of his needs during the cruise. Larkin didn't want a stranger in his immediate circle, not when what he was doing was so crucial. Isaac had been a loyal employee for years; he always did whatever was asked of him without complaint, no matter how demeaning it might be. Whenever it looked as if the man had had enough and was about to walk, Larkin would throw him a bone: a raise, a gift, maybe a vacation. Isaac would spend his final days sleeping in cramped crew quarters and doing as he was told. He'd die here, loyal to the end.

Maybe he should feel sorry for good old Isaac, Larkin thought, then gave a contemptuous laugh. If Isaac had had any balls, he'd have left a long time ago. Why should he feel sorry for a fool?

Isaac couldn't handle everything, though. Room service, for instance, would take twice as long if Isaac had to go to the kitchen and fetch the food, so he was relieved of that duty and Larkin tolerated the room service personnel. He was in the suite when he ordered room service, obviously, so it wasn't as if anyone would be coming in while he wasn't there.

A young man—his name tag read "Matt"—delivered Larkin's dinner. Larkin hated him on sight. Not only was he pretty in a tennis pro, surfer kind of way, with curly blond hair and the innocent eyes of the terminally stupid, he looked as healthy and in shape as Larkin himself had always been. He hated the kid for his health, for his complete unawareness of his own mortality. What would it be like to not realize you were dying? Everyone was dying, but most people carried on in blissful ignorance. Larkin no longer had that luxury, and the unfairness of it made him want to slap the kid's stupid, pretty face.

"Good evening, sir," the idiot said cheerfully. "Where would you like your dinner?"

Shoved up your ass, Larkin thought, but didn't say it. Instead he indicated a small table near the doors that opened onto the balcony. "Put it there."

The kid unloaded the tray's contents, said, "Is there anything else I can get for you, sir?"

"No, just get out," Larkin said, his fists clenching as pain shot like a nail through his head. Sometimes it did that, the chronic headache turning hot and sharp before subsiding again. A wave of nausea followed hard on the heels of the pain.

The kid looked startled by Larkin's rudeness. "Uh . . . yes

sir," he said, hurrying to the door. He was in such a rush that he tripped over his own big feet and fell, thudding to his knees. He dropped the tray and it rolled away from the klutz with an ear-shattering clatter, finally spinning to a noisy halt against the tall artificial ficus tree that had been placed against the wall near the door.

"I'm sorry," the kid blurted, scrambling to his feet. He popped up, reached for the tray, and damn if he didn't stumble again, barely catching himself on the container that held the tree, almost turning it over. He caught the tree, but dropped the tray again.

"Sorry!" he yelped.

"Oh, for God's sake!" Larkin yelled over the din. "Just get out!"

"Yes, sir. Sorry, sir. I'm sorry." The boy lurched for the tray, grabbed it, and this time managed to get out the door without falling again. He even collected himself enough to say "Enjoy your meal, sir" as he launched himself into the passageway.

After the door had closed, Larkin stood there breathing hard, his eyes closed as he waited for the nausea to subside. When it did, he looked at the food with loathing. Enjoy it? "I wish I could."

Out in the passageway, Matt resisted the urge to whistle. Some things were just too easy.

With the way the evening was structured, with different sections of passengers being allowed in the casino for an hour at a time for the big Charity Gamble, there were times when none of the team was actually in the casino area keeping an eye on Larkin. Cael swore some to himself, then accepted the situation and adapted as best he could.

He and Jenner were in the first group, Larkin's group. The evening started out with the charity organizer, a buxom woman who glittered and sparkled and showed a lot of teeth, introduced Larkin as the host of the cruise and thanked him profusely for everything he'd done, blah blah blah. Cael felt Jenner's attention perk up when Larkin was introduced, and he inwardly rolled his eyes. Great. Now she had a name, and one she probably recognized if she paid any attention to politics at all. Still, she had been bound to learn his name eventually, so it wasn't really a big deal.

Larkin went to the blackjack table, where he began winning consistently though he didn't seem to be having any fun doing it. Jenner eyed him for a minute, then headed for the blackjack table herself. Cael grabbed her arm, reeled her back in. "Not on your life," he muttered, steering her toward a nearby slot machine.

"But I want to play blackjack."

"Uh huh. Play Double Diamond instead, and act like you're having fun." No way would he let her at the table with Larkin. She narrowed her eyes at him but began dutifully punching buttons and pulling levers, winning a little and losing more, while he surreptitiously watched Larkin.

Larkin was hosting the cruise, but for a host he didn't seem to want to mingle very much. Though he'd produced a big smile when he was introduced, after that he barely acknowledged most of the guests. To Cael, it looked as if he didn't like his fellow passengers very much, if the veiled contempt with which he watched them was anything to go by.

That in itself was surprising, because the people on the cruise were movers and shakers in their own right, with a lot of money behind them. If Larkin pissed off enough of them they could start talking to people in Washington with whom they had influence, and Larkin could very swiftly find himself on the outside, looking in at the power circle to which he had once belonged. If Larkin took no pleasure in hosting this cruise, he could've handed the duty over to someone else, one of the other co-owners. Why spend two weeks on the *Silver Mist* if hosting the cruise was such a chore?

Even the destination, Hawaii, and the possible meet with the North Koreans didn't explain why he was putting himself through an experience he didn't enjoy. Hell, he could have chartered a private jet and flown to Hawaii, then back the next day. There had to be another reason why he was on the cruise, because he sure as hell didn't look as if he were enjoying himself.

They had studied information on every passenger aboard the *Silver Mist*, and at first glance there was no one who could be an industrial spy or a North Korean operative, but appearances and background information could be deceiving; he and his own crew were proof of that. So far Larkin had interacted with very few people, speaking mostly to his head of security, Dean Mills, but the ones he had spoken to, they had gone back and looked at again, to see if there was any detail they'd missed. Maybe investments had taken a particularly hard hit; maybe some photographs had been taken that someone wished to stay hidden. But there was nothing, and frustration ate at Cael because his instincts told him he was missing something.

Larkin hadn't so much as turned on his laptop yet, so Faith's key-logger program hadn't yielded any results, pertinent or otherwise. Still, it was early.

After the hour for their group had passed, they had to leave the casino. There had been some big winners, but Jenner wasn't one of them; in fact, he'd seldom seen anyone who lost as consistently at a slot machine as she did. Faith and Ryan were in the next group, so Cael was confident Larkin would remain under close surveillance. Then there was a gap, with no one in the third group, or the fourth—two hours without anyone in the casino area watching him. But a number of people were standing outside the casino, watching the gaming, shouting encouragement or groaning with disappointment when a friend failed to win, and he intended to join them. He'd be able to photograph anyone Larkin spoke to, even though he couldn't get close enough to catch what was actually being said.

With Faith and Ryan on duty, Cael slipped his hand around Jenner's waist and steered her toward the bar next to the casino. "Want something to drink?"

"No, thanks," she said, probably because he'd asked her if she wanted anything. If he hadn't asked, he had no doubt she'd have demanded a drink.

"Then how about some ice cream?" There was a twenty-four-hour soft-serve ice cream bar, and it was already one of the most popular places on the ship.

"Thanks, but I'm not hungry."

Goaded, he said, "Just as well. If you ate a single bite, you'd probably burst every seam in that dress."

"Probably," she agreed. Damn it, what was wrong with her? He'd been in her company for only a little over twenty-four hours, and he already knew she gave as good as she got. But she seemed a little distracted, which made him wonder what she was thinking. Whatever it was, nothing good could come of it.

He found them two seats at a small table and got her settled. A cocktail waitress immediately appeared and without asking he ordered a teeter-totter for her and a beer for himself. He could have done with something stronger, but he wanted to keep his head clear. When he glanced back at Jenner, he found that she was leaning forward to see around him as she watched the action in the casino. She hadn't seemed all that interested in it when she'd actually been in there, so he looked around to see what had her interest.

A cold chill ran down him when he realized she was watching Larkin. Damn it all to hell, the little witch was getting too interested in what they were doing, and God only knew what she was capable of doing to satisfy her curiosity. Why couldn't she have stayed nicely frightened, the way she'd been at first . . . for all of, say, five minutes? After that, she'd been nothing but trouble.

He shifted his chair to block her view, and coincidentally to keep Larkin from perhaps realizing Jenner was staring at him as if he were a zoo exhibit. The last thing he wanted was to put the bastard on guard.

Jenner gave him a bright smile. "You know, you could leave me in Hawaii," she said, leaning forward so her low voice was almost lost amid the annoying jangle and singsong ringing of the slot machines adjacent to the bar. "I promise not to give away whatever it is you're doing. I'll get a hotel room, spend a week on the beach, and I'll be out of your hair. You could let Syd go, she could join me, and we'd all be happy. Perfect solution."

He mimicked her motion, leaning closer to her. Damn, she smelled good, and from this angle the low cut of her midnight blue cocktail dress was interesting—and that was putting it mildly. She didn't have much in the boob department, but what was there caused his gut to knot up, low and hard. He should get away from her. He *needed* to get away from her, but the job kept him there, on the front line, in harm's way. "Why would I let you go?" he asked, nuzzling her ear. "The entertainment value alone is worth the risk of pain and injury."

The green glint in her eyes promised retribution, but once again she refused to rise to his bait, which was just as well. The last thing he wanted was for her to deck him in public.

As much as he'd like to release her, for both their sakes, he needed her right where she was, to provide cover for him. Without her there, he'd have no reason to be in that suite— and the general policy of a cruise ship was that the staterooms weren't transferrable by the passengers. A passenger could cancel, but assigning anyone else to a stateroom was up to the cruise line. He couldn't take the risk that he might not be allowed back into the suite.

She would just have to suck it up.

The night wore on. Larkin greeted every group, then retreated back to the blackjack table, where he kept on steadily winning. For all the excitement or life in his face, he might as well have been watching grass grow.

When Tiffany's group was allowed in the casino she planted herself beside Larkin and tried her best to interest him, without even a hint of success. Frank Larkin had escorted some beautiful women in the past, had something of a reputation in that department, but even as exotic and eye-catching as Tiffany was she couldn't pull more than an irritated glance from him. Maybe her scene had scared him off, because Cael knew for a fact that Larkin had been watching; maybe she just wasn't his type. Getting her close to him would have been a bonus, but it wasn't happening.

Staying so close to Larkin could make him suspicious— just about anything could make the paranoid bastard suspicious—so Tiffany moved on and began flirting with a man whose wife was winning big at craps, not because she had a thing for older, married guys, but because that gave her a good angle to photograph anyone Larkin talked to.

As soon as the hour for the last group was over, Larkin tossed his cards on the green felt of the table and walked away, leaving his winnings there as all the proceeds were going to charity. They couldn't follow him en masse, so Tiffany said good-bye to her new friend and followed Larkin at a distance, moving through the crowd smoothly and naturally. Her prowling walk drew more than one appreciative glance from some men and a dagger or two from the women with those men, but on a ship filled with beautiful people she fit seamlessly. Faith and Ryan stayed at the nearby table they'd taken, as did Cael and Jenner.

A soft voice, transmitted through the earbud Cael wore, said, "Ghostwater Bar," as Tiffany informed them all of Larkin's destination. The man did drink, though not to excess. Last night he'd limited himself to two drinks, and not the ubiquitous Ghostwater, either. His preferred drink was scotch, straight up. He had no routine established yet— this was just the second night—so they had no idea what to expect.

"He's moving," came Tiffany's voice just minutes later. "I don't know why he came here, because he didn't get anything to drink. He's coming back toward the casino. Someone else needs to pick him up."

They all went on alert. Larkin reappeared very shortly, his expression blank, but Cael thought his eyes looked a little spacey. Was he on drugs? He walked with purpose, though, if a little stiffly.

"Come on," Cael said to Jenner, urging her to her feet. Maybe Larkin was going to his suite, maybe not. God knew it was late enough, and the man had put in some long hours in the casino. Regardless, he wanted to keep Larkin in sight.

If he didn't go to the suite, Faith and Ryan could shadow him, alert Cael to his destination.

He gripped Jenner's elbow as she looked around with interest, trying to spot what had galvanized him to action. She spotted Larkin in just a few seconds, and her attention riveted on him, her expression reminding him of a hound on the hunt.

Just to distract her, he said, "Smile."

She flashed him a very wide, very phony grin that reminded him of a shark.

He sighed as he increased his pace. "Never mind, Witchiepoo."

"Witchie who?"

"Look it up," he said.

Larkin went to the elevator, and the car left before they could reach it. Cael took out his cell phone and sent a swift text to Bridget, alerting her that Larkin was on the way up. His pulse kicked up a notch. If Larkin didn't go to his suite, they'd have to locate him. He didn't like having his target out of sight, even for a short while.

He stood with Jenner waiting for the next elevator, and before it arrived his cell buzzed a text alert. Swiftly he checked it, and breathed out a sigh of relief. Larkin had entered his suite. Everything was good.

A few more people hurried up and got in the elevator with them, so he and Jenner didn't talk, but he could tell she was bursting with questions. As soon as he unlocked the suite door and ushered her inside, she turned to face him, backing up as he moved forward. "So, why are you spying on Frank Larkin?" she asked.

"Get away from the door," he said, and swiftly turned around to open the door and check if anyone was in the passageway who might have overheard her. The hall was blessedly empty. Shaking his head, he closed and locked the door, then chained it.

Jenner still stood there, her eyebrows lifted as she waited for his reply.

"Well?" she prompted.

"None of your business. Get ready for bed while I check that everything's working."

He wanted to do more than that, he wanted to know if Larkin was on the phone with anyone, or if he'd finally fired up his laptop. Jenner gave him a frustrated look, but grabbed a pair of pajamas and disappeared into the bathroom, which meant he had a few peaceful minutes to himself. Earbud in place, he watched Larkin get ready for bed. When the light went out in the bedroom next door, Cael removed the earbud. Nothing. So far, they had squat.

Jenner was still in the bathroom, so he used the opportunity to strip out of his own clothes. He had the handcuffs ready when she reappeared, face shiny clean, and clad in another pair of pajamas with one of those flimsy tank tops—this one was pink, and had glittery stars all over it—and without a word he indicated the chair.

She glared at him as she sat, and he cuffed her to the chair. Irritated, she jerked at the cuff. "This isn't necessary. As long as you're holding Syd, I'm not going to do anything. You're doing this just to show me who's boss."

"Yeah," he agreed, going into the bathroom and taking the handcuff key with him.

There was a moment of stunned silence, then she half-shrieked, "You mean you *admit* it?"

"I get a lot of pleasure from it." Smiling to himself, he took care of business, brushed his teeth, and left the bathroom to find her still fuming. Oh, yeah. The truth was the truth.

She kicked at him as soon as he was within reach. He

dodged back, laughing, though he wouldn't have found it funny if her foot had landed where she was aiming.

"Don't you *dare* laugh!" she spat, and kicked at him again. He caught her foot, then the other one, and deftly jerked her butt out of the chair onto the floor. He was holding enough of her weight that she didn't hit hard, but the jolt got her attention.

"Asshole! Numb-nuts!"

While she was down he freed her from the chair, and just as swiftly cuffed her to his left wrist. He picked her up and half-placed, half-dropped her on the bed. "Leave my nuts out of this," he said as he dropped the key into the drawer of the bedside table, then got in bed beside her and turned out the lamp.

Chapter Eighteen

Jenner woke, and in the darkness for a moment—a blissful moment—she forgot where she was. Then she moved and the handcuffs pinched her wrist, and reality came crushing down. Truly, reality wasn't as terrifying as it had been twenty-four hours ago, but it still wasn't a picnic, either. For one thing, Macho Man couldn't seem to accept that she wasn't going to go running to the ship's captain, she wasn't going to try to hide from him, she wasn't going to do anything that would endanger Syd. She didn't know what the situation was like where Syd was being held; her captor might be the type of jerk who looked forward to hurting people, and was being held in check only as long as she herself behaved.

Actually, she thought, Macho Man probably *did* know that she wasn't going to do any of those things, but he'd told the simple truth that he enjoyed bossing her around. That, or he'd decided he simply couldn't take the risk, that whatever they were up to was so important, or so financially huge, that literally nothing was being left to chance, no matter how small the odds.

She rolled over enough to look at the clock. She'd had two hours of solid sleep, which was pretty good considering she was handcuffed and couldn't move without twisting her arm into a pretzel. Now, however, courtesy of the teeter-totter she'd had in the bar, she needed to pee.

She tried ignoring it. Cael hadn't awakened when she'd moved, and she didn't want him to. He'd tossed back the covers, again, and lay there wearing nothing but a pair of boxers. Even in the faint glimmer of light that came from the living room, he looked big and intimidating.

She sighed. This was going to be the longest two weeks of her life. Curling on her side, she squirmed around trying to get comfortable, then forced herself to lie still once more. She was cold, again, and she *really* needed to pee. Getting comfortable was impossible, between being cold, not being able to pull the covers up, and a full bladder, and all three of those things could be laid right on his doorstep—not that he cared. He'd probably enjoy making her beg to be allowed to go to the bathroom.

The key to the handcuffs was right there, in the drawer of the bedside table. Had he thought she wouldn't notice where he put it, within easy reach if he needed to get to it in the middle of the night in case she, say, set his hair on fire? She really, really wanted that key. He hadn't even attempted to be secretive about where he put it, as if he didn't see her as a potential threat—or as if he were daring her to try anything.

Either scenario was annoying. She didn't like being helpless, and she didn't like being written off as helpless. Even worse was the idea that he might be expecting her to go for the key, that this was a test to see if she could be counted on to not cause any trouble.

Well, hell. She didn't want to cause trouble, at least not the kind that could get Syd hurt. Neither did she want to ask him for permission to pee. What she'd really like to do is get the key, unlock the cuffs, go to the bathroom, then slip back into bed and let him find out in the morning that she'd been free for hours and hadn't taken advantage of the situation to go running down the passageway screaming for help. That would, logically, go a long way into proving she wasn't going to do something stupid, which should, logically, also result in more freedom. The problem was, she didn't know if numb-nuts responded to logic.

Another aspect was that she really, really wanted to thumb her nose at him and show him he wasn't as much the boss as he thought he was. Was it really too much to ask that she could go to the bathroom without asking permission? That she could have one truly private moment without a man standing on the other side of the door listening to her pee?

The key was within reach. The problem was in reaching it without waking him.

She moved smoothly, easily, taking her time, listening carefully to his breathing in case the rhythm changed. The room was too dark for her to make out his expression, but still she watched for signs that she was disturbing him. She wasn't exactly still at night, so subconsciously he might already be used to her movements. He might be accustomed to sleeping with someone anyway; Tiffany came to mind. After all, they'd been sharing a stateroom before he forced his way into hers.

Gradually she lifted herself onto her elbow. He didn't stir, didn't grumble. He wasn't snoring, either, and she wished he was, because then she'd know for certain he was asleep. She balanced there on her elbow for what seemed like fifteen minutes, giving him time to sink back into deep sleep if she had disturbed him.

Slowly, careful not to touch him, she reached over and across his bare chest, her fingers stretching toward the drawer handle. *Crap.* She wasn't nearly close enough.

She shifted position, got a knee under her for balance, lifted herself higher. All the while she struggled not to tug on the handcuffs, because that would wake him for certain. Or would it? If he'd awakened any of the times she'd changed positions, he hadn't said anything.

Hovering over him, she stretched even more. She could almost reach the drawer. Impatience bit at her but she resisted it. Calm control was the key to a successful bathroom run. Very gradually she got to her feet, though she had to stay bent over to keep from putting tension on her cuffed arm. Just as gradually she placed one foot between his spread legs, for better balance. The thought of what might get kicked if he woke while she was in this position gave her a moment of unholy glee, and she almost hoped he would.

She waited some more. Thank goodness for all those Pilates and yoga classes! Core strength was important when twisting one's body into unnatural positions for clandestine purposes.

If she slipped now, she'd fall straight down onto a half-naked Cael, and she didn't want to know how a man like this one would react to being awakened that way. He wasn't the average guy; the shape he was in testified to that. She saw a lot of gym rats, and his muscles weren't like that; they were longer, more sinewed, and she'd seen scars that hadn't come from falling off the monkey bars in grade school. He was hard and capable, and power was in every move he made.

She was much too close to him in this position. She could feel his body heat rising against her skin, hear his even breathing. For a moment she almost chickened out, almost shifted back so she could lie down beside him again. Yes, she still had to pee. Yes, she'd have to wake him up and ask permission.

No, by God, she wouldn't. The drawer handle was so close, she couldn't give up. Besides . . . enough was enough.

It wasn't just that she wanted to go to the bathroom without asking his permission; she wanted, needed, to show him that she could get past his ridiculous precautions. She wanted to rub his face in the fact that he wasn't such hot shit, after all. *Boss*, her ass.

She grasped the handle with her fingertips and held her breath as she slowly pulled the drawer open. The angle was bad, and her muscles were beginning to tremble from being held so tense for a long time. If she could have pulled the drawer straight toward her it would have been a lot easier, but she had to ease it out in a sideways motion that made her arm cramp.

There! That was far enough. She froze, to make certain the low sound of the drawer sliding hadn't awakened Cael. He slept on, and carefully she reached out to snag the small key that lay on top of a notepad. She wasn't home free, she still had to get the cuffs unlocked without waking him, but a pure, sweet sense of victory shot through her. *Gotcha, numb-nuts!*

He shot up without warning, grabbing her with his cuffed arm, flipping her onto her back, then his heavy body crashed down onto hers and they bounced. Before she could do more than squeak, he easily pried the key from her clenched fist. *What the hell?* His breathing had never changed; he'd given her no clue that he was awake. That wasn't fair; it wasn't *right*.

"Going somewhere?" he asked in a slightly gravelly voice.

True desperation made her push frantically at his shoulder. Oh, God, he'd jostled her around and—"I'm going to pee on you!" she cried frantically.

He froze for a second, then said in a musing tone, "I don't think I've ever been threatened with that before."

"It isn't a *threat*!" She pushed again. "Let me *up*!"

Finally he seemed to realize she wasn't joking, and he practically vaulted off her to stand beside the bed, which of course pulled her with him. Gritting her teeth, she fought for control. "Stop bouncing me, you moron, and unlock these cuffs!"

Quickly he turned on the lamp and unlocked the cuffs. As soon as she was free, she rushed to the bathroom and slammed the door. She barely made it, as she was sure he was aware because he'd probably followed her and was waiting just outside the door.

A few minutes later, having thought the situation over, she shoved the door open and barreled out, fire in her eyes. As she'd expected, he was standing right there, and she plowed into him before he could do more than get his hands up to catch her around the waist. She dipped her shoulder and drove it into his mid-section, not that she had to dip it very far, and not that it did a lot of good, but at least he fell back a step before catching his balance.

"It's all your fault!" she said furiously, so angry and embarrassed she was almost jumping up and down. "I didn't want anything to drink, but no, you thought I needed a teeter-totter to make things look good, so of course I had to pee! Then you handcuffed me so I couldn't get to the bathroom. I swear, if you *ever* do that to me again, I'm just going to pee on you as soon as I wake up and save myself the wear and tear."

A slow smile began to curve his mouth.

"Don't laugh," she warned him, tucking her chin and clenching her fist. "Don't you dare laugh."

He reached out and caught her fist before she could swing it, and, damn him, snapped those damned cuffs around her wrist again. Seething, she let him lead her back to bed. If he made a joke about it, she'd kill him with her bare hands.

He didn't stop smiling, but at least he had sense enough not to say anything. She crawled into bed and he flipped the covers off the floor where she could reach them. He turned out the lamp and got back into bed beside her. They were both settled before he asked, "Why didn't you just wake me?" Maybe it took that long before he could get his voice under control.

"Because a grown woman shouldn't have to ask permission to go to the bathroom," she shot back. She wasn't anywhere near being settled down, and the way she felt now, a couple of months would come and go before her temper cooled.

"Under these circumstances, for now, the grown woman most certainly does." Exasperation crept into his tone. "Did you really think you could shake the bed, crawl on top of me, and steal the key without waking me up? Just shaking my shoulder would have been a lot faster, and a lot less, uh, dangerous."

"I didn't want to touch you. Jackass."

"You ended up touching me a lot, so I'd say your plan didn't work."

She didn't want to remember those moments when he'd crushed her into the mattress, his heavy, mostly naked body on hers in a perfect sexual position. Her legs had even been spread, and for a few heart-stopping seconds the hard bulge of his penis had pushed against his groin.

Did it say something about him that he hadn't taken advantage of the situation? She hadn't been afraid that he would, she realized. She hadn't been afraid at all. Sometime during the past day, she had stopped fearing him.

Chapter Nineteen

Jenner woke still in a bad mood. For the second day in a row she was alone in the bed, and she'd slept through the removal of the handcuffs when she hadn't even been able to retrieve the fricking key without waking Cael. He seemed to delight in proving to her again and again that she wasn't in control of even the smallest thing, that she was completely helpless. It had been a very long time since she had been dependent on anyone for anything, and she didn't like it at all. But, like it or not, Cael was forcing her to be dependent on him for everything until the cruise was over and she got off this damn ship.

The jackass was probably sitting out in the parlor, slugging down the last of the coffee and eating the last croissant, rather than waking her so she could eat, too. If he wasn't here, one of the others would be, to make certain she didn't poke her nose outside the suite without a guard by her side. She hoped he was gone, because dealing with Faith or Bridget would be easier right now than dealing with him.

She took her time showering, then dressed in one of her favorite outfits, cotton and silk blend teal capris with a skimpy white top trimmed in the same teal. Little sandals, which cost more than she used to earn in two weeks, decorated her feet. From her jewelry roll she took out platinum earrings, a couple of bracelets, and a tiny diamond toe ring. The outfit gave her confidence, because she knew she looked good in it. *He* wouldn't know it, but how she was dressing was a sort of flip-off to him. She was damned if she'd give up, damned if she'd try to fade into the background, *damned* if she'd be Miss Meek and Mild. Oh, she'd play along with him in public, because she had to—*Remember Syd*, she reminded herself—but in private . . . that was a different matter entirely.

She sailed out of the bedroom and found Cael seated at the dining table, a round pedestal table with four upholstered chairs grouped around it. A large oblong serving tray sat on the table, filled with coffee service and two covers. A mostly empty plate sat to his left, a cup of coffee to his right. Directly in front of him was the laptop, and his earbud was in place.

He looked up when she entered, tapped a command on the laptop, and removed the earbud. "Breakfast," he said, indicating the two round covers on the tray. "Still fairly warm. It was delivered while you were in the shower."

She didn't know which was worse, not having any breakfast, or having a breakfast that he'd ordered without consulting her. Opting for coffee first, she upended the second cream-colored porcelain cup—no polystyrene for the *Silver Mist*—and filled it with coffee. He watched in silence as she sipped appreciatively before lifting the covers to check out the food.

The ordinariness of the meal was a little disappointing: whole wheat toast, scrambled eggs, potatoes, bacon. She'd been expecting something disgusting, like cold oatmeal, or soft-boiled eggs. Oatmeal was okay when it was hot, but there was nothing that would ever make her like soft-boiled eggs, no matter how fancy the little utensils used to crack the egg and scoop out the contents. She wouldn't have put it past him to have burdened her with both cold oatmeal *and* a soft-boiled egg, but he'd surprised her. The plain old breakfast was almost a . . . peace offering?

"Have a seat," he invited genially, getting to his feet and pulling out a chair for her. She gave him a suspicious look as she sat down; she'd become accustomed to good manners, but she didn't expect courtesy from him. On the other hand, there was something . . . Continental about him, little things that were somehow different, like his clothing. As well as he dressed, her life was filled with people who dressed well, and expensively, so it wasn't that. It was more the cut of the clothing, the fluidity and drape that spoke of . . . Italy, maybe? His accent was pure American, but she couldn't identify the region. It was as if he'd traveled so much that his original accent had long since evolved into something more homogeneous.

"Where are you from?" she asked as she began buttering her toast.

He didn't answer, merely gave a half smile as if acknowledging her effort to dig information out of him.

"Not where you live now," she explained. "Originally." She started to add that she meant what area of the country he was from but at the last second some little frisson of instinct had her saying, "What country?"

His blue gaze lifted, and the smile was gone now. *Bingo!* She barely hid her sudden satisfaction; a blind thrust had hit home.

"What do you mean?" he asked softly.

It occurred to her that Cael Traylor could be a very

dangerous man, that prying into his affairs might not be a smart thing to do. She was teasing the beast, just to show him that she wasn't some stupid pawn to be moved hither and yon at his whim. At least, she wasn't *stupid*, because right now she was definitely a pawn.

As casually as possible, she took a bite of toast. "Your accent. There's something about it—"

"Don't let your imagination run away with you," he said, leaning back in his chair. "I'm American."

Uh-huh. Sure.

Letting the subject drop, she devoted herself to breakfast. Despite the covers on the food, the eggs had gotten too cold for her to choke down, especially when he sat there watching her. The bacon and toast were tolerable, because even cold bacon and toast were pretty damn good, but with him sitting there watching every move she made, each bite became harder and harder to swallow. Finally she dropped the slice of toast on the plate and said, "Stop staring at me! I'm not a monkey in a zoo."

His mouth quirked. "Then there's no reason for me to duck?"

"I didn't say that." In fact, she wished she had something gross to throw at him. "Just . . . stop watching me. Don't you have something more important to do?"

"Nope."

Maybe going after the key last night hadn't been such a good idea, because he didn't seem inclined to cut her any slack. Continuing to eat was impossible, though, so she grumbled, "Show's over," and got up. She refilled her coffee cup from the carafe and took it out onto the balcony, not looking back to see if he was following but certain that he would.

She sat down in one of the deck chairs. She craved a

moment alone, a precious sliver of time to take a deep breath and gather her wits about her, but he seemed determined not to allow her any more time alone than it took to shower and dress, take care of the necessities. Bathroom time was important, but she didn't want to spend hours in there. Besides, she was afraid that if she lingered in the shower too long he'd think she was up to something and walk in to check on her, to make sure she hadn't found a way to make poison out of mascara and shampoo, or something else even more heinous.

She didn't know what to make of Cael, and that bothered her. Normally she had pretty good people-instincts, but she couldn't make up her mind about him. He and the others were obviously spying on Mr. Larkin, whom at first glance she didn't care for but he might be one of those people who improved on acquaintance. The big question was, who was the bad guy: Cael, or Mr. Larkin? Or was there no good guy at all? Maybe there was bad, and badder.

Last night's revelation had confused her even more. Cael was maddening and annoying and bossy, unyielding, arrogant, and he'd had Syd kidnapped—some might even say he'd kidnapped her, too—but she wasn't afraid of him, as any right-minded woman should be. She'd been terrified at first, but over the course of two nights she'd lost that fear. If she'd been truly afraid, she never would have gone for the key. She wouldn't have been able to sleep a wink with him beside her. Then again, it wasn't as if her track record was flawless where men were concerned. There had been times in her life when hormones had knocked common sense and good instincts right out the window. It had happened before, and it could happen again, though no one had slipped under her guard since Dylan. She was older now, more wary. So had she lost her mind, or were her

237

instincts telling her Cael was the good guy here—or at least not the worst?

She sighed as she stared out at the blue water, wishing she knew what was going on, hoping Syd wasn't frightened, wishing Cael would fall overboard, hoping she'd have a chance to help him over the railing . . . wishing and hoping, like the old song.

The balcony was private, or at least gave the illusion of privacy as there were floor-to-ceiling walls between this balcony and the ones on either side. In other circumstances, she might find the view and the fresh air a real pleasure, but these circumstances didn't leave room for even the simplest pleasure.

Her first cruise. And her last one, damn it. There was no way she'd ever willingly set foot aboard a ship again. She hated being in a position where she literally had nowhere to go.

She wasn't surprised when she heard the door onto the balcony open, and Cael step out. He sat in the other heavy lounge, stretching out his long legs. Taking a sip of his own coffee, he gazed out at the ocean much as she did. If she didn't know better, she'd think he was relaxed. No, he *was* relaxed, but he was still alert. She wondered if he ever truly let his guard down, if some part of him wasn't always on duty. Even now, on this protected balcony with nothing but the ocean in view, he was as watchful as if he thought an attack could materialize at any time.

After a moment, she realized that he did expect an attack—from her. The thought amused her so much that her mood immediately lightened. What did he think she could do? The only way she could toss him overboard would be if he climbed on top of the railing first. She'd taken those judo classes, true, but she didn't think Cael would just stand there while she tried to remember how to flip him, then practiced her positioning and balance. Expert, she wasn't.

She got a great deal of pleasure imagining him tipping over the rail, though. He'd make a nice, big splash.

"Finish your coffee and come inside," he said, as if he'd read her thoughts. She wasn't trying to guard her expression, so maybe she'd looked unexpectedly gleeful.

Obviously he didn't trust her to even sit out here on the balcony alone, though what she could do or where she could go was a mystery.

The power between her and Cael was so out of balance— he, after all, had all the power—that it was frankly amazing she could get under his skin at all. He could crush her like a bug, and she'd have to let him. No matter what he wanted to do to her she had no way of stopping him. She couldn't hurt him, couldn't give him up to the shipboard authorities, couldn't foil his mysterious plans.

She could needle him, though, and take great delight in doing so—but not out here. She didn't know if Larkin was out on his balcony, sitting quietly, enjoying his morning coffee or his morning Ghostwater, listening to every word they said. She didn't know how well sound carried out here on the balconies. Other than that little while the first day, right after departure, she hadn't been out here.

She took a tiny sip of coffee. She wasn't about to gulp it down. In fact, this cup of coffee might last until lunchtime. Sweetly she asked, "What are our plans for today? Do you have anything in particular you're interested in?"

He put his cup down and stared at her as if she'd morphed into an alien. Jenner took great pleasure in indicating the direction of Larkin's balcony. In the spirit of cooperation she continued, "This weather is so great, though, it's almost tempting to stay right here all day."

239

Like velvet rubbing her skin, Cael said in that smooth, deep voice, "There's something I'm always interested in, sweetheart, and the balcony is fine with me."

Sydney tried her best to relax, because being in a constant state of anxiety was eating at her to the point she could barely sleep or eat. Having a heart attack at this point wouldn't serve any purpose. In fact, it would defeat the purpose, which was to survive.

She stood at the window in her bedroom, staring out at the scenery. San Diego was a beautiful city, and she hoped she never saw it again. She was never visiting Caro again; assuming she survived, Caro could come to south Florida to visit *her*.

So far her captors hadn't shown any signs of violence—well, other than shoving a pistol in her side in the limo. The weapons remained, always in evidence unless a maid or room service person was in the suite. Her kidnappers never allowed her to be alone in the same room with any of the hotel employees. When the maid came, Syd was hustled to the other side of the suite, and she was always in her bedroom with one of the kidnappers when food was delivered to the parlor.

Other than the fact that she'd been kidnapped and frightened out of her wits, the kidnappers seemed concerned that they make this as comfortable for her as possible, which was so at odds with what she'd expected that she had no idea what to think. They'd made it plain, though: So long as she didn't give them any trouble, Jenner wouldn't be hurt. They didn't want money. She had no idea what the hell they *did* want.

Yesterday she'd talked to her father and explained that

she'd missed the trip because of a particularly nasty stomach bug. After satisfying himself that she wasn't seriously ill, he'd suggested that she fly to Hawaii and join Jenner there as the *Silver Mist* sailed between the islands later in the week. Syd had told him that was a good idea, if she was over the bug she'd think about it. She'd also had to assure him again that her illness wasn't serious. It was a fine line, to convince her father that she was too sick to go on a cruise, but not so sick that she needed him to fly to San Diego, nor did she need to be in a hospital, and she didn't need for him to send someone to take care of her. All the while she talked to him, Kim watched and listened intently to make certain Syd didn't try to send any coded messages or something.

As if she knew *how* to send any coded messages.

Her lack of ability to do anything about this situation was frustrating. She knew how to put on a formal affair, how to coordinate outfits, how to juggle a thousand and one social obligations. Other than driving a car, however, she didn't have a single skill that could be considered useful—and even if she did, she probably wouldn't have the nerve to do anything, so the question was moot.

Being able to talk to Jenner had helped calm her nerves. Their two conversations hadn't lasted long, just long enough to reassure each other, but just hearing Jenner's voice and knowing she was all right gave her hope that they'd both see the end of this alive and well. Jenner's captors were letting her call, at an ungodly hour, which probably meant she'd been pestering them nonstop and they'd finally caved. She liked that scenario, because it meant that Jenner was winning, even if it was in something small.

Syd could even envision how Jenner had convinced them to let her call. Jenner didn't trust easily; just because they told her Syd was all right didn't mean Jenn would believe them, and she was perfectly capable of digging in her heels and refusing to cooperate unless they proved it, every day.

That was Jenn: not tough, but definitely prickly. She'd be frightened, but she'd get in there and fight anyway. In other words, almost the polar opposite of Syd herself, who had never fought for anything in her life.

She was suddenly ashamed of herself. She'd had all the benefits a life of comfort could provide. She'd never done without, never been threatened, had never been hungry— unless she was dieting—and still she'd let life walk all over her. She'd had a broken engagement because she'd found out the so-called love of her life had been more interested in her money than in her. Big deal. Jenner's life had been a lot tougher than that, and she hadn't let it cow her. Instead she sucked it up, and came out swinging.

Out in the parlor she heard a knock and a voice singsonging, "Room service!"

Within seconds, Kim slipped into the bedroom with her, and closed the door. Syd barely looked around from her stance at the window. Even if she had the nerve, she wouldn't raise the alarm, because of what the people who held Jenner might do to her. That was a good excuse to not be brave, but it was also true.

Kim stood listening until she heard the room service guy leave, then she said, "Lunch is here."

"So I heard," Syd said flatly, not exactly snapping but close to it. "What did you order for me?"

"A BLT." Kim hesitated. "If you want something else, just say so. We can order in a pizza, or Chinese, Mexican— whatever you want."

Wasn't that accommodating of them? The prisoner got to choose her food. She looked down at her hands as a thought occurred to her. Actually, yes, that *was* accommodating of them. Prisoners all over the world would like to be able to order any food they wanted. So why were her captors being so nice? Why were Jenner's captors letting her call every day?

Because they needed her. The answer slapped her in the face. How obvious could it be? They needed Jenn, and they were using Syd's safety to coerce her into doing whatever they wanted. Jenn, of course, had realized that, and was using their need for her in order to make demands of her own.

That worked both ways, didn't it? If Jenn wouldn't do what they wanted unless she was assured Syd was all right, then . . . what if she, Syd, refused to talk to Jenner unless she got some concessions, too? They'd want to keep her as happy as possible, so she'd continue talking and keeping Jenn in line.

The problem was, she didn't know at what point she and Jenn would become more trouble than they were worth.

She'd have to be careful. She wouldn't demand anything outrageous. She knew she couldn't just walk out of the suite any time she wanted, but, damn it, she wasn't going to cower in this room like a ninny.

"I want some books to read," she said. She'd brought one, thinking she and Jenn would be too busy with all the activities onboard for her to have much reading time, but she'd finished it the first day.

"Okay, fine," said Kim. "We'll get some."

"And I'm not hiding in the bedroom anymore," Syd continued. "Jenn won't do whatever it is you want unless she talks to me every day. And unless you back off, then I'm not going to talk to her."

With that she went into the bathroom to wash her hands

before eating. Kim stared after her for a brief, befuddled moment, then she went out into the parlor where Adam and Dori were waiting. "Shit," she said softly, not wanting Sydney to hear. "She called our bluff."

Chapter Twenty

On the third night, at the captain's cocktail party, where the ship's captain made himself available to the passengers, Jenner turned around and found herself face-to-face with Frank Larkin.

She'd been standing with Faith and Cael, making enough conversation to give the impression that she and Faith were at least friendly acquaintances, smiling enough at Cael to give another impression entirely. For once Cael didn't have a death grip on her elbow, mainly because he'd been forced to release her to shake hands with someone Faith introduced him to. Afterward she'd linked her arm through his, so he wouldn't suffer from anxiety and his issues with trust— namely a complete lack thereof. She had leaned against him very slightly, tilting her head to smile up at him, hugged his arm to her breasts. In short, she'd acted like a besotted fool.

The captain, Emilio Lamberti, was making an amusing little speech in a charming Italian accent, and they were listening to him. Half-listening, anyway. As it was at most cocktail parties, the din of conversation had died down only a little when he began speaking.

Then, in one of those almost-accidents that happen in crowds, Jenner heard a loud laugh somewhere behind her and automatically turned to see what was happening, at the same time Frank Larkin had abruptly decided to move from the spot nearby where he'd been most of the evening, which was why she and Cael and Faith had been stationed where they were, though only Faith had been turned so she could see him. He had stepped to the side to avoid someone who inadvertently moved into his path, Jenner turned, and they each stopped short of plowing into the other.

She felt the sudden tension in Cael's arm as he, too, turned around, but he couldn't move her away without being conspicuous about it. Without hesitation she laughed at the close call and held out her right hand. "Mr. Larkin, I've been wanting to meet you. I'm Jenner Redwine. We've seen each other in passing because I'm in the suite next to yours. Thank you so much for hosting the cruise. It's been absolutely marvelous, and of course it's helping so many worthwhile charities. The *Silver Mist* is a ship to be proud of. Have you always been interested in ships and sailing?" If there was anything she'd learned since moving to Palm Beach, it was how to bullshit with the best of them.

Larkin took her hand and shook it, clasping his other hand on top of hers as if to hold it in place. A practiced smile wreathed his face. "No, I've never been a sailor," he said genially. "The ship is an investment, but she's a beautiful one."

His hands were clammy, Jenner noticed. And . . . was there something wrong with one of his eyes? No, when she looked again, she couldn't see anything different about it, so it must have been a reflection from the crystal light fixtures overhead. On the other hand, there was no mistaking his expression, and she didn't like it.

Gently she withdrew her hand under the guise of making introductions, as she indicated Faith. "Have you met Faith Naterra?"

"We've met, very briefly," said Faith, smiling her lovely, charming smile as she, too, held out her hand. "But it's always nice to meet again."

"And this is my friend, Cael Traylor," said Jenner, because it would be too odd if she didn't introduce him when he was standing right there. The two men shook hands, said the appropriate things, then Cael slid his hand around her waist.

"Are you ready to leave, sweetheart?"

There was a warning glint in his eyes as he smiled down at her, but it wasn't needed. She had no intention of doing anything that would jeopardize whatever he was doing. "Yes, please."

"I was just about to leave, myself," said Larkin, but before he could say anything else the captain finished his little speech with a reference to Larkin, holding out his hand to indicate the host. Larkin had to smile and accept whatever compliment the captain had given, and Cael used the opportunity to steer Jenner out of the lounge, his hand moving from her waist to its customary grip on her elbow.

She was getting damned tired of being dragged around like a recalcitrant child. At the first opportunity she angled her body so no one could see what she was doing, then jerked her arm as she stooped to pretend she was picking up something from the floor. Cael had to release her arm or twist it out of place, as well as make it obvious to anyone behind them that he had a death grip on her. When she stood up, with a smile in place, she took his hand and laced their fingers together.

He slanted another of those warning glances down at her, but another couple was following them to the elevators so he couldn't say anything. Instead he lifted their clasped hands and brushed a kiss across her knuckles, then lightly bit.

The bottom dropped out of her stomach at the touch of his warm mouth.

Cold panic wound itself around her spine. She knew that feeling, knew what it meant. Damn it, she was *not* going to be that galactically stupid. Captive falling for captor was such a cliché, such a moronic thing to do. Not that she thought she was falling in love with him, but lust was something different, and could make a woman act just as dumb.

She'd been in almost constant contact with him since the first night on the ship. She'd fought with him, kissed him, slept beside him. She'd read once that a woman's pheromones were transmitted by air but a man's were transmitted by touch, in which case she had Cael Traylor's pheromones all over her, interfering with her thinking and making her want to get naked with him so he could transfer even more pheromones.

"I need a shower," she muttered to herself.

"He's slimy," Cael agreed absently as they stepped into the elevator. He held the door for the approaching couple, then punched the button for their deck.

Thank God he hadn't had any idea what she was thinking! Then she mentally paused, and rewound. That was the first thing any of them had let slip about Larkin, and it wasn't anything to do with why they were spying on him, but the comment was still telling. Cael thought Larkin was slimy.

Odd, because she hadn't liked him, either. Neither had she specifically disliked him, though she was inclined more toward that side of the fence, but he hadn't done anything to make her fall one way or the other. That said, there was something slightly off about him that made her want to keep her distance.

There were more implications in that simple, two-word sentence than she could immediately wrap her brain around. The first, most obvious one, was that if Cael thought Larkin was slimy, then he considered himself the good guy in whatever scenario they were working. The second one was, good guys didn't kill innocent hostages.

Maybe.

One of the advantages of his cover was that no one thought twice if he and Jenner "retired" early in the evening.

Earbuds in place, Cael watched the monitors and listened. The button camera Matt had affixed to the plant container gave him a nice view of the parlor, where Larkin now stood alone. He'd returned to the suite not long after Cael had brought Jenner back. Faith and Ryan had had the honors of keeping track of him until then. Damn, he wished Jenner hadn't bumped into Larkin, because he didn't want to become too prominent on the bastard's radar, but the meeting had been accidental and unavoidable.

She'd handled herself well, far more smoothly than he'd expected. If he'd expected anything, it was that she would seize the opportunity to bust his chops, but she had been pitch-perfect in her response. She'd surprised the hell out of him, and scared him to death, too. Any time Jenner behaved, his instincts started screaming at him to watch out.

As he watched and listened, he glanced at Jenner now and again. She was trying to get comfortable in the chair, where she was presently cuffed, but it wasn't easy. Tough shit. He'd tried letting her go to bed unrestrained—at least until he turned in himself—thinking he could watch her *and* do his job, but damned if she hadn't been up and down, flitting around in the bathroom, going to the parlor for a book that had obligated him to stop what he was doing and follow her. She'd read for maybe five minutes, then she'd been up again, rearranging the clothes in the closet and whatever the hell else she could do to take his attention from the job at hand. Finally he'd grabbed her, pushed her skinny little ass in the chair, and cuffed her to it. He couldn't afford to be distracted.

Not that she wasn't distracting enough already.

She'd looked good enough to eat—in both senses of the word—tonight, in a pink dress with sparkles all over it, held up by two tiny straps that he could have snapped with one finger. That's what he'd kept thinking about: how easy it would be to break them and peel the top down to bare those pert little breasts that kept tormenting him from under the skimpy tanks she wore as pajama tops.

Last night had been a mistake. Throwing her down and landing on top of her had been a miscalculation, a moment when sheer instinct had overridden cool intellect. His heart had almost stopped when her legs parted, and his erection had pressed hard against the soft heat of her groin. If she hadn't had her pajamas on, he'd have been inside her without thinking twice, and that was the worst part of it, that he *wouldn't* have thought twice, or even once.

Since then, he could barely drag his mind away from the subject. He'd realized from the beginning that she had the ability to get to him, on a purely physical level, like nothing he'd ever experienced before, but there was a big, deep trench between them that he couldn't let himself cross. The psychology of their situation meant that she had no power, so any intimacy between them smacked, at best, of coercion. She'd recognized it, too, or she wouldn't have said that about the Stockholm syndrome. He wasn't a rapist, full stop. There was no wiggle room on this.

But, God, he wanted her under him. He wanted to see her naked, he wanted her to kiss him the way she had the first night, when she'd been so hot and angry she'd almost set his shorts on fire. The intensity of the way he wanted her made him feel like a caveman, intent on nothing else except grabbing her ass and holding her still for that first heart-stopping stroke of his penis into the hot clasp of her body.

Wasn't going to happen. He couldn't—*wouldn't*—let himself do it.

On the laptop screen, Larkin turned on his cell phone and walked toward the balcony. Cael jerked his mind away from Jenner and focused on the task at hand. Watching Larkin, he leaned forward and tensed, said a little prayer. If Larkin went outside they'd be lucky to catch every other word. The wind, combined with the distance from the mike, would play hell with their reception. Fortunately, Larkin didn't go through the doors but stood there, punching buttons; then he lifted his head to stare into the darkness through the glass door.

What he wouldn't give to have a bug on that cell phone so he could hear both sides of the conversation, Cael thought. But they couldn't even capture the call by other means, because Larkin's phone was encrypted just like theirs were. He made a note of the time. Maybe his contacts would at least be able to get the number Larkin had dialed, if Faith couldn't pull it herself.

"I call you on my schedule, not yours," Larkin said coldly, into the phone. "I have the information you need to make the payment." He rattled off a long number from memory, probably a bank account and routing number.

After that, he was silent for a few moments. Who was on the other end of the line? Just a business associate, or the contact they'd been searching for?

"Hilo, as arranged," Larkin said carefully, as if he didn't

trust the phone's encryption and being cautious about offering too many details. "Don't be hasty. All things in good time." He listened awhile longer, then ended the call without saying good-bye. Did that mean he considered himself superior to the person he'd been talking to, or had the other person disconnected first?

Larkin turned off the cell phone and set it aside. He removed his tie as he walked toward the bedroom, turning off lights as he went. As he walked into the bedroom, the camera and transmitter Cael had threaded into the room caught the action. The angle was from the floor, pointed up.

Thank God Larkin didn't sleep naked.

Cael watched as Larkin rubbed his temples, frowning deeply before swearing for no apparent reason. Was he sick? Stressed? Betraying your country should give a man a headache. To Cael's way of thinking, the fact that Larkin was a naturalized citizen made treason even more heinous, because he wasn't a citizen by accident of birth, he'd actively chosen to become one, he'd sworn an oath to the country.

Larkin went into the bathroom, where, thankfully, Cael couldn't see him, though the earbuds did pick up the sounds of teeth being brushed and the toilet being flushed. He came out of the bathroom and went into the closet, where he changed clothes and emerged wearing gray silk pajamas that shimmered in the lamplight. Then he got into bed and turned out the lamp, plunging the room into darkness.

When all had been silent for a few minutes, Cael removed the earbuds. Any sound would be recorded, in case something unexpected happened during the night, but so far once Larkin went to bed he stayed there until morning.

Cael turned toward Jenner. "You might as well get some sleep. I have some phone calls to make."

She gave him a look that should have drawn blood. "You think I can sleep in this chair?"

"I gave you a chance to sleep in the bed while I worked," he pointed out. "But, no, you had to jump around the room like a Chihuahua on speed. Up and down, here and there, you weren't still for two minutes. It's your own fault you're cuffed to the chair."

She jerked on the cuff. "So uncuff me now, and I'll go to bed."

She had to be both uncomfortable and tired, but he didn't feel guilty; this was his job, and he'd damn well do whatever needed to be done. That said, he understood why he might not be her favorite person on the planet, which was good. He didn't want her feeling friendly toward him.

On the other hand, he didn't want to completely alienate her, either. There wasn't much he could actually tell her, but he could offer her some reassurance. "Look, I'm doing my best to make this as easy for you as possible, but you keep getting in my face. Your friend is fine, she'll continue to be fine as long as things go okay, and when you get back to San Diego you'll"—he lifted his hand in a dismissive gesture— "go out to lunch, pick out some new diamonds, get your nails done—whatever it is you do to recover from a slightly upsetting experience."

"*Slightly* upsetting?" Her voice wasn't exactly a shriek, but it definitely came close.

"Yes, *slightly*." Now there was an edge to his tone. This job was a walk in the park, even for her. She hadn't been hurt, she had good food, she slept in a real bed at night. She didn't know what rough conditions really were.

She glared at him, with a strength in her gaze, a pure force of will, that he was always surprised to see in her eyes. They were nice eyes, hazel green, smart and sharp. He tried to imagine going through this experience with any of the many other women he'd met on this cruise, but it didn't work. An ordinary woman would probably be too scared to function, and would cry. A lot. Like most men, crying women drove him nuts. Jenner didn't cry. And when she got scared, she got mad. That might not be the most comfortable reaction for him to deal with, but he sure as hell didn't get bored.

Pain in the ass that she was, he'd take Jenner Redwine over any of the other possibilities, any day.

He left her there in the bedroom, handcuffed and pissed, and walked into the parlor. He dialed a number he knew by memory, and when his contact answered, Cael said, "Hilo."

Chapter Twenty-one

They were sitting at a table by the pool. Jenner was so glad to be out of the suite that she had been behaving herself, even when Cael put his arm around her shoulder as they walked from the elevator out to the pool. She stayed close, as he'd instructed, and didn't do anything to draw attention their way—other than the little bit of attention he wanted. Not that she didn't enjoy giving him a hard time every chance she had, but that was in private. Maybe, after last night, he'd get the idea she wasn't going to give them up to Larkin, or anyone else. She had her doubts Syd was in any real danger, but she didn't know, so she'd play it safe. If Syd wasn't in the equation . . . who knows? Maybe, maybe not.

She still didn't know who was who in the good guy/bad guy field, but Cael's "slimy" comment had given her a solid hint. Could bad guys feel morally superior to good guys? They might feel smarter, tougher, etc., but would the moral aspect even occur to a bad guy?

Then again, she'd heard that the murderers, thieves, and con men in prison really hated the child molesters, so did that mean anything other than that child molesters were the lowest of the low? Could she say that gave a murderer a sense of moral superiority? Again—maybe, maybe not.

What she *was* certain of was that she didn't care for Frank Larkin, and that was a purely personal instinct. Something about him set her Jerry-radar pinging like crazy. She couldn't put her finger on what it was about him, exactly, but one of the first life lessons she'd learned was to listen when her radar sounded the alarm. Maybe she'd caught some tiny flicker of expression that reminded her of dear old dad when he was about to fleece someone out of something, maybe it was that association and nothing else, but as far as she was concerned she'd been officially warned about Larkin.

They sat at the table for a while, watching the sunbathers, the sardines in the pool, and the others who, like them, had opted to sit at one of the umbrellaed tables. A handsome young deckhand with curly blond hair brought them iced tea and towels. His name tag said his name was Matt. As he leaned over to set the glasses of tea on the table, there was something about the way he and Cael looked at each other— a brief glance that nevertheless seemed loaded with meaning—that made Jenner wonder if Matt might be another one of them.

Then again, maybe Matt was gay, and like a lot of other people at the pool he was admiring the available views. A swim-trunk-clad Cael was definitely worth looking at. His olive-toned skin was smoothly tanned, and, hell, was a six-pack ever *not* worth gazing at? The view was the same one she saw at night when they went to bed, and it still made her heart gallop.

After Matt left, Jenner took a sip of her iced tea and said, "Does he work for you?"

"Who?" Cael asked, reaching to the top of his head and

sliding his sunglasses down into place as he squinted at the pool.

"Matt," she said, without explaining who "Matt" was. If a detail like that had slipped by Cael Traylor, then she was a monkey's uncle.

A slow grin spread across his face. "You're paranoid, aren't you?" They were keeping their voices low, but the noise around the pool area was such that they could have used normal speaking voices without worrying about being overheard. A live band was blasting Jimmy Buffett music at the sunbathers, people were shrieking, laughing, chattering. Cael had selected a table as far from the music as he could get, but the noise level was still high.

"I'll take that as a yes," she said, and looked away because his grin was making her stomach do flip-flops. How many days left until they got back to San Diego? They hadn't even made it to Hawaii yet. She didn't know if she could bear up under the pressure of being so close to him, because already she felt as if she were about to jump out of her skin.

She rubbed the back of her neck, felt the sweat. The weather was very warm—or *she* was very warm—so Jenner kicked off her beach thongs and stood. Cael lazily reached out and snagged her wrist. "Where are you going?"

"Swimming." She indicated her swimsuit, a hot pink tank with cut-outs on the sides, then the pool. "Swimsuit, pool— *hello!*" She wished he'd stop touching her. Damn it, evidently even her wrist was an erogenous zone. She just hoped he didn't feel how her pulse was galloping.

"It's too crowded to swim."

That was true, but swimming wasn't her goal; cooling off was. She said as much, though she didn't expect him to relent. To her surprise, he sighed and got to his feet, kicking off his own deck shoes. Taking her hand, he walked with her

257

to the pool's edge. "Are you going to get your hair wet?" he asked.

"Do I look like a woman who won't get her hair wet?" she countered, flipping the choppy ends of her hair, which was barely long enough to cover her ears. "I go snorkeling and parasailing whenever I can."

"Then hold your breath," he said, and stepped off the side of the pool still holding her hand. The pool wasn't a diving pool so it wasn't deep, maybe six feet at the deepest part, but it was still over her head where they were. He tugged on her hand and brought her back to the surface, then wrapped one arm around her to keep her there.

The cool water felt wonderful; his hard, muscled body felt even more so. Jenner took her time wiping the water out of her face, to hide her reaction to the sensation of his wet skin against hers. Muscles and water had to be one of the most potent combinations known to womankind. Had she lost her mind? What in hell had she been thinking? Actually, she hadn't been thinking about being in the pool *with* him, she'd been thinking about getting in the cool water *away* from him. That plan hadn't worked.

"Put your arms on my shoulders," he said, his face so close to hers she could see the individual black eyelashes, clumped together in wet spikes that made the blue of his eyes even more vivid. Automatically, her mind having turned sluggish by his damn pheromones, she did as told, which brought her against him from breast to thigh. Getting in the pool had to be one of the worst ideas she'd ever had, and definitely the one she'd enjoyed the most. She was a fool and a nitwit, to fall in lust with her captor—though, in her view, any woman worthy of the name would be fanning herself at just the sight of him, more rough than pretty, and tough in ways most men would never even consider.

The buoyancy of the water sent her legs sliding against his. Bracing her hands on his tanned shoulders, she tried to find purchase by pressing her feet against the side of the pool, but so many people were jumping in and out that the water was in constant turbulence and kept pushing her against him. The back and forth reminded her almost unbearably of another back and forth, one that had nothing to do with water and everything to do with getting naked.

"This was a bad idea," she said, caving in before things got any worse and she found herself with her legs locked around his waist.

His expression said *I told you so*, though he hadn't, not in so many words. "Ready to get out?" he asked.

"Yeah."

He hoisted himself out of the pool, water sluicing off his body, then he bent down and bodily lifted her out of the water to stand her on the edge of the pool. That careless strength made her stupid stomach tie itself in knots again. She was skinny, yeah, but she wasn't bony skinny, and she actually weighed more than it looked like she did because all of her activities gave her muscle. For him to so easily lift her like that . . . She couldn't look at him; she couldn't bear to. If she did, she might never look away.

They returned to the table and toweled dry, and Jenner used her fingers to arrange her hair. It would dry quickly in the breeze, and the cut deliberately made it look choppy and messy, unless she went to some pains to smooth it down. She gulped down some of the tea, then turned her chair slightly so she was looking more at the ocean than she was at Cael. Sun didn't normally bother her eyes, even living in south Florida, so she often had to remind herself to wear sunglasses. Now was one of those times, and she gratefully seized hers from where she'd tossed them on top of the table. Hiding her eyes was a damn good idea.

They sat there a little while longer, not speaking much. Her swimsuit stopped dripping, and her hair dried enough that it began to lift in the breeze. The gentle motion of the ship began to make her sleepy, and she thought how nice it would be to stretch out on one of those padded deck chairs and take a nap.

"Let's go," Cael said, pushing back his chair and standing.

"Hello, neighbors!" came a cheerful voice, and they looked around to find the two women in the suite across from theirs, Linda and Nyna, smiling at them as they approached. Jenner had spotted them at a distance at the various functions, but they hadn't spoken since the lifeboat drill.

"Hello," she said, smiling back because both of them seemed genuinely nice. They made no pings at all on her Jerry-radar. "Are you enjoying the cruise?"

"Yes, we are," said Linda. "Join us for lunch, and we'll tell you all about it."

"I'd love to," Jenner said quickly, before Cael had a chance to come up with an excuse. The last thing she wanted was to be alone in the suite with him right now. She wanted to give her hormones a stern talking to, as well as a chance to settle down.

He could've begged off and had lunch with his buddy Ryan, but of course he didn't. Cael wasn't going to leave her on her own even with two perfectly harmless older women; Jenner thought *she* had trust issues, but Cael was in a league of his own.

She pulled on the almost-knee-length coverup that made her bathing suit perfectly acceptable for lunch, and stepped into her sequined beach thongs. Cael put on his shirt and buttoned it up. *Thank God.* She could breathe easier now, even though a part of her wished he never put on a shirt. The important thing was to not let him see how he affected her.

Linda and Nyna were having lunch in The Club, one of the casual indoor restaurants. They were shown to a table for four near the center of the room. The two older women seemed to have made acquaintance with almost everyone in the restaurant, because their passage was slowed by people greeting them.

When they were seated, Nyna unfolded her napkin and said, "It's so nice to see you two again. Of course, there's so much to do, and the ship is so large, you might have been roaming the ship from stem to stern and we wouldn't know it." Her smile made it clear that she thought exactly what Cael wanted everyone to think—that they were spending the cruise in her suite, and mostly in bed. That explained away all the hours he spent spying on their *other* neighbor.

"Have you been to the spa?" Linda asked, her question directed at Jenner.

"No, I'm afraid not. I'd planned to, but ..." She shrugged, letting the sentence trail off. Let them draw their own conclusions. "Have you?"

"Twice." Linda grinned. "The masseur is *very* good. You should make an appointment."

"I don't think so," Cael drawled, and both women laughed.

Nyna said, "I prefer the yoga classes. You should join me in the morning. It's a wonderful way to start the day."

"I'd love that," said Jenner, who sincerely could use something, anything, to help ward off cabin fever. Before Cael could come up with a plausible reason why she couldn't, she turned to him and put on her most innocent face. "You should come with me," she invited. "Yoga would be so good for your bad back."

He started to shake his head. "I don't think—"

"You have a bad back?" asked Nyna. "Jenner's right, you know. Yoga does wonders for that. What sort of problems do you have?"

"It's a pain in my lower back," he said, looking at Jenner instead of her. "Very low. And dead center."

Jenner's chin wobbled with the effort it took her not to laugh. She reached out and laid her hand on his arm. "C'mon, give it a try. If it hurts too much, you can always stop. No one will hold a gun on you and force you to do anything you don't want to do." Take *that*, sport, she thought. He could scarcely forbid her to attend the yoga class, not without making it appear that they were in a weird, sick kind of relationship, which wasn't what he wanted. She was giving him what he wanted: the illusion of a relationship. It was fake, but he needed to realize that any relationship, fake or not, came with concessions.

"We'll see," he finally growled.

"Tomorrow, then," Jenner said, turning to smile at Nyna. "What time are the classes?"

"I prefer the six a.m. class, with the sun just coming up. It's wonderful."

When Jenner attended her yoga classes she always took the early ones, too, for just that reason. Cael, however, looked horrified, and all three women laughed at him.

A uniformed waiter took their orders. The two older women ordered the ubiquitous grilled chicken salad with dressing on the side. Jenner chose a BLT and fries. Cael ordered a cheeseburger and fries, but Jenner uttered a quick, horrified, "What?" and once again placed a caring hand on his arm, which she gently patted. "No, he won't have that," she said to the waiter. "He'll have the salad, as well. No dressing, cheese, or croutons. Please bring lemon wedges."

The waiter didn't question her order, and Cael was evidently too stunned to countermand her. She smiled. "Lemon juice makes a wonderful substitute for fatty dressing. Really, Cael, with your cholesterol, you shouldn't eat red meat or fries at all. I don't know what you were thinking."

"Neither do I," he said, his meaning clear to her, if not to the others.

They passed the rest of the meal in relative peace, even if Cael did glance longingly at her BLT and fries—but only once. Linda and Nyna both thought it was hilarious, that love influenced a bruiser like Cael to let himself be bossed around. He ate his salad, and Jenner figured it wasn't the worst sacrifice he'd ever made in the name of getting what he wanted. If she could be a prisoner, he could eat a salad. That didn't even come *close* to evening the scale. But for the first time since stepping aboard the *Silver Mist*, she truly enjoyed a meal. She ate well, and didn't once feel as if she was going to choke. She actually tasted the food on her plate, especially the fries, which she made a subtle production of enjoying.

The meal came to a close and conversation began to morph into comments about what they were about to do, which were meant as a gentle way of parting company. Cael's beautiful manners were still holding up but Jenner could almost feel the tension rolling off him—he was so ready to escape before she did something else to him. Served him right.

As she was placing her napkin on the table, Frank Larkin walked in. She didn't spot him immediately, but she was so attuned to Cael that she felt the abrupt focus of his attention shift and she automatically looked around to see what had gotten his attention.

Most people in the restaurant looked at Larkin, so she

wasn't doing anything unusual. It was the same as if they'd been in Hollywood and Spielberg had walked in. Larkin wasn't a celebrity, but he was a mover and shaker, with access to incredible power over and above what his own monumental fortune gave him. He didn't take a table, but strolled through the restaurant speaking to particular passengers. From what Jenner could tell, he gave his attention to the richest, most powerful men in the place. No women seemed to be worthy. Her radar pinged again as she picked up an almost indiscernible air of contempt about him.

"There's our host," she said, unnecessarily. She turned to Linda and Nyna. "Have you found out anything about him? What does he do? Other than host charity cruises, that is."

Cael got to his feet and reached for Jenner's hand, under the guise of assisting her from her chair. He squeezed her fingers in warning.

"What doesn't he do?" Linda answered. "Politics, finance, all sorts of business. I've been asking questions, and evidently he's one of those behind-the-scenes people in Washington, the ones who can make the president jump."

Well, wasn't that interesting, Jenner mused.

"I forgot to bring my pills with me," Cael said, all but hauling her away from the table. "We have to go back to the stateroom."

"We'll see you in the morning," Jenner called over her shoulder. "Five forty-five!"

When they were well away from the restaurant, Cael grabbed her arm, turned, and backed her against the railing. There was no one close by, no one listening in, which was why he'd chosen this spot to stop. The stiff breeze blew Jenner's hair away from her face, and she lifted her head to catch more of the sensation.

He caged her with his arms, gripping the railing as he

leaned down until his blue eyes were on a level with hers. She met his gaze with a look of total innocence.

"You're a demon, you know that?" he said with feeling. "When your feet hit the floor every morning, I'll bet the devil shudders and says *'Oh shit, she's awake!'*"

She smiled. She didn't doubt that Cael would do whatever needed to be done to meet his objectives, but she no longer believed that he'd hurt her or Syd out of spite, or for revenge. He was still in control, but for a little while, a few precious minutes, she'd taken that control away from him. She'd led the way. Maybe she'd pay for it later, but she'd gotten what she wanted: She had him flustered.

She also knew more about Frank Larkin than she had. Politics and finance, huh? That left the field of possibilities for spying wide open, so she wasn't exactly in the loop yet, but she was catching up.

"Let's go get those pills, honey," she said as she patted Cael's chest and pushed him slightly away from her.

"There aren't enough pills in the world—" he began, but then he stopped and closed his eyes as he shook his head.

She'd done it. She'd shut him up. This was turning out to be a good day, all things considered.

Chapter Twenty-two

Larkin opened the door to his suite, hoping for a respite, some peace and quiet, but instead of blessed silence he was assaulted by an unbearable noise.

Isaac, his private steward, was hard at work and hadn't heard the door open. How could he hear anything with the roar of the damned vacuum cleaner drowning out everything else? Larkin slammed the door; Isaac heard that.

He lifted his head and turned off the vacuum. "Mr. Larkin. I didn't expect you back so soon."

"Obviously," Larkin said as he stepped into the room.

Isaac was about Larkin's age, but he looked a good ten years older. He was too thin, his hair white instead of a distinguished gray, and he had deep wrinkles around his eyes and mouth. He wore years of hard menial labor on his face; his shoulders were stooped, his hands gnarled with arthritis. And yet Larkin was the one in pain, the one who was dying. Where was the fairness in that?

But if he had to die, he'd make sure he wasn't alone. Like everyone else on this fucking ship, Isaac was about to die, too; he just didn't know it yet. The satisfaction of that thought made Larkin feel a little better. Even his headache seemed to ease.

"Get me some aspirin and a glass of water," he said, crossing the room to the sofa and gingerly sitting down. Every movement, every *sound* hurt, but he couldn't let his pain show beyond this room. "I have a headache," he said softly as Isaac disappeared into the bedroom to fetch aspirin from Larkin's Dopp kit in the closet. Through the open door, Larkin noted the made bed and realized that Isaac's chores were almost done. Thank God.

Isaac did as he'd been instructed, as always, quickly delivering two aspirin and a bottle of water.

"Would you like a glass and some ice for the water, Mr. Larkin?"

"No, this will do." Two aspirin wouldn't make a dent in his pain, but he didn't want to rouse even Isaac's suspicions about his physical condition—though it was unlikely Isaac would be alarmed, even if Larkin had demanded the entire bottle. Isaac was not particularly intelligent.

After he'd swallowed the aspirin, Larkin snapped, "Come back later to finish your chores." He didn't need to offer a reason or make an excuse; Isaac simply followed orders, as always. He silently left, taking the damned vacuum cleaner with him.

When he was alone, Larkin went to his Dopp kit and grabbed a small handful of aspirin. He popped them all, washed down with long swallows from the water bottle. At this point, what did it matter if he ended up with an ulcer? Enough aspirin sometimes made the pain fade, and he needed that now. He needed just a few damn minutes with no pain.

Cancer had ruined him.

The sound of a knock on his door shot through him like a

knife in his temple. If Isaac had come back, if he'd returned knowing that Larkin had wanted to be alone . . . he wouldn't live to see the bombs go off.

But it was Dean Mills at the door. Larkin let Dean into the suite, and gently closed the door behind him. A slam would've relieved some of his temper, but the sound . . . he couldn't take the noise.

Dean said, "Sir, a couple of the men have some questions about the getaway after the—"

"We're not going to discuss this," Larkin said sharply. "I have everything organized."

"But—"

"Do you think I'd leave anything to chance?" he snapped.

"No, sir," Dean replied, maintaining his composure as always.

Larkin never left *anying* to chance.

He'd needed assistance in carrying out his plan, and since none of the people he required for help were suicidal, he'd had to concoct a reason for their presence and what they were doing. A handful of security personnel, who had helped him bring the bombs onboard and place them, thought there was going to be a robbery on the high seas, during the return trip to San Diego. They believed they were going to rob all these rich people of their jewels and cash and then escape. The jewels and cash alone wouldn't make such a heist worthwhile, but added to the artwork that was supposed to be auctioned off, it would all add up to millions.

A million wasn't what it had once been, but it was still enough to entice a few morons.

Larkin had assured them that he'd taken care of all the details. They'd take a lifeboat, then be met by a larger boat that would take them all to South America. Once they were well away, the bombs would be detonated, so there would be no one left alive to identify the robbers.

The plan was full of holes, but that didn't matter, because the bombs would be detonated before the planned robbery, not after. So far he'd handled any questions he couldn't answer with an offhand or irritated assurance that he had the matter under control. Who were these idiots to question him? So far, the lure of a big payoff had kept them all satisfied.

There were nine bombs, all carefully placed to take the ship and its passengers to the ocean floor. When the time came, the would-be thieves would arm the bombs. A couple of them, Dean included, thought they had the triggers for those bombs, but in truth, Larkin had the real trigger. He'd choose his own exact moment of death . . . and the deaths of so many of the rich idiots who had either inherited their money or, like the Redwine bitch, won a fucking *lottery*. Stupid fools. None of them had earned their money, worked for it the way he had. They didn't deserve to have it, any of it. They didn't deserve to live.

After all the trouble Jenner had caused him at lunch, Cael didn't think twice about handcuffing her to the chair that afternoon, and she hadn't asked him not to. She knew better. She still looked very pleased with herself, as he retrieved and set up his equipment so he could catch whatever had been digitally captured from Larkin's suite while he and Jenner had been on the deck, lounging around and lunching with their new friends.

"Yoga, my ass," he muttered under his breath.

"What's that?" she asked sweetly. "I didn't hear you."

He didn't respond, but sat down with his equipment.

Larkin had been on deck for a while, so there shouldn't be much catch-up work required. Cael watched Larkin's private steward cleaning, making the bed, vacuuming. Exciting stuff. Then Larkin arrived.

The exchange between Larkin and his steward was telling, personality-wise. Basically, Larkin was a shithead . . . a shithead who was taking a shitload of aspirin. Cael had already noticed that he often cradled his head when he was alone. Was he ill? Or just prone to headaches?

Then Dean Mills came in, and that was much more interesting from Cael's point of view. Getaway? What in hell did Frank Larkin have "in hand"? Other than his own dick, of course. Was Larkin planning on disappearing after the meet in Hilo?

Cael removed the earbud, retrieved the cord for the stateroom phone from his locked briefcase, and reconnected it as he did each time he ordered room service. He dialed, and in a calm voice requested extra shampoo, at the steward's convenience.

"What's going on?" Jenner asked as he removed the cord and once more locked it in his briefcase.

"Nothing," he replied.

"Seriously, you look as if you're worried about something."

He ignored her and went into the parlor, just in time for Bridget's knock on the door and her entrance on the heels of that knock. She carried several miniature bottles of shampoo in her hands.

"I think Larkin is up to something other than the Hilo meeting," he said in a lowered tone. The less Jenner knew, the better.

"Such as?" Bridget went into the bedroom area and Cael followed. She turned left, to go into the bathroom and deposit the shampoo. He glanced at Jenner, who was sitting cuffed and annoyed in her chair, spine straight, expression openly curious. Bridget came out of the bathroom and glanced at Cael, wondering about his silence. He nodded toward Jenner, and a light of understanding came into Bridget's eyes.

Jenner got it, too, and she didn't like it at all. "I'm in this as deeply as either of you," she argued as Cael and Bridget returned to the parlor. "Deeper!" she called after them. "And I didn't have a choice about it, either!"

Bridget grinned, and Cael briefly closed his eyes. He moved farther away from the door and lowered his voice even more. Trust her? That would be like trusting a teenage boy to drive across country the day after getting his license. "Have Sanchez keep an eye on Dean Mills and any other crew members he meets with on a regular basis."

"What did you hear?" Bridget asked.

"Treason may not be the only deal Larkin has going." He told her what he'd heard about the "getaway," and everything else Larkin had said. As he finished, he heard a thump, a scraping sound, then another thump. He froze. Surely not. She wouldn't. Oh, hell, who was he trying to fool? Of course she would.

He turned his head and there she was, clumsily lifting and dragging the heavy chair with her, moving it into the doorway between the two rooms of the suite.

"I saw the expression on your face," she said, sitting down in the chair as if its placement was perfectly normal. "Don't expect me to stay in the dark while you rally the troops." She narrowed her eyes at him. "Do I need to be worried about something or someone other than you? How bad is it?" Looking from him to Bridget and back again, she added, "I've never seen a weapon on any of you, and I think if you'd had them I would have. Do you need help?"

"I don't need *your* help," he said pointedly. "And I don't need a weapon." Though, damn, he'd love to have one right about now.

She snorted. Yeah, he had her intimidated, all right. "So you're telling me if I get out of hand you'll kill me with a paper clip?"

That was actually possible, but he didn't think she needed to know it. "I make do with what's available, when I have to."

Bridget was trying to keep from smiling, and in an effort to deflect the argument she said lightly, "Anything's possible. Samson slew a thousand men with the jawbone of an ass."

"What a coincidence," Jenner exclaimed, then jerked her head in Cael's direction. "We can use his."

Bridget's eyes almost bugged out in her struggle to hold in a laugh. "I'll get word to our man in security," she said, which was way more than she should have said in front of Jenner, and all but tore the door off its hinges in her haste to get out of the room before she exploded.

Cael scrubbed a hand over his face, hiding his own expression. He had to laugh, or he'd kill her. She thought he was worried? Larkin was selling classified stuff to the North Koreans, something else besides that was going on, and in the meantime he had to deal with her. Why should he be worried?

He really didn't like the idea that Jenner could read his expressions so easily that she'd looked at him and immediately realized something was wrong. It wasn't as if he was running around in a panic; he was concerned, but in control. Most people would say he pretty much had a poker face. Unfortunately, she wasn't most people.

"You aren't part of this," he finally said. "So don't make demands. I'll tell you everything you need to know."

"No, you'll tell me what tiny bit you think I need to know, which up until now has been nothing."

She wasn't afraid of him anymore, he realized, and if there had ever been an unwelcome thought, that was it. She was worried for her friend, but the fear was gone. That was a problem, since only fear would truly keep her in line. He didn't think he could seriously threaten her with physical harm, at least not seriously enough to make her believe it, because he'd have to go further than he was willing to take something like that—at least with her. But he did hold the key to her cooperation.

He said coolly, "One more word, and you won't talk to Syd today."

She knew him well enough to see that he wasn't bluffing, and she clamped her lips shut.

Oh, yeah. He was worried.

Chapter Twenty-three

On the morning they reached Hilo, Hawaii, Jenner woke with her nose almost pressed to Cael's chest. They were lying facing each other, one of his legs inserted between hers. Familiarity was a terrible thing; she'd become accustomed to being handcuffed to him while she slept. He still kept the room too cool at night for her, so when she went to sleep she ended up rolling into him, instinctively seeking out his warmth. Several times during the night a movement restricted by the cuffs would wake her, a little; she'd move away from him as much as possible, and when she woke again she was in the same sort of position, all but on top of him.

He didn't seem to mind. Hell, he didn't even stir, though she knew if she tried to go for the key again or smother him with a pillow, he'd be awake and aware in an instant.

In the past couple of days they'd come to an uncomfortable truce. She didn't push for details he refused to share, even though it galled her to be left out of the loop; he continued to let her speak to Syd. Yesterday the conversation had even gone on a few moments longer than usual. She'd had the chance to really hear Syd's voice, and note the lack of fear. They didn't exchange details that might endanger the precious concession their captors had made, but it was clear that Syd was surviving the ordeal as well as Jenner was.

Cael had even gone to yesterday's early-morning yoga class, though he'd made it clear to her that one class was to be the last. Just as well. She'd been looking forward to watching him try to contort himself into knots, and keep his balance at the same time, but she'd been disappointed. As muscled as he was, he still hadn't had a bit of trouble with any of the positions, which made her think he'd done some yoga or tai chi before. He was, however, a definite distraction in a room full of women—a pleasant distraction, but still . . . he threw the entire class out of whack just by being there, and being who he was.

The world was filled with all sorts of men, but damned if she'd run into any quite like this one.

She moved away from him and dozed off again, because it was still dark out, but morning was coming and according to the schedule they would reach Hilo at about seven a.m. When she woke the next time, light was peeking around the heavy curtains and she was once again curled up against Cael's side. There had been a time when she'd have panicked at being so close to him, but not anymore. Unfortunately, she liked it. There was no way in hell she'd ever let him know it, but she liked the dip of the bed where his big body lay, the warmth she got from him, even the way his skin smelled.

This time, she didn't roll away. She couldn't; he'd thrown one heavy arm over her body. Her face was tucked close to his chest, again, and her feet were entwined with his. It was as if her body wanted to be close to him and every time she let her guard down by going to sleep, it automatically moved closer.

He'd kidnapped her, bullied her, scared her. She had no idea what he was up to and he refused to enlighten her; he made it clear day after day that even though she'd done her best to do what he demanded without giving him too much grief—not too much by *her* standards, that is—he didn't trust her. Damn it, that wasn't fair. *She* wasn't the kidnapper here; she wasn't the one who had proven to be untrustworthy.

And yet, she wasn't afraid of him; hadn't been for days. She was wary, as any right-minded person would be in these circumstances, but she wasn't afraid. Did that make her a good judge of character, or a fool who was letting her hoo-ha do her thinking for her?

But she *was* thinking. She was thinking that, no matter how she provoked him—and God knew she'd done her best to really tie him in knots—he hadn't hurt her, and had in fact responded with sharp humor that slipped under her guard. The "slimy" comment about Larkin, coupled with the "treason" she'd overheard, made her think Cael was one of the good guys. His hat might not be white, but it definitely wasn't black. Gray, maybe. She could handle gray.

When she realized that Cael was waking up, she crept out from under his arm and turned her back to him, as best she could considering her restraints. She had to pull on his arm, which completely woke him up, and in a matter of minutes he was unlocking the cuffs, and their day was under way.

Less than an hour later she was standing at the railing on the private balcony, sipping coffee on a gorgeous morning, as they neared Hilo. She could allow herself a moment to relish the illusion of being alone, even though Bridget was on the other side of the door, keeping an eye on her while Cael showered. Jenner was tired of telling them that she had no intention of causing them any trouble. Well, no serious trouble. When she knew that Syd was safe, she'd do her best to cause them all kinds of grief.

No matter what their intentions, no matter what Larkin might've done, they'd kidnapped her and Syd, and she couldn't just let that go. It wasn't in her nature to take a beating, figuratively or literally, and slink away. She wouldn't go to the authorities, but she'd do *something*. She just had to figure out what.

For now, though, she enjoyed the moment. If she was in another situation, she'd get lost in the magnificent view before her: the water, the lush green of the island, the crisp blue sky and puffy white clouds. She made a point of taking it all in, because once she got off the *Silver Mist* she was finished with sea travel. If she ever returned to Hawaii, she'd be admiring the view on approach from the window seat of an airplane.

Her illusion of privacy was interrupted when the door behind her opened. She turned as Cael stepped out to join her. She almost smiled. He wore khaki pants and a traditional Hawaiian shirt, loose fitting and brightly colored. The outfit was a far cry from his usual silk shirts and exquisitely tailored pants, but he looked perfectly comfortable, and of course the whole point was for him to look like every other tourist. To her he didn't look anything of the sort, but then she knew him.

She wondered if she'd even be considering that he was more than he claimed to be if he didn't look this way. If he was short and scrawny and ugly, would it even cross her mind that he might be one of the good guys? That there might be a reason for his behavior? She didn't want to be so shallow that her hormones affected her judgment, but what red-blooded woman wouldn't look at Cael Traylor and fantasize just a little bit.

"Get a quick shower and get dressed," he said bluntly. "You have thirty minutes. We're going ashore."

"Why you silver-tongued devil," she said. "What an invitation."

"It isn't an invitation, it's an order. You're a part of the costume."

Oh, yeah? She was on the same level with his atrocious flowered shirt?

As she went past him he caught her hand, forcing her to stop and look up at him.

His expression was deadly serious when he added, "And today you *will* be on your best behavior."

They followed Larkin in shifts, he and Jenner, Faith and Ryan, and Matt—who'd sneaked off the boat wearing a pair of baggy shorts and a T-shirt, a dark wig, and sunglasses, as well as a large well-worn backpack—trailing for a while then breaking off when another team had him in sight. All they knew was that Larkin had a meeting set for Hilo, their first stop in the islands. They didn't know where or when, but as Larkin had been one of the first passengers to disembark, maybe they'd get lucky and the meeting would take place soon.

The man they were following might not think twice about catching a glimpse of a few of his fellow passengers while he was out and about, but if that went on for too long and he continued to see the same people again and again he'd get suspicious, and might even call off the meeting. If that happened they were back to square one, so they were careful to stay out of sight as much as possible, even though they were swapping out the lead in following him.

Tiffany, who'd spent so much time near Larkin in the past

few days that he probably would think twice if he caught sight of her in his orbit on the island, was staying aboard the ship. Bridget would keep an eye on the suite, as usual. Sanchez remained on board, as well, but Cael didn't trust the hired man the way he trusted his own people. The rest of the team followed Larkin, communicating through a state-of-the-art system that was all but invisible, the components were so small.

Larkin usually had a bodyguard with him wherever he went, but this morning, when his rented car dropped him off on a street corner, he'd continued on alone, walking briskly, taking quick, frequent glances over his shoulder. Cael and Jenner, who'd been in a cab close behind Larkin, notified Matt—the least recognizable of the group in his disguise—of the subject's whereabouts, and had watched from a distance until Matt informed them that he had Larkin in his sights. For two hours this had continued, the three teams leapfrogging, keeping Larkin in view, until Cael found himself, with Jenner on his arm, at the colorful and crowded farmer's market.

Larkin weaved in and out of the crowd, stopping now and then to admire flowers, exotic fruits, and even exchange a word or two with the locals who had set up shop to sell their wares. He even stopped at a table of homemade preserves and nuts, spent several minutes admiring the offerings, and eventually made a purchase. Cael carefully watched the exchange, wondering if this was it, but he saw no exchange other than cash for what looked to be a jar of jelly.

Thank goodness the market was bursting at the seams with people. Cael had no trouble keeping a buffer of several customers between him and Larkin. A gray-haired man in a dark suit was easy to spot in the marketplace, which was teeming with casually dressed locals and tourists. It struck

Cael that it was a stupid mistake on Larkin's part, to dress in a way that made him stand out in a crowd. Either he didn't care, or he thought he was smarter than everyone else and would spot anyone trying to follow him.

Maybe Larkin wore the suit because he needed the jacket to hide a weapon. Cael and his people hadn't been able to get weapons on the ship, hadn't thought they'd need them for surveillance, but security personnel had weapons—not many, but a few—and Larkin had connections with security through Dean Mills. While they hadn't seen him with a weapon in his possession, there had been moments when he'd been momentarily out of their sight, so it was possible. And since it was possible, Cael preferred to proceed as if Larkin was armed, especially when he and his people were not.

Cael would much prefer to do this job without Jenner in the mix, but if Larkin caught sight of him, it would be best if she were with him. They'd been inseparable since day one, a couple everyone was accustomed to seeing together. And considering where they were at the moment, he was doubly glad to have Jenner beside him. Bringing a woman to the market made perfect sense, but alone . . . alone he would stand out as much as Larkin did.

Eventually, Larkin moved through the length of the market and into open air. Cael remained beneath the cover of the tarp that shaded and sheltered the market, and spoke to Matt, who would be more easily able to move close without calling attention to himself. The kid had already changed clothes—and wigs—a couple of times, and now had longish light brown hair, jeans, and a shirt much like the one Cael wore. The backpack was slung over one shoulder, and in that backpack were the shirts and wigs—as well as the equipment they'd need to hear Larkin's conversations from a distance. A flip of a switch, and the sound of any conversation could be amplified and recorded. Matt had designed the system himself.

Beyond Matt, Ryan and Faith were playing tourist. Faith shielded herself behind other people and wielded her digital camera like any enthusiastic visitor, taking pictures of the market, the people—and Larkin, especially as he crossed the street and neared an Asian man who waited beneath a banyan tree. The waiting North Korean, if the information Cael had collected thus far was correct, was obviously annoyed and anxious.

The North Korean was also wearing a suit. Did that mean he, too, was armed? Wouldn't it be a lucky break if these two shot each other? Yeah, he should be so lucky.

Cael took Jenner's arm and guided her to a position behind a tall display of birds of paradise, among other brightly colored flowers. She'd been oddly cooperative and blessedly silent today, but then he'd warned her, as they'd left the ship, that compliance today was mandatory. If she felt compelled to needle him, it would have to wait until tonight.

He put a hand to his ear, the ear containing the earbud that gave him access to the rest of the team, and listened. Matt repeated what he heard, though they'd have clearer, more complete audio on the digital recording in his backpack.

"Kwan," Matt said.

Okay, they had a name now.

On the opposite side of the street, Faith snapped pictures and laughed. It looked as if the colorful market was her subject, but she was in the perfect position to capture the North Korean's face. Kwan was likely a false name, but it would do, for now.

"Right to business," said Matt. He'd adopted a slightly loopy persona, and to anyone watching, it looked as if the long-haired man was singing to himself. He even swayed in time to imaginary music. People in the park actually walked out of their way to avoid getting too close to him. "Kwan is pissed. He's been waiting. Larkin just handed him something small. I can't make out what it is."

If Faith had gotten a picture from the right angle, maybe they could enlarge the photo and identify whatever had been passed between the two men: a flash drive or microchip, maybe. This could be it, not just a meeting but an actual passing of technology. Why like this? Why not transfer the designs, or whatever information was changing hands, electronically? No money had exchanged hands; Kwan wasn't standing there with a duffle bag filled with cash, so it was likely Larkin's payment, at least, had been electronic.

Matt supplied the answer, keeping the team up to date on the exchange. "Seems Kwan is annoyed that the information had to be passed this way, but the weapon's designer is apparently old school, and didn't want his plans sent out over the Internet. Untrustworthy bastard, but lucky for us. Maybe he's met Faith," Matt teased.

Kwan dropped whatever Larkin had handed over into his jacket pocket, then patted it, to make sure it was well seated.

"Kwan wants to know if it's complete," Matt continued. "Larkin says no. Three months, maybe six if there are delays, and the prototype will be ready. The design he's been given is a good-faith exchange. Any decent scientist should be able to complete . . . Jesus Christ," Matt's voice sobered and dropped a level. "EMP? Did he say EMP?"

For a second, everything went still. Faith's smile faded. Ryan went very still. Cael didn't breathe. And then they all continued on as if they hadn't heard the words.

It was Kwan who turned away first. Larkin watched, seeming amused, before he headed for the street, a small brown bag containing his market purchase swinging casually in one hand.

"Ryan, you two follow Kwan while I call this in," Cael ordered, keeping his voice low. "Matt, make sure Larkin is headed back to the boat, then get busy. I want the surveillance tapes ready when I get back."

Since they'd started tailing Larkin, Cael and the others had been keeping a sharp eye out for Mills, or one of the other security guards. It was unlike Larkin to go out alone, unlike him not to have some sort of backup. Then again, it was likely that none of his people knew Larkin was a traitor. Who in their right minds would think an electromagnetic pulse weapon in the hands of the North Koreans was a good idea?

So what had Larkin and Mills been talking about the other night? If Mills wasn't in on the EMP deal, what sort of plans did the two of them have?

The job done, for now, Cael looked down at Jenner. He was surprised to find that she was watching Larkin as intently as he had been. She hadn't been able to hear Matt, but she had apparently been paying attention. Her eyes narrowed, and when she realized that he was watching her, she looked up and asked, "What the hell is he up to?"

Jenner wasn't stupid. In her thirty years she'd been up, she'd been down, but she had *never* been stupid. Larkin was into something dirty. She wasn't ready to accept without question that Cael and his people were the good guys; they had, after all, kidnapped her and Syd and they hadn't exactly been nice about it. She'd been handcuffed, ordered around, and manhandled.

But she hadn't been hurt; chafed wrists didn't count. And

283

she'd been watching Cael, seen the split second of shock in his expression as he listened to the deck boy's running commentary. Then his gaze had hardened, and all she could think was that she was very, very glad she wasn't Larkin.

She hadn't entirely discounted the possibility that she wasn't caught between the bad guys and the good guys at all, but had gotten herself into a situation with bad guys and badder guys. On the other hand, she was leaning heavily toward coming down on Cael's side. He wasn't having clandestine meetings with North Koreans—yes, she'd heard one of the others mention that, and as far as she could tell he and the entire group were merely watching.

"Are you going to tell me what's going on, here?" she asked, trying for what seemed like the umpteenth time. Sooner or later she'd wear him down.

"No."

"I could make a scene here and now," she said softly. "Scream, cry, run like hell."

"Remember your friend," Cael said, and while she was beginning to think he was on the right side of things, as right as was possible given the situation, she was also aware that he was capable of doing anything to get his way.

That didn't stop her from challenging him, pushing him. How else could she find out what she wanted to know? "I don't think you'd have Syd hurt. Threatened, yes. Scared, absolutely. But not hurt."

"Are you willing to test that theory?" He leaned closer. "Are you willing to lose your phone privileges?"

"No." If she was learning him, he was also learning her. He didn't think she'd balk if he cut off her calls to Syd. He probably didn't really need her any longer, she thought. Their so-called relationship was firmly established in the minds of more than a few people. He could keep her completely confined to the suite, and no one would know any better.

Understanding didn't make her feel any better about the situation. He knew the calls were important to her, so he'd taken to using them as a threat, like she was a rebellious teenager. Phone privileges!

He put a hand to his ear, his attention diverted. "Copy," he said, not for the first time that day, and then he returned his attention to Jenner. "Larkin is headed back to the ship."

"You mean the field trip's over? Hip hip hooray."

"I have to make a call first." Cael took her arm and steered her away from the crowd. They walked at a fast clip to a nearby park. As they walked, Cael pulled a cell phone from his pocket and punched in the number. He stopped, silently ordered her to stay put, and walked away from her, just far enough so she couldn't hear.

While she could've made a pest of herself and followed him—what the hell was he going to do in a place so public?— she didn't. She let him have his space, and enjoyed a moment of her own.

Think, think. She hadn't been entirely clearheaded lately, and why should she be? Her life had been turned upside down, all because she'd had the misfortune to be reassigned to the suite next to Larkin's. First of all, she hadn't been hurt. Second, she could see for herself that Larkin wasn't who he pretended to be, not entirely. And third, Larkin had just had a quick, clandestine meeting with an Asian man who didn't exactly look like a Boy Scout. She'd take Cael over either of those two, any day. *The devil you know . . .*

Cael ended his call, faced her knowing that she hadn't moved, that she'd remained exactly where he'd left her. Her compliance, these past couple of days, had made him less vigilant. No, he was always vigilant; he never relaxed, but he was beginning to take her compliance for granted.

"So," she said as he neared, "what would you have done if Linda Vale and Nyna Phillips had been assigned to my suite?"

"I'd have improvised."

"Do you improvise often in your line of work?"

"More often than I'd like."

"Would you have slept with them?"

A quick grin flashed across his face. "I like them, but I'm not that dedicated."

"Tell me what's going on. I'll try to help."

"No."

At least he was being honest with her. She might not like the answer, but she knew he wasn't feeding her a line of bull.

They walked back toward the market. "I talked to my people in San Diego this morning," Cael said. "While you were in the shower." For a moment Jenner thought he was going to threaten Syd's safety again, and she stiffened, slightly. She was getting damned tired of that. But he said, "Adam complained that, for entertainment, Ms. Hazlett has taken to dressing the others like Barbie dolls."

Her heart leapt, as he gave her another name, another piece of the puzzle. Of course, Syd likely knew the name Adam, so it wasn't exactly earth-shattering information. For all she knew it wasn't even the man's real name. Still, the anecdote was priceless to her. "Female guards, I hope."

"God, so do I."

She could definitely see Syd dragging out her gowns and cocktail dresses and choosing the best ones for someone else. Whenever they shopped together, Syd was always thrilled to find something that was just right for Jenner. Knowing that she was doing the same sort of thing now, even if the subjects of her attentions were kidnappers holding her an unwilling hostage, made Jenner feel so much better that happy tears stung her eyes. Syd was still Syd. She turned her head so Cael wouldn't see her emotional response. "Thank you," she said when she was certain she could speak without a telling waver in her voice.

"You're welcome."

Damn it, she wasn't supposed to like him, but when he took her arm again, she was glad of the touch.

When he returned to the ship, in the privacy of his suite, Larkin sat at the dining table in the parlor, the plate he had requested sitting in front of him. The fine china was almost entirely covered with thick slices of fresh baked bread. The smell was heavenly, awakening a remnant of a pleasant memory from his childhood. A silver spoon sat in the short, squat jar of pineapple and apricot preserves he'd purchased in the farmer's market.

For years, he'd been careful of his diet. Yes, he drank, and he'd tried recreational drugs a few times, but he prided himself on keeping fit. He worked out at an exclusive gym, and ate a rigorously low-carb diet. No bread. No preserves. No desserts. All for nothing.

He'd been indulging himself lately—hell, why not?—but nothing tasted as good as he thought it should. Some days he didn't want to eat at all. When the jar of preserves in the farmer's market had caught his eye all of a sudden he knew that was exactly what he wanted. There were plenty of jams and jellies to be had aboard the *Silver Mist*, but they were ordinary. The thought of them didn't appeal to him in any way, but the pineapple-apricot preserves were different. They were exotic, freshly made, a gourmet treat.

He was about to dip into the jar with the knife when a chilling thought occurred to him, freezing him in place. What if the preserves were poisoned? He felt as if people were watching him, all the time. Soon it wouldn't matter, but right now, having his plans go on without a hitch mattered to him more than anything else. He wanted to go out on his own terms, not someone else's. He didn't want to die writhing in pain, his insides torn apart by poison. No, when he went he'd be so close to a bomb he wouldn't even have time for a last thought, much less experience pain.

The old woman in the market might've seen him coming, and put this appealing jar of preserves right where it would catch his eye. Or else she'd swapped it for a special jar as she'd bagged his purchase, using sleight of hand. Who knew what these people were capable of? She hadn't looked Hawaiian, she'd looked more Oriental. What if she'd been a plant by that fucking Kwan?

Or maybe she was a serial killer, indiscriminately taking out tourists with her island charm and innocent-looking wares. Maybe all the pretty goodies on her table included some sort of exotic island poison?

He jumped out of his chair and stalked to the door, opening it on the guard he had posted there upon his return from Hilo. From here on out, he wanted one of his most trusted men with him at all times. He wasn't taking any chances.

"Tucker," he said, "get in here." Dean was also in the corridor, and the presence of his head of security annoyed him. Had the two men been talking about him? Did they plan something worse than poison for him? "You, too, Mills."

When the security guards entered the room, with Dean closing the door behind them, Larkin pasted a smile on his face. "You have to try this," he said in a friendly tone, Tucker the object of his attention. Dean stood back and watched with narrowed eyes, as he often did. "It's so delicious, I had to share with someone." He picked up a piece of soft, warm bread, and slathered on a thick helping of the preserves before handing it to the unsuspecting man.

"Thanks, Mr. Larkin, but I'm not hungry," Tucker said, suspicious at the unexpected overture and handling the slice of bread as if it were a hand grenade.

"But it's so good." He moved the offering closer. A slick layer of sweat sheened his grayish skin. "Try it."

"No, really, I'm—"

"Try it!" Larkin screamed, thrusting the bread at the startled man.

Tucker glanced back at his boss, and Dean responded with a subtle nod of his head. At that, Tucker accepted the bread and immediately took a large bite. He chewed, swallowed, commented on how good it tasted, and then took another bite—knowing that was what his employer required, but looking as if he really did enjoy the tastes. He finished every bit of the bread, while Larkin watched him closely, waiting for some sign that the preserves had been poisoned.

Tucker, unaware that he was supposed to have been poisoned, seemed fine. He wasn't at all bothered by what he'd eaten. Larkin talked for several minutes, about everything, about nothing, waiting for Tucker to fall to the floor and start slobbering, or writhe in pain. Nothing happened. Larkin asked questions about passengers and events, asked if Tucker had noticed anyone out of the ordinary watching him, but he barely paid attention to the man's answers.

When he was certain Tucker was unaffected, Larkin abruptly ordered, "Get out," and sat at the table once more. "You stay," he said to Dean, and his own personal bulldog obeyed, as he always did.

After Tucker closed the door, Larkin slathered preserves on another piece of bread and took a big bite, no longer worried about poisoning. He waited for a burst of fruity flavor on his tongue, but instead he tasted nothing but sugar. The preserves were too sweet, and the bread had an unpleasant yeasty taste. He took another bite, but it was as annoyingly disagreeable as the first.

He dropped the bread onto the plate, disappointed and angry. He'd rather have a Ghostwater, and he would before the night was done, but even that pleasure had to be tempered. He couldn't drink too much, because drunks talked. Too many drinks and he might let his facade slip and tell the people around him what he really thought of them, the stupid bastards. He might even tell them what he had planned.

That didn't leave many pleasures to enjoy in the few days that remained. Tiffany Marsters had tried flirting with him, soon after her break with Traylor, but she was too loud and ballsy. Even if he were was still capable of screwing her, he'd have thought twice about getting involved with someone like her. He preferred women who knew who was boss, and it sure as hell wasn't her.

"Mr. Larkin, is everything all right?"

Larkin's head snapped up. He'd forgotten that Dean was still in the room. "Do you want it?" he asked, pushing the plate away with contempt.

"No, sir. Thank you."

"It's not poisoned," Larkin assured him.

Dean was always calm and unruffled, but for some reason he looked startled. "I hope not," he said. Would he be this calm in his last moments of life? Larkin wondered. Or would Dean dissolve into pure, unadulterated panic?

The only pleasure Larkin had left was picturing the

deaths of all those around him. In a way, it was too bad he wouldn't survive long enough to see it all come to pass. But he could imagine it, and sometimes the images were so real he felt as if he could touch them.

He hurt so badly some days, he didn't know how he could wait days for the end of his life. He had to wait, though; setting off the bombs while they were in port would seriously increase the number of survivors. When the ship went down, the few passengers who survived the blasts would find themselves literally in the middle of a massive ocean, wounded and in a panic, in complete darkness except for the light from the flames on the burning ship, until what remained of the ship sank and they were left floating on bits of debris in a black night unlike any they could imagine.

He wanted them all dead. He wanted the world to remember Frank Larkin, and how he took all these stupid sheep to the bottom of the ocean.

With luck, even the survivors wouldn't survive for long.

Chapter Twenty-four

"Where are you taking me?" Jenner was nearly at a jog, trying to keep up with Cael as he moved at a fast pace down the long, deserted passageway. He held her hand, which would look better than the usual iron grip on her arm if they ran into anyone. So far, they hadn't.

When he realized that she was struggling to keep up, he shortened his stride—only a little, but enough to give her a break. "I have things to do this afternoon. You're going to stay with Faith for a while."

"You mean she's going to *sit* with me." As in, babysit. She didn't like it at all.

While she was more than ready for a break from Cael Traylor, she didn't know Faith. She knew the facade, but likely Faith was, like Cael, two people: one public persona, one private. The public woman was classy, serene, quiet, and seemingly thoughtful. What was the private Faith like? She was about to find out.

Cael knocked, the door opened, and they were ushered in. The first thing Jenner noticed was that Faith was not alone. Tiffany was also there, sitting on a blue sofa, long legs

292

crossed, eyes all but shooting daggers. Both women were dressed casually, as Jenner was. Their outfits were expensive and classically cut, even Tiffany's colorful sundress.

Remembering what Syd had said about the suite she'd chosen for them—lots of blues and two bedrooms—Jenner wondered if this was the one she and Syd would have been staying in if everything hadn't gone bat-shit crazy. For all she knew, there were a hundred staterooms just like this one, but she doubted it, because she was pretty sure she remembered Syd saying the suites were individually decorated.

"Two hours," Cael said simply, and then he left Jenner alone with the women, who stared at her as if she were a bug under a microscope.

She didn't like being in this position, and her back went up. "What, you've never seen a blackmailed, threatened, *extremely* cooperative prisoner up close before?"

Tiffany laughed; it was an honest laugh, a little throaty, not at all like the shrill laugh she affected in public.

Faith kept her composure. "We're just doing our jobs. Would you like something to drink?"

"No, thank you."

"Sit down, then, and make yourself comfortable."

So far, the private Faith was very much like the public one. Jenner was anxious to see how long that would last. She chose a chair in the seating area that put her back to the wall. "Are you always so polite to the people you kidnap?"

The two women looked at each other with meaningful and silent communication, and Jenner felt like an interloper. An unwilling interloper, but still . . . these women, this team, were close. She was the outsider, but damn it, she hadn't asked to be here.

It was Tiffany who said, "This is a first, for us. Kidnapping isn't exactly SOP."

"But you're all willing to do whatever has to be done to get what you want."

"Yes," Faith responded, calmly but with certainty. "You'd do well to remember that until this is all over and done with. Are you sure you wouldn't like some tea?"

Jenner looked from one woman to the other, and made herself remember that, like Cael, they were professionals. And dedicated, to whatever it was they were doing. She suspected either one of them could put a very quick stop to any resistance she might offer, which she wasn't going to do. She didn't want to lose her phone privileges.

She leaned back a little, relaxed. "Actually, I'd love a cup of hot tea."

Faith smiled, like any other pleasant hostess. "Of course. Tiffany?"

"Why not? Maybe we could get some little cucumber sandwiches, too?" she added with a slightly evil grin.

Tiffany was one of those women who oozed sexuality. She was gorgeous, built, exotic, and the way she moved was unconsciously sensuous. Sitting there, watching her, Jenner couldn't help but wonder if Cael and Tiffany had ever been . . . no, she didn't want to go there. She felt the heat of a blush in her cheeks. As if she cared who Cael slept with! Well, he slept with her these days, in the very literal sense, but it wasn't exactly *sleeping* she had on her mind when she wondered about him and Tiffany.

Faith ordered room service: hot tea, along with fruit and an assortment of pastries. Then she added that her guest would love some cucumber sandwiches, and while they weren't on the menu, she'd be grateful if that was possible.

When Faith hung up, Tiffany said, "You should've requested the cute blond delivery boy."

Faith wasn't smiling when she responded, "If Matt is

working delivery this afternoon, he'll keep an ear out for our suite numbers. For all we know, he's on deck."

"Poor guy, he and Bridget drew the short straws on this one." Tiffany studied her long nails. "Crew quarters aren't nearly as nice as the suites, and they have roommates to deal with. Of course, the seventy-five-cent beer at the crew bar makes up for a few of the inconveniences, but Matt has to store any gear he doesn't want nosy roommates going through in your suite or mine, and I think he and Bridget both have to shower with their cell phones."

"Tiffany," Faith said in a censuring tone, glancing pointedly at Jenner.

"It's not like she's totally in the dark," Tiffany said, and turned to look directly at Jenner. "You've been a real trooper, Redwine."

As if she'd had any choice! Jenner calmly met her gaze. "Kiss my ass."

There was a burst of laughter from both women, and as it died away Tiffany added, "Shit. I like her."

Cael listened again to the recordings from the afternoon's short meeting between Kwan and Larkin, his skin crawling as he heard EMP from the North Korean's lips. He'd talked to his government contacts several times, by secure cell. It hadn't taken the agents on the island any time at all to take over following Kwan, relieving Faith and Ryan so they could return to the ship and take up their duties here. The agents on-island would be moving in on Kwan that very night; he remained under surveillance, and as soon as the right people were in place he'd be in custody.

Though they'd located one contact, the job wasn't over. Until they discovered who the traitor on the other end of the deal was there was a possibility of another sale, another transfer of information. One of Faith's photos had identified the object being passed from Larkin to Kwan as a flash drive; it was possible that the FBI would be able to track its origins, but if not, their only lead was Frank Larkin.

Knowing exactly what Larkin was doing, Cael felt a new and bone-deep contempt for the man he was surveilling. An advanced EMP weapon in the wrong hands would be a nightmare for the entire world. He didn't know a lot about electromagnetic pulse, just that it played havoc with electronics. The modern world operated by computers. Develop an effective way of stopping those computers, and all hell would break loose. An EMP wasn't a people killer— unless those people happened to be in airplanes that were suddenly uncontrollable because all their circuits had been fried—but that kind of technology sure as hell wasn't something he wanted in the hands of a rogue nation.

Cael also mentioned to his contact in D.C. that he suspected Larkin had something else, possibly crooked, in the works. There wasn't any proof, just an odd line of overheard dialogue and a niggling feeling that something wasn't quite right.

"Keep him under surveillance," said his contact. "You need to in any case, until we know who's selling the technology. If you come up with anything concrete, pass it on and I'll get the information to the right people."

A little less than two hours after he'd dropped Jenner off, Cael knocked on Faith and Ryan's suite door, ready to collect his albatross. Before the door opened, he heard a burst of laughter that made his skin crawl. *That* wasn't right. What had the little witch done now?

Faith opened the door and he quickly stepped inside, his gaze zeroing in on Jenner. He just felt safer when he knew exactly where she was and what she was doing. At the moment, she and Tiffany were sitting side by side on the sofa, laughing together. They turned their heads his way; Jenner's smile faded quickly. There was something in her eyes . . .

He ignored it, though every instinct in him went on alert. "Ryan's not back yet?"

"No," answered Faith. "After golf, he and Captain Lamberti were having drinks. He should be here soon."

He nodded toward the sofa. "What's going on with those two?"

Faith's smile was both wry and amused. "Apparently, they have a lot in common."

God in Heaven. Cael couldn't keep the horror out of his expression. Every man on the ship should feel his testicles drawing up in fear. He knew his had.

Jenner stood and came to him, without being prompted. Despite what his testicles were doing, he liked that. He liked watching her approach, he liked the sense of all his systems going on alert.

"It's time to call Syd," she said.

He checked his wristwatch. Actually, the time was already a little later than she'd been calling.

"I don't want to be late calling, she might worry."

"Heaven forbid the hostage should be inconvenienced."

She sniffed. He hadn't gotten to her at all with that comment. "And after that, what's the plan for the evening? Dinner? A show? Karaoke?"

"*No* karaoke," he said decisively.

"I second that," Tiffany said. "Trust me, Cael's singing isn't a good thing."

He slanted a cool, warning look at her over Jenner's shoulder, for all the good it did. Tiff just waggled a hand in his direction. "Really, boss, you should show her a good time. I hear she did good today."

"She didn't have any choice." But she had. There was cooperation, and then there was doing *exactly* what he'd needed her to do. Jenner had hit the bull's-eye today.

"A local guitarist is performing tonight," said Faith. "He's supposed to be marvelous. Ryan and I will be there."

"I will be, too," Tiffany said.

"Then there's no reason for us to go, if everyone else will be there to keep an eye on Larkin."

Jenner made a derisive sound. "I'm *really* looking forward to another evening of being handcuffed to the chair while he putzes around on his laptop. Isn't that what every woman dreams of when she books a cruise?"

A smile wreathed Tiffany's face. *Uh oh*, Cael thought. She got to her feet. "I have an idea. Cael, you can stay in the suite and work, while Jenner and I make the rounds above decks."

"No way in hell," he responded without hesitation.

"I can keep her in line," Tiffany said, and he had to admit, it was true. A linebacker would have a tough time getting past her. Jenner wouldn't have a chance.

Still . . . "Considering your reputation and the scenario we set up, you don't think it would look a bit odd if you two suddenly become friends?"

Tiffany flipped her hair back. "I've been drinking a lot less in the past couple of days. A sober apology, a little girl-to-girl commiseration about a certain low-down man, and bingo, we're instant BFFs."

That sounded like a description of hell.

He looked down at Jenner, who wore a smug half smile. She knew damn well he wasn't going to let her and Tiffany loose on an innocent population. He could keep her locked in the suite, but he wasn't going to do that, either. He sighed and gave in, except—

"No karaoke."

Dean Mills watched Larkin from a distance as his employer made his way through a crowded bar. It was a little early in the day for one of those damn Ghostwaters, but Larkin was already sipping on one as he made his rounds. Larkin had always been twisted and unpredictable, but in public he'd put on a smooth, sophisticated act that had fooled a lot of very smart people. He wasn't doing that now, but he should have been. Instead, he seemed to be falling apart, day by day, hour by hour.

Dean understood why he and the others had agreed to participate in the robbery, which would take place in just a few days while they were at sea, but what did Larkin have to gain? He said he was having financial problems—wasn't everyone?—but to a man in Larkin's position that was dealt with by taking out loans, adjusting investments and financial deals, and selling a big-ass house or two. True, he might get some satisfaction in taking from these people he despised, but it seemed that he would lose more than he'd gain, with the plan as it stood. Larkin said he had mounting debts and wanted to get away from it all, that people would think he was dead if the ship went down, but with so many cell phones, laptops, and a large crew with the latest in communications equipment, it seemed logical to assume that someone might get the names of those involved out before the bombs exploded.

Maybe there was a detail or two Larkin wasn't sharing, a separate plan of some sort. That would be just like the bastard.

The episode with Tucker and the bread earlier in the day had set Dean's teeth on edge, and he hadn't been able to dismiss the image of Larkin shaking a piece of bread in Tucker's face and demanding that he take a bite. Obviously Larkin had suspected the food was poisoned, which didn't make any sense at all.

One's partners in crime should be rational. A raving lunatic on the team wouldn't increase their chances of pulling off the job and getting away clean—if you could call burning and sinking a ship, and killing a shitload of rich people, "clean."

What Dean wanted was simple: He wanted the money. He was tired of taking orders from bastards like Larkin. The money he would get from this haul would set him up in a South American country for life.

Larkin's recent behavior made him uneasy, but it was too late to alter the plan. The bombs were in place; the trigger mechanisms were in good hands. But damn, he'd be relieved when it was over and he was sailing away from this fucking death trap.

When they returned to the suite, Jenner was surprised to see a man still posted at Frank Larkin's door. Great. Usually there was no one in the hallways, but now it looked as if someone would always be aware of their comings and goings. She didn't like it, and she imagined Cael liked it even less.

Entering, they found Bridget there, neatly laying evening clothes on the bed: his tux, her strapless black dress, which meant either Faith or Tiffany had already been on the phone to alert her to the plans for the evening.

Hours later, they were on deck, the evening breeze refreshingly cool, Cael's grip light on her arm as if he no longer felt the need to physically hold her in place. Jenner found herself relaxing as she listened to the guitarist perform a haunting version of a classical tune she couldn't name. Song followed song, some upbeat, some breathtaking in the intricate work required on the strings, another more melodic. Despite years in Palm Beach, she didn't know much about classical music, because she avoided symphonies. Give her a Bon Jovi test and she'd ace it every time. Ask her if the tune currently being played had been written by Bach or Beethoven or some other long-dead dude, and she'd fail miserably.

But she liked it. The entire moment was magical. The music, the breeze, the man on her arm. Though she could never admit it to Cael, or anyone else, he was an important part of the package that made this moment special.

The guitarist sat on a chair that had been placed on a small, raised dais, and listeners sat in neatly arranged chairs near the stage, or milled about. She and Cael stood near the back of the crowd, letting the notes drift to them. It was a formal evening for most: tuxes and evening gowns, jewels and fabulous shoes. Cael looked great, though there was no way she'd tell him that she noticed. There was something special about a hard man in a tuxedo. She tried to ignore that something, but it wasn't easy.

The musician ended his set with a fast-paced song that should be impossible to pull off on an acoustic guitar. Jenner found herself holding her breath as he finished, and then, like the others, she applauded enthusiastically. She looked over at Cael, who like her, appreciated the music. Maybe he was actually glad he'd given in and escorted her to the event.

Abruptly she felt his body stiffen slightly, and his gaze shifted to someone just behind her, otherwise she would've been surprised to feel the gentle tap on her shoulder.

Keeping her smile in place, she turned to face a familiar-looking woman.

"Chessie!" she said, doing her best to sound delighted, which was helped by the fact that she truly did like the woman. "How nice to see you here."

Chessie Fox and her husband, Mike, were not what Jenner would call close friends. They were ten or so years older than she and more involved in their children's activities than in the charities Jenner and Syd embraced, but they did run in the same circles, on occasion.

Chessie was dressed in a pink gown that screamed "money doesn't necessarily equal good taste," but the diamonds in her ears and resting on her massive chest were real enough. Her blond hair was arranged simply and had been sprayed into submission; the breeze coming off the water didn't ruffle a single strand. Mike's suit was expensive and cut for his trim build. They were nice people who lived their lives as they wanted, and didn't worry about anything else.

Jenner introduced Cael to the Foxes, and he was his usual charming self. He could be devastatingly charming to everyone but her, it seemed. He smiled, shook Mike's hand, then placed an easy arm around Jenner's waist. Just a couple of days ago her heart would have been pounding at being put in this situation, to be forced to play this role, but tonight it seemed natural enough.

"I would say I'm surprised I haven't seen you sooner," Chessie said, laughing, "but I spent the first three days in bed, upchucking, then the last couple of days trying to find my way around. This ship is supposed to be extremely well-built and stable, but you can't prove it by me."

"I hope you're not still seasick," Jenner said. She'd been worried about that herself, but she hadn't had a moment's trouble. Beside her, Cael and Mike were having one of those men conversations, about sports or investments or politics. She tuned them out, much as Mike had probably tuned out her and Chessie. Cael, though, would be aware of every word she said.

"No, I'm fine now. I hit the gift shop and stocked up on Dramamine and ginger, and this magnetic bracelet seems to help." She showed off a small, plain bracelet that hugged her wrist. "So far, so good."

"I'm glad. Being sick on your vacation is the pits."

Chessie beamed. "It's so nice to see someone I know here. I've seen some familiar faces, but I honestly haven't known nearly as many people as I thought we would."

"I know what you mean." She'd been surprised herself at how few people she'd seen that she actually knew.

"Is Sydney here?" Chessie's gaze scanned the immediate area.

"No, Syd got sick with a stomach flu right before we sailed. I talked to her just a little while ago. She's feeling better, but she said she still wasn't completely over it."

"I'm sure she's upset to have missed the cruise." Chessie continued with a friendly, "Would you two like to join us for dinner?"

Jenner smiled. "Thank you, but we already have plans with a couple of friends." She turned to Cael, whose expression had not changed one bit. "Is it almost time to go?"

He glanced at his watch. "We're already a few minutes late."

The Foxes said good-bye, and Jenner promised them that they'd have dinner together another time. As they walked toward the restaurant, Cael said softly, "You handled that very well."

"I *can* be reasonable," she said.

His answer was a strange, brief, strangling sound deep in his throat.

She saw Faith and Ryan on the other side of the room, Ryan in a tux, leaning on his cane, Faith in a stunning bronze gown that gently hugged her curves. They were a beautiful couple, with a sort of easy, comfortable sophistication. If she didn't know better, she'd never dream they were not exactly who they appeared to be.

The evening wasn't all fun and games. Frank Larkin was also there, with his bulldog bodyguard close by . . . but not too close. She didn't like the way Larkin looked at the other passengers. Even when he was talking to them, smiling, to all appearances one of them, something was off. He made it easy to choose sides.

Something was wrong with him, she thought, and wondered why none of the people he talked to seemed to see it. He seemed to be deteriorating before her eyes, getting more and more antsy as the days passed. His clothes, while expensively cut and made of the finest materials, didn't fit him exactly right. He seemed to have lost weight, and hadn't bothered to buy new clothes or have the old ones tailored, which didn't make sense for someone who went to the trouble of having those clothes made in the first place.

Everyone else on the cruise had someone with them; a friend, a spouse, a lover . . . a Cael. But Larkin was alone. He not only had a large stateroom to himself, and was making the two-week trip without a traveling companion, but he kept all others at a distance.

Even as he made small talk, walking through the crowd playing the gracious host, he was separate and alone. It was sad, in a scuzzy kind of way.

She and Cael had been talking to Faith and Ryan for just a

short while when Tiffany joined the group. She wore a very short and snug black dress that left little to the imagination, and five-inch heels that lifted her to a height equaling Cael's; how she could walk in those heels was a mystery to Jenner. While not everyone had witnessed Tiffany's scene on their first night at sea, most had at least heard about it. All eyes were on their little group as Tiffany turned to Jenner.

"I owe you an apology," she said, her voice calm and at normal level, so some people could overhear but it wouldn't look as if she were putting on a show. The smile she flashed was brilliant. "You'll be glad to know I've given up alcohol for the duration of the cruise, and if I never see a Ghostwater again, it'll be too soon." The smile softened. "I don't like being a mean drunk."

She even nodded to Cael, though her attitude was outwardly more dismissive. "I'm sorry. I'm glad the cruise is working out well for you, even though I did my best to make a mess of things."

He nodded politely, said nothing, and drew Jenner a bit closer. The look he gave Tiffany was one of relief and, more strongly, suspicion. Was that a part of the act, or was he truly surprised by this new development?

Tiffany returned her attentions to Jenner. "Again, I'm so sorry I dragged you into my drama. Am I forgiven?"

"Of course."

Tiffany offered her hand for a handshake. Jenner took that hand, and felt something being pressed into her palm. It was small, square . . . a note? When the handshake was over, Jenner waited a few seconds before she surreptitiously glanced at what she was holding. Her heart leapt into her throat; her mouth went dry.

It wasn't a note. It was a plastic-wrapped condom.

Chapter Twenty-five

Jenner clutched the condom in her hand, feeling as if she couldn't get enough air. What the hell—? The plastic wrapper crinkled, and she prayed no one else heard the very soft noise. She gave Tiffany a quick look, then said, "Excuse me, please. I have to visit the ladies' room."

"I'll go with you," Tiffany said brightly.

Cael gave her a long look. Jenner had never had anyone pay such close attention to her as he did. It was as if he knew every breath she took, as if he caught every flicker of expression. She just hoped she didn't look as panicked as she felt. She sensed he didn't like her going off with Tiffany, but what was he going to do? There were too many people close by, still listening in, and he couldn't forbid her to go to the bathroom, for God's sake. He released her, his fingertips trailing over her arm in a way that said *Hurry back*.

She and Tiffany fell into step, and behind them she heard Faith say, "I need to powder my nose; I think I'll join them."

Ryan made some offhand comment about women going to the restroom in a pack. Cael remained silent. Jenner didn't

306

look back, because she knew what she'd see: a very suspicious man.

She had more important things than his happiness on her mind. Why the hell had Tiffany passed her a condom? Did she think it was going to be necessary, or was it a sick joke?

When they entered the nearest ladies' room, there was one other occupant, a white-haired lady who was reapplying her lipstick at the mirror. The woman smiled, nodded, and left. As soon as she was gone, Tiffany checked the five stalls to make sure they were alone, and when that was done, Jenner held out her hand, condom sitting on her palm. "What the hell?"

Faith saw what Jenner was holding and said, "Tiffany!" Disapproval was plain in her voice.

Thank goodness *someone* realized the "gift" was inappropriate under these circumstances, Jenner thought.

And then Faith continued. "One? What good is *one* condom?"

Jenner stared at her in disbelief, then shook the small, square, crinkling package in Tiffany's direction. "What are you not telling me? What makes you think I'm going to need this?"

Tiffany sighed. "Shit. You're scared, aren't you? Sorry. It's just . . . I saw the way you looked at Cael today, and I figured if you decide to jump his bones you should be prepared." She looked at Faith. "And honestly, if she needs more than one, she can buy more in the gift shop. This one is for a dire emergency."

Jenner gaped at her. "And you decided the best way to pass it to me was with a handshake, in public?"

Her grin was diabolical. "That was just for fun."

"Fun!"

"You should've seen the expression on your face."

"Yeah, funny. Ha ha. What makes you think I want to jump Cael's bones?" Maybe the fact that she *did*. She was resisting for all she was worth, but it was a real effort, especially when she woke up in his arms and he was mostly naked, and— *Don't go there!* As long as the circumstances were what they were, jumping his bones wasn't going to happen . . . she hoped. The temptation was so strong it was almost painful.

Tiffany said, "Please. The way you two look at each other?"

"As if there's going to be a murder at any second?" Jenner said drily.

"Is it really possible to die from sex? Because it's looking more and more like it's going to happen, and one of you has to make the first move. You're going to have to do it, because it won't be Cael."

That made Jenner freeze, her mind momentarily thrown off track. Indignantly she thought: *Why the hell not?*

The silent question must've shown on her face, because Faith gently explained, "He kidnapped you. You're entirely in his control, so he won't make any move on you, no matter how much he might want to. It wouldn't be fair. Cael has some faults . . ."

"Don't let him hear you say that," Tiffany muttered. She was ignored.

"But he won't take that kind of advantage. He just won't," Faith finished. "Tiffany's right. If you want him, you'll have to make the first move."

"What makes you think I want—" Both women looked at her as if she'd lost her mind, so she didn't even finish the question. Okay, they were observant. It was part of their jobs, she supposed. She threw out her arms, so frustrated she wanted to hit something. "Would you even consider getting involved with a man in this kind of situation?" she asked, incredulous.

Calmly Faith asked, "What makes you think I didn't?"

There was something about the expression in her eyes that told her this was no joke. Something had happened with Ryan, something Jenner never would have suspected, given Ryan's suaveness. Not the same situation—was any situation ever exactly the same?—but they hadn't met in the produce section of the supermarket or been introduced by a friend.

She blew out a breath and looked back at Tiffany. "While we're apparently laying it all on the line, what about you and Cael?"

"What about—?" Understanding flooded her face. "Oh, no. Never. No way. He's *so* not my type."

How could Cael not be any and every woman's type?

With a smile, Faith clarified. "Tiff prefers a . . . different type of man."

"I like nerds," Tiffany said defiantly. "So sue me."

Faith gave a ladylike snort, if a snort was ever ladylike. "What Tiffany's saying is, she prefers men who let her be the boss in *all* areas—and that so isn't Cael Traylor."

"I got it," Jenner said. She held the condom out, getting back to the subject at hand. "What am I supposed to do with this? I don't even have an evening bag with me." There hadn't seemed to be any point in bringing one, as she didn't have her cell phone or even a key card for the suite. Her lipstick was in Cael's pocket.

Tiffany shrugged her shoulders. "Your call. Do what you want with it. Stick it down in your bra, or throw it away."

Another group of three well-dressed women entered, so the conversation ended. "I'm starving," Faith said, leading the way from the bathroom. Jenner glanced briefly at the trash can near the door, hesitated, then tucked the plastic wrapped condom into her strapless bra.

The ship sailed during the night from Hilo to Honolulu. Ryan, Faith, and Tiffany went ashore that morning, while Cael stayed onboard with Jenner. He'd expected her to rant and rave, to give him grief about staying onboard when they were in freakin' Hawaii, but she'd been oddly quiet since going to the ladies' room with Faith and Tiffany the previous night, which made him wonder what they'd said. Jenner hadn't even complained about the handcuffs last night. When they'd gone to bed she had simply stuck out her hand, a solemn and begrudging offering. A thoughtful Jenner Redwine scared the shit out of him. What the hell was she up to? He didn't for a minute think she'd suddenly and meekly accepted the situation, because that wasn't in her DNA.

She didn't do anything, which made him even more wary. It was like waiting for a volcano to blow.

They were in Honolulu only that one day, and sailed that night back to the Big Island, to Kona, which was on the opposite side of the island from Hilo. Kona was their turn to go ashore. Their movements couldn't mirror Larkin's, or even each other's. Someone on the team would be aboard at all times, someone would be on Larkin at all times, but it couldn't always be the same person, or group of people.

His original plan had been to take Jenner to a restaurant or coffee shop with a great view, and kill a few hours there. They could've gone along with the Kona group tour, which would've been great cover, but also a special kind of torture. Linda Vale and Nyna Phillips had met two other women who were traveling together, and the four of them had hit it off. Penny and Buttons—Buttons, what kind of name was that for a woman?—were staying in one of the smaller staterooms on another deck, but in the past couple of days they'd been spending a lot of time in Linda and Nyna's suite across from Jenner's. He knew, because a couple of times he and Jenner had run into the foursome in the hallway, and they'd also heard them out on the balcony, laughing and evidently having a blast.

Yesterday they'd met the four ladies twice: once in the hallway, once on deck. Today's tour had been mentioned both times, as had meals. How about lunch? Join us for dinner? All the offers were friendly, casual, and genuine. They liked Jenner, and why shouldn't they? Instead of quickly accepting, though, as he'd expected her to do, Jenner had offered polite, reasonable refusals. Still, the four older ladies were persistent.

All four were on the group tour; hence the torture that he wanted to avoid.

Instead of the tour or the coffee shop, Cael took Jenner to a small cove that a local had recommended for snorkeling. Jenner had mentioned that she liked snorkeling, and, hell, she deserved a little fun.

They separated from the group soon after leaving the ship, and he found the dive shop Sanchez had recommended, where he rented the necessary equipment and got directions to this cove, which, according to the man who rented him the equipment, shouldn't be as crowded as Kealakekua Bay.

The shallow water was an unexpected shade of blue; the half-circle of trees around the water were lush and thick, cutting them off from the rest of the world even though Kona bustled just beyond those trees.

Jenner stood a few feet away, her cover-up discarded to reveal a black bikini that looked as if it had been painted on her body. Seeing her in a bathing suit had made him realize she wasn't skin·ıy, at least not as he thought of skinny. She was thin, but her bones were covered by some sleek muscles. Her breasts might be on the small side, but they were firm and high. They were perky. She'd probably take his head off if he ever referred to her, or any of her body parts, as perky.

Those little breasts made his mouth water, and his hands twitched with the need to touch them. Her nipples would be— He jerked his thoughts away from the path they were racing down. His willpower was already stretched thin from sleeping with her. He'd woken the past couple of mornings to find her wound around him like a vine; his morning erections made the situation particularly dicey. If he were smart, he'd ditch the handcuffs, except then he wouldn't wake with her almost on top of him. Trade-offs were a bitch.

Her flip-flops and hat were sitting on the sand with her cover-up neatly folded and laid on top of the hat to keep it from blowing away; her snorkeling equipment dangled from her hand. She stared at the water before her, lost in its beauty—or maybe wondering if he was going to drown her once they got into the deeper water. It wasn't as if she hadn't given him cause.

"Don't worry," he said as he walked toward her. "If you disappear while we're together, it'll raise too many suspicions. You're safe here."

She rolled her eyes. "Thanks so much. You're *such* a gentleman."

There was more than a hint of sarcasm in her voice. By now she knew that he wasn't going to hurt her, and he knew that she wasn't going to cause him the trouble she continued to promise. Not in public—and not until this job was over, at least. Afterward . . . afterward, he and Jenner Redwine would settle the accounts between them.

That promised to be one hell of a battle. He looked

forward to it more than anything else he could remember in his life, even his sixteenth birthday when he'd gotten his first car. He pulled on his mask and walked into the water, looking back to make sure that Jenner was following. She was, and like him she pulled on her mask as she moved into deeper water.

His eyes followed the lines of her body, because he couldn't *not* look. It wasn't as if he hadn't seen her in form-fitting clothes before. Some of her gowns hugged her curves, and there had been the other bathing suit for sitting by the pool. But a bikini was the same as underwear, at least to a man, and the amount of skin visible was nothing short of torment.

Soon. This would be over soon. Then he and Jenner would have themselves a long talk.

Jenner tried to dismiss all her worries and enjoy the snorkeling, but it was difficult when Cael was always so close. What did he think she was going to do, swim to safety? She gave herself a stern talking to. No, he wasn't hovering over her, not today, he was staying nearby for safety. She should be accustomed to him being constantly close at hand, so his closeness shouldn't affect her at all. But it did, and there was nothing she could do about it.

Like it or not, the condom she'd hidden in her underwear drawer was on her mind. How could it not be? It made the possibility of what might happen, what *could* happen, very, very real.

She floated on the water as colorful fish darted past, under her body, right before her eyes. She loved the feel of the ocean against her skin as she pushed through the water, propelled forward by her arms and the gentle kick of her feet. It was like swimming in a huge tank of tropical fish, like being a part of the ocean instead of an observer. Eventually she almost forgot that Cael was with her. She couldn't entirely dismiss him, but she almost forgot that she'd been sleeping handcuffed, held prisoner, made to play a role as Syd's life was threatened, too. The water flowing over her skin, the abundant fish all around, was too soothing. If only she could stay here . . .

She lifted her head, and glanced behind her to see that she'd drifted farther from shore than she'd imagined. Still, when she straightened, her feet touched the sandy bay floor. Cael was close by—naturally—and when she stood, so did he. She pulled off her mask, deeply inhaling the fresh air.

They were far away from everything, truly alone in the world, and she was tired of guessing, tired of playing games. Her life was not a game; neither was Syd's. They needed some truth between them.

"I'm not stupid," she said.

Cael removed his mask and shook his head, sending droplets of water flying. He was a head taller than she, wet, and in better physical shape than any man she'd ever seen in the flesh. She loved the way he looked right now, more bare than not and soaking wet. He wiped away the water that dripped down his face. "I've pretty much figured that out for myself."

"You can trust me," she said. "Stop treating me like I'm a prisoner."

"But that's what you are, like it or not."

"Don't be a bonehead," she muttered, exasperated. She was trying to make a gesture, call a truce. "You're the good guys, all right? I can see that. I can put a puzzle together. Larkin's slime, and he's involved in something dirty. You're trying to get the goods on him. *I get it.*"

His expression was so controlled she couldn't read a thing from it. "I appreciate that, but it doesn't change anything."

She thought she might explode from frustration. He had to make everything so damn difficult. "Why don't you go swim over there?" she said between gritted teeth, flinging her arm out and waving.

"I like it here."

"I can make things easier for you, or I can make things difficult."

"Ditto."

He was maddening. She shouted "Numb-nuts," then put her mask back on, turned her back on Cael, and gently reentered the water. Even with the water around her ears, she heard him laugh right before the muted splash that told her he was joining her.

She floated on top of the water, not working, not paddling, just *there*. She wanted to trust Cael; she wanted to be trusted. Was that too much to ask? Floating in the water, reaching toward a brightly colored fish that darted away from her, she let herself let go and just drifted. She did her best to stop worrying, to stop thinking. The problem was, when she let her guard down, old memories always shot to the surface and she got lost in another time, another breach of trust.

It surprised her, that her mind went back so quickly and easily. She hadn't realized how she'd carried the betrayals of the past so strongly within her, all these years. She was always waiting to be hurt, to be used, and that had kept her from forming close bonds with any but the most trusted, who were Syd and Al. She didn't allow anyone else to get close, didn't allow herself to let down her guard long enough for anyone to break her heart. Not a man, not a friend.

She didn't mourn the loss of Dylan, or even her own father, but Michelle was a different story. Jenner doubted the woman she'd become and the woman Michelle was now would have anything in common, but suddenly she missed her old friend as much as if they had had their falling out just yesterday.

With all the stress of the past week, suddenly it seemed unimportant to carry a grudge for long ago indiscretions. Michelle had been an important part of her life for a very long time, and even if those days were long gone, even if she couldn't get back what she'd once had, her life had been richer for having Michelle in it. She wouldn't take back a single day even if she had the chance.

Years ago she'd walked away from Michelle and she'd never looked back. When this was over—and with every day that passed she was more certain that it would end with her and Syd unharmed and together again—would she walk away from Cael as easily as she had walked away from her old life? Would she cut him out of her mind and, yes damn it, her heart?

Would she even have the chance? The choice? She'd probably wake up one morning and he'd just be gone, leaving her life as abruptly as he'd entered it.

She thought of Michelle again, their celebrations and conversations and arguments, and she smiled. There had been more good times than bad, and though she'd denied them, she hadn't forgotten. They were a part of who she was, even though she'd changed so much since those days. Even Dylan and Jerry had served their purposes in making her who she was today. She didn't have any desire to see either of them ever again, but in her own way, she forgave them as she swam in this place that was like another world.

When she came up out of the water, Cael was, as always, close by. There was no one else in the cove, though that might not last.

She walked toward him, her movements slow and easy as she worked against the water, which lapped around her breasts. She pulled off her mask, shook the water out of her hair.

"The first night we were onboard, you made me kiss you."

He pulled off his mask, too, watching her with hooded eyes. "People were watching," he said flatly. "It was necessary."

"No one's watching now," she said as she came to a stop, so close she was almost touching him. She tilted her head back and looked up at him. She pushed away her anger, her frustration, her hurt, and tried to let herself look at Cael as nothing more than a man. From the beginning she'd been attracted to him, drawn to him in an instinctive way, but she'd fought her response to him—as would any right-minded woman who found herself in the same situation.

But everything wasn't as it had initially seemed, she knew that now. And she didn't want to lose him. What a kick in the ass that was!

"Kiss me again," she said. "Not because anyone's watching and you have to, not because it's necessary but just . . . because."

He blew out a breath. "That's not a good idea." His smooth voice had a rough edge to it, one that made everything in her tighten in response.

"Agreed," she said. "Do it anyway."

He didn't move. She laid her hand on his chest, feeling the crispness of hair, the warmth of his skin, the pound of his heart.

"Kiss me," she said again, and her own heart was thudding so hard and fast she could barely breathe. "With no one to sell it to but the fishes."

She took the half-step forward that brought her against

him, he put his arm around her and pulled her close, and he closed his mouth over hers.

There was no fear this time, no panic. She leaned into him, got lost in the sensations of his mouth on hers, his wet body against hers. His heat was a sharp contrast to the coolness of the water, of her wet skin, and she drank it in.

The isolation, the water, the feel of Cael's skin against hers and the pleasure his mouth gave made her dizzy with sheer pleasure. For this short moment, she wasn't worried about tomorrow, revenge, or once again being the outsider when she wanted desperately to be on the inside. It was just a kiss, a kiss for them and no one else.

He cupped her bottom and lifted her, fitting her to him, wrapping her legs around him. He was rock hard, his erection pressing into her. Slowly he moved her against him, undulating her back and forth. A soft cry clogged her throat as she clung to his shoulders, and "just a kiss" changed so rapidly into something else that she felt as if she were spinning out of reality. The throbbing between her legs went from pleasurable to frantic in just a few seconds. Her second cry was taut, aching.

He shoved his hand down the back of her bikini bottoms, his long fingers reaching down and in. She jerked as two of them penetrated her, hard and rough, and just like that everything in her tightened and peaked and she began coming, her raspy cries floating over the sound of the waves. Frantically she tried to stop the cries, tried to stop her body from moving against him so obviously, tried to control the rhythmic tightening around his fingers. This wasn't happening. This couldn't be happening. All she'd wanted was a kiss, something to tell her she wasn't in this alone. She hadn't expected things to blast out of control that way.

He let her down gently—physically, at least. When she

could breathe again, think again, when her legs would hold her weight he uncoiled her legs and let her slide down his body. She leaned against him for a moment, her eyes closed, caught between acute satisfaction and embarrassment.

He solved that dilemma, though. He said, "I thought you said you weren't going Stockholm syndrome on me." Shock and humiliation roared through her. His breath came as hard-fought as hers did, but that was a tiny detail when compared to what he'd just said.

"Do you really think that's what happening here?" She managed to be calm. She managed to keep her voice even. What she couldn't manage to do was look at him. She didn't know if she'd ever be able to look him in the eye again. She had never felt so sick as she did right then, and the plunge from exquisite pleasure to humiliation was so breathtaking it was like a punch in the gut.

"What the hell else am I supposed to think?"

"A kiss and an erection really shouldn't annoy you so much," she said, determined to keep her voice cool even if it killed her. "I think you have issues."

"I wasn't the one having the orgasm."

She *could* look at him, she found. Enough anger worked wonders. "That," she said, "is entirely your problem. I got what I wanted. Too bad you didn't."

He took her hand in his and headed for shore, practically dragging her along. "We're going back to the ship, and you're moving in with Faith and Ryan. Today."

"No," she countered, "I'm not. "

He ignored her. "I'm not sure how we'll explain it, but we'll think of a way."

"I'm not going anywhere. That's my suite. If you don't want to stay there, then move your ass out. *You* go stay with Faith and Ryan."

They walked out of the water, the last of the cove washing against their feet. She jerked her hand out of his, and they faced off like two gunslingers.

Surprisingly, a sudden grin flashed across his face. "Why am I not surprised that a climax makes you cranky?"

Unbelievable.

She opened her mouth to blast him, but a family—mother, father, two teenage boys—arrived at the beach, their snorkeling equipment and bags of assorted beach stuff in hand. Her conversation with Cael was over . . . for now.

Except for the last word. The last word was hers. She said, "There are other people present. Maybe you should wrap your towel around your waist, big boy."

Chapter Twenty-six

The trick to successful, long-term surveillance is blending in, becoming invisible. In a way, the cruise ship situation created the perfect cover. If you were living your everyday life and kept seeing the same handful of people near work, on the streets, close to your home, in various restaurants, you'd naturally get suspicious. When you were basically living together in a floating luxury hotel, you *expected* to see the same people day in and day out.

That didn't mean they didn't need to be careful, work in shifts, and maintain their cover.

Cael knew what he needed. He needed to concentrate on work and get the woman who was in the shower out of his head, and out from under his skin.

Like it or not, he and Jenner would be on deck tonight. A Roaring Twenties costume party was scheduled. He hated fucking costumes, even if they did come with a fedora. At some point during the evening there would be a bachelor auction, which he intended to steer clear of. The auction was one of the charity events, so Larkin would likely be there. Life of the party, that one was.

The knock on the door surprised Cael, but when he heard Matt's voice—"Room service, Ms. Redwine"—he relaxed and crossed the room to open the door. Something must be up; he hadn't called room service. If Larkin was in his suite he now had a guard outside the door all the time, so he'd told Faith and Tiffany to stay away.

The increased security puzzled him. Why have it now, *after* the meet in Hilo, *after* Larkin had passed off the memory stick? Something else was definitely up, though as of now they still had no clue. On the other hand, it wasn't impossible to imagine that Larkin had more than one buyer lined up.

Matt came into the room with a domed silver tray balanced on one hand. "Sanchez says there's definitely something going on," he said in a lowered voice, after the door had closed behind him.

"Dean Mills is in the middle of it, but there are several other security guards who've put their heads together a few times in what Sanchez says is a suspicious manner."

"Larkin?"

"Not involved, that Sanchez has seen."

That was surprising. If Dean Mills was involved, how could Larkin not be? He needed more eyes on the inside, but that wasn't going to happen. If he'd had time he would have placed more of his people in security, but the background checks for those employees were even more stringent than they were for a deckhand and a steward. Given enough time he could have done it, but the security team had been set when this job had come along. He'd been lucky to find Sanchez. So far the man had been steady as a rock, and everything he said a hundred percent reliable.

Matt placed the tray on the dining table. "Compliments of your steward, sir."

He removed the lid with a flourish.

The bed of the silver tray was covered in an assortment of individually wrapped condoms.

Cael stared down at the tray. "What the hell is this?"

Deadpan, Matt responded, "They're called condoms, sir, a commonly used prophylactic for the prevention of . . ." He stopped talking when Cael caught his eye, fidgeted, and finally said, "Bridget thought they might come in handy."

"Bridget, huh."

"Actually, she said if these weren't necessary before the end of the cruise, she'd eat her steward uniform, which she really hates."

Cael lifted a hand, which Matt correctly read to mean silence. Now.

He couldn't have sex with Jenner, no matter how much he wanted to—and he did, damn it, he wanted it so much he could barely think of anything else. He'd kidnapped, threatened, and frequently handcuffed her, and basically used her to do what had to be done. Logically, he knew it would be all kinds of sick to screw her under these circumstances. His brain was in line; his dick had a mind of its own. The last thing he needed was members of his own group undermining his self-control. They weren't the ones who had to deliberately say things that would drive a wedge between him and what he wanted most. They weren't the ones who had to see the hurt and fury in her eyes.

The shower stopped, which meant Jenner could walk into the parlor in a matter of minutes. It wouldn't do for her to find him standing over a shiny pile of assorted condoms. He glared at Matt. "What the hell am I supposed to do with these?"

"I understand they go on your . . ."

This time his look would have cut steel.

Matt shrugged his shoulders. "Hide them or tell me to take them away. Your call, boss."

Cael's brain knew getting the condoms out of the suite was the right thing to do. He fought another battle with himself, but this time his dick won.

Jenner had never been a huge fan of costumes—she avoided Halloween parties like the plague, because Halloween was creepy, and not in a good way—but this party was oddly fun. She'd never dressed up like this before. Her fringed red flapper dress and close-fitting cloche hat were actually cute, and Cael dressed as a gangster was hot, so hot she couldn't stop looking at him even though she wanted to completely ignore him. Some things were just not going to happen. The black suit, black shirt, and white tie looked good on him; she even liked the hat.

Judging the different costumes of those around them, as they milled about on deck, she decided she and Cael had lucked out. There were outrageous zoot suits in all colors, Gatsby Girl outfits that had a softer appeal than the flapper dresses, and a couple of World War I uniforms. A few of the flapper girl dresses were a virulent shade of yellow that really stood out in the crowd, and Jenner was glad to have a hat, instead of a headband and attached feather that danced in the breeze. There were even a couple of cigarette girls, complete with candy cigarettes in their trays; better them than her.

The music that had been playing all night wasn't strictly from the twenties, but how many times could you listen to the "Charleston" and "Singin' in the Rain"? It was all old, though, from the twenties, thirties, and forties. Now that the Charleston lessons were over, a handful of couples were on the dance floor, but she and Cael stood by the rail, where Larkin, dressed in a gangster suit much like Cael's, though on him the look was more sleazy than dashing, was in Cael's line of sight.

While Cael watched Larkin, she watched Cael. She was still mad at him, but watching him was still a visceral pleasure. She hadn't told either Faith or Tiffany what had happened while they were snorkeling, but they weren't dummies; they knew something had. Tiffany had caught her eye and shrugged. Now that her temper had cooled somewhat—not much, but some—and her humiliation level had dropped a few degrees, Jenner was able to maybe see the morning from a slightly different angle.

She was going to have to make the first move if she wanted this fake relationship to go anywhere real, right? Well, she had, and gotten a breathtaking orgasm as a result, but then Cael had pulled back when any normal man would have been all over her like slick on butter. She didn't know if she could take another rejection like that, no matter what his reason. If he was being honorable, then that sucked. She needed him to be honorable only if she needed someone else to take care of her, which she didn't. She was an adult. She could make her own decisions, good or bad, and accept the consequences. On the other hand, while she was willing to step out on a limb, that didn't mean she was going to set herself up for more rejection. If he didn't want her . . .

His body said he did. More accurately, his body said he wanted sex. Maybe he disliked her so much—God, why should he?—that even though he was horny he didn't want to have anything to do with her. Or maybe he was *married*, or seriously involved. Tiffany wouldn't have given her that condom if he was, would she? Maybe. Tiffany had her own rules. But Faith would have had a different outlook, and she hadn't been at all disapproving.

So, no marriage, no significant other. Either he was brushing her off to protect her from herself, in which case she might kill him because that was the last thing she wanted, or he seriously didn't want her.

Damn it, how was she supposed to tell the difference?

She gave up trying to make sense of the situation and looked at the rest of the group. Tiffany was as flamboyant as ever, dressed in a black-and-white flapper dress, and didn't seem to mind the dancing feather on her head. She wore a multitude of long necklaces, and often swung them about as she flirted outrageously with every man in her path. Faith's Gatsby-style dress was a soft champagne color, as was the matching hat. Ryan, leaning on his cane, was dressed in a military uniform; the sight of him in that costume gave Jenner a moment's pause. He had the look of a soldier; he might've just stepped out of World War I. He was so urbane she hadn't noticed it before, but there was definitely something military in his posture, despite the cane.

The five of them weren't hanging out together tonight, as they had the night before. She supposed that would've been a pattern, and Cael didn't like patterns. Apparently there were a *lot* of things Cael didn't like.

Larkin was coming in their direction, and as he drew closer Jenner noticed that he was smiling. It wasn't the tight, false smile she'd seen on him before; this looked like a real smile. Either he'd gotten better at putting on a show, or something had truly amused him. He stopped to greet a couple—the man was in a green zoot suit, the woman wore a classy dress much like Faith's, only in a soft pearl—and while they were talking, Larkin smiled as if he were very pleased with himself.

The idea of him being pleased with anything sent a shiver up Jenner's spine.

Linda Vale, wearing a black flapper outfit that was two sizes too big for her thin frame, walked between Larkin and Jenner. It was all Jenner could do not to jump out of her skin.

"There you are," Linda said brightly. She was holding a clipboard, which was not in keeping with her costume. "I've been looking for you two." She smiled at Cael. "Very handsome," and then at Jenner, "and you look like a doll!"

"Where's Nyna?" Jenner asked. She always saw the roommates together.

"She's with Buttons and Penny, getting drinks." Linda lifted her clipboard. "I've volunteered to help out with the bachelor auction." She looked significantly at Cael. "I'm afraid we don't have many bachelors onboard."

He smoothly placed his arm around Jenner. "I'm taken," he said.

Linda sighed. "Every man onboard is taken, that's not the point. It's for charity. Maybe Jenner will bid on you."

"And maybe she won't. Then what'll I do?" Cael teased, though he had to know Jenner not bidding on him was a distinct possibility, as things stood between them.

"Then Nyna will." Linda laughed, but it was probably true enough.

"What does the winning bidder get?" Jenner asked. Cael's arm tightened very slightly.

"The remainder of the evening with her bachelor. What you do with the evening is up to you."

"There's no obedience clause in there? If he had to do whatever I wanted, for an entire night . . . that might be worth bidding on." She gave Cael a shark smile. "I might bid on you after all, honey," she said. "Wouldn't you like to know what you're worth?"

Linda said, "So, I can put you down . . ."

"No," he said flatly.

Linda was disappointed, but she didn't give up. "Be a sport," she said. "It's for a good cause."

Cael looked around, a flash of frustration in his expression. They were drawing attention, and that was never good. Even Larkin was looking their way, curious, listening to their exchange with Linda. Jenner wasn't a spy, but even she knew it wasn't a good idea for Larkin to realize that Cael had her in an iron grip and had no intention of getting more than a few feet away from her.

"Go ahead, sweetheart," she said, and then she went up on her toes to give him a quick, soft kiss that sent her head reeling. "I'll be fine here by myself. I promise not to get jealous if someone else buys you."

Everyone in the area was watching, waiting. Cael leaned down and kissed Jenner on the cheek. He pressed his rough cheek to hers and whispered in her ear, "Come on, tell me the truth. You were hatched, weren't you? That's the only explanation."

Damn him. She couldn't stop herself from laughing, a genuine laugh that went a long way toward easing her tension and worry. So much for sweet nothings! She said, "Trust me."

"Like I have a choice," he murmured, before he surrendered and followed Linda's lead, weaving through the crowd toward the dais.

It would've looked suspicious if Tiffany had rushed to join Jenner, after Cael was all but dragged to the front of the room, but as soon as possible she joined Jenner by the rail. "I thought I'd keep you company while he's occupied."

"Not to mention it'll keep him from freaking out because I'd be standing here by myself," Jenner said.

Tiffany shrugged. "Men."

That said it all.

"You look great," Jenner said. Tiffany twirled around to show off her outfit. Fringe danced, and so did the ridiculous feather.

"So do you." Tiffany leaned against the rail and looked out on the water. "I'm surprised Cael didn't trip over his tongue."

They both turned to face away from the crowd, facing the ocean. Jenner said, "I don't think he's all that interested."

"Trust me, he's interested."

"He's not, like, married or engaged, is he?" Even though she'd already decided he wasn't, she had to check. No matter how attracted she was, she wasn't going to be a home-wrecker.

"Nope," Tiffany said without hesitation. It certainly sounded like the truth. "So, what happened today? Did you make your move?"

"He made a crack about Stockholm syndrome." That was the tiniest portion of what had happened, but Tiffany didn't need to know everything.

"Bummer."

"Yeah."

She realized that, behind them, the auction had already started. They turned to watch the handful of men who were gathered at the front of the crowd. There were a few crew members, two gray-haired guys, a blond she didn't know, and Cael; not exactly a stellar showing, even though Cael looked mouthwateringly good. Matt must be working; if he was up there she imagined he'd fetch a pretty penny with his beach-boy good looks.

Tiffany nodded toward the bachelors. "Are you going to let Cael twist in the wind up there or are you going to save his ass?"

"I'm not worried. Some fool will bid on him."

Tiffany laughed, and so did Jenner. The possibilities were rather funny, she had to admit. What *would* Nyna do if she had Cael to herself for the evening?

Once her duty had been done, Linda Vale made her way back to the two girls. Jenner made introductions, watched Linda's eyes as the older woman studied Tiffany carefully and then apparently decided that while she looked like a high-class gold digger, she was all right.

Some people were simply a good judge of character.

"I can't believe you got Cael up there," Tiffany said to Linda. "That's so not his kind of thing."

"It's for a good cause," Linda responded. "I'm sure he won't regret participating."

A man wearing one of the old-style military uniforms passed by, and Linda's gaze followed him. She shuddered, her smile dying, and she went a little pale.

Concerned, Jenner focused on the older woman, placing a hand on her arm. "Are you all right?"

"I'm fine." Linda placed her hand over Jenner's, squeezed. "I just wish they hadn't included soldiers in tonight's costumes."

"I like a man in uniform," Tiffany said, and Jenner glanced her way. From what she understood, Tiffany preferred a man in a lab coat. Still, she was playing a part, and maybe this was part of it.

"So do I," Linda said wistfully. "My husband was a soldier. Vietnam. Wayne was killed when I was eighteen, just a couple of months after we got married. He was only nineteen."

Chills crawled up Jenner's arm; Tiffany's easy smile faded.

Linda had a look on her face that was both dreamy and painful. "Wayne was it for me, he was the one. I never

330

remarried, never got over his death. We had just a few months together, not years, and there are times when I feel like I'm drowning because it was so incredibly unfair . . ."

Tiffany laid a comforting hand on Linda's shoulder. "I'm sorry. That really sucks."

"I never talk about this." Linda wiped away a tear. "What's the point?"

"Because it helps, sometimes," said Jenner. "You can talk to us about it, any time you like."

"I suppose I can." Linda tried a smile, which didn't work well. "Once we're off this ship we might never see each other again. Who better to confess to than a stranger?"

"We're hardly strangers, not anymore."

"That's true." Linda sighed. "There really isn't much to tell. I loved Wayne with all my heart, he died, and ever since then I've been in a kind of limbo, just waiting for the day when I'll join him."

"No!" Tiffany said explosively, then she cranked it down a bit. "Don't talk like that. You have a lot of life left in you. You should enjoy every day."

"I do. I have a good life."

"The uniforms upset you. It's understandable," said Jenner.

"Things are a little close to the surface today. I dreamed about Wayne last night," she added. "God, it's been years since I've dreamed of him that way. You know how some people will say that they've forgotten exactly how a lost loved one looked, or how his voice sounded. I never forgot. Never." She shook off her melancholy. "You girls don't want to hear an old lady go on and on."

Their conversation was interrupted by a sudden eruption of noise from the crowd around them, and they looked about to see that one of the gray-haired gentlemen had been bought by a woman who was boogying up to the dais to fetch him.

"Maybe you should buy yourself a man for the night," Tiffany suggested.

Linda gave a slight smile, and in a very soft voice said, "That never worked."

Chapter Twenty-seven

Cael hoped his head would be put on the chopping block first so he could get this ordeal over with, but no, they decided to save him for last. A bartender and then a popular steward went first, then a couple of widowers, then a shy man who was there with his fiancée, who dutifully bid on him until he was hers—for the evening's record sum of seven thousand.

There were a couple of catcalls as Cael was introduced. From what he could see, they all came from rich, primarily white-haired, giggling widows. Playing along, he tipped his hat to the crowd. He even winked at one blushing matron. He looked for Jenner, but she and Tiffany were no longer standing where he'd last seen them. Great. They were probably in Tiffany's suite or in one of the bars, yucking it up at his expense.

Somebody was going to pay for this.

The bidding started, and quickly escalated. He passed the five-thousand mark within a few minutes. Still no Jenner. Cael caught Ryan's eye; he and Faith were amused, and a little worried, but there wasn't much either of them could do.

If Jenner or Tiffany didn't step up to save his bacon, he was going to end up the property of either the plump, lascivious granny in the lime-green fringed dress and matching fishnets or the scary-looking broad with too much makeup and unnaturally blue-black hair. They were the only two left in play, as the bid passed eight thousand.

A flash of red in the crowd caught his eye. Jenner was making her way toward the front of the crowd, with Tiffany close behind her. Jenner raised her hand and got the auctioneer's attention.

"Fifty thousand," she called in a clear, steady voice.

The crowd murmured, a few people applauded. The scary broad looked pissed as she and the lime-green granny conceded the bid—not that either of them couldn't have offered more, but there was only so much money they were willing to part with just for a little bit of fun.

"Poor baby," Jenner said confidently as she reached the dais. "Did you really think I would share?" The crowd burst into laughter and applause as she claimed him. He was the only one in a position to see how cool her gaze was, and he knew she was still pissed off.

Larkin had left the costume party and escaped to the quiet of his suite. If he'd had to listen to more of that fucking music, he'd have thrown the musicians overboard. He sat at the desk in the parlor, writing a letter on his e-mail program. He wouldn't send the e-mail until the last possible moment, but he wanted to be prepared. He still wasn't sure who to send it to. The *New York Times*, the *Washington Post* . . . but newspapers were going the way of the dodo. How many people bothered to read them anymore? He should also send the e-mail to a couple of television networks.

I take full responsibility for the destruction of the Silver Mist *and its passengers. If I could take more of you assholes with me . . .*

No, if he wanted the letter published in its entirety, he'd have to watch his language. Fucking pussies.

If I could take more of the worthless parasites of the world with me, I would. Gladly.

He could die with a bang or he could fade away; he really wasn't a fading kind of guy. Serial killers, bringers of mass destruction, they were remembered long after they left this earth. He would be remembered, too.

When the Silver Mist *blew out of the water on the tenth day of her maiden voyage, I made my mark on the world. At the end of the day, money means nothing. Power is reduced to the simple control over life and death.*

Yeah, that sounded about right. Powerful. People would remember what he'd written until their own deaths. When the time came, he'd turn on his computer, set the e-mails to be sent at a certain time—perhaps 9:55, five minutes before the bombs would explode—and then he'd put everything in motion. Some bombs were on a timer, simply for logistical reasons, and he had the triggers for others. While Dean and his idiot team of would-be robbers got ready to move in on the art auction, Frank would be setting the real show into motion.

His head throbbed; eyestrain caused by the computer screen was a bitch these days. Suddenly unsure, he checked to make certain he hadn't accidentally logged onto the Internet, because sometimes he did things that he didn't quite remember. He didn't want to send the message yet, so he hadn't even gone online. There was no e-mail of any consequence headed his way—very little was of true consequence now. There was no reason for him to surf the 'net. He didn't care how the stock market was faring, or what news of the day might be interesting, because the simple fact was that nothing was interesting now. Funny how certain things that had seemed so important faded to nothing when a life was reduced to a matter of days. He saved what he'd written so far into a draft file, and shut down the computer.

Larkin had already left the party by the time Jenner took possession of her winnings. Cael smiled for the crowd, but she could see past the easy grin. He was annoyed that his plans had gone awry, for a short while, and he was anxious to get back to the stateroom, since Larkin was in his.

Tonight she was the one who said, for the benefit of those listening, "I'm tired. Are you ready to turn in?"

"Sure, any time you are." Hah! As if he was ever that accommodating! Smiles in place, he took her arm and they walked at a leisurely pace toward the elevators.

They were silent in the elevator, each of them too pissed at the other to engage in their customary verbal joust. They stepped off the elevator, headed toward the suite—and the guard posted next door. The man ignored them, didn't even glance their way or nod when Cael slipped the key card in the door to unlock it, as any other member of the crew would've done.

Cael went to the bedroom, stripping off his jacket as he went, tossing his fedora aside. He didn't guide Jenner to a chair and handcuff her, didn't look back to make sure she wasn't making a run for it. She followed him into the bedroom, kicking off her shoes and removing her own hat, twirling the cloche on one finger as she headed for the bed. Cael was already setting up his laptop to review anything he might've missed.

Finally she broke first, mainly because she couldn't leave

well enough alone. "Are you really mad because I didn't save you from the horrors of the auction block?"

"No," he said curtly. She'd prefer that he make a joke or insult her in that funny way he had, but he was deadly serious. She sat on the side of the bed, as close to him as she could get. After a few seconds he glanced up, frowning, and tensed at what he saw in her face. "Don't look at me that way."

"What way is that?" Like she wanted to eat him up, which she did. She was tired of trying to hide the way she felt.

"You know this is a bad idea," he said, trying to turn his head away and ignore her.

"I know no such thing."

Sighing, because she obviously wasn't about to let him work, Cael set aside his equipment and stood to look down at her. Maybe he was trying to intimidate her. "The situation is . . . difficult."

She had to snicker. "Couldn't say *hard*, could you?"

He ground his teeth, which he seemed to be doing a lot lately. "Jenner . . ."

"I know, I know. You kidnapped me. You're afraid I'm having some sort of nervous breakdown, or that I might feel obligated to sleep with you so you won't kill me when this is all over, or—"

"I'm not going to kill you," he snapped.

"I know that," she said softly. "But the situation isn't exactly normal."

"No, it isn't."

"I know how to fix that."

He crossed his arms over his chest and narrowed his eyes. "Yeah? How's that?"

"Let me go."

He remained silent, but his eyes narrowed.

She continued, "As long as we're still cruising around the Hawaiian Islands I can get off the boat, go to a hotel, lay low until the cruise is over. If I give you my word that I won't betray you, if I swear that you can trust me . . . you can let me go."

"So that's what this is about," he said curtly, temper flaring in his blue eyes. "You think if you flirt with me, I'll suddenly lose my common sense."

She sighed. "No. I'm thinking if you let me go and I stay of my own free will, everything changes."

She stood, because being seated made her feel as if she were in a subservient position. Cael was still taller than her, bigger than her, stronger than her, but in every way except physically she was his equal, and it was time he acknowledged that.

He stared down at her, evaluating, calculating, and she couldn't help but think about Linda Vale and her Wayne, the only man in her life, the only man she'd ever wanted. Jenner wanted to know what it was like to love that deeply. Cael got to her. He made her angry, he made her laugh, and when he kissed her—*yowza!* He got to her in ways no other man ever had. Was that love, or just the heightened emotions of the moment? Only one way to find out.

"Fine," he said. "You're free to go."

Jenner threw her hands up. "Was that so hard?" Then she went up on her toes and kissed him, quickly and softly, as she had earlier, when they'd been on deck.

She stepped around him, collected her pajamas, and headed for the bathroom.

"I thought you were leaving," he said, sounding almost disappointed.

"Nope. This is my stateroom, after all," she said. "They'd probably kick you out of this room if I left the cruise, and wouldn't that be a pain in the ass. The difference now is, I'm not a prisoner, I'm a partner."

"Like hell you are."

She gave him a very satisfied smile. "And honey, I'm not nearly as easy as you seem to think I am. Once we get off this damn boat, where are you going to take me on our first date?"

Chapter Twenty-eight

Jenner came out of the bathroom in her pajamas, her face freshly scrubbed, her nipples pebbled against her thin tank. It was all Cael could do not to groan. He had to be the biggest fool on earth, to think he was in control of anything where she was concerned. He'd known she was going to be trouble the first time she opened her mouth. He just hadn't known how much trouble—or what kind.

She picked up the conversation they'd been having before she'd changed as if there had been no break. "So," she mused. "CIA? NSA? FBI?" A hint of a smile teased the corners of her lips. "Coast Guard? Since we're partners now, there's no reason for you to hold out on me."

He had to set her straight, sooner rather than later. "We're *not* partners."

She was unshaken, completely unaffected by his edict. "I say we are. So, details, please. What have you gotten me into?"

He considered turning his back, but that could be dangerous, and ignoring Jenner Redwine was getting more and more difficult. In the end, he didn't even try. Maybe she'd earned the truth. "Let's just say that not everyone who does work for the government actually works for the government."

"That's as clear as mud."

"No dental, no pension plan . . ."

"Contract work," she said, without even a hint of alarm in her voice.

It was dangerous for her to know too much, but she was already in a dangerous position. She already knew too damn much. He nodded once, and returned his attention to the audio and video he'd been reviewing before she'd interrupted him. Larkin had opened his laptop tonight, but it was hard to tell if he'd signed onto the Internet or not. If he had, Faith would have the details shortly. Might be nothing, but then again, maybe there would be a clue about what he was up to with Mills.

He didn't handcuff Jenner to the chair. Why bother? She'd had several chances to blow his cover and she hadn't done it. If she'd headed out the door when he'd told her she was free, would he have stopped her? Maybe, maybe not. Didn't matter; she was still here.

A *date*?

She crawled into bed, pulled the covers to her chin, said good night, and closed her eyes.

Like it or not, she was into the shit damn near as deeply as he was.

Jenner woke a couple of times, realized Cael still wasn't in the bed with her, and opened one eye to see that he still sat in the chair by the bed, watching and listening to the man next door. What could be so important that he'd rather be over there than in bed with her?

341

She sighed. While she knew very few details, she knew what he was doing was truly important. She'd heard enough, seen enough to know that much.

The bed dipped, waking her, when Cael finally came to bed. She sighed, rolled toward him, and found him propped on his elbow watching her. "What is it?" she asked, then blinked when she saw he was naked. Completely.

"My turn," he said, and pulled her under him.

She shot awake, her heartbeat going from normal to shuttle blastoff in something like a tenth of a second. His heavy weight crushed her into the mattress. "What? Wait!"

"Wait, my ass," he said in a goaded tone as he grabbed the hem of her tank top and dragged it off over her head. The sudden exposure sent her senses reeling, and she would have done something totally silly like covering her breasts if he hadn't shackled her wrists with his hands and pinned them to the pillow on each side of her head as he looked down at her. In the lamplight she could see the way his features clenched, and her nipples pinched tight in response—not from the cold, not a simple reaction to being touched, but a response to *him*, all heat and power and dark sex.

He slid farther down in the bed, still holding her wrists, and clamped his mouth over one thrusting nipple. Pleasure so sharp it was almost pain shot through her breast. She made a keening sound as his tongue stabbed at her nipple, circled it, before he sucked hard and deep. She bucked under the lash of sensation, straining against his grip, his weight, those wilds sounds still coming from her mouth.

He made a rough sound against her breast, and released one hand so he could reach down and give a mighty tug at her pajama bottoms, shaking her out of them as if he were shaking a pillow out of a pillowcase. He had to completely turn her loose to accomplish the job and she tumbled to the other side of the bed. He dragged her back into position and covered her, putting his hands behind her knees and lifting them around him.

If the past few tumultuous minutes counted as foreplay, that was all she got. He reached down between them, said, "*Fuck!*" in a strained voice, and reached for the bedside table. Blinking in confusion, Jenner turned her head and stared in amazement at the number of foil packs scattered across the tabletop.

"Holy hell," she blurted.

He tore open the foil, rolled the condom on with a few fast, rough motions, and pushed into her—that fast, that hard, that intent.

She sucked in a deep breath, half-closing her eyes as she absorbed the sensation. She was just barely wet enough to take him, and he was so thick and long . . . another of those helpless, keening sounds burst from her throat. Her fingers dug into his shoulders as she tried to anchor herself, but he was taking exactly what she had offered. As he'd said, it was his turn, so she wrapped her arms around his shoulders and gave herself over to him.

He thrust hard and deep, no finesse, just a raw drive to climax. The power and heft of him pushed her over the edge almost before she realized she was there. She came hard, clenching around him, and with a muffled curse he came, too, his almost savage rhythm changing to something slower and deeper as he rode the crest.

The silence in the bedroom after was broken only by the gasps of their breathing, as if they'd both run a marathon. Cael pulled out of her and collapsed beside her, his body gleaming with sweat. Jenner felt as if her entire body were throbbing from the force of her heartbeats. That hadn't been like anything she'd experienced before. It hadn't been amazing, or great, or any of the other adjectives she'd heard used to describe sex. It had been powerful and primal, stripped down to the simplest form—no polish, no technique, though she was certain he had them. He had fucked her. He had *mated* her.

Until now, until this final step, she would still have been able to step back, but not now. This had gone too far. A man didn't make love to a woman like that and walk away unscathed.

Panting, she lifted her head and met his gaze, brilliant blue under narrowed lids, his expression both hard and extremely satisfied with himself. Then she looked at the bedside table, estimating the number of condoms. Looking back at him she said, "You're in big trouble now, cowboy."

"You think so?" he asked, reaching out for a fresh condom. "Brace yourself; you're in for a rough night. We'll count coup in the morning."

*　　*　　*

Larkin couldn't sleep. He got out of bed and paced the suite, feeling as if ants were crawling on him. Something was wrong. Something was out of kilter, but he couldn't put his finger on it. Finally he realized what it was, and went to the suite's main door to jerk it open and stick his head into the hallway. The guard on duty, Johnson, straightened with a jerk. "Is anything wrong, Mr. Larkin?"

Larkin glared at him. "You can go," he said sharply.

Johnson looked surprised. "But Mr. Larkin, I thought . . ."

"Don't think," Frank said. "You might hurt yourself."

He hadn't been thinking clearly himself, apparently. While the suite was more secure if there was a man at the door, and he worried less about the eyes he sometimes felt on him, it would also be harder to find the privacy he needed when the time came for him to set the timers on the bombs. These yahoos thought all the bombs would be detonated by manual triggers, but that wasn't the case. The bombs they'd planted below deck, in places he couldn't access without arousing suspicion, were operated by the trigger in his possession. The incendiary bombs on the public decks were on a timer, which he would set himself, early in the morning of his last day on this earth.

The morons also thought the triggers they had in their possession were operational, but they were merely toys. He had the single working trigger, and he'd use it at the proper time, well before they were expecting it. If there was a guard on his door at all times, how would he get away to set those timers? He hadn't been thinking clearly when he'd ordered Mills to set up the constant watch. It was the tumor, the damned cancer that had stolen his ability to reason.

Johnson left and Larkin closed the door, reveling in the seclusion that had become his life. He trusted no one. He needed no one. And that was a good thing, because he had no one.

*   *   *

The next morning, Cael watched, narrow-eyed, as Jenner got dressed. The night between hadn't eased the stress of being around her. He was beginning to feel a real sense of terror that this particular stress would never ease. They'd done normal things this morning: showering, eating breakfast, and still all he could think about was getting back inside her. After the night they'd spent, logically he should be hours, maybe even days, from being ready for sex again. She was trying to kill him. Slowly, painfully. He'd rather be shot; it would hurt less.

"What the hell are you wearing?"

Jenner glanced down. "It's just a sundress."

That was like saying they were "just breasts." The thin fabric of her blue sundress draped over her like a second skin; the skirt was knee length, showing off fine legs. Even her feet, in another pair of those ridiculous sandals, were sexy as hell.

Yep, she was trying to kill him.

They were going ashore again today, to Kauai this time. Tiffany was joining them, since she was single and Tiff and Jenner were new best buds. The rest of the bunch would keep an eye on Larkin, all four involved with the surveillance if their subject stayed onboard, which seemed to be his preference since the Hilo meeting, Faith and Ryan tailing him if he decided to go ashore.

After today, there would be only one more day of splitting up his team to watch Larkin. Tomorrow night they'd be back at sea. Cael was more comfortable with that scenario. Once they were at sea, Larkin wasn't going anywhere.

He'd decided to stick with the arranged tour for this excursion. At this point, it was a good idea to stay in a crowd, and keep Jenner out of bikinis before he fucked himself to death. What was it about her? It definitely wasn't her curves, because she didn't have that many. She had a smart mouth. She was diabolical. Logically, his intense reaction to her shouldn't be happening.

Unfortunately Little Cael didn't function on, or even recognize, logic.

Dean asked Tucker and Johnson to meet with him privately, in the water treatment facility where they could be certain not to be disturbed. In a narrow corridor between two separate series of twisting pipes, they could be assured of privacy.

Asker and Zadian were also in on the robbery, but Dean had known Tucker and Johnson for years, and he trusted them to do as they were told. It was no mistake that they'd been given two of the three triggers for safekeeping. He had the other.

He could trust them with this.

"I think Larkin is losing it," he said, his tone heavy.

"No shit," Tucker said.

For the past couple of days, the guard Larkin had once insisting on having at all times had been called off, ordered back on again, and then once more called off. Even if the incident with Tucker and the bread hadn't proved to Dean that his boss was a nutcase, Larkin's increasingly erratic behavior as they sailed among the islands would've done the trick.

"We're going to follow him in shifts, just the three of us. Maybe if we keep our eyes open we can figure out what he's up to."

Johnson, who was thinner and older and usually more serious than Tucker, asked, "Do you think he's planning a double cross?"

"It's crossed my mind."

Tucker ran nervous fingers through his hair. "But we've got the bombs and the guns. He can't do anything without us. All he did was plan the getaway."

A getaway that was looking less and less likely to Dean, less and less clean, though he didn't say so aloud. A part of his brain whispered *this isn't going to work*, while another part said, more loudly, *millions*.

He was so tired of taking orders, so tired of taking shit from men with money, while he never had any, to speak of.

"Once we get off the ship and the bombs have done their work, we might have to take out Mr. Larkin." A bop on the head and a swim in the drink would do the trick.

Neither of the men had a problem with that scenario; one less man to share the haul with meant more money for all of them.

"Until then, we keep an eye on Larkin," Dean said. "I suggest you don't let him see you."

Jenner could honestly say she'd had a lovely day. Tiffany was funny and honest to a fault, and the foursome they'd come to know so well—Linda, Nyna, Penny, and Buttons— embraced life, truly enjoying the exotic beauty of the island and the company of new friends. Linda didn't mention her confession from last night, and neither did Jenner or Tiffany. It had been a private, touching moment, one that had affected Jenner more than she dared to admit.

Cael didn't say much as the day passed, which should've been a relief but was not. For one thing, the look in his eyes as he watched her made her as flustered as a virgin the day after her wedding. When you knew how a man looked naked, when he'd had you naked, it changed things. Once she wouldn't have thought so, but now she knew better. She was so attuned to him now a simple stroke of his finger on her arm could make her almost jump out of her skin.

Tiffany was fast at figuring out what had happened, and she kept grinning at them, which made Jenner even more self-conscious. Damn, she hadn't been this edgy when everyone had thought she was having sex with him but she wasn't. Now that she really was, she felt stripped naked, so to speak. His silence was probably explained away to the others in their group by discomfort over the fact that his old girlfriend and his new girlfriend were so chummy, but Jenner knew the truth: He was thinking about sex with her. Again. Soon.

At the end of the day, though, when they were back on the ship, instead of taking her straight back to bed Cael went to speak with Ryan. To her annoyance, he wouldn't tell her what had happened while they were gone. While they were getting ready for dinner, she tried to get some information. "What's the plan for tonight?"

"It all depends on Larkin," Cael said as he buttoned his cuffs. "Since he might've caught sight of Ryan and Faith several times today, I'll need to keep watch if he's on deck and let them lay low."

"You mean, you and *I* need to keep watch," she corrected.

He shot her a look. "No, you don't watch. You don't do anything but stand there and look gorgeous."

"If you tell me not to bother my pretty little head . . ." she began, more than a little annoyed. When was he going to get it through his head that she was a part of this? She wasn't just a passive pawn any longer.

He snorted. "We all have our duties. Yours is to be silent, cooperative, and obedient eye candy."

"Aren't cooperative and obedient pretty much the same thing?"

"It's a point I can't drive home often enough."

She turned her back on him and walked into the closet to choose her outfit. "If I'm only supposed to be decoration, what on earth should I wear?"

It was hard to be sure, but it sounded as if one of the words he muttered was "turtleneck."

Chapter Twenty-nine

Syd sat in the parlor with two pairs of attentive eyes—Adam's and Kim's—on her as she talked to Jenner on Adam's cell. Their frequent and always too short conversations had gradually changed in the past few days, to the point where the exchanges were almost normal. Neither of them was terrified anymore. Confidence had returned to Jenner's voice, and that was a huge relief to Syd. If Jenner was okay with this, then she could be, too. After more than a week of being held prisoner, with the threat of harm to the other keeping both of them hamstrung, it was becoming more and more apparent that there was an end to this. A good end, where no one ended up dead.

The *Silver Mist* would pull out of Maui this evening, and was scheduled to dock in San Diego in five days. Five days, and this adventure would be over.

"I'm fine," Syd said in response to Jenner's question about her well-being. "I'd love to go for a walk and get some fresh air, or sit down in a restaurant, or shop, or go to a movie, but other that that, all is well. I never thought I'd see the day where I was tired of sleeping late and ordering room service." Jenner laughed lightly; that was a very good sign.

"Is the ship lovely?" Syd asked. She'd so wanted to see the *Silver Mist* in action.

"It's very nice," Jenner responded. "Which is a good thing, since I'm never getting on a ship again as long as I live."

Syd wanted to apologize. After all, it had been her idea to take the cruise, her father who'd booked the suite. An apology over the phone would be insufficient, so she didn't even try. When she had her arms around Jenner's neck, when she knew without a doubt that this escapade was over, then she'd apologize.

"The food is good," Jenner said.

Syd sighed. "I'm jealous. Right now I'd kill for a decent cheeseburger and some good fries. The room service restaurant here serves great salads and grilled shrimp, but their cheeseburgers are truly subpar, and the fries are soggy. I should be eating the salads and grilled shrimp, but with the stress of this whole situation I'm feeling the need for something more substantial. You know, comfort food."

"I have to go," Jenner said briskly. "I'll talk to you tomorrow. And when I get there we'll gorge ourselves on cheeseburgers!" The connection ended.

Syd stared at the cell phone for a moment, then childishly stuck out her tongue. She was accustomed to their conversations ending abruptly, as whatever cretin who was holding Jenner insisted that she hang up, but that didn't mean she had to like it. The tongue was for *him*, not Jenner. She'd heard his voice a time or two, in the background. He sounded like a jerk.

But Jenner sounded like Jenner again, so maybe he wasn't all bad. Not that Syd didn't want to kick his ass. Well, she'd *hire* someone to kick his ass. No one would ever be afraid of her, but she could certainly hire scary people, and when this was over she intended to make a point to find some. She would *not* go through this again.

Maybe her kidnappers could help. Syd knew her captors much better than she had a week ago. Spend enough time with a person—or people—and it happened. Dori looked scary, she had a terrifying scowl and a hard demeanor when it suited her, but if you caught her off guard she had a very nice smile. She laughed at the silliest things on television. She'd probably be thrilled to find a Three Stooges marathon playing when she pulled the night shift. Not that Syd cared to cross her, but still, she wasn't nearly as frightening as she'd been that first day.

Strong, usually silent Adam was obviously sweet on Kim, and from what Syd had been able to tell, Kim didn't have a clue, though when it came to other matters she didn't miss much. Kim, knives and all, was so like Syd's other friends, in personality, it was sometimes difficult to mentally keep her in the role of kidnapper. Dress her up and take away her knives, and she might be a perfectly ordinary pretty woman.

She thought about escape often, daydreamed about it in her recent hours of boredom. But even knowing that her captors were more than the thugs she'd initially thought them to be, she realized there was no way to escape. Maybe they wouldn't kill her—maybe—but they would definitely stop her. If she simply ran, they'd catch her. If she tried to latch onto one of the service people, a maid or a room service delivery guy, she'd only be putting the innocent hotel employees in danger—not that her diligent bodyguards ever let her get all that close to anyone other than the three of them. In her fantasies she was as tough as Dori, as skilled with knives as Kim, as physically strong as Adam. In her fantasies, she would sneak up on them and knock all three out with a series of skilled karate chops, and then she'd be free.

But those were only fantasies. She didn't know anything about karate other than what she'd seen in the movies. If she tried to run she'd get caught, and then she'd end up in a basement somewhere, thrilled at the very prospect of room service. If she was lucky.

And who was she kidding? She wasn't the ass-kicking type, by any fashion.

Syd found a movie on television—she'd seen it before but it wasn't horrible—worked most of the crossword puzzle in the *USA Today*, and when neither appealed to her any longer she retired to her bedroom and took a nap. When she woke up close to six o'clock, she heard the front door to the suite close. It was probably room service. Again. More grilled chicken or quesadillas, most likely. She washed her face, combed her hair, and entered the parlor, determined to eat a bit even if she had to choke it down. Adam stood by the dining table, with a couple of large white paper bags in his hand. "Cheeseburgers and fries," he said simply. "I asked the concierge, and he said this place made the best burgers in town."

He'd overheard her phone conversation, and gotten a cheeseburger for her.

Dori, who'd been kicked back on the couch watching something on TV, jumped up. "I'll get some sodas from the machine. Diet or regular?" she asked, nodding toward Syd.

"Diet, please." And at that moment, she hated her captors a little bit less.

It was a relief to Cael when the *Silver Mist* pulled away from Maui. When they were at sea all six members of his team—

if she could read his mind Jenner would say *seven*, but thank God she hadn't figured out how to do that yet—could be used at all times. No more taking turns going ashore, watching and waiting for Larkin to decide without warning to take off to a beach or volcano somewhere. He hadn't done that, but they'd always had to be prepared in case he did.

Jenner was in the bed; not sleeping, he could tell, but headed in that direction. Maybe he wouldn't wake her when he went to bed himself. Yeah, right. He was going to stop breathing, too.

He was up later than usual tonight because Larkin seemed restless, jumpy. What would make a man who'd calmly hand over EMP technology to the North Koreans, stopping to buy jam along the way, jumpy? The possibilities were not good.

Not for the first time, Cael wondered about the aspirin Larkin took so often, the constant hand to his head, as if he had a persistent headache. Obviously he wasn't well. How sick was he?

It was just past two in the morning when Larkin abruptly jumped up like he'd been shot out of the chair and headed for the door. He was alone. No Mills, no bodyguard at all. Maybe this was it; the meeting they'd been waiting for. Was it possible that the man on the other end of this deal had been onboard all along? Or that there was another buyer, another memory stick?

Cael jumped up. There was no time to call anyone else on the team. He was the one on duty. By the time he woke Ryan or Matt and got them here, it would be too late. Jenner, of course, immediately woke and came up on her elbows. "Where are you going?" she asked sleepily as he headed for the door.

"Stay here," he commanded.

"But where are you . . ."

"Stay!" he hissed, and then he stepped into the hallway. Larkin wasn't in sight; Cael heard the ding of the elevator. Up or down? He sprinted to the elevator bank and checked the indicator.

Up.

Cael headed for the forward stairs at a run, glad there was no one else in the hallway at this late hour as he went up them two and three steps at the time. As he entered the stairwell he heard what sounded like footsteps a level higher, at the Lido deck. He stopped to listen, decided it was an echo, and continued upward.

Jenner threw back the covers and jumped out of bed. Stay? Was he kidding? She wasn't a dog. She didn't *stay*. She didn't roll over or play dead, either.

Besides, she knew Cael better than he realized. The expression on his face, as he'd left the room, had been intense. Something was going on, and if *he* didn't like it, *she* didn't like it.

It didn't take her two minutes to pull on a pair of capris and a T-shirt, and step into a pair of tennis shoes. She didn't take the time to put on a bra, but it wasn't like she had a lot to harness. Putting on a bra would take precious minutes she didn't want to waste. If she was certain she wouldn't run into anyone, she would've followed Cael in her pajamas.

Damn it, if only Bridget and Cael hadn't completely cleared the suite of anything that might be used as a weapon! Maybe Cael could kill bad guys with a paper clip, but if she was headed into dangerous territory, she wanted something more substantial. Considering this was Frank Larkin's ship, and that Cael was obviously worried, she hated to go out alone without some kind of protection. As she was tying her shoe, she had a thought and glanced up. On the top shelf of the closet, several pairs of shoes sat. Most were casual, sandals and flip-flops, but there were a few pairs of dress shoes. A couple of them had narrow, very high heels. She reached up, grabbed a shoe, and ran for the door.

Larkin got out of the elevator on the sports deck, which was thankfully deserted at this hour. He hadn't been sure it would be; there were a couple of insomniacs and quite a few night creatures on this cruise. But fortunately, most of those who were still awake were in the ship's various bars.

Even though the spa and golf activities were closed at this hour, the sports deck was well lit. The *Silver Mist* was a bright, shining city, an expensive amusement park for adults. There were long shadows, dark recesses, but most of the deck was as bright as day. Once, he thought he heard a step behind him, but when he whirled around nothing was there. Was the damn cancer playing tricks with his hearing now?

He walked toward the putting greens, unconcerned. If anyone was watching, they'd think he was enjoying the peace and quiet of the night. He wasn't, of course. Larkin didn't care much for peace or quiet; he never had. In his mind he was picturing the display that would begin in less than forty-eight hours. One of the incendiary bombs was hidden in a closet, disguised by the false bottom in a storage bin, in the men's steam room at the aft end of this deck. When it went, the sight would be spectacular. He could almost see it. Flames would burst into the air, spreading and climbing, incinerating anyone who had the misfortune to be on that end of the deck, sending a tower of flame into the night sky as, at the same moment, a different type of bomb destroyed a portion of the hull and a large part of the crew, and other bombs added their fire and roar of destruction. What a display it would be . . .

He didn't want to wait any longer, but it would be better if the *Silver Mist* was well away from Hawaii, and the navy vessels there, when she blew. He wasn't going to make it so easy for those who would survive. Let 'em wait for their rescue. Make 'em bleed and scream and wonder if help would arrive in time. God, he hated them, hated every minute he wasted in their company. All these years he'd put up with them, and now it was almost over. Everything was almost over.

A few months ago he hadn't known anything about explosives, but thanks to his wealth he was in a position to obtain and learn about anything that struck his fancy. The bombs had been constructed by a man who'd participated in a few arms deals Larkin had put together over the years. The same man had instructed Larkin on how to arm the bombs, when it was time, and had been the one to suggest that some devices be set to go off by timer alone, while others that were in close enough proximity to one another could be set to respond to the same trigger device. Why put all his eggs in one basket? If for some reason he wanted to get the party started earlier than planned, he had the power to do so. The timed devices could be programmed well in advance, and if something happened to him before he could trip the switch on the others, the *Silver Mist* would not continue on unscathed.

Larkin was torn. He'd intended all along to die quickly, and he doubted he'd change his mind. But oh, he did want to see the *Silver Mist* and the people aboard her burn.

He didn't stay on deck very long. His impatience was growing; being outside didn't make his pain any better, it didn't make the time pass any faster. Instead of heading back for the aft elevator bank, he walked to the forward stairwell, which was closer. His floor was just two stories down. Even in his condition, he could manage that much. At least being close to the bombs had given him a little bit of satisfaction.

Cael stood in shadow and watched Larkin from a distance. There was no one else up here; no meet, no contact. Shit. He'd taken the chance of blowing his cover because the nut job wanted a breath of fresh air.

As he watched Larkin disappear into the stairwell, a touch of cold metal brushed his neck, and a deep voice whispered, "Don't do anything stupid, pal. Why are you following Mr. Larkin?"

Cael didn't give any hint that he realized the metal touching his neck was a gun. He turned, stumbled slightly. "I'm not watching anybody," he said, sounding a little bit drunk, reeling back when he saw the gun. It was unlikely that the security guard would take the chance of firing the weapon. There was no suppressor, and it would make a helluva noise. "Whoa. You shoot people for pissing off the top deck?"

The guard wasn't buying it. "Funny, you didn't walk like a drunk five minutes ago."

So, the security guard had been watching for a while. The footsteps from the stairwell. He'd probably taken the elevator one floor up and walked from there; he'd been here all along.

"I think Mr. Larkin might want to talk to you. He doesn't like being followed."

Couldn't happen, Cael thought coolly. Larkin absolutely *could not* find out that the man who was staying in the stateroom next to his had followed him onto the sports deck in the middle of the night. He and Jenner and everyone they'd talked to during the cruise would end up shot and tossed over the side, noise be damned.

Cael evaluated the man before him—thin but strong, calm, not easily distracted, armed—and looked for weaknesses. For one thing, he was one of Larkin's underpaid, overworked security guards. He couldn't be the cream of the crop.

The guard had waited for Larkin to leave before he made his move. Was it a power play, a chance to shine as he delivered a spy to Larkin's door, or was he worried about maybe irritating his boss in a public place, where someone else might see his instability?

The ping of the elevator arriving was loud on the all but deserted deck. The security guard didn't waver; the gun he held on Cael remained steady as he stepped to the side and turned his body so he could see Cael as well as whoever was arriving by elevator.

Cael looked over his shoulder, expecting another guard, Larkin, or an innocent passenger who was about to find himself in the wrong place at the wrong time.

He did *not* expect to see Jenner, armed with a fucking shoe.

Jenner had taken a chance. Up or down. Fifty-fifty she'd end up going in the same direction as Cael. Maybe sixty-forty. Odds were up, she guessed, because that was where all the action was at night. The Lido deck was the most crowded, so she decided to check out the sports deck first. If Cael wasn't there, then she'd walk the Lido deck. Inside the elevator, she fidgeted. Maybe she should've stayed in the room, but she was certain something was wrong, and she was damn tired of being left out of the loop. It was more than curiosity that spurred her on. She didn't like being helpless or worthless.

The dinging sound the elevator made as the doors opened surprised her. So much for stealth. She'd remember that next time, if there was a next time, and take the stairs.

She stepped off the elevator and just ahead, there they were—Cael and a man in a security uniform. The man in the uniform had a gun, and it was pointed at Cael. Oh, Jesus, a *gun*. Her heart leapt into her throat; her knees went weak and she began to shake. But she didn't lose her ability to think. Panicking wouldn't help Cael at all. She'd blown her chance to be stealthy, so she might as well charge onward and pretend she'd never intended not to be seen.

"You're arresting his ass. Good!" She shook her shoe at Cael and walked boldly toward him. "A three-way? The nerve. I thought you were *different*. I thought you *loved* me." She sniffled loudly and turned her attentions, and her shoe, on the man with the gun. He wore the somber uniform of a security guard, along with a brass name tag that read Johnson—yeah right, *Johnson*. On this ship nothing was as it seemed. If the security guard was innocent, Cael would say something, he'd tell her, somehow, to back down. He didn't.

Johnson didn't let the gun waver at all. It was still aimed at Cael's chest, and that sight made her knees feel weak again. The weakness didn't last; she wanted to be a partner, not a hindrance. "Maybe I'm being too hasty," she said, letting the shoe fall a bit. "A lot of people think three-ways are just peachy. Maybe I should give it a try. What do you think, big boy?"

Johnson looked a little shaken at that question. Finally, the gun shifted, just a little. Johnson looked at her and his eyes narrowed. "Hey, I recognize you. You two have the suite next to Mr. Larkin's."

Cael moved like a snake striking, grabbing the guard's arm and pushing his gun hand away, then he delivered a cross to the man's jaw. Jenner stumbled back a half step as she tried to get out of the way of the blow to the man's jaw. Johnson stumbled back, too, into the rail. He gathered himself, the gun came back around and Cael went for it, but Johnson wasn't letting go so easily. He shifted, freed his gun hand from Cael's grip, swung out, and popped Cael in the side of the head with the weapon.

Cael's head snapped around; Jenner choked on a cry as a streak of blood bloomed just above his temple, she instinctively rushed toward him as he began to go down, dropping, as if he were falling to his knees. This wasn't how it was supposed to go. Johnson shifted his aim until the gun was pointed at *her*. He actually smiled.

And Cael's direction shifted. Instead of going down he shifted his weight and surged upward, hitting the armed guard under the chin with his head and sending Johnson reeling backward so hard the armed man slammed into the railing and almost tumbled over. Cael helped, grabbing one leg, lifting, and giving a shove.

Johnson went over, but fighting for his life gave him strength and speed; he managed to catch the rail with one hand as he fell. He hung there, which couldn't have been easy, considering how fat the railing was. Two hands might give him a chance, but as Jenner looked over the rail she saw that he still hadn't let go of his gun. Cael lunged toward her, the words ripping out of his mouth as he reached for Johnson. "Are you all right?"

Yes. No. He was going to shoot *you.* She couldn't find a voice to answer, could barely breathe. She forced herself to nod, then gave a stifled shriek as she caught the movement out of the corner of her eye, saw the gun coming up. Johnson wasn't going down if he could help it, he was going to shoot. Her. Cael. One of them, or both, if he could. Instinctively she swung around and down with the shoe, ramming the point of the heel into the hand that gripped the rail.

Johnson screamed. He couldn't hold on. He, his gun, the shoe . . . they all fell.

Chapter Thirty

It was everything he'd feared. For a split second he'd been looking at Jenner, not the armed security guard, and that distraction could've cost them both their lives.

"I killed that man." Jenner looked over the side, then turned and buried her face against his chest.

"You didn't kill him, I did," Cael said, holding her close. Her body trembled and she felt too cool, but she was far from in a panic. "I tossed him over the rail, not you."

"But I . . . I finished him off." Her voice was soft. Logically, Jenner had to realize that she'd saved their lives, but she'd just played a part in killing a man and that shouldn't go down easy, no matter the circumstances.

Damn, he wished he'd been able to get his hands on that gun before Johnson had gone over the side. He had a really bad feeling that said he was going to need it.

"Come on, let's go back to the room."

She let him lead her, his arm tight around her shoulders. They took the elevator; if anyone got on at the Lido deck, they'd just think the lovers had been out for a late-night walk. The cut on his head wasn't too bad; if anyone noted the blood and asked, he'd tell them he'd fallen and hit his head on the rail. It was a plausible explanation. He didn't want Jenner to have to deal with putting on a false face even for the short time it took to get from one floor to the next, but he wasn't going to make her walk down the stairs, either, not as shaky as she was.

Fortunately, they didn't run into anyone in the elevator, so he just held her, silent until they walked into the stateroom.

"I told you to . . ." he began.

"Don't," she said, turning in to him, pressing her face against his chest. "Not now."

He needed to tell the others what had happened, but that could wait until morning. No need to wake them up; it wasn't like there was anything they could do.

Jenner's tremble gradually eased. He tried to release her, but she grabbed his shirt with both hands and held on tight.

"I'd do it again," she whispered into his chest.

"Don't think about it."

"He was going to *shoot* you."

Maybe. Maybe not. "I know."

"So I'd do it again." She tilted her head back and looked up at him. "Your head's bleeding."

"It's not too bad." If he wasn't unconscious and his vision wasn't affected by a river of blood, he was okay. A tap on the head wasn't going to stop him now.

"I have a first-aid kit . . ."

He kissed her. Without thought, without command, without any reason other than he wanted to. For a long, heart-stopping minute he thought he'd lost her, and the only thing he'd been able to think was that he wasn't ready to let her go. Not now, and probably not for a long, long time.

*

The next day, Tiffany smiled at the bartender and accepted the virgin Bloody Mary she'd ordered. The tomato juice and celery stick fit with her new "on the wagon" persona, as did the outrageous flirting, which wasn't tough. The bartender was cute. Neither he nor anyone else could tell from her actions that anything was out of place.

Surveillance only, Cael had told her when he'd recruited her for this job. Yeah, right. Now a security guard—admittedly a bad security guard, since good ones didn't pull guns on passengers and pop them upside the head with the butt—was food for the fishes, and when word got out there would be hell to pay.

But it was well into the afternoon and she hadn't noticed even a stir among the crew or the passengers. Frank Larkin was picking at his lunch in the outdoor cafe near the bar, where he was dining with one of the movers and shakers on the cruise, a man whose bank account put Larkin's to shame. She turned that way, fiddled with her necklace and took a picture of the two with the tiny camera concealed there. And then, before he had a chance to notice that she was paying too much attention, she walked away, because last night's escapade put them all at risk. They'd have to be extra careful from here on out.

She made a half turn, and immediately spotted the security guard who was watching Larkin from a distance. Her eyes scanned right past him; she saw Buttons standing by the rail, enjoying the view, and she headed that way.

Surveillance only, my ass. Every instinct she possessed told her there was more to this job than any of them knew. In the way of the biz, they'd probably know more than they cared to before it was all said and done.

*

Getting involved with Jenner had been a bad idea. Cael knew better, but he didn't regret a minute. Not a single minute, even though he'd let his dick complicate things beyond hope. He'd never before cared about anyone he'd been on a job with, and now he knew how dangerous it was. Faith and Ryan managed, but damn if he knew how.

He sat in a deck chair, legs stretched out, his mind on the days ahead. If Larkin's bodyguards were not only armed but willing to use those weapons at the drop of a hat, what was going to happen when one of them came up missing?

Jenner walked onto the balcony wearing another of those sexy sundresses with almost no top, and he felt as if the air was sucked from his lungs. Damn, this was so incredibly bad.

She sat on his lap and gave him a too-quick kiss. His arm went around her waist. She smelled good, tasted good. He could almost forget why he was here, and that wouldn't do.

"You should've stayed in Hawaii," he said, a tickle of warning crawling up his spine.

"No way. The return trip has *got* to be better than the first leg. I don't want to miss all the fun." Her smile dimmed. They'd made their own fun, that was the truth, but she wasn't going to forget last night's adventure anytime soon.

"This isn't exactly a pleasure cruise."

"From here on out, it could be," she promised, and everything in him tightened.

He narrowed his eyes and glared at her. "What are you up to?"

"About five-four, barefoot. Why?"

"God, you're a smart-ass."

She smiled. "I know. Lucky for you, because otherwise you'd be bored stiff. Oh, speaking of stiff. Would you be interested if I told you I wasn't wearing any underwear, and I brought this, just in case I got lucky?" She reached into a pocket of the sundress and withdrew a condom between two slender fingers.

Cael drew in a harsh breath, pulling her close and pushing up her skirt. He slid his hand slowly up her thigh, and verified her lack of underwear for himself. Bad idea or not, he was in so deep he might never see daylight, and he didn't want out.

It was as if Cael had literally flipped a switch, bringing to life needs she'd buried for so long they'd been almost entirely forgotten. There was no trust to compare with putting her body in his hands, to opening herself up, letting herself go.

It would be very easy to confuse the intensity of her feelings for love, as she straddled Cael and leaned down to kiss his throat while he caressed her. She didn't want to let him go, but that was strictly a physical response. She could so easily imagine how they'd spend their days when they got off the ship, when in reality she suspected there would be no real first date, no ordinary days. She'd take what she could get while the getting was good. Reality be damned.

"You're so easy," she said, as she laid her hand on his erection, beneath khaki pants.

"I'm easy?" he slipped a hand between her legs, caressed the wetness there. One look from Cael, and she was half ready. One touch, and the other half joined in. "Guys are supposed to be easy. It's in our DNA."

She unfastened and zipped down his pants.

"Easy *and* impatient," he said.

"You talk entirely too much." She kissed him on the mouth, to shut him up and because, damn, she loved kissing him. As the kiss deepened she stroked his penis, driven by the need to feel him in her hand before she unwrapped the damn condom. She was beginning to hate them. If there was a date on dry land, if they stayed together after the cruise and the job was done, she was going to get a prescription for birth control pills. She didn't want anything between them. The thought of him slipping inside her, hard and hot and bare, made her moan deep in her throat.

When he was inside her she forgot everything but the way they felt coming together. She didn't think about anything but pleasure and warmth. Everything else went away, for a while. What they'd found was sex—really good sex—but it was also more than that. It was Cael, the way he made her feel with a look, with a word. He was maddening, bossy, unrelenting . . . and hers, for now.

With the sea breeze wrapping around them and the afternoon sun slanting onto the balcony, she rode him. She swayed, rose, and fell, while he held her hips and guided her.

If they never had to leave this room for the rest of the trip, she'd be content.

Tiffany gladly passed Larkin over to Faith and Ryan. The man they were surveilling was always looking around as if he expected someone to be watching. He was very aware of where he was and who was close by, which made their job much more difficult than it should've been. Instead of returning to her room when her shift was over, she continued to sit by the pool with Penny and Buttons. It was true that it never hurt to take care that it didn't look as if they were literally passing the baton, but it was also true that she had no reason to rush to her suite.

Even though they had nothing in common except for the fact that they were on the *Silver Mist*, she liked Penny and Buttons, and the other ladies, too. Linda and Nyna were taking a Pilates class this afternoon, leaving their new friends to sun by the pool.

Buttons looked to be maybe ten years younger than the women she'd been spending time with on the cruise, but she fit right in. Rich widows, out for a good time. Penny was always on the prowl for a man, but Buttons seemed content with her life.

It hadn't taken Tiffany long to realize that Buttons was a natural-born peacemaker. She wanted everyone to get along. If she could get all the passengers to hold hands and sing camp tunes—"Kumbaya"—she would've been happy as a clam. Tiffany hadn't thought she'd actually like a woman with Buttons's unrealistic traits, but she did. She hadn't made fun of the woman's name once, and was quite proud of herself.

Sitting on the other side of Buttons, Penny was asleep in her deck chair. It struck Tiffany that shortly she'd have to wake the fair-skinned woman to get her out of the sun. Sunscreen or no sunscreen, a nasty burn on that superpale skin would be painful in the morning. And *why* was another woman's sunburn her concern? She was turning into a freakin' caretaker!

"I'm glad you and Jenner are getting along so well," Buttons said, "in spite of the unfortunate circumstances that brought you together."

She stole my man was hardly an ordinary starting point for a solid friendship.

"Yeah, me too. What can I say? When I'm sober I like her." And that was the truth. One tough woman recognized another, and it had not escaped Tiffany's attention that she knew a lot of women who, in the same circumstances, would've thrown the Hazlett broad under the bus without a second thought. Jenner hadn't.

She just hoped Jenner was tough enough to get past killing her first man—and tough enough to handle Cael.

"Where are the lovebirds today?" Buttons asked.

Hiding until Jenner can show her face without also showing too much of the truth. "Oh, you know those two," she said suggestively. She lifted her hands to demonstrate, but realizing what she was about to do, Buttons gently slapped her hands down, laughing.

"It's like one of those old movies," Buttons said with a gentle smile. "You know, the shipboard romance, the two beautiful people who find each other in a crowd and . . ."

"Doesn't someone always end up dead in those movies?" Tiffany interrupted.

Buttons laughed. "I guess you're right." Penny stirred, then slipped back into her afternoon nap.

Tiffany sighed. How had she gotten into this mess? "Hey," she said, sitting up. "We need to get Penny out of the sun before she's extra crispy."

Dean was rarely at a loss when it came to handling a situation, but even as he knocked on the door of Mr. Larkin's suite, he wasn't sure he'd made the right decision.

"Come in," Larkin called, and Dean used his key card; Larkin was expecting him. He wouldn't dare let himself in otherwise, pass key or no pass key.

It had been more than twenty-four hours since anyone had seen Johnson, who should've been keeping an eye on their paranoid employer last night. So, had the bonehead jumped ship before they'd left Maui? Or had Larkin caught the security guard tailing him and tossed him off the boat? You wouldn't think, at first glance, that Larkin could take Johnson in a fight, but Johnson wouldn't expect resistance,

caught following Larkin or not, and truth be told, crazy people could surprise a man.

Larkin was hunched over his laptop computer; he seemed more annoyed than usual.

"Sir, I have some bad news," Dean said after he'd closed the door behind him.

Larkin slapped his computer closed. "Just what I need. What now?"

If Larkin had killed Johnson, and Dean told him that the man had stayed behind, then he'd know it was a lie. If he found out one of his employees, one of his partners in the planned crime, was simply gone, he might panic. This had to be handled just so.

"Johnson's missing," Dean said simply.

Larkin rose up out of his chair. His face turned an odd shade of red. "What do you mean, he's *missing*?"

"He hasn't been seen since we pulled out of Maui. I'm afraid he might've had second thoughts and found a way to stay behind."

"How the hell could that happen?" Larkin was so upset, it seemed unlikely that he knew more than he was letting on.

"He's in security, he could have pulled it off, found a way to bypass being accounted for. The main thing is: Can we handle the job one man short?"

Larkin's face returned to a normal shade, and he sat. "Of course we can." He looked up at Dean, his eyes steadier than they had been a moment ago. "It'll be more difficult, of course, but we can't let Johnson's absence stop us. Too much planning has gone into this."

"He knows too much," Dean said, thinking that Johnson might have truly jumped ship, after all.

"When this is all over, you might want to track him down down and slit his throat."

"Yes, sir. Good idea."

"Now get out. I have things to do."

Dean nodded and slipped into the hallway, sighing once the task was done. All in all, it could've been worse.

The letter still wasn't quite right, and he had the five bombs that were above deck to program. It wouldn't take long, and the tasks could be done at any time in the next twenty-four hours, but there would be some risk involved. He couldn't be seen, couldn't get caught. Not that he could trust anyone else to do the job.

Maybe he'd take his time getting the timers set. The one in the theater tonight; the one under the bar on the Lido deck very early in the morning. The others as the day went on. If he did the job gradually, casually, *piecemeal*, no one would be the wiser. It wasn't as if he could run from deck to deck setting them all at once without raising someone's suspicions.

Fucking Johnson. He knew about the bombs; he was supposed to be here when they went off. Larkin hadn't even gotten started, and already there was a survivor.

He opened his draft file and read what he'd written, then deleted it all and began again.

You fuckers, I wish I could blow you all to hell.

Maybe that simple truth would do.

Part Three

NO LUCK AT ALL

Chapter Thirty-one

Cael couldn't get Larkin's conversation with Dean Mills about Johnson out of his mind, as he dressed for the night's big event, the art auction. The upside was that Johnson's disappearance wasn't going to cause a ripple. The downside was that he'd been right all along; something was up. *Second thoughts. One man short. Slit his throat.*

The only thing that immediately made sense was a robbery, to be pulled off at some time before they docked in San Diego. With all the security on a cruise ship you'd think the passengers would be safe enough, but if members of the security detail were in on the deal, it could certainly be done.

Cael had already informed his people by phone that something was likely to happen, tonight, tomorrow night, or the next. Matt was going to talk to Sanchez to see if there was any way to get weapons for their team. The ship security team would have access to a few weapons, but it wasn't as if there was an arsenal onboard, so getting some weapons was a long shot. Still, with Mills and his men armed, Cael would feel better if they had some kind of backup.

She continually surprised him in a world he'd thought held no more surprises. She'd never backed away from him, never shied away—not after that first night, at least. But now she stared at him even more boldly, as if she could see into him.

He'd never expected this; he'd never expected *her.*

"Look at me like that and you can forget about leaving the stateroom tonight," he teased, though damn if it wasn't the truth.

She smiled. "Works for me."

He didn't tell her what he suspected. She'd only worry. Worry, hell, she'd want a gun. Or a shoe.

Besides, it wasn't like he was going to let her out of his sight.

Frank finally decided on a letter of responsibility that suited him. There were no words to convey his contempt for the people he was taking with him, as well as those he was leaving behind, but this would suffice.

The Silver Mist *will be my funeral pyre, and I suppose that's fitting. I don't give a damn about the passengers. They're sheep, too stupid to realize they're being led, and I'm tired of being their damn shepherd.*

I take full responsibility for the destruction of the Silver Mist. *I planned the attack and planted the bombs myself. Fuck you.*

If they didn't like that last part, they could cut it out of the news coverage. He thought it was important, because it conveyed exactly what he thought of them all. The e-mail would go to three major newspapers, an all-news network, and the three major networks.

He decided to write one more message, since he was in a mood for confessing.

He wanted Johnson's gun more than ever. Damn, what a waste that it had gone over the side with him.

If the robbery, if that's what it was, proceeded without violence, it was possible that the best course of action would be for him and his people to hang back. Stuff could be replaced. A shootout between the pirates—sea robbers was more accurate, and sounded less romanticized—and his people would likely lead to innocent people getting hurt or killed. If they simply took their loot and made their escape, he wouldn't move a muscle. Let them go; it was safer that way.

Might have to use his handcuffs on Tiffany, though. She wasn't particularly good at hanging back.

There was to be an art auction tonight, and the oil paintings that would be on display were worth a pretty penny. Might be just the right time for a robbery. Then again, the paintings weren't going anywhere.

If he were staging a robbery, he'd choose one of the formal events to hit. That's when the diamonds would be out, on display as surely as the paintings were. The artwork could be cut from their frames and stored in waterproof tubes. Cash? There wouldn't be much, since so many of the expenses here were prepaid, or simply charged to one's room, but these were rich folks who didn't travel without cash, and some might have a hefty wad. Was there something else onboard that he didn't know about? Some valuable item—or, God forbid, *someone*—worth taking this kind of risk?

It was the getaway that stumped him. There would have to be another ship of some kind nearby. The robbers could get there by lifeboat or helicopter, if the other ship was so equipped. It would make more sense to wait until they were closer to land, because as soon as the call went out, every

vessel in the area would respond. Coast Guard, na
there was no way to tell who would be in the vicinity.

He could see the security guards getting the drop
passengers at one event or another, but what about the
This was a big ship, and there were crew mer
everywhere. It would be like trying to rob an entire
city, and even if all the security guards were in on the
and that was very unlikely, there were too many holes ir
scenario he tried to imagine, too many things that coulc
wrong.

A mass kidnapping? A demand for ransom from hundre
of wealthy families and high-profile companies? That thoug
caused a chill to run down Cael's spine.

Tonight he had to find a way to speak to Captain Lamber
about his concerns. He'd take the man aside, tell him wha
he suspected, and if necessary why and how he'd found out
and perhaps suggest precautions that could be taken to stop
the robbery or kidnapping before it started. Sanchez already
had a good idea about a handful of security guards who were
in on the deal. Cael considered phoning the captain now, but
unless he was looking in the man's eye, how could he know
if Lamberti was taking him seriously or writing him off as a
nut? Ryan had established a relationship with the captain,
and they had Sanchez on their side, too. Maybe that would
be enough to get his attention.

If not, a viewing of a bit of the surveillance footage and a call
from someone in D.C. who could vouch for their credentials,
and the captain would have no choice but to believe.

Jenner caught his eye, as she walked out of the bathroom
where she'd been fiddling with her hair. Her gown—black
trimmed in white—hugged her torso, showing off her small
but finely shaped breasts. The low scoop of the neckline
teased him.

Chapter Thirty-one

Cael couldn't get Larkin's conversation with Dean Mills about Johnson out of his mind, as he dressed for the night's big event, the art auction. The upside was that Johnson's disappearance wasn't going to cause a ripple. The downside was that he'd been right all along; something was up. *Second thoughts. One man short. Slit his throat.*

The only thing that immediately made sense was a robbery, to be pulled off at some time before they docked in San Diego. With all the security on a cruise ship you'd think the passengers would be safe enough, but if members of the security detail were in on the deal, it could certainly be done.

Cael had already informed his people by phone that something was likely to happen, tonight, tomorrow night, or the next. Matt was going to talk to Sanchez to see if there was any way to get weapons for their team. The ship security team would have access to a few weapons, but it wasn't as if there was an arsenal onboard, so getting some weapons was a long shot. Still, with Mills and his men armed, Cael would feel better if they had some kind of backup.

He wanted Johnson's gun more than ever. Damn, what a waste that it had gone over the side with him.

If the robbery, if that's what it was, proceeded without violence, it was possible that the best course of action would be for him and his people to hang back. Stuff could be replaced. A shootout between the pirates—sea robbers was more accurate, and sounded less romanticized—and his people would likely lead to innocent people getting hurt or killed. If they simply took their loot and made their escape, he wouldn't move a muscle. Let them go; it was safer that way.

Might have to use his handcuffs on Tiffany, though. She wasn't particularly good at hanging back.

There was to be an art auction tonight, and the oil paintings that would be on display were worth a pretty penny. Might be just the right time for a robbery. Then again, the paintings weren't going anywhere.

If he were staging a robbery, he'd choose one of the formal events to hit. That's when the diamonds would be out, on display as surely as the paintings were. The artwork could be cut from their frames and stored in waterproof tubes. Cash? There wouldn't be much, since so many of the expenses here were prepaid, or simply charged to one's room, but these were rich folks who didn't travel without cash, and some might have a hefty wad. Was there something else onboard that he didn't know about? Some valuable item—or, God forbid, *someone*—worth taking this kind of risk?

It was the getaway that stumped him. There would have to be another ship of some kind nearby. The robbers could get there by lifeboat or helicopter, if the other ship was so equipped. It would make more sense to wait until they were closer to land, because as soon as the call went out, every vessel in the area would respond. Coast Guard, navy . . . there was no way to tell who would be in the vicinity.

He could see the security guards getting the drop on the passengers at one event or another, but what about the crew? This was a big ship, and there were crew members everywhere. It would be like trying to rob an entire small city, and even if all the security guards were in on the plan, and that was very unlikely, there were too many holes in the scenario he tried to imagine, too many things that could go wrong.

A mass kidnapping? A demand for ransom from hundreds of wealthy families and high-profile companies? That thought caused a chill to run down Cael's spine.

Tonight he had to find a way to speak to Captain Lamberti about his concerns. He'd take the man aside, tell him what he suspected, and if necessary why and how he'd found out, and perhaps suggest precautions that could be taken to stop the robbery or kidnapping before it started. Sanchez already had a good idea about a handful of security guards who were in on the deal. Cael considered phoning the captain now, but unless he was looking in the man's eye, how could he know if Lamberti was taking him seriously or writing him off as a nut? Ryan had established a relationship with the captain, and they had Sanchez on their side, too. Maybe that would be enough to get his attention.

If not, a viewing of a bit of the surveillance footage and a call from someone in D.C. who could vouch for their credentials, and the captain would have no choice but to believe.

Jenner caught his eye, as she walked out of the bathroom where she'd been fiddling with her hair. Her gown—black trimmed in white—hugged her torso, showing off her small but finely shaped breasts. The low scoop of the neckline teased him.

She continually surprised him in a world he'd thought held no more surprises. She'd never backed away from him, never shied away—not after that first night, at least. But now she stared at him even more boldly, as if she could see into him.

He'd never expected this; he'd never expected *her*.

"Look at me like that and you can forget about leaving the stateroom tonight," he teased, though damn if it wasn't the truth.

She smiled. "Works for me."

He didn't tell her what he suspected. She'd only worry. Worry, hell, she'd want a gun. Or a shoe.

Besides, it wasn't like he was going to let her out of his sight.

Frank finally decided on a letter of responsibility that suited him. There were no words to convey his contempt for the people he was taking with him, as well as those he was leaving behind, but this would suffice.

The Silver Mist *will be my funeral pyre, and I suppose that's fitting. I don't give a damn about the passengers. They're sheep, too stupid to realize they're being led, and I'm tired of being their damn shepherd.*

I take full responsibility for the destruction of the Silver Mist. *I planned the attack and planted the bombs myself. Fuck you.*

If they didn't like that last part, they could cut it out of the news coverage. He thought it was important, because it conveyed exactly what he thought of them all. The e-mail would go to three major newspapers, an all-news network, and the three major networks.

He decided to write one more message, since he was in a mood for confessing.

378

The surly engineer who'd designed the EMP weapon was cautious to the point of being paranoid. Kyle Quillin didn't like to use the Internet for any exchange of sensitive communication. He thought people were spying on him all the time. Larkin had made a nice profit—profit he'd never see—from the EMP sale, and so had Quillin, who could no longer complain that he was underpaid and underappreciated.

But truthfully, Larkin despised the punk. Hell, he despised everyone, but Quillin was such a self-important little bastard. The EMP technology was out there now. It was almost complete, and already in the North Koreans' hands. If the e-mail was tracked and they arrested the kid, the completion of the weapon was still a given. And it would be kind of funny, that the technology Quillin had always feared led to his downfall.

Frank wrote one last e-mail, addressed to Quillin, this one without days of thought and rewriting. *Fuck you.* When something was worth saying, it was worth saying twice.

He'd set his e-mail program to send the messages at a preselected time, which meant he'd have to log onto the Internet and walk away, leaving his laptop on with the incriminating messages just sitting there. He didn't care. He had the trigger for the bombs below deck in his pocket, along with a weapon he probably wouldn't need, and the incendiary bombs on the higher decks, all five of them, had been activated. He glanced at his watch.

One hour and seven minutes.

He smiled, and for a moment, one precious moment, the pain in his head faded almost to nothing.

Ryan looked fabulous in his tuxedo, as usual. Faith smiled at him as she slipped the posts of her eye-catching emerald earrings into her ears and fastened them. The earrings had been a Valentine's Day gift, one of many. She had to admit, her husband did things right.

Her own attire for the evening, a pale champagne silk gown that was draped elegantly on her body, was one of the more comfortable she owned but also one of the most expensive. There were days when she was willing to pay a pretty penny for comfort. The fact that this gown drove Ryan wild was a nice bonus.

A soft ping from the computer, which was sitting on the desk in the parlor, alerted her to the fact that she had a message. Maybe Larkin had finally signed on to the Internet and the key-logger program was paying off. Then again, it was more likely a message from her sister, who was determined that the two of them would go on a cruise together before the year was out, and had sent several messages to that effect.

Faith didn't rush into the other room, but slipped into her shoes and straightened the emerald necklace, a birthday present, that matched the earrings, before she walked into the parlor to check the laptop. Before she left for the evening, just in case, she'd program her iPhone to capture anything that came in while she was out of the room. She didn't sit, not wanting to wrinkle her gown just yet, but bent over the desk and opened the laptop.

Jackpot.

She smiled as she opened the program so she could see what Larkin had typed into the computer. The luck she was having with this program so far, it was probably a note to his mother. Did men like Larkin *have* mothers?

She read the message, and her smile disappeared.

"Ryan!" she shouted.

Recognizing the urgency in her voice, he ran into the parlor. "What's wrong?"

Her heart was pounding so hard she could feel it; her knees felt suddenly weak. "Larkin is going to blow up the ship and everyone on it."

"When?" Ryan asked pragmatically, already reaching for his cell phone.

"I don't know. Tonight, I think. He didn't give a time, but it looks like the e-mails are set to be sent in an hour, so . . . shortly after that, maybe. He won't want anyone to have advance warning."

"I'll start calling the others, you call Cael."

"Then what?" Faith asked as she dialed.

"Then we get the hell off this ship."

Larkin had called Isaac earlier in the evening and told him to take the night off. His steward had been surprised but grateful. Frank had suggested that Isaac spend some time in the crew bar, maybe sit around the sad little crew hot tub. He'd even told Isaac that he'd been doing a good job and deserved a break.

Truth was, he didn't want to take the chance that Isaac would get nosy and look at the laptop and the messages there. The only other man Frank might have to worry about walking into his room uninvited was Dean Mills, and since he was sitting across from Dean at the moment he wasn't concerned about that.

They were alone, at a small table in the corner of the Fog Bank. Dean was anxious, worried about his boss's plan to make an escape, a plan he didn't quite buy into. Greed had kept him on a leash thus far.

"Relax," Frank said as he sipped at what was probably his last scotch. "In just two hours, the excitement will begin." In two hours the excitement would be over, for most of the people on this ship. But Dean didn't need to know that.

Frank was prepared for anything and everything. His gun—a .40-caliber PM40 Dean had provided, when Frank had insisted that he needed a weapon for the big event—sat deep in one pocket. It was a smallish gun, but it was heavy and the bulge ruined the line of his suit. Who the hell cared? He hated the way a gun felt tucked in his waistband, and was always afraid he'd shoot his balls or his ass. Unlike Dean, he didn't own a shoulder holster. The pocket would do. Sitting here, directly above one of the incendiary bombs that would explode in less than an hour, no one could see the bulge in his pocket, anyway.

But if he needed it . . .

"I'm worried about Sanchez," Dean said in a very low voice.

"Who's that?" Frank truly felt no concern. Knowing he was about to die was more freeing than frightening.

"A security guard. I swear, I run into the guy every time I turn around. I think he's watching me."

"Don't be paranoid, Dean." Frank took a leisurely sip of his scotch. "If he gets in your way tonight, shoot him."

That slut Tiffany Marsters was sitting at the bar, drinking water and laughing with the bartender. She'd been more entertaining as a lush, but sobriety hadn't improved her tastes. The short, skintight bright blue dress she wore might've been painted on her, and how the hell did she walk in those shoes? Dean had cast more than one appreciative glance her way, even though he was worried about the plan for tonight and should have other things on his mind. Tiffany reached for a small gold clutch purse and opened it, pulling out a cell phone. He hadn't heard it ring, but then she was a good distance away. She didn't strike him as the sort who'd set her phone to vibrate out of consideration for others.

Dean was looking that way again.

Frank leaned forward. "After tonight, women like that will flock to you," he whispered, hoping to ease Dean's fears. "Money is a powerful aphrodisiac."

Judging by the expression on the man's face, the comforting words did the trick.

"Where are you?" Ryan's voice was unusually sharp on the phone.

"Excuse me," Tiffany said, smiling at the bartender as she slipped off her stool and walked away, searching for a bit of privacy. It wasn't like she could talk freely, though Ryan knew she was watching Larkin at the moment. "Fog Bank," she said, as if she were setting up a meeting with a friend.

"Is he there?" Ryan asked.

"Yes. What's up?" she asked casually, in case the bartender was paying attention, even from a distance.

"Don't look at him, don't react."

Tiffany stiffened. This couldn't be good.

"Larkin has planted several bombs on the ship." Ryan's voice was crisp, and she didn't interrupt him to ask questions. This wasn't the only call he'd have to make. "We don't know how many or when they're set to detonate, but it looks like tonight. Since he set his e-mail program to send out a couple of e-mails in approximately forty-five minutes, we should have at least that amount of time to get things under control."

"Shit." It took all her willpower not to turn and look at Larkin, to stare at the monster. *I can take him*, she thought.

Ryan knew her too well. "Don't make a move. Cael's

calling the captain, and Sanchez is trying to get some weapons for us. For now, stay on Larkin. I'll be in touch."

The call ended, and Tiffany dropped the cell back into her purse. With every fiber of her being, she wanted to run across the room and strangle Larkin with her bare hands. But she didn't. She returned to her barstool, smiled at the bartender even though her heart was pounding, and waited. Her self-preservation instincts were shrieking *Bombs! Bombs!*, but what the hell could she do? She was in the middle of the freakin' ocean with nowhere to go.

Cael hadn't spoken to her directly about what was happening, but Jenner had heard his end of the conversation, and she knew enough. More than enough.

Bombs. That psycho Larkin was going to blow up the *Silver Mist*. Jenner thought about the people she knew, the passengers and crew she had never met, the friends she had made here. Friends, not mere acquaintances.

If Cael and his team weren't following Larkin, if they hadn't kidnapped her and Syd and set up surveillance, Larkin would've gotten away with this. It wasn't a given that he might not still get what he wanted.

It took Cael precious minutes to get the captain on the phone, and they didn't have a minute to lose.

"Captain Lamberti, this is Cael Traylor. There are bombs on this ship and they're going to blow tonight. You need to begin evacuation procedures immediately." Cael grit his teeth as he listened to the captain's response. "No, this isn't a bomb *threat*. It's a warning." He looked at Jenner. "Fine, arrest me. Lock me up. But before you do that, please get the passengers off this floating death trap." He listened a while longer, his patience fraying, and then he said two very important words, "Frank Larkin."

Cael hung up the phone, and two seconds later, the alarm sounded. A voice—the captain's—spoke loudly over the shipwide intercom. *"This is not a drill. Please proceed to your Muster Stations. Repeat, this is* not *a drill."* Cael ran into the bedroom and grabbed the two PFDs, then he took Jenner's arm and led her to the door. "Move it, sweetheart. You're getting off this ship now."

"You mean we, right?" she said as he ushered her into the hallway. Her heart was pounding. Well-dressed people who hadn't yet moved to the upper decks for the evening were beginning to leave their rooms, some with PFDs, others empty-handed and confused. "You mean *we*."

She freed herself from his grip and knocked on Linda and Nyna's door, hoping to hurry the ladies along.

No one answered, and Cael wasn't in any mood to wait. Knowing how important this was to her, he stepped back and kicked at the door Jenner had been knocking on. It splintered, cracked, swung open crookedly.

She called out; received no answer. Linda and Nyna weren't there; their stateroom was empty. Cael grabbed her and half-dragged her to the stairwell where they joined the others who were fleeing. Holding on as best she could, she prayed the ladies were already on deck and headed for safety.

The siren continued to blare; some of the passengers in the stairwell were crying, and one man pushed another aside.

"Don't panic," Cael called in a calm but inflexible voice that carried well. He gave the man who had pushed the other a look that said he'd toss his ass to the bottom of the stairs if he didn't settle down. "Everybody will get off the ship if you all remain calm. We have time." Not a lot of it, but some.

"Time for what?" one of the more impatient men shouted. "What do you know that we don't?"

"I know if you keep shoving, someone's going to get hurt," Cael said. Jenner wanted to kick the man's ass on general principle, but Cael was right. Panic didn't help anyone.

Without warning there was a deafening blast from below. The boat shook, lurched wildly to one side, and Jenner grabbed onto the stairwell railing to keep from falling. Some dust and debris filled the air as she bent down and wrenched off her shoes. She should've gotten out of these heels before leaving the suite, but changing into running shoes hadn't been on her mind. In front of her, Ginger Winningham stumbled and almost fell. Her husband, Albert, caught her; so did Cael, offering a steady hand.

Then he turned and looked at her with those deep blue eyes she'd come to love so very dearly. And she saw in those eyes what she, and all these other people, suspected.

They might not make it off this damn ship alive.

Chapter Thirty-two

Frank was happy, content, excited . . . and then the alarm sounded. Dean jumped to his feet. "What's happening?"

"You idiot," Frank said, his voice tight but calm. "Obviously someone's found one of the bombs." He suspected that one of the devices that had been placed below deck, those he hadn't personally hidden, had not been properly hidden. This was what happened when you were forced to leave important tasks to morons.

Most of the handful of customers in the bar were heading for the exits, but some remained. One old man insisted he wasn't leaving until his drink was finished. A couple on the other side of the room thought it was just another drill. The Marsters woman had become hysterical, and was apparently trying to call someone on her cell phone instead of following instructions and making her way to the lifeboats.

"Let's go," Dean said softly. "Our only chance is to act like we don't know anything, like we're as surprised as everyone else. I need to get you into a lifeboat."

"No," Frank said, remaining seated. He glanced at his watch; in a little more than half an hour, the incendiary bombs would explode. Half an hour! Sudden fury shook him. He wasn't about to sail away and watch the ship burn without him. His plan was falling apart before his eyes; people were already making their way to the lifeboats. Dammit, he wasn't going to die alone.

Frank stood, drew his gun from his pocket, and pulled the trigger. He wasn't a particularly good shot, but Dean was close and the single shot did the trick. Dean crumpled. With his free hand, Frank removed the remote from his pocket and looked at it for a moment. If the drill continued, everyone would get off the ship before the bombs went off. That wouldn't do at all. The bastards! Someone had fucked up his plan. He braced himself, flipped back the safety trigger, and punched the button with his thumb.

Captain Lamberti had ordered some of the crew to search for the bombs, in case any of them could be disarmed, or maybe he didn't really believe there were any bombs and he wanted to prove it. Bridget had moved from the water treatment room to the storeroom, wondering where she'd hide a bomb on a ship, if that was her job. The place was huge; there were so many possibilities. Where would a bomb do the most damage? Electrical areas, engine room, control room, water treatment, anywhere near the hull . . .

The crew was divided. Some were headed up to help with the evacuation, and to escape themselves. Others were sticking with their jobs, for now, tying up loose ends, planning to head up in a few minutes. It wasn't like crew would be evacuated first anyway, no matter what the reason for the alarm.

They didn't know what she knew—that there were explosives hidden under their very noses.

According to Faith, they had some time. Larkin wouldn't

blow up the ship until his e-mail messages were off. Otherwise, why bother to write them? They had at least half an hour. Maybe more. If they could find and defuse the bombs in that thirty minutes, they wouldn't need to abandon ship.

Not that they knew how many bombs Larkin had placed, or where the hell they were. She and Matt were searching on the lowest levels, and would work their way up. She didn't have the capabilities to defuse a bomb, but Matt did. Matt was one level up, on the level where the majority of the crew resided. That floor would be all but deserted during a crisis like this.

Unfortunately, she couldn't use her cell to call Matt if she found a device, since the cell signal might detonate the bomb, particularly if she was right on top of it. She'd have to go old school—running and screaming. Given the circumstances, she could handle that.

They were going to give it fifteen minutes, then head up to get the hell out of Dodge.

Then . . . success. Or failure, depending on how she looked at it. She would have preferred not finding anything. Wedged between a tall stack of cases of Coke and a similarly tall stack of boxes of crackers, a device sat, clumsily disguised by an empty cardboard box. She very carefully moved the box aside.

Bridget was no expert when it came to explosives, but she recognized the blocks of Semtex. A simple detonator was strapped to the explosives, and there was a tiny red light that blinked at a slow, steady rate.

One down . . .

Without warning there was a clicking sound from the bomb, and the light turned a steady red. Bridget instinctively backed up, but she knew it was too late.

"Our Father . . ."

*

Linda Vale walked briskly down the hallway, realizing, too late, that she should've gone to the aerobics class with Nyna this afternoon. Instead she'd taken a nap, spent time dolling herself up for the evening, and then headed down to meet Penny and Buttons in their room. Penny wanted help doing her hair, and while Linda thought it was rather like the blind leading the blind, she'd agreed to do what she could. After her class, Nyna would shower and dress quickly and meet them in the stateroom on the lower level, then they'd all go to the art auction together.

Nice plan. Too bad it had fallen apart. The alarm had sounded while she'd been in the elevator. It had stopped on this floor and she'd exited with the couple who'd been on with her. The elevators had stopped working because of some safety system, she supposed. She was going to have to take the stairs down another level—or was it two?

It was so easy to get turned around on the ship, and it was all but impossible to make her way down while everyone else was headed up. People trying to escape pushed, they refused to step aside and let her pass, so she sometimes took one step back and then two forward. She looked for Penny and Buttons, but didn't see them in the crowd. Had she already missed them, or were they waiting for her? Poor Nyna was probably in a panic, on the top deck all by herself. Linda felt more than a touch of panic herself. Of all the times to be alone!

She kept going down, pushing her way past fleeing passengers, her progress maddeningly slow. Many of them tried to convince her to head up with them, but she shook her head and kept going. If she saw her friends, she'd gladly head up to the Muster Station. Muster Station Three, she remembered. If she could just remember where it was . . .

She squeezed past a frantic couple and slipped into a

hallway, taking a deep breath, glad to be out of the crush. This was the floor where Penny and Buttons's room was, wasn't it? Most people had already fled, so there was only one lagging couple in the hallway. Linda ran half the length of the hall, then stopped. She wasn't going in the right direction. The elevator she usually took would've put her in the corridor in a different place.

Linda was standing in the middle of the hallway when an iciness shot through her body. Her neck tingled, as if someone had blown cool air there. A man whispered her name and she spun around, certain, even though it should be impossible, she was going to see Wayne standing there. She even called his name, held her breath expectantly, and then a blast beneath her feet deafened her, blew her up and back, stole the air from her lungs. And she realized that she'd been right.

"Wayne . . ."

Without any prior indication that it was coming, Larkin shot Mills. Tiffany turned, looked directly at the psycho as he pulled another object from his pocket. A remote trigger. Shit! He thumbed the device and, after a momentary pause, a couple of seconds at most, the ship shook; below, there was a terrifying rumble. The sirens continued to sound for a moment and then they stopped. The lights in the bar flickered and went out, and a moment later, emergency lighting came up.

Larkin was pointing his weapon at her, and as he fired she instinctively ducked, then rolled on the floor, making herself small and looking for cover. Had he made her? Was he shooting at her because she'd seen him hit that remote and shoot Mills?

391

She soon realized he was shooting not at *her* but at everyone who remained in the bar. The bartender. An older man who had refused to take the drill seriously until the explosion. A crew member who was trying to get everyone out of the bar. A couple who'd been cool before but were now in shock.

A dark-haired, stocky woman stumbled into the side entrance, near to Larkin. She'd been crying; the skirt of her long black gown was torn, as if she'd fallen to her knees, hard. "I'm looking for my husband," she said. Larkin turned toward her and fired again. A neat black hole appeared in her forehead. Her head snapped back, she fell, and Larkin calmly stepped over her body and walked out the side door.

Those around her were shocked, either screaming or looking as if they were about to faint, but Tiffany acted. She took her cell phone, stuck it in her bra, and ran. She reached Mills, crouched down, and grabbed the gun she knew he always carried.

He wasn't quite dead, but he would be soon. "Wait," he whispered.

"Honey, I can't do a thing for you," Tiffany said without sympathy. Mills had chosen the wrong side, and this is where it got him.

"I know, but . . . there are more," he said, his voice almost gone.

"More people? More bombs?" Tiffany pressed.

"Both."

She grabbed her cell phone and tried to call Cael, but she couldn't get through. She didn't think the cell tower itself had been damaged, but the bombs below had done a lot of damage and the power was out. Apparently there was only the most minimal auxiliary power. At least she wasn't completely in the dark.

Tiffany returned her cell to her bra, on the off chance the power was restored. What were the odds she'd run into Cael, or one of the others? Slim, but not none. Until then, she'd do what she did.

She followed Larkin. "That psycho fucker's mine," she muttered as she stepped onto the Lido deck. Maybe Larkin was a terrible shot, but she wasn't.

The blast from below threw Matt back. He landed hard, hitting his head against the wall. His arm took a good shot as it banged against a metal shelf in the storage closet he'd been searching, and then he landed on it funny, and pain shot through his entire body. His ears rang, filling his head with a high-pitched humming that drowned out everything else.

But he didn't lose consciousness, and urgency got him to a sitting position, then he staggered to his feet. His first evaluation said he wasn't bleeding too much, he didn't think. The power had gone out, then the emergency lighting came up, casting sad, insufficient illumination over one of the least impressive parts of the ship. He couldn't see very well, but he didn't think he was hurt all that bad.

He was still stunned though, and it took him a few seconds to reclaim his ability to think past the ringing in his head. He hadn't found a single bomb, but it was a big-ass ship, and judging by the blasts, they'd all been placed one deck down.

Where Bridget was conducting her sweep. *Shit*. Bridget!

Matt jumped up, and his arm protested. He glanced down and realized he hadn't gotten off so lightly after all. His arm was obviously broken, which meant he wouldn't be able to dig his way out if he got trapped down here. He gripped his wrist to keep the arm still, until he could find something to fashion a sling with, and he ran into the corridor and toward the stairs. He burst into the stairway, which was filling with smoke. Black smoke drifted up the stairs. He shouted, but the sound was odd to his own ears. If he'd lost most of his hearing one level up, any survivors below would likely be deaf.

There had to be survivors, and it was possible Bridget was one of them. Maybe. Hundreds of crew members had been below, while he'd climbed one flight to begin his search. Then he saw movement in the smoke and he waited, expecting a stream of people to emerge.

Four. Only *four* had made it out? Surely to God there'd be more. This was just the first bunch, wasn't it? He stared at them in disbelief. All of them were injured in some way. Cuts, mostly, some of them serious, others less so. Two of the survivors had blood seeping from their ears.

"Bridget," Matt called loudly. "Did any of you see her?" Two women and one man just looked at him, dazed and deaf, thinking only of getting to the top of the ship. They continued on without stopping. Jane, a pretty blonde who worked the deck as he did, was at the end of the line. He caught her eye and she stopped on the landing.

"Bridget?" he shouted, dazed. A rivulet of blood ran down one side of Jane's face, but she didn't appear to be seriously injured.

Jane pointed to her ears and shrugged her shoulders. Tears sprung to her eyes.

Matt pointed to his mouth, hoping she could read lips. "My friend, the steward," he said slowly. "*Bridget.*"

Jane grimaced. "I saw her earlier." She spoke loudly, shouted as Matt had, and placed one palm against the side of her head, maybe trying to ease the ringing. "Bridget was headed into the storeroom. I think she was really close to one of the blasts. At least, she went that way and I didn't see her leave . . ." The tears trickled down her cheeks. "What happened? What went wrong? Matt, there are *dead* people down there!"

"Keep moving," Matt yelled, pointing up to direct her. "Get yourself on a lifeboat asap."

"Are you coming?" Jane screamed.

"No," Matt said, and he continued downward, into the thick smoke.

Ryan's only intent was to get his wife off the *Silver Mist*.

It was bizarre, to see all these people in evening dress running for the boats. This was nothing like the lifeboat drill, where women had giggled and men had been bored and irritated that they'd been pulled away from their putting practice or card game. Tonight order was forgotten—and then, the blast shook the boat and changed everything.

Passengers were already in a couple of unlaunched lifeboats—good-size vessels that could easily hold forty to fifty passengers—orange PFDs in place over tuxedoes and evening gowns. After the blasts women screamed; men showed their stripes, either assisting or shoving others out of the way. After the explosions below, the usual bright lights of the ship went out, and a moment later were replaced with emergency, battery-powered lights. What had been crisis became chaos.

He steered Faith toward one of the crew members and a lifeboat. "I'm going to find Cael."

"I'll go with you."

He kissed her briefly, wondering if it would be the last time. "You're not a fighter, Faith."

"But . . ."

"And you'll distract me when I can't afford distraction."

Her lips tightened. She looked at him with her heart in her eyes. She didn't like it, but she knew he was right. "I love you," she said. "Be careful." And then, tears streaming down her face, she allowed the crewman to take her hand and assist her into the lifeboat. He watched as the boat was swung away from the larger ship and lowered. The first group was away.

Cael held Jenner's hand as they burst out of the stairwell and onto the Lido deck. Behind them people pushed and shoved, screamed and cried. He separated from the group, protecting Jenner as much as he could with his body, steering her away from the crush.

The blasts had done serious damage, but the ship was extremely well built. The *Silver Mist* wasn't going to sink, at least, not for some time. Though damned if she wasn't listing a bit.

"You're getting on a lifeboat," he directed.

"Not without you," Jenner responded, her voice steady.

He looked into her eyes. She was stubborn, determined, immovable. Damn it, he didn't have time for this. "For me," he said, playing the only card he figured he had where she was concerned. Apparently it wasn't enough.

She gave him a scornful look. "Not on your life."

Poor choice of words. "I can't leave until I know my people are accounted for, and I'd like to make sure Frank Larkin doesn't blow anyone else up. And damn it Jenner, I'd really like to know you're safely away from here when I do what has to be done."

On all sides, there was mayhem, and he didn't know what had happened to his team. Behind him, someone screamed

"He's been shot!" and a chill walked up his spine. Jenner still kept it together, though. She realized the seriousness of the situation, but she wasn't falling apart.

"I know you better than you realize," she said in an even voice. "You're a damn hero. If I'm right behind you, if you know without a doubt that I'm not getting on a lifeboat until you do, then you'll take better care of yourself."

The hell of it was, she wasn't wrong.

Chapter Thirty-three

After taking a few minutes to walk among the panicked passengers and enjoy the upheaval he'd created, Larkin slipped into the side entrance of a restaurant, The Club, which was barely lit by the auxiliary lights mounted on the walls. He walked past the empty tables, which still showed the evidence of the passengers who'd been sitting there until a short time ago, toward the kitchen. Hidden deep in a storage closet in the kitchen, one of the incendiary bombs sat armed to go off in, he glanced at his watch, twenty-three minutes.

The sounds of passengers screaming pierced the walls. Unfortunately they were primarily screams of fright, not pain.

Not yet.

He walked into the deserted kitchen, past the food prep area. Passengers had been eating, or waiting for their food, when the alarm had sounded. The kitchen had been abandoned as the crew made their escape. The grill had been turned off, but no one had bothered to put away the food, and there had been no one remaining in the dining room to consume the finished meals.

There was some indignity in dying in a closet, but in the end it wouldn't matter. Besides, it was quiet here. There was no traffic in and out. He could die in peace.

The headache that had faded for a while was back with a vengeance, like nails shooting through his skull. Thank goodness the sirens had been silenced.

He knew the procedures for such emergencies. And since events had not gone as planned, the captain had no doubt contacted the Coast Guard via the Amver system. How soon would rescue arrive? Likely not within twenty-three minutes. He glanced at his watch again. Twenty-two, now. The Pacific was a big ocean, with miles and miles and miles to be covered before anyone would reach the distressed *Silver Mist*.

So, a few more people would escape than he'd planned. At this rate not everyone would make it off by lifeboat, though. The idiots were panicking, costing themselves precious time. He wondered how things had gone below. Had Isaac been near the blast? Was he dead? Injured? Ignorant that his employer was responsible? He could only imagine the surprise of the security guards who'd been counting all this time on a robbery that had never been a part of the master plan.

For years, Larkin had been a success in every venture he began. He'd made deals happen, he'd influenced politics and finance, he'd secretly brokered arms deals that had affected the entire world. What was wrong with the fucking world that he couldn't pull off his suicide in the way he'd planned?

He glanced at his watch again. Twenty-one minutes.

Jenner stayed close to Cael, but she made a point not to get in his way. She didn't say a word when Ryan found them, and informed Cael that Faith was already off the ship, having gone on one of the first lifeboats to launch. And he didn't take the time to needle her because Faith had cooperated and she had not.

Maybe later.

Captain Lamberti found the two men in the crowd. His distinguished face was set with purpose. "The Coast Guard has been informed," he said. "Every ship in the area, if possible, will come to our rescue." There was no telling what kind of ships were nearby: fishing boats, freighters, other cruise ships. The problem was, they were currently hell and gone from any other ship. It was going to take precious time for rescue to arrive. Lamberti didn't linger. Maybe it was true that the bombs hadn't sunk the ship, as had been intended, but people had been killed—and he didn't yet know how bad the toll was. No one did.

It was after the captain had moved on that Cael and Ryan put their heads together. "We need to find Sanchez," Cael said.

"If he was below when the bombs went off—" Ryan said, then stopped and shrugged. They had no way of knowing where he'd been. Security personnel could have been anywhere on the ship at the time of the explosion, so his fate wasn't a given. Larkin was still unaccounted for, and so was Tiffany, who'd been tailing him. Matt and Bridget had both been below when the bombs had been detonated, and with the cell tower out there was no way to check on them.

Cael turned once to look at her, and she saw the hint of a plea in his eyes.

"I'm not leaving until you do," she said, gentle but firm.

A couple she knew ran past, dressed in evening wear and PFDs. Though they passed by so near they almost ran her

400

down, neither of them looked at Jenner closely enough to recognize her. Their attention was on the lifeboats.

"Sanchez!" Ryan suddenly shouted, and Cael's head snapped around. He immediately spotted the Hispanic man, who was a head taller than those around him, trying to make his way to them. He was hard to miss. With his wide shoulders he could've easily forced his way through the crowd, but he gently moved panicked passengers aside, and directed several to the boats.

When Sanchez finally reached Cael, he reached beneath his jacket and pulled out a pistol. He handed it to Cael, keeping the movement furtive. The passengers would panic again if they saw weapons being passed around. "You guys are easy to spot in the crowd," he said with a strange sort of sigh, and Jenner realized it was the truth. They were the only ones not running for the lifeboats.

"Tucker's dead," Sanchez said in a voice lowered so only they could hear. Not that anyone around them cared what was being discussed. They were only interested in getting off the ship as fast as possible. "He was killed in the blast; that's his weapon. I was on my way down before the explosion but got delayed. I wasn't near the blast, as Tucker was."

"The others?" Cael prompted.

"Asker and Zadian are on the loose, as far as I can tell."

"That's it?" Ryan asked. "Is anyone else besides Larkin and those two involved?"

"Not to my knowledge."

Cael nodded to Sanchez. "Thanks for your help. You can head to the lifeboat station . . ."

"No thank you, sir," the security guard responded. "I'd like to see this through, if I can."

Cael nodded, and then a furious voice made them all turn

their heads. "There you are." Tiffany had a gun in one hand, but it was down at her side and in the crush no one seemed to notice—or care. Her exotic eyes were snapping with rage. "Larkin's on this deck somewhere, at least he was last time I saw him, and according to Mills there are more bombs and more people in on this shit."

"We know about the people," Cael responded. "But we don't have any information about more explosives. Where's Mills?"

"Mills is dead, so he's not going to be any more help." Tiffany looked down at Jenner. "Why aren't you on a lifeboat?"

Jenner didn't hesitate. "You first."

She took a moment to study the people gathered together, a sea of control in the midst of the chaos. Cael, Ryan, Tiffany, Sanchez, and her. They were, in effect, a small army. It annoyed the hell out of Jenner to recognize the fact that she was not a part of this army, but she'd always been pragmatic. She wanted to be one of them, an asset in a crisis, and if they got out of this in one piece maybe she would be. But now . . .

"We can assume Faith's original estimation on time was correct, which means we have less than twenty minutes," Cael said. "We can probably count on fifteen. We're going to split up. Much as I'd like to get my hands on Larkin, the bombs are our first priority. He'll know where they are, and so might Asker and Zadian. Do we all know what they look like?"

Everyone nodded, except Jenner. She hadn't been in on their briefings until this point. She hadn't even heard the names Asker and Zadian before this moment.

"Jenner!" She spun around at the sound of that voice, coming face-to-face with a teary Nyna.

402

"Nyna, why aren't you on a lifeboat!"

"I can't find Linda," Nyna said. She wasn't dressed in evening clothes, like most of the others, but was in one of her workout outfits. Tears streaked her face. "I was supposed to meet her in Buttons and Penny's suite, but they're sealing off the stairways, not letting anyone go down."

Jenner took the woman's hand and looked her in the eye with confidence, though she felt no confidence at all. "Linda's probably already evacuated."

Nyna shook her head. "I don't think so. She has no sense of direction at all."

Jenner looked at Cael. She didn't like it, she didn't like it at all, but he had something to do that she couldn't help him with. She had to accept that, if she stayed, she was going to be in his way, she was going to distract him when he didn't need distraction. She wanted to be useful, to make a difference in this crisis, and she couldn't do that by hanging on to Cael's coattails.

What she could do was get Nyna off the boat before more bombs started going off. Less than twenty minutes! Maybe she could find Linda, and make sure Penny and Buttons got onto a lifeboat.

Their eyes met. Cael realized what she was thinking, he knew she was about to take charge of Nyna and leave him to do what he had to do. She didn't have to explain, but she went up on her toes, kissed him, and then whispered, "Muster Station Three, fifteen minutes. Get yourself hurt and I'll kick your ass."

It wasn't like she had any place to hide a gun.

With Sanchez directly behind her, Tiffany followed Cael's directions and took the stairs up to the sports deck. Unlike

403

the stairs coming up from the staterooms and the theater level below, these were deserted. There had been plenty of time for anyone who'd been up here when the alarm sounded to get to their Muster Station.

Larkin was likely either on the Lido deck or the sports deck. He wouldn't have taken the risk of taking the stairways down when so many people were surging up and the crew was doing their best to make sure everyone moved upward.

She wasn't afraid of doing what had to be done, but honestly, this was not what she'd signed on for. "It's a cruise," she said in a soft, high voice, mimicking Cael even though he'd never spoken in such a squeaky voice. "It'll be fun."

Tiffany stepped into the open, eyes peeled for movement where there should be none. Sanchez was directly behind her; they instinctively separated. She headed for the fitness center; he walked toward the putting greens.

Since there was so much open space on this deck, and no one was jockeying for position, it should be easier to search than the Lido deck. Not that there weren't plenty of places for a man to hide. She was determined to get her hands on Larkin, but she wouldn't mind grabbing Asker and Zadian, too. According to Cael, they were in on the planning, had probably been in on planting the bombs.

How many more, and when were they set to blow?

Though the deck was not well lit, she was alert, on edge, and when she saw a bit of movement out of the corner of her eye, she spun around. Her gun hand popped up, and the other came with it, a steadying hand. Two figures were in shadow, so she didn't fire. Could be lost passengers, confused folks who were so panicked they'd decided to hide up here instead of evacuating. Unlikely, but before she pulled the trigger she had to be sure.

A man, not Larkin, yelled, "She has a gun!" And fired.

Tiffany returned fire as she quickly moved to cover behind the decorative pressed concrete of the elevator bank. The two men moved into the dim light as she scooted out of their line of sight. Asker and Zadian, looking very much like the pictures Faith had pulled up online, after Sanchez had given them the names of those he thought were involved with Mills.

The gunfire brought Sanchez running, his own weapon drawn. He drew fire, and Tiffany took the opportunity to take aim at the dark-haired man who was shooting at Sanchez. Her shot took Asker down. Sanchez got Zadian.

With both men down, Tiffany left her cover and joined Sanchez. Asker was dead, a bullet between his eyes, but Zadian had a bit of life left in him. Sanchez collected their weapons while Tiffany stood over Zadian and glared. "Where is he?"

"Who?"

As if he didn't know. "Larkin."

The man turned his head and spit. "Larkin lied to us. He never intended for us to get away before he set off the bombs. Why would he . . ." He stopped, breathing heavily. If there were a hospital nearby, he might survive the shot to the gut. Unfortunately for him, there wasn't.

Tiffany asked. "Were you looking for Larkin up here?" She had them pegged as men who'd push old ladies out of the way in order to get off a sinking ship, unless something very important delayed them.

"Yes." Zadian laid a hand over his wound, but didn't look at it. "He's not here. Maybe he escaped, leaving us . . ."

"Larkin didn't go anywhere." Too many people were looking for him. Cael and the captain had taken care of that. Besides, according to the e-mails, Larkin intended to die here tonight, and take as many people as possible with him. He wasn't thinking of escape.

"Where are the bombs?"

Zadian panted, then shook his head. "I planted one in the control room below, and another in the storeroom. I don't know where the above-deck bombs were placed."

"Who placed them?"

"Mills and Johnson."

Two dead guys. Great. Larkin was their only chance to get to the bombs before it was too late.

"Larkin must be on the Lido," Tiffany said as he turned back toward the stairway. "We need to get one of those weapons to Ryan and . . ."

"Kill me," Zadian said, drawing her attention. "Please, kill me."

She glanced back at him, then snorted. Like she'd do any favors for a fucker like that.

Cael got more and more pissed as he searched the bars and cafes on the Lido deck.

The evacuation procedure had reached a calmer level, but the crew members who were loading the boats and lowering them didn't realize there were more explosions coming. Since they were working at maximum capacity, it wouldn't do any good to tell them. In fact, they'd panic and the procedure would probably suffer.

He heard the distant ring of gunfire. Larkin, or the security guards who were on the loose? His gut told him Larkin was close.

Damn it, he and his team weren't here for wet work, they were a surveillance crew. *Surveillance!* All of this felt too damn familiar to him, but his team hadn't signed on for this. Neither had he, but what the hell; you took what came at you. In a few minutes, according to the plan he'd set with the others before they'd split up, they were going to get off the ship themselves. By that time it would likely be too late to find and defuse the bombs. Let Larkin blow himself up.

There were too many places on this ship to hide a bomb, too many possibilities. Since these were likely civilian bombs, IEDs that could be any size or makeup, he didn't even know what to look for.

Only Larkin would know, and they were about to pass the time where that knowledge would do them any good.

He kicked in a kitchen door, raised his weapon, and there was the bastard, sitting on the floor in the doorway of a pantry of some sort. There was little light in the kitchen, but it was enough to cast a shadow across Larkin's face.

Cael raised his weapon, aimed at Larkin. "Stand up."

"No," Larkin said in a calm voice.

He was too confident, Cael thought. He must know there wasn't much time left. "Where are the bombs?" Cael asked. "How many? When are they going to detonate?"

Larkin looked at his watch, moving it into the light to read the hands. "I'm not telling you," he said, sounding like a petulant child. In the weird light, his eyes were strangely shiny. "There are too many of them; even if you found them, you don't have enough time to disarm them. I'd say you have a little less than five minutes. Give or take."

Cael swiftly calculated. Last time he'd seen Jenner, she'd been standing by the lifeboat station with a frightened crew member, helping others onto the boats. She should be off the ship by now—he hoped. God, he hoped.

"You're the one who screwed this up for me, aren't you?" Larkin asked, as he put the pieces together. "Who the hell are you?" Without waiting for an answer, he lifted one hand, revealing a small weapon.

The old instincts kicked in and Cael fired—and at this distance he couldn't miss. The bullet tore through Larkin's arm and the pistol went spinning away. He fired again, aiming for the knee. He didn't want the bastard deciding at the last minute to make it to one of the lifeboats. Larkin screamed and fell forward, writhing in pain.

And time was up. Screw Larkin. He had to get Jenner and the rest of his team into the lifeboats. Now.

Jenner was frantic; she'd gotten Nyna on one of the lifeboats, but there had been no sign of Linda Vale, or of Penny or Buttons. The women might've gotten off the ship before Jenner had arrived at the station, as many of the passengers had, but she and Cael had gotten to the Lido deck so quickly, that seemed unlikely. Surely she would've seen them, even in the crowd.

There was so much to worry about, so many very real concerns, that she felt some control when she concentrated on one problem at a time.

Diana, a very young crew member who'd valiantly stayed at her station even though she obviously, desperately, wanted to escape, was beginning to show the wear and tear of the last horrible . . . how long had it been? Half an hour? An hour? She had lost complete sense of time. The lifeboats were filled, then swung away from the ship and lowered into the water, where they automatically detached and the process began again. The process was quick, and went smoothly as long as everyone cooperated. There were only a few people left onboard, and Diana was befuddled.

Large lifeboats filled with people floated on the water,

moving away from the *Silver Mist,* waiting for rescue that should arrive no later than morning. It was going to be a long, scary night.

"There should be more passengers, and lots more crew," Diana said as she looked around, asking the unspoken question of the older man who was assisting her. There were other stations, other crew members—and Captain Lamberti, at the aft lifeboat station—asking the same questions. Where was everyone else?

Jenner suspected that the earlier blasts had taken more lives than anyone yet knew. "It's hard to keep track of people in an emergency," she said calmly, while inside her chest her heart was pounding and she felt like screaming in an agony of fear. Where was Cael? They didn't have much time before the arranged meet. She couldn't leave without him.

"Get in the boat," she said to Diana. There were no other passengers waiting in line at this station.

"But . . ."

"I'm right behind you," Jenner promised, not adding *as soon as Cael arrives.* She definitely didn't want to tell Diana the truth, that there were other bombs on this ship and there wasn't much time left.

She heard the sound of footsteps and turned. Tiffany came sprinting into view, still wearing those high heels, still carrying a gun. Sanchez was directly behind her, his powerful stride matched to hers. Ryan approached from another direction. Where the hell was Cael?

"Get in," Tiffany said brusquely as she reached the lifeboat.

"Not until Cael—"

"Sanchez," Tiffany said sharply. "Help Ms. Redwine into the lifeboat."

Jenner held up a hand. "That isn't necessary." Nausea

gripped her as she climbed into the boat, and she felt so weak that at the last minute she almost fell. *Where was he?* Tiffany and the others climbed in right behind her, and Diana was ready to launch the boat, which was filed primarily with crew members who'd been the last to evacuate via this station.

"Wait," Jenner said desperately as Diana started to lower the lifeboat. "There's one more coming."

Cael was coming, wasn't he? Larkin hadn't gotten to him, hadn't shot him, hadn't come up behind him and hit him on the head and . . .

Tiffany took her hand and squeezed. "He'll be here," she whispered.

"I know." But she *didn't* know. She couldn't be sure. Would she *feel* it if something bad happened to him? Shouldn't she? Her breath hitched. She couldn't lose him now. Damn him, she'd found him just a little over a week ago and they'd wasted so much time in fighting each other . . .

Then she heard it, the sound of pounding footsteps approaching at a run, and took a deep breath. But when a crew uniform and a blond head came into view, she almost cried.

"Thank God!" Tiffany stood, and when Matt reached the side of the boat she offered a hand to help him.

"No, don't touch me," he panted. One arm was in a sling he'd fashioned from what looked like piece of a singed tablecloth. He was banged up pretty badly, bleeding and bruised, and his clothes were torn.

"Bridget?" Ryan asked, and Matt shook his head.

"She didn't make it." His voice was too loud; he shouted even though he was standing close to Ryan. "I looked as long as I could . . ."

"We have to go," Diana said, and it was the truth. They were out of time.

"I said I wouldn't leave without him," Jenner said, and gripped the side of the lifeboat as she began crawling out.

Tiffany grabbed her and hauled her back in. "Keep your ass here," she said sharply. "We don't have time for this kind of shit."

The blast from the sports deck made everyone duck. Diana screamed, and a fireball shot into the air. From the aft end of the deck, there was another explosion that took out the lifeboat station there, as well as the people who were manning it. The heat of the fire reached them in a stinking wave and the lifeboat they were sitting in shook violently. Diana began to lower it.

"No," Jenner said, sobbing. "Wait!" Diana looked at her, hesitated for a few precious seconds, then began lowering the boat again. Jenner jumped up, but Ryan grabbed her hand and pulled her back down. He held that hand tight. She didn't know if that strong hand was meant to keep her in place or offer comfort.

The lifeboat lowered in slow, jerky movements. Just as it sank below the railing, she saw him, coming at a dead run. "There he is!" she shrieked, and Diana hesitated again. The lifeboat jerked to a stop.

Cael didn't hesitate. He literally dove over the rail and into the boat, looking for all the world like some sort of rabid James Bond, tuxedoed, singed, sweating. Jenner grabbed him and held on tight, ducking as low as possible as yet another explosion rocked the upper decks of the ship.

Larkin tried to suck in air, but there didn't seem to be enough oxygen. The burning sensation in his arm was bad enough, but his knee, or what had been his knee, was excruciating. He wouldn't have to endure the pain for much longer, though. Sitting propped up on the floor of the closet, he listened with more satisfaction than pleasure to the first explosion. He'd had to set the timers separately so there would be a few seconds, perhaps even a minute or two, between explosions, but he didn't have long to wait.

Another explosion sounded, and he imagined the fire racing across the deck, fed by chemical accelerant, feeding on everything and everyone in its path. He closed his eyes. There was the third explosion, and the fourth, which seemed to be the one in the theater below, as it felt more distant, rumbling from beneath his seat in a kitchen closet. He could feel the heat from encroaching fires, heard the crackle and pop of the burning ship, as well as a scream in the distance, and still the bomb he was all but sitting on hadn't yet exploded.

He waited. One moment. Two. And then, in a rage, he moved the boxes under which he'd hidden the bomb. It ticked away, inert, the timer showing an hour yet to go. An hour! He stared at it in disbelief. He couldn't have set it wrong. Someone had seen him, had come back and changed the time. He didn't make mistakes like this.

If he'd stayed in the Fog Bank he'd be dead now, blown up in an instant as he'd planned. He wouldn't be in this pain. He'd have simply disintegrated, the way he'd planned. Instead he was stuck here, almost vomiting with pain, waiting for a release that hadn't happened yet. He yanked at the wires on the bomb beneath him, hoping to make it explode. Instead, the timer simply stopped blinking. Nothing happened.

The heat around him was building to a suffocating level. Cursing, he dragged himself up, tried to stand, but his shattered knee collapsed under him. He howled in pain, rolling on the floor. Finally, panting, he began pulling himself along. He found his gun and stuffed it in a pocket. Searing pain licked at his foot and he looked around in horror to find his shoe on fire. Screaming, he beat at the shoe, then finally took it off and hurled it away. His hands burned, his foot burned. His leg and arm were nothing but agony.

With furious, single-minded purpose, he dragged himself out of the kitchen and onto the deck, where flames were leaping into the night sky. He managed to reach the railing and looked below, where a large number of lifeboats filled with people floated on the ink-black ocean. Not everyone had made it out, he had that satisfaction, but this was hardly the spectacular event he'd planned.

Fire raced across the aft deck toward him. He turned, suddenly afraid in the face of that unnatural flame, but fire raced at him from that direction, too.

The bastards. The fucking *bastards*. They were going to live! After all his careful plans, they were going to live and instead of going out in a blast he was going to *burn*. He hated them, he hated them all. Pulling out the pistol, he draped himself against the rail and began firing blindly at the lifeboats, at the water, at anything and everything. The flames reached him again, and he screamed.

It hurt. It hurt everywhere, worse than he'd ever imagined, and for what seemed like a very long time . . . he suffered.

Chapter Thirty-four

The night was lit by the raging fire that consumed the listing *Silver Mist*. Soon it was obvious that no one could possibly be left alive on the ship. No one could've survived the blasts and the resulting fire that swept through the boat so quickly.

Cael sat and watched the red reflections dance on the ocean's black surface. He was silent, furious . . . and deeply grateful that he and so many of the others had made it off that damn ship. Jenner sat next to him as the lifeboat rocked gently, her head resting on his shoulder, her arm around his waist. They held each other. Tears dripped down her face, tears for Bridget, as Matt explained how he'd looked for her, how he'd stumbled across so many bodies in the areas damaged by the initial blasts.

Ryan searched the boats for Faith, who was easy to spot, even at a good distance, with the emergency lighting on each boat. She was standing, as Ryan was, searching for him. When she saw her husband Faith waved, blew a kiss, and then sat. Even from a distance Cael saw Faith then drop her head in her hands and sob—in relief, in pain, in sorrow.

Tiffany and Sanchez were comparing weapons, but he could see that it was a defense mechanism, as they were both strongly affected by all they'd seen but were reluctant to let their feelings show. After telling them about Bridget, usually happy-go-lucky Matt sat alone with his head down, silent.

A couple of crew members eventually fell asleep in the lifeboat, exhausted.

Jenner watched them all. She looked around at the people she'd come to know so well. If it hadn't been for them, the carnage would have been a lot worse. They had found out what Larkin was up to, they'd started the evacuation early, and, ignoring the danger to themselves, they had set about finding and disarming as many of the bombs as possible, as well as tracking Larkin down.

She'd spent six years trying to blend in with the Palm Beach crowd, but it wasn't happening—not because of anything they did, but because of something inside herself. She'd been looking for the place where she fit, and Palm Beach wasn't it. Why else did she change her hair color so often? Subconsciously, maybe, she'd thought that if she changed herself enough she would find the Jenner who belonged.

Screw that. She wasn't going back. She knew where she belonged now.

She looked up at Cael and said, "I want to do what you do."

It wasn't easy to rattle Cael Traylor, but she'd succeeded with that one. His eyebrows went up, then snapped down as he frowned at her. "What? You're not serious—"

"I am." She sat up, her gaze steady in her sooty face. "I took judo lessons awhile back; I'm not very good, but I can always go back for more training. And I'm really good at skeet shooting so picking up how to shoot a different type of weapon shouldn't be all that difficult. As to whatever else I need to know . . . I'm willing to learn."

"Sweetheart, you don't—" He sighed. "I do surveillance, that's all."

She pointed toward what was left of the *Silver Mist*. "Surveillance, huh?"

Cael's gaze remained on the burning ship for a long moment. Bridget's body was in there somewhere, as were a number of passengers and crew.

"If you hadn't been here," Jenner said, "if you hadn't kidnapped me and Syd and set up your surveillance, all these people would be dead. Syd and I would be dead. Frank Larkin would've gotten exactly what he wanted."

Cael couldn't imagine a world without Jenner Redwine in it. So soon, so strongly, she was necessary.

"Teach me," she whispered.

"We'll see."

She sighed and snuggled more closely against him. "That'll do, for now." She was silent for a while, thoughtful—or else dozing—and then she asked, "Do you have a boat?"

"No."

"Good." She gave another sigh that sounded like a breath of relief.

A short while later he heard it . . . the unmistakable sound of a helicopter, most likely a Coast Guard rescue helicopter, headed their way.

There was one other thing, something she had to get out of the way now. "I'm really rich, you know," Jenner confessed in a lowered voice. "Buy-a-small-country kind of rich."

He thought it was an odd thing to say. "I know. So? I'm not in the market for a small country."

"Some men get weird about it, that's all."

"I don't care about your money," he said honestly. "Besides, I have enough for us. Give it all away, burn it, save it for the kids . . ."

He probably shouldn't have said that yet, but when he looked down at Jenner she was smiling, so maybe it wasn't too soon, after all.

Jenner was wearing someone else's pants, which were held up with an oversize belt and rolled up at the cuff so they wouldn't drag on the ground, and an oversized Coast Guard T-shirt. The flip-flops on her feet were unadorned, had no arch support, and were borrowed. She hadn't slept in thirty-six hours or so, and her makeup was at the bottom of the Pacific—or ash in the air above it. She felt like crap, she *looked* like crap, but Cael didn't seem to care. Syd certainly didn't.

Syd squealed and ran toward Jenner, leaving her three guards standing on the shady front porch without looking back, running down the sidewalk with long, anxious strides. Jenner wondered if Cael had chosen this isolated spot, a small house well outside the city limits of San Diego, in case she and Syd decided to join forces and retaliate in spite of everything that had been said since they'd sailed away from the *Silver Mist*. She wasn't going to do anything that might be considered retaliatory, and Syd, well, it was definitely unlikely.

With open arms, Jenner met Syd near the middle of the long sidewalk. They hugged. They hugged for a long, long time.

Still holding on tight, Syd said, "Oh, Jenner, I was so worried . . . and then I saw the news about the ship and I didn't know if you'd survived or not and I just lost it . . . and

I slapped Adam because he was standing right there, and I had to hit *someone* or something, but he didn't hit me back, which I guess was pretty nice if you think about it . . . and then I tried to run but he wouldn't let me and . . . and . . . they made me pay for my own kidnapping, which is really just wrong." She sighed deeply, wiped her eyes, and finally said, "Are you really okay?"

Jenner held Syd tight. "I'm fine. Well, maybe not entirely fine yet, but I will be." Her emotions were in turmoil. She'd found Cael, but had lost a friend in Linda Vale, who had not been in one of the lifeboats as Jenner had assured Nyna she would be, and in Bridget, who had died trying to save others. Penny and Buttons had been reunited with Nyna aboard a freighter that had responded to the rescue call, but so many others had been lost.

There still wasn't an accurate death toll, but it looked as if well more than three hundred people had perished with Frank Larkin, which was far short of what he'd planned yet still a terrible tragedy.

Syd let Jenner go and pinned her gaze on Cael. She didn't know his name, but she still knew who he was. He was the one behind all of this. Her eyes narrowed. "And *you*, you kidnapped us, you threatened us, and . . ." she faltered, obviously thinking better of saying too much before she was truly away from her kidnappers. Her lips trembled and she quickly controlled them. "You just wait. You'll get yours," she added in a low voice.

Jenner put an arm around Syd and led her toward Cael, who had given her some distance for the reunion with her friend. "Syd, this is Cael Traylor. Cael, Sydney Hazlett." She really did want the two most important people in her world, the two people she loved most, to get along. All things considered, it might take awhile.

Cael seemed cautious. Maybe she should tell him that Syd didn't bite.

Nah. Let him worry.

"I'll reimburse you for all the bills that were incurred while you were with us," he said, his voice businesslike and kind.

Syd looked at Jenner, her eyes widening. "He makes it sound like I had a bad vacation and am asking for a refund."

"I know. He annoys the shit out of me, too," Jenner said. She leaned in and whispered, "But don't worry, he's one of the good guys." She winked at him. "He's *my* good guy."

Five weeks later

Kyle Quillin nearly jumped out of his skin when the doorbell rang. Ever since that nut Frank Larkin had blown himself up, Kyle had been waiting for someone to show up at his door. Had Larkin confessed before he'd died? Had he given anyone the name of the weapons designer who was putting together the revolutionary EMP weapon?

He'd changed his e-mail address, moved the money he'd been paid three times, from overseas account to overseas account, and he'd quit his job with the defense contractor who didn't pay him shit. He was weeks away from finishing the weapon—weeks! So far, no one had connected him with Larkin, and still, he worried that something, somehow, would lead to him.

Kyle looked through the peephole and was relieved to see a pretty redhead standing on his doorstep. No police, no men in dark suits and sunglasses. He opened the door. The woman on his doorstep had spiky red hair, and was dressed in a skimpy tank top and shorts. She was jumping up and down, just a little.

"I'm sorry to bother you," she said, "but my husband and I are helping my sister move into the house across the street, and *naturally* she didn't get the water turned on, and I have to pee."

"There's a gas station . . ."

"I can't wait," she interrupted. "No way will I make it back to that gas station. Pleeease."

Kyle looked across the street, where two men were unloading a moving van, while a gorgeous, stacked, eye-catching black-haired woman stood with her backside resting against a car as she watched the proceedings without lifting a finger.

"That's your sister, and she's moving in across the street?" Wow, this was his lucky day. Most of his neighbors were retired, or married with annoying kids and dogs that crapped in his yard.

"Yep, that's Tiffany." The redhead offered her hand. "I'm Jenner. Jenner Traylor." She lifted her eyebrows in silent question.

"Kyle Quillin." He shook her hand briefly.

"Nice to meet you, Kyle," Jenner said. "You'll probably be seeing me and my husband around for a few days as we get Tiffy settled." She rolled her eyes. "God forbid she should have to get her own water and power turned on." Again, she jumped up and down. "Bathroom?"

"Sure." Kyle stepped back and let the Traylor woman into the house. He pointed. "Down the hall, first door on the right." His eyes stayed on her sister for a moment, until Jenner got his attention as she stumbled, squealed, and caught herself by grabbing the bookshelf.

"I'm such a klutz," she said with a laugh, as she disappeared into the hallway.